Philip Boast is the author of LONDON'S CHILD,
LONDON'S MILLIONAIRE, LONDON'S DAUGHTER
and GLORIA as well as the panoramic CITY, all of
which are set in London. He is also the author of
WATERSMEET, a West Country saga, and PRIDE, an
epic novel set in Australia and England. He lives in
Devon with his wife Rosalind and their three children,
Harry, Zoe and Jamie.

The Foundling

Philip Boast

HEADLINE

First published in 1995
by HEADLINE BOOK PUBLISHING

First published in paperback in 1996
by HEADLINE BOOK PUBLISHING

10 9 8 7 6 5 4 3 2 1

ISBN 0 7472 4882 6

Typeset by CBS, Felixstowe, Suffolk

Printed and bound in Great Britain by
Cox & Wyman Ltd, Reading, Berks

HEADLINE BOOK PUBLISHING
A division of Hodder Headline PLC
338 Euston Road
London NW1 3BH

For
Simon and Sara

Part One

The Hidden City

Book One

The Alchemist

Chapter One

I

4.15 p.m., Friday 9 December 1870
Evening was falling, dark with rain, so that the
setting sun struck across the docklands and
graveyards of Paddington from beneath the clouds,
and London was going home. Nobody in the sea of
faces hurrying along Watling Street noticed the
man hurrying forward with them, whether he wore
a hat, or the colour of his coat, or whether his skin
was pale or dark. For a moment he was beside them,
sharp eyes and quick fingers, but he never bumped
or knocked them, and they never felt anything. In a
moment he was behind them again, crossing the
road. Near Turnham's Alley a woman sneezed,
searching in vain for her kerchief, but he was already
gone.

The rain began to fall, and a swirl in the crowd
carried her away.

Arthur Albert Simmonds pressed his body deeper
into the doorway that almost concealed him. The
alley was a dead end. A mound of scenery and old
playbills lay heaped against the back wall like
discarded dreams. The kerchief was cheapest cotton

with frayed edges, fifty of them wouldn't fetch a penny in Field Lane, but he tucked it in his belt anyway. You didn't get lucky twice in one day: his head pounded guiltily, remembering. Mrs Oilick's rum had been salted with Condy's crystals, he reckoned, and brown boot-polish for colour. He'd been took.

Arthur groaned. He'd drunk the whole five shillings he had got for the watch. He had let Elsie down, again, as he always did, and he always would, but it would be all right if she never found out.

'Can't get no worse!' he sighed, but he knew it could. The gang of children worked harder than ever at the road-crossing, their elbows flashing as if steam-driven. There was the boy. His name was Monkey, because his short legs were bent like a monkey's. He had a monkey's rolling gait. No one cared what his real name was.

St Mary's Church bell tolled half-four across the rubbish-tips behind the fine buildings. Plenty of time.

Yer'll wait fer me on the corner of the Met, Arthur, an' yer'll bring a boy wiv yer.

Arthur waited. It was the same old London story, he saw. Beyond Turnham's Grand Concert Hall night and smoke pressed down between the jungle of rooftops, enveloping the gas-globes so that they swelled like brilliant, steamy eyes overlooking the shimmering thoroughfare. The glare of the theatre foyer made a golden steam of the people rushing past Arthur's hiding-place. He saw golden umbrellas bobbing over golden pavements, golden heads and golden shoes, soldiers sporting son-of-a-bitch

4

sidewhiskers and a girl hanging on each elbow like painted jewellery. And beneath the bright show, he saw, the poorest plodded on anyhow, men, women, children, and he knew they'd never get those rags dry tonight. Arthur watched the golden mob shrink in the distance, losing their glow, fading like shadows into the huge mass of London.

Not one of them had realised how black it was in here, or seen him watching them, waiting.

The rain bucketed into the alley from the theatre roof above him. The gutters and drains poured silver spouts down the black walls around him. Arthur waited. He felt as miserable as a shag on a rock. He let the water stream off first the back of his hat-brim, then the front, the only choices open to him. He pulled up his plum-coloured coat to his ears. Three years ago Simeon, his father, had died penniless and mad as May-butter at the enormous age of ninety-six, wrapped in this same coat, on the stone floor of the Marylebone Parish Workhouse. The coat had been the old crim's proudest and last possession and he had begged his only son, shivering and clutching these same lapels to his throat, to be allowed to go into the earth in it, and died believing he would.

But a pauper's shroud was warm enough for a corpse, and Arthur wore his father's coat.

A slant of gaslight caught Arthur's face, for a moment making him look exhausted and careworn, casting a net of shadows around him. He was thirty-five years old today. The light made a blade of his nose and a handle of his chin, and the curve of his pot-belly looked like a new moon settling its horns into his pockets. Despite the good impression his coat made, his shoes were held together by their shine, and his spotless collar was threadbare. What could be seen of his carefully trimmed hair gave the impression of a clerk down on his luck, trying to keep himself neat, worthy of work. Such men were ten-a-penny on the streets, common enough to be beneath notice.

Masters of the art like Bamfylde Moore Carew or Sixteen-string Jim changed their appearance at will, but to be overlooked was the best disguise. Only his fingers gave Arthur away, and then only to a policeman experienced in such tricks. They were shaved as silky as a girl's, the backs of his hands plucked smooth to slip light as a kiss into even the roughest serge or tweed pockets. Even so, he was not half the man his father had been. Arthur stood on the shoulders of a giant.

In his prime Simeon Simmonds had been a criminal of substance. Born and bred under the name Giddings, Dad's blood had been steeped in generations of Devon smugglers, the Giddings thieves, murderers and opportunists who built Lynmouth on their success. He sent goods as far as London aboard his 'Cabriolet Service' wagon. Hauled before the Western Circuit Assizes, Sir Alexander Thomson presiding, for handling stolen goods, he had the presence of mind to take the name Simmonds, and so was transported to Botany Bay for only the smallest of his crimes. Shipwrecked on King Island, discovered by the authorities in his retirement and deemed to have served his sentence, of course the old crim smuggled himself back to England and picked up merrily on his former ways. An indomitable figure stumping the streets of London – one leg of meat, the other of hard Huon pine – Simeon had married a child, and sired Arthur in his sixty-fifth year.

Twenty years later, growing up stunted and dull in the old man's shadow, little Arthur plucked up the courage to do one remarkable thing in his life. He married, legal and proper and against his father's wishes, furiously expressed, sweet Elsie Hawkins.

Rather, she married him. The sea-captain's daughter was the loveliest girl on the street, living in the corner house that put her a cut above Arthur in class, and she could have had anyone else. Fifteen years ago she'd seen something in Arthur. 'You wouldn't say boo to a goose,' she'd laughed, 'yet you try to look so fierce!'

With his quiet demeanour and puppy-dog eyes, Arthur would be her very own man. She would make something of him.

He'd married a busy young tyrant full of schemes. When they were rich they would live in *that* house, they would do this, do that, they would be happy. Arthur loved to hear her talk, he'd do anything for her. For her he sold ham-and-mustard sandwiches on the steps of the new Covent Garden Theatre, but when he lost them (and her tray, and the leather neckstrap too) he was afraid to face her. He made a few pence carrying baskets of vegetables in the market, and of course a pineapple fell into his pocket, and though of course he had not the faintest idea how it got there, of course he got caught. However often it happened he couldn't stop himself, there was

7

always a next time. His excuses were wonderful. Gangs of youths – the weather – tripped over a dog! She never knew he let her down.

The birth of her baby did not have the settling effect on her husband Elsie hoped for. To Arthur it seemed every child was called Bert or Bertie that year, after the Royals, and he could not find his infant as lovable as its mother did. To him it was another mouth to feed, a child growing up with dreams and questions, who must be deceived, just like his mother, about his father's failings. The truth was that for Arthur every year was worse than the one before. Each year he dragged them down. The harder he tried to make a success of his life, the more he could not mend his old ways. Even now Arthur's hands fretted at his lapels, his earlobes, the hairs in his nose, snatching flawlessly at the drips from the drainpipe, practising their skill while his mind was distracted.

Because of Arthur's devotion to his wife and son, his excuses had long ago turned into stories. Because he truly loved her, and he thought Elsie didn't know how hard his life was, he lied to her. He was always bright, always cheerful, always lying because he knew the truth was a terrible darkness that lay around them, everywhere.

But still she loved him.

He was lying to her right now, just by being here, and he closed his eyes. The night and teeming rain felt solid around him. Elsie would have screamed if she'd known he was here . . . if she'd known whom he waited for.

It had been a horrible day. But it had begun

perfectly, with her kiss. His tongue moved in his mouth. He remembered the salty taste of her lips.

II

8.00 a.m. that morning
She woke him with a lovely cockly kiss.

'Happy birthday!'

'Wha'?' Arthur muttered, blinking.

Elsie sat beside him on her heels, her hair over her shoulders. 'Don't worry – my sister's gone to the baths, and Bert and Peter went with her. I arranged it.'

Arthur was suspicious at once. That elder sister of hers never did something for nothing. Nobody did.

'Just the two of us,' Elsie said.

What was she up to? No one was stranger than women, Arthur thought. It was a perfect sunny morning, and she'd taken down the curtain that divided their half of the room from her sister's, as though the whole room was her own, for a little while at least. She'd thrown open the sash-window and through the gap came the slow clop of country traffic. The toll-booth bell sounded across the marshes of Barn Elms, then the train whistled in Putney station and set the cows lowing as they were led back from milking to the fields.

'I'm freezin'!' Arthur shivered. 'Don't yer know it's winter?' He clutched the blanket around him, squinting against the daylight. Elsie wore only a linen shift. ''Ere, yer mad!' he said. 'Wot's that doing in public? Yer'll catch yer death!'

'Better warm me up,' she said, but he scuttled

across the bare boards to the window, kneeling to hide himself from the street, and slammed the glass closed.

'Shameless,' he said. 'Yer age too.'

'Close your eyes,' she said playfully. 'You've got lovely hands, you have.'

'It's not right,' he said. 'Being together in the daytime. It's French.'

She laughed. 'I do love you, Arthur!'

He stared at her, then held the blanket around him with all the dignity he could muster. She had a son eleven years old, she took in washing, sewing, any old work to make ends meet, her face was weary with care. Yet she was looking at him like a girl.

'You look so surprised!' she giggled. 'Oh, Arthur!'

He realised he was out of his depth. Her greatest fault was that she was more intelligent than he was. 'Wot's brought this on, then?' he muttered, and she laughed again.

'Why shouldn't I say I love you, and show it?' Then she looked into his face and said seriously, 'Present for you.' She'd saved her pin-money for a half-pint of cockles, his favourite treat – spending it on him not the ever-open mouth of their boy for a change. Arthur sat. He breakfasted on the straw mattress with his legs crossed like a potentate, and his mood began to sparkle. Not getting enough meat was the reason he usually felt so weak, he thought. Jauntily he offered Elsie the juiciest cockle, but she said, 'I ate earlier.'

He realised she'd just rubbed the taste of it over her lips, she couldn't fool him, she wasn't so clever after all. He persisted, asserting himself. 'I don't really like them . . .' she said.

Then she ate it to please him, and he smiled.

'If only every day was like this,' he said, relaxing. 'Sit beside me, don't cost extra.'

'But we mustn't talk about money,' she said firmly.

'It's what makes the world go round, old dear!'

'Don't go on about it.' She touched him appealingly, but he didn't respond. He was always saying, one way or another, that if only they had a little more money they'd never fight. When it came down to it her work brought in more money than his, it must hurt him. He was so touchy and vulnerable that she wanted to cuddle him, but he flinched away. 'I like you just the way you are, Arthur.'

'Something'll turn up,' he told her. It never did, but he raised his eyebrows. 'Promise.'

'I don't blame you because we're short at the moment,' she said. 'I really don't. Why should I?'

'Because I've dragged yer down in the world,' he blurted.

'You have not!'

'Me and my bad luck,' he said bitterly. He hated her opening up the room into her sister's territory like this, it had the opposite effect she intended. It reminded him of all he did not have. He stared at the other side of the room, which had a table and two chairs, old but neat, and a proper bed, and a truckle-bed squeezed into the box-room for the boy. Prim and sensible Miss Edna Hawkins, with no husband, no children, and absolutely no income of her own, had acquired legal charge of her ten-year-old nephew, Peter Aloysius Lucan Hawkins, his mother having died in childbirth. Edna's ward received an allowance

11

from his father at sea, paid to her. Small though this sum was, irregular though it was, it sufficed to keep the fortunate aunt and her valuable asset on the good side of the curtain, the patterned side. Not only that, Edna had the bow window for light and the little box-room that Elsie coveted so as a bedroom for her own child. The territory was usually fiercely defended.

Arthur longed for enough money to give Elsie a room of their own with her own bow window, and a proper bed, and a box-room too if it meant so much to her, if it would make her happy. But he couldn't even give her the patterned side of the curtain.

'Put it back!' he said tersely. 'I mean it.'

She gave him a weary look, then picked up the dull curtain and pegged it to the line that bisected the room, and they stood in the shadows as usual. Suddenly he took hold of her and kissed her to get her going, then sat her on the mattress. He got on top of her and took her, showing all that needed to be shown, it didn't have to be put into words.

Her voice came. 'Do you love me?'

He stared at her as if he couldn't believe what he'd heard, then put his arms around her and hugged her so tight that she arched her back.

'I'd die fer yer!' he said. 'Go out of me mind wivout yer.'

She smiled, understanding that he meant he did love her. 'I'm the luckiest woman,' she said. 'Nothing else matters. The very luckiest.'

'I'm lucky ter 'ave you,' he said simply, and found he had said the truth.

In companionable silence she got up and bustled

around him, laid out his shirt for him, freshly washed, and his socks, darned. She touched his shoulder with her hand, brushed his arm with her elbow, watching him dress. 'You'll be lucky today, Arthur,' she said.

'Live in 'ope.'

'I believe in you.' Elsie was always telling him that if you said something often enough, and hoped it enough, and believed in it enough, then it came true.

'I'll be all right, don't worry,' he said. He polished his shoes, the man's job, requiring concentration.

But she wanted to talk. 'Where will you try for work today?'

'I'll give the 'Dilly a go.'

'That nice Captain Combuskle,' she said comfortably.

Arthur cleared his throat. Naturally Elsie always thought kindly of sea-captains. During the day she liked to hold a vague mental picture in her mind of what Arthur was doing, cleaning a carriage maybe, or on a corner selling handkerchiefs or song-sheets, imagining the interesting people he met in town while she was stuck at home. So he'd come up with the rolling figure of dear old Captain Combuskle, who was short with white sidewhiskers, his loud bark hiding a kind heart, who had been good to Arthur and tipped him a shilling once.

Captain Combuskle didn't exist, and neither had the tip. Arthur had lifted the shilling from someone's pocket. He'd never owned up to Elsie and never could, his stories having by now piled up to make a whole fantastic web of lies. She remembered them

13

better than he did. The truth about himself was so mean and shabby that if she ever found out, he'd lose her. The Arthur Simmonds she believed in was as false as Captain Combuskle.

She picked up the plum-coloured coat and Arthur shrugged it on. She waved to him from the door and he set off for work.

Putney was a proper village, clean, hardly like London at all. In the lane people acknowledged him by his coat, called him Mr Simmonds, and believed he was a clerk walking to Fulham or the City. That he worked north of the river was the only remarkable thing about him, for the southern villages of London lived their own lives, sundered from the teeming mass of the north bank by bridge tolls. Arthur had paid his halfpenny, the turnstile clicked, and he'd walked into a different world.

Arthur still crouched in the doorway. Faintly through the rain and dark St Mary's tolled six o'clock in the evening, but the iron-shod traffic streaming past his hiding-place overwhelmed almost every sound with its rumbling, racketing roar. Four-wheeled growlers pounded the brilliant stretch of Watling Street, a gleaming rainy river of horse-omnibuses swaying top-heavy as galleons, umbrellas and shoulders crammed along the upper decks, feather-hats and flower-hats and women's pale faces squeezed against the windows below. Around them milled carts, drays, dog-carts and barrows, the barrow-boys risking the heavy wheels and weaving through the crush as spry as fleas. Through every gap costers, walking side-ways, heaved their unsold wares home from the stalls, or kicked the stuff into the gutters to stink with yesterday's.

Still Arthur waited.

Smoke and sparks thundered from a chimney disguised as a wall. Somewhere below the street a locomotive was dragging its human cargo along the new underground railway, which locals called the Drain, because a sewer had been built down there too, and water pipes to serve the new streets around the railways and the canal. People moving into the district gave themselves away calling Turnham's by its new Railway name, the Metropolitan, and knew Watling Street as the Edgware Road. But Arthur had been born not a mile from here by Portobello Farm, countryside in those days before the Great Western, the Kensington & Richmond and the West London Railway lines boxed the land in, and carpenters had knocked up the first Paddington Station in a field nearby. His earliest memories were of the secret paths through the marshes of Wormwood Scrubs, a fine training for the backstreets of Marylebone. He'd always had more sense than to live where he worked, and no honest person knew London from Paddington to Piccadilly as well as he did, or would have known there was so much to know.

He belched, and tasted Mrs Oilick's rum. Down by the New Road the crossing-sweepers' children worked back and forth like little demons. Jack Riddles's voice came to him again, and he remembered the dancing flames. He wiped his hand across his ear as though feeling Jack's spittle still hot there.

I'll need a skinny-isaacs boy, Arthur me old choom. A loofer boy.

15

The bell tolled eight times and Arthur slipped from his hiding-place towards the boys.

It had been midday today in Piccadilly when the old gentleman walking past Arthur tripped on the kerb and went down with a fearful wallop.

Arthur had looked round him suspiciously. It seemed no one had pushed the old duffer, no tripwire was stretched from the lamp-post, no half-brick had come flying from the alley or one of the deep doorways. No gang of children flocked out like birds to strip the body in a trice, leaving him dazed and half-naked, worth nothing to anybody. No one filched the old man's stick, in fact one passer-by actually stepped busily over it, on his way to an appointment in one of the excellent shops no doubt. The shop-tickers all looked the other way, touting for business among those who could spend their money, uncaring of a man who wore a black mourning band on his arm and lay flat on his face.

Arthur could hardly believe his luck.

''Elp yer up, sir!' he said, fetching the old gent's stick, which had a plated knob and ferrule, not worth running off with. And his left shoe had come off, but it was worthless without the other. Still, Arthur was not in a position to be a chooser, and he almost ran with them out of habit. Instead he dropped on one knee and spoke with gruff kindness. 'Let's get this shoe on, poor old feller, yer look silly wivout a shoe. There. 'Ere's yer stick, careful now. Tripped on a matchstick, I 'spect. Let's get yer on yer pins – one, two, hup we go.'

Something flashed in the old man's pocket.

Arthur swallowed, resisting the temptation.

Helping the old man solicitously to his feet, of its own will Arthur's hand flicked into the old man's pocket like a trick of the eye, almost too fast to see, and with consummate skill came out empty in case someone was watching. 'Call yer a cab ter take yer 'ome, sir!' He whistled, and the driver of a growler lowered his whip at once, pulling over.

'Have I suffered a fall?' the old gent said, confused.

'Pleasure ter be of service, sir,' Arthur said genially, and slammed the door. The vehicle disappeared into the traffic and he breathed a sigh of relief, and shame.

Turning into a sidestreet to examine his prize, he opened his hand as though to click his fingers, and the old man's watch slid smooth as silk from his sleeve into his palm. The silver closed-case reflected gleams into his eyes. He clicked it open, revealing a railway face, raised seconds, and tiny script beneath PATENT LEVER claiming a jewelled movement in four holes. Only four. But that hallmarked case was a quid's worth of anybody's money, engraved with a woman's name in a heart. Obviously a gift from her.

Arthur's hands trembled to have had such luck.

Perhaps Elsie was right. If you believed in something enough, maybe it really did come true.

'I'm the luckiest man in the world,' Arthur said. 'The luckiest man in the world. I am!'

Slipping open his coat, he stored the watch safely in his sloured hoxter, a buttoned-up pocket where it would be safe from men such as he. Whistling cheerfully as he walked, inventing stories in his mind to explain Captain Combuskle's generosity to

Elsie, he crossed the elegant circle of Piccadilly Circus. He emerged on the far side having palmed a hothouse carnation for his buttonhole and a Spanish orange for his belly. Slipping the orange from his sleeve, he ate the segments as he walked to Holborn, wiping his lips luxuriously on his lapel.

He left the broad thoroughfare before reaching Smithfield, avoiding a tangle of roadworks, and took to the backstreets of Saffron Hill. On his right, beyond herds of lowing cattle and the roofs of the abattoirs, the City's fine boulevards spread down to the Thames. But he turned uphill, and when he saw the strangely shaped spire of St Luke's church ahead of him, only just beyond the City's northern border, he crossed the last proper road.

The maze of the St Luke's rookery closed around him.

No vehicles here, only soft footsteps. Urchins padded after him, barefoot even on such a winter's day, their jackets held together by tape. They begged for a scrap without shame, if they were very young. 'Not today!' Arthur laughed. 'Find another one!' They fell back as he pushed through. Older boys leaned against the walls, their mouths shut and their eyes hard. Most of them had a girl with them, or fetching beer for them. The next alley was empty, only a woman lying wrapped in a cape as faded as a shroud, her breathing showing she was alive, her baby bundled at her neck.

Arthur stepped over her and walked on quickly.

Crouching beneath an archway, he climbed some steps over a wall. There were none on the other side, it was a 'one-way street', and he jumped down. He

18

must leave by a different route.

He wended his way through a queue of children carrying water from St Thomas's burial ground, the smallest dragging the buckets between two of them.

At the coiner's Arthur turned downhill past the dye house. No wider than a paving stone, these back-alleys looped in every direction, joining and rejoining in deliberate confusion. The paths jumped foul ditches, open sewers, on planks that could be lifted to foil pursuit. Other ways lost themselves underground, deliberately blocked by walls, or sometimes old houses slumped like weary animals with age. But there was always a way through, if you knew it. In one corner, he saw, a nest of ragged boys had set up home in a coil of old rope, where they lay curled asleep as comfortably as eels in a dish. He smiled to see their harsh little faces innocent with sleep, and walked on before they woke.

Here Arthur felt at his best. Here in St Luke's he was someone, and he gave a hallo to anyone he knew. Among these people he was a successful man. He had family, shelter, hope. He had escaped. Yet despite his fine coat he remained one of them, and he was troubled by no one.

Honest men did not venture into St Luke's maze of alleys and courts, public houses and gin-shops, damp and filth. Most people had no idea such places existed, but Arthur knew they were everywhere, especially closest to the richest districts.

St Luke's fed upon the City.

Here, within yards of the international banks and great guilds of the Square Mile, fathers sold their children into prostitution, and mothers worked at child-skinning. They lured middle-class children from their parents in the street, or in shops, or in the park. Here in St Luke's they stripped them for their clothes, sold them into brothels or got rid of the bodies, and drank themselves blind. When the Red Lion was knocked down the workmen found bones beneath every floor, in every cupboard, in every bolt-hole.

The women muttered as he passed.

"Ow's yer face, Smart Arthur,' someone called, and a baby cried.

'Good afternoon!' Arthur responded cheerfully, but did not stop for a moment. Now that the Fleet River had been covered in, this row of tenements was the place for baby-farming. In streets like this unwanted babies were taken in from good homes for 'fostering'. Here they were fed two drops of chlorodyne. They were carried out again well bundled in the swaddling they had arrived in, as though they were still alive, to be disposed of somewhere.

Without bodies there was no murder.

Arthur fell silent, looking behind him often as the walls crowded more narrowly around him, passing through several houses where he was known as a precaution against being followed. He skirted the foul yards, rubbish-tips, cesspools that overflowed from the housebacks. So moist had the soil become, over the years, that the people's houses were subsiding into their own waste and decay. Doors and windows no longer fitted, roofs were twisted and bent. Past the Blue Anchor he found the walls tumbled together overhead, sometimes propped up by beams, otherwise left slumped wearily against one another like old drunks. Arthur crept through caves of mossy plaster shutting out the sky. When he banged his head he wiped his hat fastidiously. Someone heard his footsteps and called from the doorway of the Shears. "Oo's that then?' and Arthur replied, 'It's me.'

'It's Smart Arthur,' someone called, and someone else called, 'Wot yer got fer us today?'

As always with slums, this warren was really a fortress.

Arthur descended a last, steep set of steps, bare of railings and worn into scoops by age, and stood in the cobbled street known as Rookery Row. He had no kerchief, or he would have held it to his nose against the stench. Here was the heart of the place. Here you could buy and sell anything, a woman, a child, a life, a set of silver spoons, a soul. Nowhere in London had so many flash shops, fence shops, doll-shops, and filthiest brothels of the fourth rank. Arthur set off, threading scrupulously between the piles of manure in his shiny shoes, then screamed as a hand grabbed his lapel. He was dragged down without warning, biting his tongue. He glimpsed the flash of a Bowie knife.

Arthur cringed, squeezing his eyes so tight shut that he showed all his teeth.

'Don't hurt me, Jack!' he cried. 'It's me!'

The fingers changed their grip to Arthur's throat, almost garotting him, strangling his cries. Wisely, he hung limp, then panted as the hand jerked at him contemptuously and let him go.

'Smart Arthur,' the voice purred.

How Arthur hated that nickname. 'Yes, Jack,' he said.

Slowly he opened his eyes. Jack Riddles filled the doorway that led down to Mrs Oilick's dolly-shop, his shoulders braced across the lintel, his head obscuring her sign.

'Yer scream like a woman,' Jack mocked him. 'Yer squat to piss, I bet.' His voice was light and fast for so big a man, but sharp as a whipsaw.

'I do if yer says so, Jack.' Arthur dropped his gaze.

'Yes, Jack,' Jack said, bending and looking him in the eye.

'Yes, Jack, I do,' Arthur said obediently.

Jack grunted, then, cocking his finger to show Arthur he should follow, bent his head, turning his broad shoulders sideways, and ducked back into Mrs Oilick's room behind him. Arthur bobbed after him as submissively as Jack's dog. But Jack did not have a dog, he hated them. Jack was the man for cats. The gloomy room down the steps stank of cats even more than it stank of spilt beer, smoke, sweat. Jack knocked a cat off his plate then picked it up affectionately, rubbing its fur against his jaw. Cats jumped from the table, the benches, the fireplace where the brown sea-coal guttered, their eyes fixed on Arthur. More cats came leaping down from the stairs, winding their bodies between Arthur's legs without affection, mewling and arching as they rubbed themselves, and one jumped on his shoulder. Arthur breathed cat-fur into his nose and sneezed.

'Cats!' he said. 'I love 'em.'

Jack stood up tall in the middle of the room near the lightwell, almost to his full height. The smoky illumination streaming down revealed a magnificent figure of a man. His head touched the ceiling, so that his long black hair was streaked with plaster dust. His hairline grew within two fingers'-width of his eyebrows, the front curls falling over his eyes in a tangle of hooks. He had close-set blue eyes and a large jaw, which gave him a wide, expressive mouth. Those eyes, difficult to see beneath the hair, shadowed in their deep sockets, examined Arthur as expressionless as those of the cat he held.

'Yer don't come 'ere fer nothing,' he said.

Jack was probably in his twenties, perhaps even his early twenties, but he looked much older. He had been born where his mother fell from a window, drunk out of her skull, into the strawyard of the Shears. Jack was born drunk, it was said, after two years in the womb, so that he pulled the birth-caul from his face with his own hands and bit through his own cord to free himself from his mother's body, and was found standing naked at the doorway to the jug-and-bottle. Liza Ketch, the innkeeper's woman, took him in, but soon he was stronger than her sons twice his age. He carried a beer cask on each shoulder like Liza's husband, big Dick Ketch. After the terrible fight between the children Liza kept Jack under lock and key but he broke out. He took to the courts and alleys, and made his life there among the hovels.

St Luke's was his home, it was all he knew. God knows who his father was. People said he must have been a horse, because Jack Riddles grew up strong as a horse. His low brow made him seem brutish and stupid, in the way big men who move slowly always seem stupid. But Arthur knew Jack could move as quickly as a cat.

He had seen it.

Jack observed him patiently, knowing what Arthur was thinking. Arthur had seen him break Dick Ketch's back.

'I was going ter take it ter Solomon's,' Arthur said, holding out the watch. He heard quiet sobs and hiccups coming from the back room. It was the sound of someone who has been crying for hours, a terrible sound, lost and hopeless. He shut his mind to it. 'I *was*, Jack, but I know yer a fair man.'

Jack Riddles's fingers closed gently around the timepiece. 'Mrs Oilick, madam!' he said. 'Take yer ear from the wall.'

Mrs Oilick bustled from the slaughter-room — Arthur heard the low murmur of bids, and knew a card game was going on — coming in as brightly as though she'd been just coming anyway. She was as small as Jack was large, her eyes set like black beetles in her red, foxy face. Like a proper Madame, she called this room her Front Parlour, and there was a Back Parlour from which came the smell of burnt charcoal, and upstairs were her Boudoirs, so small that the doors opened onto the landing like cupboards, each with room for only a rickety bed. She wore a frowsty black bonnet with a chin-strap, and a rusty cotton dress of the sort called an allbum, once black no doubt, but the colour had been worn out by its previous owners. A satin bow was tied lopsided in the small of her back. One of her shoes was black and the other brown, in a different style.

24

'Smart Arthur,' she sniffed. 'Did the cat bring yer in? Got more rubbish, I s'pose.' She glanced at the watch and farted through her lips.

'Listen 'ere, Agnes, yer know I don't like that nickname,' Arthur complained, grinning politely, caught between the two of them. He pulled the cat off his shoulder and put it down with care. 'I'll take a quid, not a penny less,' he told Jack, turning his back on the woman.

'"Smart as a Tart" Arthur,' she said, elbowing him aside. The cat jumped back on Arthur's shoulder. 'That's bad luck – black cat!' she cackled.

'Arthur's a lucky man, coming 'ere,' Jack said.

'Yes, Jack,' Arthur said, trying to mean it. 'My lucky day.'

'Itzy Solomon wouldn't've paid 'im a flea in 'is ear fer this metal!' Mrs Oilick exclaimed. 'Wot yer trying ter pass off?'

'Siller, 'allmarked,' Arthur said anxiously. 'Honest siller.'

'Five bob,' Jack said, breaking the watch from the case. 'Bung it in the crucible, Aggie.'

'I can't, the girl's in there.'

''Ave a 'eart, Jack,' Arthur said miserably.

'Five bob, an' a tot of best spirits.' Jack glanced at Mrs Oilick and they both grinned.

'Yer know I won't drink no drink,' Arthur said.

Jack said, 'Yer'll drink wiv me.'

'On the 'ouse!' Mrs Oilick opened the closet and pulled out a bottle of navy rum. She unsealed it, uncorked it, poured it. Arthur drank it. Jack banged down five shillings in front of him. Arthur drank another then closed his hand over the money. It

25

grew warm under his fingers and he dreamed of taking it home to Elsie. He must go straight home to Putney and give it to her. He tried to get up, stumbled.

'Great stuff!' he said.

'Penny a totter now,' he heard Mrs Oilick say distantly. 'Only the first comes free.'

'I got – I got ter go,' Arthur said.

'Finish wot yer got.' Arthur drained his glass. 'One fer the road,' she murmured, 'looks like rain afore dark. Keep yer warm.' Arthur drank the glass until he could read the maker's name on the bottom. He sat unsteadily, his elbows spreading out helplessly beneath him on the table. He rested his forehead on the rim of the glass and found it was somehow full again, though he thought he'd drunk all it contained. He emptied it into his mouth in confusion, swallowed, and brushed his hand across his eyes. *'Present fer yer!'* he imagined telling Elsie. *'Cap'n Combuskle got me some work up Piccadilly, God bless 'im.'*

And Elsie would believe him.

He imagined handing her the five bob, imagined the look in her eyes. Nothing too special. Respect.

That was enough for Arthur.

Jack had gone into the back room, and Arthur saw heat shimmering above the crucible that such places always kept on the go. Mrs Oilick leaned back in her chair, one eye on the bottle and two red dots on her cheeks, looking as merry as a rocking-horse. Then her eye snapped closed and she snored.

Arthur stood to go. He held onto his thumping head with both hands, then stared at the table. He saw no money there. He looked at his hands, then patted his pockets, then held his head again. The five shillings Jack had given him for the watch was gone.

'Jack?' Arthur quavered.

He shuffled to the back room, but he didn't dare go in.

The door was so bent with damp it was hardly a door, and through the gap he glimpsed pawnshop articles, unredeemed, scattered higgledy-piggledy, umbrellas, shoes, but mostly hats – hundreds of hats of every shape and size, piled against the walls like a silent crowd. Surrounded by the hats, a pair of thin, grimy heels stuck from the end of a couch.

The toes were blackened and rough as roots. Rucked up to the thin knees he saw the hem of a dress, frayed rotten by use, once red or purple. The girl was twelve or thirteen, and very stinky, the ripe smell of those once used to washing but now unwashed. He could smell her from here, and see the fleas swarming in her dress, the lice in her hair. But her hands lay lifeless in her lap and she'd stopped crying. Her face was slack and dull, she didn't even swing her legs. Her eyes stared unmoving at the hats.

Jack moved about the room without seeing her, and the smell of melting metal mingled with the smell of the girl.

'Jack, there's been a terrible mistake,' Arthur called ingratiatingly.

'Yer made it,' Jack said. He knocked the girl. 'Maggy, do yer spiel.'

'Yes, Jack.' The girl contorted her mouth into a grin that didn't touch her eyes. 'Pleased to make the pleasure of your acquaintance, sir.'

27

"Ain't she got class?' Jack grunted. 'I only use 'er fer bilking, she's not a prostitute yet. Soon as 'er mark takes 'is trousers down I'm on 'im. A man wiv no trousers is 'appy ter pay double or thrice the price, 'an throw in 'is false teeth too.'

'Does she know wot might 'appen?'

Jack poured silver from the crucible. 'Wot's got into yer, Arthur?'

Arthur knew he wouldn't remember her face. None of them had a face, in Field Lane or Regent's Street or a hundred neighbourhoods you saw girls like her standing in ranks, as passive and indifferent as stands of hackney cabs.

'About me necessary,' he said. He stood back as Jack knocked past him, then followed him into the front room.

'Yer drank it,' Jack threw over his shoulder.

'Not it all, surely, Jack.'

Jack roared. 'Mrs Oilick, madam!' She woke with a snort and dragged her feet off the table. 'Go on,' Jack said irritably, 'tell 'im wot I told yer.'

'Drank it ter the last penny,' she muttered, scratching the insides of her knees. 'Couldn't stop 'im. Drunk as a lord 'e was.'

'In the old days Smart Arthur was a man to admire, Mrs Oilick.' Jack shook his head, yawned. 'No one 'ad sharper eyes or quicker 'ands for fine drawing – the fine drawing of fings from gennelmen's pockets, that is. 'E could always 'old 'is drink. But 'e 'ad a weakness. 'E fell 'ead over 'eels fer a partickler girl, an' married 'er.'

'Married 'er proper?' Mrs Oilick asked.

'I love my Elsie,' Arthur said simply.

'Wot a tragic tragedy!' Jack picked up a cat by its ginger scruff. 'A wife slowed 'im, see. 'E started ter doubt 'imself, got responsibilities, wasn't 'alf the man 'e was. But fer 'er, Arthur, yer could've been king of us all, an' ended swinging.'

'Shame on 'im!' Mrs Oilick condemned Arthur.

'Elsie made a fool of our Arthur, an' now the drink's making a fool of 'im too. *She* done it ter 'im.' Jack stroked the cat once, from head to tail. It hissed as though sensing his anger.

''Cause of 'er, demon drink's got its 'ooks in Arthur!'

'I stopped,' Arthur said. Tears filled his eyes. He told himself it was the effect of the rum. 'Never, never again.'

'After one sip yer can't never stop,' Jack said.

Mrs Oilick laughed. 'No one's clever like yer is, Jack. No fleas on yer! Yer got 'im good'n'proper!'

Arthur wiped his eyes. Jack bent down, fondling the cat's head, speaking close. 'In Abbey Place there's big 'ouses, right? Right, Arthur? That's wot my knife-grinding pal told me.' Arthur flinched from the flecks of his spittle.

'Leave it,' he said. 'Abbey Place is St John's Wood, it's not yer ground.'

'I got legs, don't I?' Jack spoke closer, his lips creaking moistly, breathing in warm gusts. 'Time fer a change. Got ter use 'em. The good stuff's worked out round 'ere.'

'Calm down, Jack. Stick ter wot yer know.'

'Me pal tried 'is luck, went ter the front door accidental-on-purpose, kept 'is peepers peeled. The butler took 'im below-stairs through the 'all, lazy bastard. Mahogany doors! Silver in the front rooms, candlesticks, bowls, cutlery, I don't know, solid stuff worth its weight. More in the family rooms upstairs no doubt, the master's a strut in the City, an' the missus got jewels more'n she can stand up straight in, there's paintings of 'er. Photographs too.'

'Children?'

'Two, one of 'em witless, the butler said they can't do nuffink wiv 'er. Both asleep in the attic, why should they wake?'

'Dogs?'

'Only next door, behind a 'igh brick wall. We won't be on their patch, so 'oo cares? 'Ere's the clincher. Wot should my pal spy on the 'all table but two tickets fer the opera. Covent Garden. Ternight! So no gennnelman or lady in the 'ouse. The butler's night off an' the cook an' maids early ter bed.'

'Windows?'

'Tighter'n a cat's arse. I'll 'andle it. It's an evening's tommy-work fer yer sharp eyes, Arthur, an' five bob in yer pocket.'

'That's a Jack-deal!' Mrs Oilick crowed. 'Give the poor sinner 'is own money back! Oh me achin' sides!' The more she laughed, the more her eyes were cold and watchful, set on Jack. 'St John's Wood. Yer getting too good fer us. Really yer are.'

'I'll be there,' Arthur said, rubbing his ear as though to rub Jack's voice out of his hearing.

'Eyes is all, Arthur. Any pickin' on yer own account, I'll chop yer fingers off.'

'Yes, Jack.'

'Yer'll wait fer me on the corner of the Met, an' yer'll bring a boy wiv yer. Eight o'clock. Let me down an' I'll 'ave yer guts.' He jerked his arm. 'Now get off

the earth!' He cursed, surprised, as the cat scratched
him. Five slits swelled on the soft underside of his
forearm, opening, filling with blood. The blood
trickled down to his elbow. 'Blooded me,' Jack said.
The look in his eye did not change. He swung his
arm.

He threw the cat in the fire.

Arthur shouted. The cat yowled and streaked
upstairs trailing thin smoke from its fur. Arthur
stared after it, appalled.

Mrs Oilick got up. 'I 'ate that smell.' She wiped
her hands on her dress and crossed to the door. 'I'm
like a mother ter 'im. 'E don't care, do 'e? Jack
Riddles don't care about nothing nor nobody. God
bless 'im.' Then she grinned up at Jack, and left the
room.

Jack ignored her. He put his lips to Arthur's ear.

'I'll need a skinny-isaacs boy, Arthur me old choom.
A loofer boy.'

St Mary's tolled eight times, and down by the New
Road the crossing-sweepers' children worked back
and forth like little demons. The rain had stopped
but under the gaslights their small round faces
shone with sweat, smeared and spattered with
horseshit from the long-handled shovels and brooms
they wielded, which stood taller than they. Across
the pavement the youngest children were slumped
on the doorsteps, exhausted, a swaddled baby
sleeping peacefully among them like a chrysalis.

Shadowed by the bright shop-fronts, part of the
thinning crowd, Arthur drifted towards them
unnoticed.

31

There he was. The loofer boy.

Monkey was the smallest and skinniest of the children, though he was nearly thirteen years old. He darted this way and that between the rumbling carts and buses, his bare legs so bent by English disease that he scampered like a monkey, but his joints were as limber as grease. His elbows were said to be double-jointed, so he could reach behind his armpit to scratch the back of his head if he was told to. A loofer boy's life hung on such tricks. But for now his filthy hands snatched eagerly for ha'pennies from the silks and velvets pushing past him in the mêlée of the crossing, depositing the coins in pockets secreted all over his person, and he was always cheerful. 'Thank 'ee, sir! 'Bliged, ma'am!'

The elder tearaways and gonophs waiting along the walls would knock Monkey's takings out of him later, unless his ma got to him first, but Monkey always had another pocket.

All at once the children's angry chirping cries rose like a flock of birds, reddening the ears of a miser who tried to bluster past, and quick expert flicks of slimy manure peppered the back of his coat and trouser-legs. 'Yer got that fer free too, yer skinflint!'

Those old men's faces on children's shoulders missed not a trick, Arthur knew, and sadness dragged at him like a weight.

Coming up silently on the left behind Monkey, he reached across, tapped the boy's right shoulder, and grabbed him when the boy ran to the left.

'Aw,' Monkey gasped. 'I thought yer was a rosser. Blimey!'

'Yer get paid when yer open the door on the inside,' Arthur said, 'an' see us standing outside.'

'It's me night off,' Monkey said, brightening. 'I was going ter be a good boy.'

'Not now yer ain't,' said Arthur. "Ow's yer dad?'

'I got lots of dads,' Monkey said blithely. 'Yer might've used me crossing!' he added, hopping as Arthur pulled him across the filthy part of the road.

Everything was falling quiet now, the best business of the day gone over. Men were paid on Saturday, tomorrow, no one had money tonight, the thinnest evening of the week. The pubs and gin-palaces that made every street-corner brilliant were turning down their lights, changing, becoming dull and tawdry. Men hung about in knots, then drifted away. The darkness seemed to seep out of the ground as the lights went out. Turnham's Grand Concert Hall lost its glow. Last week's posters proclaiming the high-kicking spreesters Lily Alhambra and Wiry Sal were peeling and streaked with damp, yellowing, their magic lost. 'Just keep yer fingers away from me pockets, Smart Arthur,' Monkey said cheekily. Long gaps showed in the traffic along Watling Street, though occasionally they jumped aside as an unlighted cart rumbled past them out of the darkness. Above the black rooftops the clouds cleared away in pale feathers, letting the moon's cold radiance pour down. They heard footsteps and a tall figure crossed the pavement in front of them.

'Jack?' Arthur called. 'Jack, is that you?'

The figure stopped, outlined with moonlight. Then as it turned its head the shape of its hat-brim changed, its face shadowed beneath.

Monkey rubbed his thin shoulders, then skidded on the frost, behaving for a moment like the child he was. The Asylum for the Houseless Poor would be opening its doors tonight, he said. Monkey knew such things, and his voice prattled on.

'Jack?' Arthur called. A cart rattled loudly past them, then the echoes faded away and the usual silence fell.

The figure seemed made of stone by the moonlight. Suddenly it turned and crossed the empty road away from them as though it had not heard them, or considered them of no importance, or had its mind set on another task and had already forgotten them.

Monkey wrapped his arms around his shoulders and stood on one foot, keeping the other warm behind his knee.

'If I 'ad a pair of shoes like that!' he swore. 'Did yer 'ear 'em? Proper 'obnails. An' steel tips, front an' back.'

Arthur stood in the doorway that almost concealed him, his collar up, grateful for the warmth of his coat. The temperature was dropping fast, the sky deep black around the brilliant ball of the moon, and the rubbish piled at the back of the alley gleamed stiff and hard with frost. He moved uneasily, listening, as St Mary's struck a quarter past the hour. Between nine and two was the worst time for police. He breathed out a pale cloud, rubbing his hands. Where was Jack?

The pavements would be treacherous tonight, and in the morning horses would fall. In such rock-hard conditions there would be no work for crossing-sweepers, and their standby, doors and windows,

34

could not be cleaned. Arthur nodded as Monkey crawled under the hem of his coat and stood up inside. Only the boy's peeping face and white puffs of breath showed between the buttons. He put his feet on Arthur's shoes, which were warmer than the paving-stones of the alley. And so they waited.

Monkey stopped breathing. He jabbed Arthur's leg with his elbow.

The pile of rubbish was moving. Suddenly it cracked open, bits of old sandwich-board sliding down, and Jack stood up. He wore a shabby Army greatcoat, very long, almost to his ankles.

He scratched his fingers back through his hair, yawning like a man who has rested well.

'I was 'ere before yer, keeping me eye on yer,' he said. 'I was 'ere all the time. Let's go get it done.'

Chapter Two

I

My dear friend.
Here's a gift for you. No, don't laugh, take it! Best
butcher's steak for those noisy dogs of yours. What,
no servants?
I forgot. I asked for our discussions to be private.
I'll feed the dogs myself.
I know the way.
Then we'll talk in peace.

II

'Joy Briggs, what *do* you think you're doing!' Tom
shouted. He chose his words just like Mama to make
his little sister obey him. 'Get away from that window
this *very* minute!'

Joy knelt at the attic window. She held her breath.
She shifted, rubbing one of her knees which had
gone stiff from the hard windowsill. Her eyes did not
move from the street four storeys below.

Shut up, Tom, she thought.

They were not allowed the lamp after bed-time.
Nanny had bundled her to bed in the white silk

nightgown just like Mama's, impossible to wear without pleasure, though the attic was too dark to show colour. Joy, sneaking to the clothes-trunk by the window, had put on her favourite pink satin dressing-gown by herself, and her pink lambswool slippers by herself. They were one size too large, but she knew she would grow into them. She loved dressing up. She made herself wedding rings out of wooden beads, and around her neck she'd hung a string of silver coins for a necklace. Tonight she was a pagan princess.

Joy was five years old, a fact which she understood perfectly. She could not have said so. She could put almost nothing of what she felt into words. Five years was *old*, five years knew almost everything, but adults talked down to her in their slow mumbling voices, repeating the same things over and over, as though she were stupid. I know, she always wanted to shout. I know that, I do understand!

Tom, still yawning, didn't even understand that she was a princess, or what she had seen on the moonlit pavement. The stones still gleaming with wet from the rain made everything down there into a shadow.

She breathed through her nose, motionless, staring.

New shadows came moving into the shadows far below her, their dark shapes drifting as slowly and smoothly as fish in a deep pool.

Suddenly Tom, who must have come up behind her, knocked her against the windowpane. 'Get back to bed or you'll get in real trouble!' she heard him threaten.

38

Joy looked over her shoulder.

Her eyes were a beautiful fox-brown, deep and still, and her gaze was steady and direct. Confused by her, Tom stepped back. Even by moonlight Joy's hair was red, the curls lying like embers on her shoulders, flowing like flames down her back. 'Bed or trouble,' he repeated uncertainly.

She knew he meant *he* would get into trouble. You're afraid Nanny M'Kenzy will hear you shouting at me, she thought. Because you *are* shouting, aren't you, Tom.

But she could hardly hear him.

Anyway, he certainly wasn't treating her like a princess, so she turned her back on him.

Joy pressed her nose against the glass. She was flying. Her face was level with the tops of the plane trees that lined the road, their bare branches looking like huge upthrust arms towards her, brilliant with air-frost and moonlight. Deep shadow stretched down beneath them, and as her breath fogged the glass they glowed like giant moon-coloured candles growing out of the darkness below. The scene looked so lovely that she wished Tom would watch them with her and understand what she was seeing. She tried to make him understand, but Tom's lips were pinched white with anger and frustration.

'You're stupid!' he said, his voice muffled as though he were shouting into a pillow. He tugged her from the window.

Joy faced him.

She tried to tell him about the figures moving below. In her mind's ear she heard herself saying, Tom, there's some men in our street. *Tom, there's*

*some men in our street, and they're looking at our
house.*

She took a deep breath.

'T-T-Tuh,' she stammered thickly. Her lips
trembled. 'Tuh-Tuh—'

'Uh Uh!' Tom grabbed his chance. 'Uhuh, ooh-
ooh!' He gibbered his usual ape-noises spitefully, his
mockery making her attempts to utter the words
even more clumsy, and now her tongue refused to
form the sound-shapes. Yet Joy could see so clearly
what she wanted to say, even the patterns and
colours of the words, but still they would not come,
and the more she tried to bring them forward the
more they shrank, slipping away from her, circling,
whirling away like brilliant foam down a plughole.
She could not grasp them however hard she tried.
Tom rolled his eyes and dribbled, as she did.

She gave up and watched him without tears.

Tom limped the length of the attic bedroom
brushing the carpet with his knuckles, his lower jaw
thrust forward, and she couldn't help beginning to
smile. He was the orang-utan at the Zoological
Gardens in Regent's Park, where Nanny sometimes
took them. His mouth moved and she knew he was
singing a snatch from the popular song, 'Walking in
Zoo is the OK thing to do . . .'

'Tuh-Tuh—' she stammered. Then it came. '*TOM!*'

'That's my name, don't wear it out.' He had no
idea what it felt like to be her. 'Who are you tonight,
Joy? The Princess of Stuh-Stuh-Stammer?'

She pressed her face to the glass to make him
follow her.

'Your nose will go flat and you'll never pull it out,'

40

Tom said. 'You'll have to walk around like that for ever and ever, looking like a pug-dog.'

Why are you so afraid, Tom, she wondered.

'Snub nose,' Tom went on. 'I'm going to call you Snubbie.' His voice came more loudly, blurring, as he shouted close to her ear. 'Snubbie! Snubnose Pug-dog! Flatface!' He gave up. 'Joy, I know you can hear me,' he mumbled sadly, 'I know you can, even if it doesn't make much sense to you. Go back to bed, please, then we can both go.' When she did not move he said, 'You cretin. You're so absolutely cretinous. Mama doesn't love you.' He had overheard Papa say something. 'You're such a terrible embarrassment, Joy.'

She tried to say, *Mama does love me! She DOES!*

Sometimes Mama allowed Joy to watch her dress. Mama was very beautiful. Her tummy was white and flat even after two children. Her breasts were round and her nipples bloomed bright blood-red like fruit, not darkened by infant feeding. She was very lively and vivacious in company, all the men at Papa's parties adored her. Sometimes a carriage would be sent round the next day, with hothouse flowers or a basket of oranges, and Mama would talk to the man in a room with the door closed. The men called her 'Lydia'. At first Joy was given little prizes when Mama came out, but once Mama shouted at her that she was a spy. A spy received the switch, and the switch left a stripe.

Both mother and daughter had been horrified. 'Look what you've made me do!' Then Mama had put her finger to her lips in the universal gesture of silence. 'Sssh . . .'

Mama does love me, Joy tried to say, but Tom laughed, because he couldn't hear her.

Joy thought angrily, he's afraid of the dark. He's being nasty to me not because he doesn't care about me, but because he does. A boy can't admit that he is afraid to his little sister.

Tom's so much bigger and stronger and older than me, she realised, but he's so afraid of being alone. Inside his heart he's just like me.

She reached out her hand, but Tom turned away.

'Why won't she do what I say?' he muttered. He wasn't a cruel boy, he was normal. It was Joy who was not normal. He waited barefoot in the slant of moonlight between the window and his bed, looking at her, wondering what was going on in that head of hers.

Slowly he realised that she was not thinking of him at all.

Joy held her breath until the glass cleared of mist. She knew the difference between her left hand and her right hand, and she knew numbers. The large pebbledash house beyond her right hand, she knew, was number seventeen. The windows were dark, and a frightening old witch lived there. On her left hand was number thirteen. It rose beside them looking like their own redbrick house seen in a mirror, with high chimneys, and steep tile roofs, this side of it in the blue moonlight, the lighted windows looking very yellow. She and Tom were allowed to eat Sunday lunch with Papa and Mama, and Papa had sneered at their plump neighbour's ways, calling him Mr Sparkles, or Our Friend Sparkle-Stein. Once from her window Joy had seen the two men setting off on their different ways to work, raising their silk top hats to one another so politely that she knew they were being rude. That night Tom, following Papa's example, had told her the man was a fat Jew, and that his house was full of jewels because he worked in a place called the Garden, and he shouldn't be allowed to live in this street, because it was an English street. Sometimes when the fat man came home from work Joy had seen two broad-shouldered bullies squeezed beside him in the carriage, escorting him to his front door before turning back. His door was lined with steel, and she had seen workmen fitting it with shiny new hinges twice the size of the old ones.

'You're always looking outside!' Tom grumbled. He gave in to her fascination. 'What's there, anyway?' She moved aside eagerly as he pushed beside her. But instead of seeing the men, he stared upwards. 'You're just a silly little girl with only half a brain, gazing at the moon,' he said.

Joy understood half. She had heard Dr Warren say *half* to Mama when he presented his large bill, and Mama had said *half* to Papa. Only Nanny M'Kenzy had said nothing, hugging Joy silently into her big white arms, and Joy had cried because she sensed she was supposed to cry. As she was taken out she heard Mama tell Papa one of those kindly meant things that were so difficult to understand. 'I think we should keep this under our hats, don't you?'

'It's such a terrible embarrassment,' Papa had muttered. 'Yes, best kept quiet . . .'

Far below, in the shadow beneath a tree, Joy saw another shadow move. She pointed, but Tom did not respond. He stared up vacantly. 'I can see his face,' he murmured. 'I wonder if there really is a Man in the Moon.'

Joy was sure that these men were not interested in their neighbour's house, like the other man. That man, who'd arrived earlier, had been welcomed next door by the unmistakable figure of Papa's neighbour dressed for the evening meal, glossy celluloid collar to the chin, white tie and tails, his belly in a tight scarlet band, his plump hand waving a lighted cigar in greeting. Who the stranger was Joy did not know, the light streaming past them had showed on his face for only a brief moment when he took off his hat, then he had followed the fat jeweller inside, and the door had closed.

These men outside were different.

'There's nothing to see,' Tom said, yawning. 'Get into your bed now, or I'll tell Mrs M'Kenzy on you.' He faltered. 'Why are you looking at me like that?'

Didn't he know Nanny M'Kenzy lay on her back in her room at the other end of the corridor, a bottle that had held something as clear as water clasped between her breasts, asleep and dreamless beneath the picture of Jesus?

'Who are you really tonight?' Tom blustered. 'Princess Pocahontas again? Redskin princess! Whoop, whoop! Grow up.' He turned away from the look in her eye.

Joy saw two men in the street now, perhaps three. They were definitely looking up at Papa's house, seeming to gaze above the attic windows, and she imagined what they must be seeing – not her, Princess Pocahontas was safely hidden behind the shadowed glass, but the chimneys above and behind her, some still smoking. The third figure was much smaller, a child probably, and took no interest. She smiled to look at him hopping from one leg to the other as though his feet were cold. Joy wondered why he should feel cold. Surely he was well wrapped in socks and boots.

She gripped Tom's elbow, tugging him, pointing.

But he hugged her. 'Sometimes I worry about you, little sister. I wonder sometimes if you're not silly at all. You might be almost as clever as me, except you're a girl.'

She pushed him away impatiently, and Tom looked wounded.

Suddenly the figures came forward, crossing the pavement as quickly as hunting-dogs, throwing shadows behind them. The short man wearing a hat slipped through the gate and turned aside at once, collar up, merging into the darkness behind the gate-pillar and ornamental bushes, where he could see the road but not be seen.

Joy had seen Tom and his friends play these games. The man was the lookout. Boys like Tom's friends called it keeping *cave*, kay-vee, which was an easy word to hear.

The man in the ankle-length coat – like soldiers wore begging on street-corners – came loping with long strides across the lawn. Joy realised that the gravel of the drive and the carriage circle made a noise that ordinary people could hear. Even to them the man would be silent. The boy in the cloth cap scampered nervously in those huge footsteps, taking two or three jumps between each one, and Joy grinned to see what they had both forgotten, their trail following them in the frost that was forming.

They weren't perfect.

She looked down on them from above, and their size seemed to shrink as they ran beneath her towards the side gate, until all she could see of them was the tops of their heads with their shoulders sticking out below. Abruptly the angle of the roof hid them.

Out of her sight, she knew, they had found an arrowed sign on the gate for the benefit of the shop-boys, tinkers, knife-sharpeners and itinerants who were always calling, TRADESMEN'S ENTRANCE. Joy was never allowed in there, but she had seen the entrance discreetly half-hidden by oleander bushes. Beyond the gate a passageway led down the side of the house, locked at night. She knew no one could open locks without a key. So the huge man would give up, and she would see him and the tiny boy go running back across the grass, defeated.

But she did not see them go running back.

Joy held her breath.

Suppose he knew how to make the lock give up? Suppose he was working on it now? The gate would squeak if it opened, she knew – Papa, changing for the opera, had complained about the noise to Worth.

But Joy would not hear such a quick, light sound.

Still, she listened.

Tom jerked. 'What was that?' he said.

III

Give me the key.
I know you do have a key. Quiet now, don't cry. I

46

*know everything about you, my friend . . . because
that's what I do.
Give me the key.
Hush, old man, don't lie to me. I know you keep it
here, with your family, in your home, with everything
most precious to you, because that's the way a man's
mind works. And her mind, too – but of course, you
don't believe I would really hurt her, do you?
Give me the key.*

IV

Joy imagined the man and the boy slipping down the
narrow concrete passageway between the house and
the redbrick boundary wall. The fat man's dogs
would bark – they were trained to bark at any
disturbance, and did, so that Papa often complained.

The dogs did not bark.

The man and the boy would be skirting quietly
around the dustbins, and she thought of them
tripping over coal-lumps dropped near the bunker –
Worth was always shouting at the coal-heaver to be
more careful, and his dray pulled by two black horses
had delivered this morning, blocking the passage, so
Worth had had to walk the knife-sharpener down
through the house.

The knife-sharpener had seen Joy watching him
and winked one eye in his filthy face, very friendly,
but Worth had not let him say anything insolent.

The man and the boy must have passed the coal-
lumps by now. Joy remembered to take a breath.
Her heart was hammering.

'I thought I heard something, that's all,' Tom said.

He grinned, but his eyes were wide. 'Second time tonight.'

She imagined them going down the concrete steps at the end of the passageway, coming into the paved back yard walled off from Papa's garden. The yard was below ground level, and on two sides of it the windows of the rustic peeped above the paving-stones – the mysterious basement world of servants' quarters, workrooms, and the kitchen. Cook treated the kitchen like her personal property. On a sunny day like today the washing would have been hung out to dry around the yard, but when the rain had threatened it would all have been taken inside and hung from the kitchen drying-racks, which were pulled up to the ceiling by ropes. Joy had glimpsed the scene once – over the heads of the busy maids cutting and chopping, and saucepans boiling with steam, it had seemed to her that the kitchen was full of flying people.

The kitchen door was always locked at night. The two iron bolts, top and bottom, echoed like the ones on the front door as Worth shot them closed last thing on his rounds. It was part of Standing Orders. Tonight was the second Friday of the month, so he would have finished his duties early before going out.

Joy imagined the huge man staring at the outside of the door, his shoulders slumped in defeat.

Like all houses, Papa's house had its rustic windows screwed down to deter petty thieves or tradesmen taking an opportunity. Only the kitchen windows opened, to let out steam, and they were barred. The maids' rooms, somewhere beneath the front of the house, had no windows at all, or even a door to the outside.

There was no way in to Papa's house. They were safe.

'Don't you realise?' Tom said. 'We're alone.' He frowned as Joy went to the bedroom door. 'I mean, except for Nanny M'Kenzy. What are you doing!'

Joy put both hands around the brass doorknob, knowing it was stiff, and twisted with all her strength. The door opened.

'You can't,' Tom said. 'It's not allowed.' Then he said, 'Don't.' He licked his lips. 'Something woke me earlier – in my sleep I heard dogs barking. I woke up and saw you looking out of the window, but it was something else I heard outside that woke me . . .'

The children's door had an elephant and a mouse drawn on it. Joy looked along the corridor. One lamp glowed at the far end, beyond the narrow stairwell, outside Nanny M'Kenzy's room.

'I was woken by a scream,' Tom said.

V

These are such terrible times we live in. Give me the key to the safe, and I needn't hurt her.
Don't force me. You'll be the guilty one. It won't be my fault.
Give me the key. Right now. Right now.
Now.

VI

'I thought the scream was brakes,' Tom said. He had

49

put his lips close to Joy's ear. 'I thought it was a brake-shoe screaming on a cartwheel. But it sounded more awful than you can imagine.' He reached after her towards the attic stairs, but she slipped out of his grasp, knowing he was trying to frighten her, it was all part of the games boys played. Tom was very pale. 'Then I saw you at the window,' he said. 'Let's go back to our room and look, shall we?' Then he said, 'You'll get us both into trouble. I didn't really hear anything.'

The steps were narrow and steep. Joy peered down them. Tom was the only person she knew completely, apart from herself. She knew he had heard something.

'I'll get Mrs M'Kenzy,' Tom said. He was too old to call her Nanny, nearly twelve, supposed to be an almost-man, a string of a boy in striped pyjamas with a boy's straight pale hair, hands that had never worked, a boy's sensitive eyes, and from the way he showed off to her Joy realised he knew he was being brave. He sauntered along the corridor, stopping nervously halfway as he realised he was barefoot, then carried on. Raising his fist, he tapped on Nanny's door without sound.

Joy could not hear it. She saw him knock harder and this time heard, almost felt, the muffled thuds.

The door swung open, unlatched. Tom looked apologetic and put his head inside.

He glanced back at Joy, drew a breath at the smell, then went into the room. In only a few moments he came out. The lamp flickered in his eyes. His hair had fallen over his forehead.

You really didn't know, Joy thought, amazed. You

tried to shake her awake, and you were surprised when nothing happened. Don't you keep your eyes open, because you have ears?

'She won't stir,' Tom said. He tried to sound in charge like Papa. 'Back to our room with you, young lady, right now!' He lifted the lamp off the wall so that they wouldn't be frightened of the dark.

Joy took a step downstairs. Tom's hand closed on her shoulder, tight, pulling her back. He was hurting her. Joy twisted away and gave him an angry stare. His fingertips had left a half-circle of grubby marks on her dressing-gown, and she saw that he must have been secretly eating chocolate beneath his bedclothes earlier, thinking she'd never know.

Tom looked guilty, then he jumped, and she knew he'd heard something move.

'Nothing,' Tom said, but his throat worked. He was swallowing.

Silently, Joy peered at the broad landing below. Mama's bedroom door stood to one side of the wide stairwell down there, Papa's on the other side. The moon's glow from below made a confusion of light and shadow that tricked her eye. The carpet had big dark patterns that Tom always thought were snakes and spiders. The walls were darkly wallpapered and thick with watercolours, country scenes, and photographs hidden behind glaring rectangles of picture-glass, so that she could hardly tell what she was seeing. Perhaps they really were snakes and spiders.

Tom jerked her round, the lamplight yellow on his face. He put his finger to his lips, pointing. His lips moved as though he was whispering but she could not pick out the words, then he pointed again at the wall. It was a bare, blank wall. Mama's room was on the other side of it. What was he trying to say?

Joy went down to the final step. Rather than tread on the snakes she reached out her slippered toe until she could almost touch the plain mat outside Mama's room, got a grip on the doorframe with her outstretched fingers, and swung herself across.

Tom hissed at her. She grinned, wildly excited, half expecting – no, almost *certain* – that the bulk of Nanny M'Kenzy would appear any moment at the head of the stairs and spoil their fun. A cuff round the ear for them too, especially Tom, for not being able to control his little sister.

'Stop it!' Tom hissed. 'It's in the wall. *They're inside the wall!*'

Joy opened Mama's door, and slipped inside.

The moonlit room was empty, made of stone. Nothing moved, only her footsteps.

It was taken for granted that Mama's room was out of bounds, but now, having started, she felt unable to stop. She was entering the secret territory of the woman she would one day grow up to be. Joy lost her childish quickness, her steps slowed. She held up her hands and parted her hair in the middle like Mama, and now she even walked like Mama, as if she were wearing one of Mama's gorgeous flounced dresses, the emerald-green one perhaps, and everyone was admiring her. With instinctive grace she nodded her head first to the left, then to the right, acknowledging the compliments of the guests at the Ball.

But she could not hear a word they said. The

scene dissolved. Joy stood alone in the middle of the room, the bed in front of her, the fireplace behind.

Mama's bed, standing as high as her eyes, with towering drapes sweeping from the ceiling, was made up like a gigantic spun-sugar cradle. By cold moonlight the white satin counterpane seemed as hard and brittle as the icing of a wedding-cake. Gaby had laid the fire but not lit it, awaiting her mistress's return. The grate gleamed with Brunswick black. The cinders, paper and dry wood were built up in proper layers, with coals set on top, and the brass coal-scuttle was full of equal-sized coals. There were several chairs and several life-size dolls, more by the window, prettily dressed. One sprawled in the corner, the room's only untidiness. Rose-scented perfume lingered in the still air.

Mama was not here. She was at the opera.

But Joy imagined the plain, pallid, private figure of Mama in the early morning, sometimes glimpsed through the doorway, seeming so strangely changed from dressed-up Mama. In bed Mama's face was white with grease, black hair hanging down in the way she never wore it during the day, uncombed, almost ugly she looked so different, with her elbows sticking out, eating her breakfast from the tray Gaby brought at seven-thirty sharp. Mama would look up slowly. Joy would stare at her with the child's unblinking gaze that saw everything. Mama's lips would move, a word to Gaby. Gaby's obedient bob, the door closing.

Joy turned slowly away from the empty bed. A coal rolled out of the fireplace towards her.

The piece of coal trailed a streaky black line

across the carpet as it came, then bumped to a stop against her foot.

Joy looked at the mark on her slipper, then at the lump of coal sitting on the carpet. She knew what would happen, five years old knew everything. Mama would be horrified, Worth summoned, Worth admonished for not checking the chimney-sweep's work. In the butler's pantry Worth would twist Gaby's ear and blame her for the sake of his authority.

But Joy had seen the coal come by itself, it wasn't anybody's fault.

She knew what to do. She reached out her hand for the tongs.

More soot trickled from the chimney. It blackened the tinder waiting to be lit, then the hearth.

There was a pause. Her ears heard her own breathing perfectly, but everything else was silence.

Silent lumps of soot came flopping down, puffing soundlessly over the coals and spreading out, speckling the carpet, smudging the hem of her dressing-gown.

Suddenly a hand, soot-black, and an arm, also soot-black, clothed in rags, dropped from the chimney. The dangling arm swung against the chimney-breast, more soot pouring down around it, then put down its fingers to the coals as though feeling them. Made confident, it twisted and extended itself, then bent upwards like a crab's, the fingers now feeling into the room for the mantelshelf. Joy stared, fascinated. She tried her own arm but it would not go round like that.

The face of a boy appeared, upside-down. His eyes widened, seeing her.

He swung, struggling, then in a shower of soot abruptly dropped on his head. His legs flopped from the chimney and he rolled into the room scattering coals everywhere around him. He sat up black as a golly among them, only the whites of his eyes showing.

Joy knew what would happen. When Papa finds him here, she thought excitedly, he'll hang!

The urchin sprang up. He ouched, holding his feet, hopping from one bare black foot to the other, cursing the sharp cinders with a very pink tongue in his black face. He was a dirty, ragged figure of a brat no taller than her but much older. In fact, Joy thought, this boy looked even older than Tom. He had a filthy starved face and eyes as old as a man's, as though he had aged twenty years in his boyhood, so that she could not sum him up.

She'd never seen anything like him.

For a moment they stared at one another, the lad in sooty rags and the girl in pink satin.

'Wrong bleedin' loofer, wrong bleedin' room!' the urchin muttered, casting expert glances around him. The whites of his eyes flicked from Joy to the coal-tongs she was holding, then back again to her face. When she smiled he seemed alarmed.

Then he grinned back at her.

'Joy?' Tom called, and the spell broke.

'Burst me!' the boy swore. 'They ain't clippin' no switches on Monkey!' He dodged to the right, then ran around Joy to the left, scuttling for the door as fast as a monkey on his bare feet, leaving a trail of streaky marks and bare black footprints flying after him.

Everything happened so fast that the word burst out of her without thought, easily, *'TOM!'*

She ran after the boy, thrilled, anxious, excited, but he slammed the door after him, gone. She tugged the knob, but all the doors were made for grown-ups to open, she hated them, her hands slipped, she was missing all the fun. A thump and falling noises came from the landing. Tom had tackled the boy like he said they did at school. He'd sit on the boy's chest and call him a miserable flea.

She tried again to turn the doorknob, but her hand slipped.

She dropped the coal-tongs and gripped the knob in both hands, putting her chin on her fingers, twisting with all her strength.

The heavy adult-sized door opened with a rush, and the worst thing happened. Its weight tripped her and she tottered backwards, sat down with a bump, one leg on each side of the door. She pulled her feet to her chin and rolled away, then scrambled onto the landing terrified she'd missed Tom getting the boy.

The landing was empty.

Forgetting even about the snakes and spiders, she walked slowly to the middle. He mustn't hurt the boy! She wanted to know all about him.

Doors slammed. 'Stop him!' Tom shouted.

He sounded furious, just like Papa. He had his eyebrows together, frowning, but it was a terrific game. The boy, trapped, raced towards Joy round the other side of the stairwell, his quickness catching Tom flat-footed, and with a squeal of laughter she put out her arms to catch him. 'I won't 'urt yer!' the

boy shouted. He leapt round her somehow, banged
into the wall, then threw himself down the stairs
much too fast.

'I'll hurt *you*,' Tom shouted. 'Stop, thief!' He shoved
past Joy with an angry look, going downstairs with
the lamp, which swayed and shook, flinging yellow
rays and shadows round their two figures running
below. She leaned over the rail. Tom in his striped
pyjamas took the steps two at a time, but the boy
sprang off the last four or five steps in one jump,
swung round the newel-post with his arms at full
stretch, and launched himself down the next flight
as though he didn't care whether he ran or fell.

The boy was terrified, Joy realised suddenly. She
ran down the stairs as quickly as she could, holding
up her dressing-gown in one hand, her other reaching
up to the rail. *We won't hurt you!* she wanted to call
to the boy. *We only want to talk to you!* But no sound
came.

Tom glanced up and yelled at her furiously. 'Don't
come down!' A brass stair-rod had come loose and
he picked it up, brandishing it like a sword.

Tom, she thought, *don't hurt him*.

Indian rugs had been thrown on the polished
floors between the day-rooms and the sooty boy
tumbled onto his behind, slid along kicking to get up,
the rugs skidding this way and that from under his
feet. Tom caught him a whack across the shoulders
with the stair-rod. The boy saw Joy looking at him
through the banister rails and cried out. He tried to
protect his head with his arms. Tom caught him and
whacked again and again, back, legs, wherever he
could have a go, and each time the boy cried, writhing

silently, and soot puffed out of him.

Stop it. Joy's lips moved. *Tom, don't hurt him!*

It was awful. Tom brought his home-made weapon whipping down. But this time the boy ducked under the blow and scampered away on knuckles and toes, pursued by Tom with the stair-rod bent almost in half. At the top of the stairs he jumped nimbly astride the banister and slid away down the rail just like Tom always wanted to but never dared.

Tom went bobbing down the steps to the ground floor, the lamp swinging. Then the light went dim. He had followed the boy into the rooms where children were not allowed.

VII

Tom stopped in the doorway.

He raised his stair-rod, surprised by how bent it was. The breath whistled in his nostrils, and he was more angry and more excited, more *alive*, than he had ever felt in his life. Papa would be proud of him.

Tonight, Tom was no longer a child.

'I'm going to give you a good thrashing,' he called.

He stepped into the room and lifted the lamp above his head, making the light gleam on the brass rail raised in his other hand. He must look very frightening.

A scuttling noise, muffled, came from behind the long table. The cutlery, already set ready for tomorrow's soirée, made a chinking sound, and a silver épergne flashed back the lamplight. Tom put out his foot and the door creaked closed behind him.

'Got you!' he said, changing his grip on the rod for

a moment, and turned the key with a loud click.

Knees scuffed the carpet. A piece of paper fluttered from the table to the floor.

'I know you're here!' Tom cried in an adult voice. 'You filthy piece of rubbish, this is *our* house.'

What made it worse was that this was one of the rooms where Papa impressed people. As a child hanging from Nanny's hand, Tom had glimpsed this table ringed by the inner circle of plain City men whose vast reputation, capital and acquaintance was cultivated by Papa, exchanging nicknames like some schoolboy code. Ziggy, the Duke, Sir Ice-Cream, Natty. Nathan de Rothschild, coming out, had tousled his hair, and Tom had never forgotten that impromptu blessing. Everard Hambro, six feet five inches tall, his head almost touching the chandelier. This room was part of the very private club in which one day, after he had entered the firm as a clerk and worked his way forward, Tom understood he would spend his life.

There was a servants' door at the far end, but only servants used that, bringing stuff from the kitchen.

'Come out or I'll kill you,' Tom panted. 'I've got a gun.'

He crouched, but underneath the table saw only a maze of chairlegs.

Something blinked. It was a pair of terrified eyes.

The scuttling noise began again. Tom raced round the table, raised the stair-rod, brought it down as hard as he could, again and again, with all his strength.

But each time the boy rolled aside somehow. He

dragged himself under the table. The yellow soles of his feet kicked. He wriggled between the chairlegs where Tom, with the lamp, could not follow. In his panic he must have tried to stand up because the table jolted, the silver candlesticks toppling then smashing down among the wineglasses before Tom could reach out.

Tom stared, horrified.

'Stop,' he said.

On the other side of the table the precious chairs knocked together, falling over as the boy's head and shoulders appeared among them.

'Look what you've done!' Tom said, aghast. He rested the lamp on the table, and it threw back its illumination on him for the first time.

'Monkey didn't mean nuffink!' the boy cried, clenching his arms across his chest as though that would stop a bullet. His eyes narrowed, seeing Tom had no gun. 'Burst me, yer only a kid!'

He raced for the far door, throwing the chairs in Tom's way behind him.

Dropping the stair-rod, Tom snagged Monkey's shirt in his outstretched fingers, but the rag tore as if only grease held it together. Monkey shrieked.

His back was white. His ribs stuck out as though he were starving.

'Oh my God,' Tom said.

Monkey skidded through the doorway.

He slammed the baize door in Tom's face.

Tom knocked it open. He fell down the steps beyond. The two boys rolled down the stone steps together, Monkey kicking and scratching. The iron railing echoed as they knocked it. They tumbled together into the moonlit kitchen.

Tom landed first. He sprawled on his back, Monkey on top of him. The boy's scrawny knees jabbed his chest, but Tom stared up, not even winded by the boy's weight.

There was nothing to him. He was skin and bone. 'When did you last eat?' Tom whispered.

Monkey spat in his face.

VIII

Sssh. She's dead.
Sssh, there now. Sssh, don't cry.
I warned you. You're the guilty one.
What? The key was in your pocket all the time?
No, don't do that. Don't—

IX

The boy ran.

Tom sat up. He wiped the spittle from his face, then got to his feet.

On the table stood a three-pronged silver candlestick put out for cleaning or repair. Above it, down the length of the kitchen, the washing had been strung in white festoons, arms and legs hanging downwards, the racks lowered to take advantage of overnight warmth rising from the kitchen range. Monkey blundered through them throwing back white shirts, shifts, camisoles, petticoats whirling up and falling down behind him, a sooty print on each one.

'Wait,' Tom said, then realised that Monkey had

almost reached the outside door.

Tom turned to ice.

Monkey wasn't trying to get out. He was trying to let someone in.

Monkey had already gripped the bottom bolt. He hauled and the bolt shot up with a loud, echoing clang. Even Joy would hear it, Tom knew. He tripped, skidding in the washing, rolling over. What had Joy been trying to tell him?

Tom, there's some men in our street. Tom, they're looking at our house.

He remembered that angry, frantic look in her eyes, fox-brown, full of fire, her desperate shout. '*TOM!*'

As though he, not she, was the one without sense.

The men who had sent Monkey down the chimney were waiting outside for him to shoot the bolts, and then they would come inside the house.

Tom scrambled to his feet. He jumped across the table. He reached out at arm's length as Monkey jumped upwards.

Their hands met on the bolt, Tom first.

Monkey hung from Tom's hand. Then he jerked down with all the weight he had. He braced both feet on the door, arching his back.

The bolt shot down. Both boys fell, sprawling.

The door burst open.

X

The scream that had come through the night was dreadful. Though faint, as if from inside a house, it was the most dreadful, agonised sound Arthur had ever heard. He pushed himself back in the oleander bushes that almost concealed him. "Strewth,' he muttered, peering through the gate. 'Jack?'

A hansom cab clopped past the gateway, whip down, going home empty, the driver yawning like his horse. The hooves and clacking wheel-rims sounded very loud, even the creaking of the axle. The sound receded and silence fell again.

Arthur rubbed his smooth hands down his face, wondering what to do. The road was still empty, the houses seemed quiet. It was an ordinary evening.

The scream rose again, muffled – obviously the screamer had a pillow forced over his or her face to keep the noise down, that was the way it was done, if noise there must be. But Arthur knew noise was the sure sign of a bungled job. Something had gone very wrong.

But if he ran for it, there was no five bob, and the thought of leaving Jack in the lurch filled Arthur with dread. He sweated despite the cold.

Still, these houses had thick walls, and the class of people who lived in them minded their own business. An Englishman's home was his castle, nothing would be heard. And at this hour, he knew, the police would be attending the closing of the pubs, not these quiet uneventful streets with gaslights guarding every intersection.

Arthur decided to get his money and get out. He ran for the passageway by the side of the house. Going down the steps, he crossed the paved area at the back. The kitchen door was down more steps. It was already open. He heard voices coming from inside.

He crept down. His eyes widened at what he saw. 'Wot – oh, Jesus Christ!'

XI

Tom wriggled, crawling away from the door for his life.

He was too late. Two heavy boots banged down behind him. He was dragged backwards with enormous force. The buttons popped off the front of his pyjamas as a man's hand caught him round the neck, heaved him up, threw him down. Tom lay with his face on the floor. He pressed his lips together, whimpering inside himself but outwardly silent. To show pain was unmanly. Like everyone else he was beaten by schoolmasters, monitors, school-prefects and house-prefects for his own good, and by Papa. He expected it, and half pulled his pyjama trousers down in readiness for his punishment.

'Wot's 'e doin'?' demanded a voice rough and sharp like a saw.

'I want 'is stripey 'jamas!' Monkey said, cocky as a cockerel now. His fear was gone as though it had never been, and Tom, glaring at him out of his single eye not pushed against the stone, despised him for changing so quickly.

'I warn you—' Tom threatened in a strangled voice, then tried to turn his head against the hand that held him down, 'my father is an important man—'

He was lifted effortlessly and a brutish face gazed into his. It was low-browed with long black hair in tangled hooks, and the blue eyes peered out of deep

64

sockets. They glanced at Tom and summed him up.

'Dead swag. Can't do nothing wiv this 'un.' Reaching under his long coat, he drew a knife from his belt. 'Where's the siller?'

Tom stared at the Bowie knife.

Monkey pointed upwards. 'Yer put me down the wrong bleedin' loofer ter the wrong bleedin' room,' he sulked. 'Not *my* fault.' Shivering in the draught from the door, plainly anxious to be going, he held out his hand for money.

'Not till I clean out,' the big man said, pulling back Tom's head by the hair, exposing the throat. 'All right, 'ave the 'jamas.'

'I don't want 'em mucky!' Monkey said, sounding sick, but he grabbed the ankles quickly, and pulled.

'Wot . . . oh cheese an' crust . . .' a voice murmured from somewhere very far away.

Tom stared down his cheeks. He knew he was going to die and he could think of nothing else. He could see his face in the moonlit knife-blade. He could see his own terrified eyes. He could see the veins pulsing in his throat. His Adam's apple bobbed for breath. He felt how much the point would hurt him as it went in, the edge slicing through arteries, windpipe, voice. He knew he would never see his Mama again, and he would never see his Papa again. He would never see Joy again in her pink satin dressing-gown, standing on the steps as real as though she were really standing there, and he reached out his hands as though he could touch her. Tom's eyes filled with tears of longing. He blubbered and begged, past words, and in the extremity of his terror his bowels emptied a stinking stream down the back of his bare legs.

Joy came down one step at a time. With one hand she held onto the iron railing, which was higher than her head. With her other hand she held up the lamp.

The little girl stared with wonderment at the scene below her.

The lamplight moved in her eyes as the light swung from side to side, as she came down step by step.

The big man who held Tom stared up at her through the railing. The bars flickered across the child's face. He blinked as though he hardly knew what he was seeing.

Joy watched Tom reach out his hands towards her to touch her, though she was much too far away. The tears streamed down his cheeks. She had never seen him cry before.

She remembered how Tom had not wanted to leave the bedroom, then he had tried to get her to go back to it, but he had followed her to look after her.

He had done it for her.

The big man did not take the knife from Tom's throat, or his eyes from Joy's face. He blinked again.

Joy understood that they were not playing a game. She had understood that when she saw Tom hit the boy. She understood how frightened Tom was now. She had been afraid that he would kill the boy, and now it was easy for her to understand how frightened he was that he would himself be killed. Whatever happened now was real.

Steps were difficult. Joy had never carried a full

lamp down steps before. She reached down her slippered feet carefully, her tongue between her teeth in her concentration. She came to the bottom step.

A candlestick had fallen from the table to the floor. She stepped over it.

The big man watched her approach. He seemed to grow in size. She saw his nostrils twitch once, like an animal searching the scent of her. She wondered if he was one of the animals from the Zoological Gardens, a tawny lion perhaps, or a wolf. He raised his head slightly, looking at her from the corners of his eyes.

His knife glittered at Tom's throat, which was very dangerous indeed, but the man did not seem to care. The man did not care how dangerous he was. He really did not.

'We got ter get on the fly,' Arthur hissed, but he couldn't shake Jack out of it. 'No time fer this, no time fer the siller. Get out while yer still can.'

'Why don't she say nothing?' Jack croaked.

The little girl came towards him. She gave a shy smile, the lamplight flashing in her eyes, and held out her hand. It was a very small hand. Jack stared at her. He'd forgotten everything else. *Give me my five bob yer owe me, yer promised*, Arthur was whining, but Jack hardly heard him. He looked from the little girl's eyes to her hand held out towards him, white, unmarked, unworked. There was a red stripe across her wrist.

'Why don't she speak?' Jack demanded. He shook Tom for an answer.

'She can't,' Tom groaned. The hand that clenched

his hair eased its grip a fraction. 'She can't, not properly!' he gasped. 'She's stupid.'

Jack stared at her. He saw no fear in her. He stared from her hand to her eyes.

Don't hurt him.

'We're ratted,' Arthur said, slipping past Jack. The candlestick disappeared smoothly under the tails of his plum-coloured coat. 'Don't yer get it, Jack? We're double-barrelled wiv someone else's play, the street'll be swarmin' wiv crushers any minute an' they might settle on us fer bein' just as sweet as—'

'Shut yer lip, just shut it! Or I'll close yer face,' Jack snarled. His voice softened. 'She's not stupid,' he said, inhaling deeply.

He released Tom another fraction.

'I'm off!' Arthur pulled Monkey, who clutched the pyjamas to his chest, after him. 'We 'aven't 'ardly done nuffink wrong yet! Yer'll get us all bunged in Clink fer nuffink.' He hissed from the doorway, 'Leave 'er, she ain't worth enough. Leave 'er, Jack!' He dragged Monkey into the dark and they were both gone.

'Take her,' Tom whispered. He looked up earnestly into the face overhanging his own. 'Exchange is no robbery. She can't even hear us. Take her, she's yours.' Tom's blubbering began again. 'Please, please, don't hurt me.' His expression screwed up, quivering, as though in reflection of a terrible pain inside himself, and his whole naked body shook in sheer misery and terror. 'Please don't hurt me.'

Chapter Three

I

Jack faced a dead loss on the night's work. He couldn't afford that, or the loss to his pride. But even so he crouched, staring into the girl's eyes, and wondered what she was thinking.

He made a simple calculation. She was worth something. The boy was not. 'Yer life for yer brother's?' Was that what she was offering? He should cut the boy's throat anyway. 'It's not 'ard to do, it's easy,' he threatened. 'It's not doing it that would be 'ard.' His eyes flicked between the two of them.

Jack had never had a family, and he had never been in love, but he had seen how love worked.

In one motion he dropped the boy and grabbed the girl's hand that she offered. He glared at her suspiciously, but she made no effort to pull away.

He let the front of his long coat fall open and stuck the knife back in his belt. He spat on his palm and slapped it against the boy's hand.

'Yer safe from me,' he growled.

Tom sobbed on the floor. 'Thank you, sir,' he wept. He lay smeared and spattered by his own slime, he'd even forgotten he was naked. 'Thank you, sir. Thank you, Joy. You won't hurt her, will you, sir?'

The boy hadn't yet realised what he had done.

Jack looked at him with contempt, then turned him over with his foot. Tom lay silenced, shuddering as though he expected to be crushed beneath the filthy leather heel.

Jack towered over the little girl. He turned her face up. She was the prettiest little thing he had ever seen.

'Why should I 'urt yer?' he said gruffly. 'Don't make sense.'

She gazed at him with a child's innocence, and Jack supposed he must seem miles tall, and as though *he* were not making sense. She knew nothing, nothing at all, only these things like pink satin and fancy dolls, born with a silver spoon in her mouth. He struggled to see past the lamplight in her deep brown eyes.

'She won't hear you,' came Tom's muffled voice. Jack gave him a kick for good measure, then another, harder, as rage filled him at the boy's cowardice in not protecting his little sister.

'And she won't speak,' Tom whimpered. He was crying his eyes out, but made hardly a sound that anyone could hear.

Jack ignored him. He sniffed past the odour of manure and the kitcheny aroma of cold boiled vegetables, copper pans and coal. He twisted his head from side to side, coming to the smell of the silver upstairs, seeing in his mind's eye the rooms full of twinkling silver. He was certain of them. They were almost in his grasp. But a draught blew from the open door behind him, and he knew Smart Arthur had put his finger on it. They were ratted all right. The whole night smelt wrong. It was time to disappear.

He crouched by Tom. 'Remember our deal. Make a sound an' our bargain's broke,' he warned.

'I'm not frightened of you,' Tom shuddered, but already he sounded more like he was talking to himself.

Jack backed to the door. He dragged the girl after him. But as he hauled her up the steps into the yard she turned. She slipped her warm little hand in his, and went with him as trustingly as though he were her dad.

Jack was so surprised that he grunted. He crossed the yard with her walking pertly beside him, the top of her head bobbing beside his hip.

His eyes were as sharp as his cats', but soon he realised that so were hers. After that first stumble coming from lamplight into dark, she did not bump into him again. As Jack's eyes adjusted fully to the moon, the wall around the yard appeared, and he saw the garden gate glimmering against the brickwork. From this side it was easy to slide the bolt that had stopped them coming in this way.

He lifted the latch and peered through the gap.

Scythed grass, pale blue with frost, stretched between a few odd-looking trees to a white wrought-iron table, and he grunted. Anyone for tea and cucumber sandwiches? There was a low hedge and a vegetable patch at the end, where the moon gleamed off a glasshouse. Behind it the boundary fence stood higher than a man, probably of creosoted planks set upright, and he thought he heard the knock of a shoe on wood. It sounded like Smart Arthur was making his escape that way, as planned, and he'd be dropping down into the Hill Road mews on the other side. Don't get no splinters in those clever fingers, damn yer, Arthur, thought Jack maliciously. Arthur had talked all the time, getting on his nerves. They'd conned that turning earlier, finding a cul-de-sac lined with stables, dead quiet this time of night except for horse farts and the snores of a stable-lad or two, but Jack knew such places could be dangerous traps with no one to lead him through a circumbendibus of back-doubles, bunk-holes, cut-throughs. In five minutes Arthur would be nipping across fields with names like William's Field and Further Seven Acres and Hither Ten Acres, knowing them all, or sitting equally at ease atop a Piccadilly omnibus, but this wasn't Jack's place. St John's Wood was foreign territory, and he wished he'd stayed in St Luke's, snug as a worm in a nut.

The little girl looked up at him as though sensing his fear.

'Wot's up wiv yer!' Jack said roughly, raising his hand to cuff her. Her calm, self-possessed expression did not change, and he wondered if she had heard him, or whether she was mocking him, waiting for him to make a mistake. Women were like that. He smacked his head. She couldn't be more than four, maybe five years old, for God's sake!

Perhaps she simply had not understood his threat.

He tousled her hair, and that did make her scowl.

But still the dogs next door did not bark, Arthur's shoe or not. Jack sniffed the night. It was the silence that bothered him more than anything. If only the little girl would speak, or scream, he would have known what to do. But she did nothing, just looking at him, resting her hand in his like a tiny trusting animal, waiting.

Was she waiting for him to let her go? Did she think he was merciful, or stupid, or what? He grinned, showing a snarl of broken teeth.

She smiled.

A surprised yell broke Jack's thrall, then the sound of a commotion carried from beyond the fence, and he heard running footsteps, their echoes thrown back from the stables so he could not tell the number. A horse neighed, another answered from stables further away, but Jack was already on the move. He tugged the girl behind him along the passageway beside the house, annoyed that his big feet tripped clumsily on the coal-lumps that she skirted expertly. From the tradesmen's entrance he checked the driveway was clear, and hurried her to the street looking around him in every direction.

'Don't make a sound,' he said. 'I'll give yer a sweet.'

She looked at his lips, and nodded.

Jack turned to the left, walking calmly. Nothing attracted attention more quickly than a running man, but a down-at-heel father and his little girl, better cared for than he, on the pad for shelter or a doorway to doss in was a commonplace, and he knew they would not be noticed even if they were seen.

Joy bobbed beside him, looking up, thinking about the sweet. He glanced at her, then searched absently in his pockets.

The pavements were deserted, tangled with shadow beneath the bare moonlit branches of the trees. Most of the houses were dark by this time of night, the Georgian façades of the old Eyre family estate rearing up like huge dim lumps of sugar lining the road. Ahead, Abbey Place was partly blocked by the ornamental gateway, lit by two gas-globes set narrow enough to forbid omnibuses and heavy drays entirely, which discouraged traffic from cutting through between Paddington Wood and St John's Wood. From the left of the gate, a small alleyway led into the Hill Road stables. Beyond the gate and old boundary ditch the name of the road changed to Abercorn Place, belonging to Harrow School, and he could see the lights of the Edgware Road crossing the end.

Jack hurried them beneath the gas-globes, their shadows swinging around them as they passed the gate. He guided her with his hand on her shoulder. His hand looked as large as her head.

'Yer aren't afraid of me, are yer,' he muttered. There were plenty of people who would pay for a child, especially a pretty one. She was still looking up at him expectantly as the light faded from her face, and he remembered the sweet he had promised her. He felt in his other pocket.

'Hoi, you!' a voice shouted behind him, sounding so loud in the quiet night that the girl jumped. 'Stop, you!'

Jack halted.

He took his hand slowly out of his pocket, and slowly turned. A policeman was walking towards them beneath the gas-globes. The crusher's gloves

74

showed up very white as he passed the gate, giving him away against the darkness behind him. He wasn't wearing a duty armband, but even at this distance the row of silver buttons gleamed authoritatively on his chest, and the distinctive Metropolitan Police badge on his tall helmet flashed.

Jack bent down, still moving very slowly.

'Stop right there, that man!' the policeman ordered at once.

Jack's lip curled.

He picked up the girl, and ran.

Jack ran with his long open coat flapping. Her head bounced against his chest, then he moved the crook of his elbow and held her to him. She weighed almost nothing. Her hair blew up into his face. Jack snorted. He held her hair down with one hand as he ran.

Behind him came three blasts on a police whistle, once heard never forgot. The policeman gave chase, his boots clapping loudly on the frosty paving-stones, then his shadow came stretching past Jack as the lights fell into the distance.

Jack glimpsed an opening in the hedge.

He twisted to the left down a path between two fences, running silent on mud which had not yet frozen. Brambles brittle with winter snatched him but he lifted the girl and hurled himself through. One of his heels tore the hem of his coat. He slipped and skidded, banged into a fence that rose in front of him, but managed to get a hand in front of the girl.

Panting, he half turned and leaned his shoulder blades against the wood, choosing between right or left. He could hear the crusher cursing the brambles.

Jack went left, anything to keep clear of the Edgware Road, they'd be over there thick as flies on dung for the pubs. He could hear the chirp of whistles responding to the three blasts. He plunged into the boundary ditch and followed its length, floundering through the frosty undergrowth.

That turn got them. The first whistle sounded again, but not so close, and Jack eased up. Quiet now. He knew how the police worked, blow a few blasts, make enough of a show to keep the ratepayers happy but not enough to worry or disturb them. The wiser bluebottles would already be returning to the back taprooms to judge the landlords' medicinal tots against the cold, very kind of you, sir, and no gaming or late drinking in your establishment I see, thanks to my blind eye. And a very merry Christmas to you, officer.

Jack knew how the game was played.

He got his breath back, crossed a row of terraced houses and slipped down the backs between old carts and rubbish. He was only jogging along now. A dog barked, but the whistles had almost stopped, sounding well off to one side. And they'd be changing the shifts soon, Second Relief off, Night Duty on. A man who wished to avoid a criminal history knew such things.

Jack looked over his shoulder and walked with long powerful strides, the icy night air refreshing on his beaded face, his sweat-streaked shirt.

'Got yer, yer bastards,' he muttered. He winked at the girl's face beneath his own as they passed by a street-light. 'Us against the world, eh, girl?' She did not reply but her eyes were bright, and he wondered if she could understand his lips.

He stopped. 'Yer know wot I'm saying!'

Of course she did, he could see she wasn't stupid. Her educated brother and her mum and dad must be blind to think she was. She'd taught herself, naturally! 'I bet they never thought it could 'appen,' he marvelled, but it was obvious to a man such as he. Every Field Lane stallholder and snatcher pattered their code of nods and winks, a whole invisible language that was nonsense beyond Goswell Street. Each parish, street, even each pub had learned its own style of flash talk, a tribal jargon of rhyming slang and back-chat to exclude outsiders, informers, police. 'Yer ma an' pa never bothered ter know yer,' Jack whispered. 'Why didn't they never believe in yer? No one believed in me neither, but look at me now,' he bragged. 'I've got where I am by me own bootstraps, an' don't let no one tell yer it was easy.'

He had hardly breathed out loud, yet he was sure she understood every word he said. Jack clasped her to him as he walked, stroking her hair. She's a real treasure, he said to himself. A real treasure!

II

'A real treasure!' Joy watched the man say. Then he carried her beyond the street-light, and if he spoke again she could not see.

He seemed happier now, and walked with a jaunty step that she heard tapping faintly with her ears, but felt clearly in her bones. She wished he would start running again, she'd enjoyed that bit the best, that feeling of speed and power as though she were flying. Even now he seemed tireless, and she wished she could see him more clearly. He confused her. He looked so unkind, but could not have treated her more kindly. His eyes were cruel, but he had been gentle, and his mouth was good at smiling now he trusted her. He had smiled even as he ran, and cut his hand on the fence rather than let her be hurt.

She realised he was not at all what he appeared. As they passed a big public house with a frosted-glass gas-globe overhanging the door, she reached up with her fingers and wiped a fleck of mud from his chin.

Once he knelt, putting the point of his knife on the stones and his ear to the handle. It was as though he were listening to the pavement. He changed direction after that, moving faster.

She wondered sleepily when he would take her back home.

III

Road junctions were always cobbled and often gaslit. Jack paused, hearing iron wheels come onto the noisy cobbles, then a tall black cart pulled up in the middle of the junction ahead of him, stopping beneath the light.

Jack thought that was St John's Wood Road, and it was where he wanted to go.

But he knew a Black Maria when he saw one. He melted into the shadows as the driver leaned back and banged on the roof with his whip-handle. The

78

rear doors were thrown open and police constables dropped out, at least half a dozen, more than Jack had hoped to see in one place in his whole life. They looked round, wondering where they were probably, then pulled their belts straight and stood around grumbling among themselves, yawning. One or two had threadbare uniforms, others worn-down shoes. A pound a week, the same as a carpenter, didn't go far.

A fat sergeant came heavily down the steps, got the constables lined up eyes-right and shuffling their big flat feet military fashion to dress the line. He gave them orders with a pointing finger, and they fanned out with a regular tread.

Jack grinned. Half a dozen coppers on his tail, he was a great man now.

He glanced around him, then sidled into the mossy alley-way behind him. He followed it at a crouching run, the girl clasped to his chest. The leather soles of his boots made little sound, and the black walls brushed his elbows on each side.

The harder they tried to catch him, the more he was determined to escape.

He couldn't get back to St Luke's now, not with the girl, but he wouldn't give her up. Somewhere to the southward of him, wedged between the Edgware Road and Regent's Park, lay a maze of poor streets sewn like knitting between boulevards of finer houses. If he could get her to the Lisson Grove rookery he would be safe, they could lie up for a few hours until the bluebottles found something better to do.

The girl smiled sleepily as he ran. She hung on

round his neck with her soft, tiny hands.

Jack slowed. Even his great strength was tiring at last. He was running uphill and the breath wheezed in his throat. The sweat poured down him and his heavy coat pulled him back. A stitch jabbed his side.

He hissed in his throat as a policeman strolled into view, patrolling the junction ahead of him. A whistle blew in the distance, short-long-short, and the policeman rapped the cobbles with his steel-tipped boots in reply. Jack waited until the man's back was turned then ducked across the street into the shadows on the other side. He was on the top of the hill, but he could smell water.

Somewhere in the streamers of fog rising ahead of him, a truncheon tapped on stone. Great North Street. Jack turned back between the shops, but on the thoroughfare he had just left a police inspector now stood. The inspector leaned to one side, careful even alone not to compromise his dignity by crouching. He touched one end of his stick to the pavement, then put his ear to the other end.

He listened.

He tapped his stick once, then walked away quickly down a side street.

'They're closing me off.' Jack moved his lips without making a sound. 'I can't get where I want ter go.' He grinned at her, then forgot himself and said aloud, 'Never say die, girl.'

'Never say die,' Joy said, then looked as surprised as he. The words had popped out of her without thought.

Jack put his hand over her mouth. 'Quiet now,' he

muttered as gently as though he were holding seed between his lips. It was as if she was a little bird and he was feeding her. 'Just yer and me, right? We can't be beat, girl.'

'We can't be beat,' she said in that funny slurred voice of hers, and he almost gave himself away by laughing out loud.

'We'll win through!' He let his chuckle show. 'Jack Riddles 'as known tighter spots than this, I'll tell yer.'

He looked at her, and she knew he was imagining what it would be like, telling her about himself.

Suddenly he snatched her up and ran. He had heard something she hadn't. His feet pounded. He changed direction as though he heard whistles, people around them everywhere.

She hung on as tight as she could and closed her eyes.

Suppose someone tried to stop them? She was afraid of what he might do to them.

His mouth was open and his eyes were full of alarm. He crouched behind a parapet, looking around him fiercely, his lips drawn back in a snarl. He looked like a cornered animal, both savage and helpless. Fog rose over the parapet.

She saw the knife in his belt.

She reached down. She felt the handle cold under her finger and thumb.

He stared behind him, then held her tight and scrambled over the parapet. He dropped down the far side. They were sliding on a steep grassy bank. Water glinted far below them. He hung onto the bricks of the parapet to stop himself falling.

As he worked his way along the slope Joy opened her finger and thumb. The knife fell away. She saw it bounce once on a tussock of grass. It span out and dropped into the moonlit water, blade first, disappearing with hardly a splash.

In the distance she saw a huge building like a palace, ice-white, topped with towers and spires. It's a palace made of ice-cream, she thought.

Jack came to some steps down. He heaved himself over the rail. There was a gaslight on the bridge above them, and below them deep shadow and gleaming water, like a mirror.

He carried her down to the towpath.

There was a bench beside the canal. He sat her on it and bent over with his hands on his knees, lungs heaving, blown. His long hair hung into the ash that had been spread on the path. Above them the bridge looked very high, like a huge wall of bricks rising to the road. The gaslight looked like a star hanging overhead.

They saw a policeman's helmet bobbing along behind the parapet.

Jack reached into his belt for the knife.

It was gone.

He cursed. She didn't know the words. He stared at her, then at the canal. He seemed to know exactly where his knife had gone.

'Maybe you're right, at that,' he shrugged silently. They hardly needed to use talk to understand one another. He hadn't put his hand over her mouth, and she could have screamed. He could no longer see the policeman.

Jack swept her up, sitting her on his shoulders.

She clung onto his hair. It was horrid and greasy. Jack sat on the edge of the canal and dangled his feet in the water. With one arm he held onto the mooring bollard beside him.

Then he swung himself down into the water.

She felt his muscles stiffen with the shock, and supposed it must be cold. She gasped as the icy water swirled over her feet. He twisted his head and gave her a look, and she realised she had pulled out a clump of his hair, but she couldn't make herself loosen her grip.

The freezing water covered her ankles as it rose to his chest. He wrapped his hands around her knees and plodded forward heavily. His coat floated behind them like a wing.

The bridge rose up in front of them, looking huge.

She realised it was not a bridge after all. It was a tunnel.

Silver ripples shimmered around them as the tunnel mouth widened, completely black. She saw no light ahead, no other end. The ripples disappeared.

For the first time, Joy was frightened. She began to cry.

Jack reached up with one hand, stroking her face as he ploughed forward into the blackness. She could see anything only by gazing backwards at the round moonlit entrance, which looked like an eye. As it got smaller the faint vee of disturbed water they were towing lost its glow and became part of the darkness.

The entrance shrank behind them. Finally it winked out as though going to sleep.

Now she could neither see nor hear. There was

only the swaying motion of Jack plodding beneath her like a donkey ride.

On sunny days there were donkey rides in the park. Tears filled her eyes.

'Don't cry,' Jack said. His voice echoed and boomed, magnified by the tunnel, and she heard him clearly for the first time. 'Don't cry, little one. We're safe in 'ere.'

She hiccuped, then was silent, hanging onto his head.

She wrapped her arms around his hair.

'That's better,' he said. 'I will never hurt you.' His voice seemed to echo all around her. 'I promised,' he boomed. 'I promised that worthless brother of yours. I promise *you*.'

She rested her head on his, almost asleep.

'*You'll have to take me back home, Jack*,' she said in her dream. '*You know you will*.'

IV

Tom rubbed himself clean with a tea towel. He did not know what else to do. Anything was better than thinking about what had happened. Papa and Mama would be back from the opera at any minute, and he knew he must erase all signs of his shame.

He stood holding the filthy towel, wondering where to hide such a brown, clotted mess when there was so much clean washing all around him. He put it in the laundry basket, neatly. That was no good. He took it out and pushed it through the range fire-door, where it lay like a dead animal on the slumbering coals, then began to burn.

He had been stepping over the faeces puddled on the floor, and now he remembered to sluice them away with water from a bucket. He mopped the place until it was spotless, and remembered to put the mop back where he had found it.

Finally he checked the range. The tea towel was no more than a curl of ash.

Tom brushed his hands. He was not crying any more.

Everything was normal. Almost normal. Except the kitchen door was still open.

He stood in the doorway looking out, wondering what he was expected to do.

He fetched the lamp and held it up. He never wanted to be in the dark again. He ran up the steps into the yard and called out hastily, 'Joy?'

No reply. He scampered back into the kitchen.

Tom went upstairs through the entrance hall. He carefully shut the doors to the rooms where children were not allowed.

He thought he heard police whistles, and when he looked from the window he saw policemen in the road.

Sheer terror filled him. He ran upstairs with the demons of hell behind him.

'What's this noise?' Mrs M'Kenzy blocked the attic stairs. She was coming down, a broad lipless woman with stumpy legs, her hair in a net. Her creased nightdress reached to her knees, revealing brown woollen bed-stockings. In the day, prepared and in control, she looked quite pretty, and her personality had weight. Now, with a sniff, she swept her cream woollen shawl across her shoulders, and looked pathetic. 'Master Tom? Is that you?' She stared at him short-sightedly.

Tom was horrified to realise he was naked.

'You stink,' Mrs M'Kenzy said suspiciously. She came down one step, squinting.

'Something terrible's happened!' he screamed. 'She's gone, and you were dead drunk!'

Mrs M'Kenzy did not move a muscle. 'I'm a heavy sleeper,' she said.

Tom panted. 'Joy's gone. My sister's gone! Men took her.' He dragged her by the arm, pointing at the sooty footprints. The old woman understood her situation at once. She backed to the banister, hardly able to stand.

'You're my friend, aren't you?' she said winningly. 'Dear little Tom, you've known your Nanny M'Kenzy all your life.'

'Yes,' Tom said. She was breathing so quickly that she alarmed him.

She raised her hands and clenched her fists. She beat them against her face. She pulled at her mouth.

'Don't hurt yourself!' Tom cried, horrified.

'You hurt me then,' she mumbled.

Tom backed away from her. Nanny M'Kenzy's nose dripped blood.

'Do it,' she said. 'Or I'm on the street.'

V

The dank tunnel seemed endless. Carefully, shrugging one shoulder at a time, Jack took off his coat. The top half was dry, though the rest was heavy with water. He couldn't bear any more of her shivering. He lifted it up to her by the collar.

'Better'n nothing,' he said, ploughing forward.

A pale line of spray appeared ahead of them, drowning his voice. She felt words in the warm breath coming from his mouth, but whatever he was saying was lost in the clatter of water pouring from the roof. He backed around the edge of the deluge, feeling his way by touch along the wall they could not see. Joy reached out with her fingertips, sensing the bricks curving over them in an invisible arch.

She saw something ahead of them now, the faint glow which had illuminated the falling water, and they realised that the light came from the tunnel roof. 'Ventilator,' Jack said, and they peered up with pale faces.

Forty feet over their heads the shaft, rendered with smooth mortar that glowed with moonlight, ended in a circle of night sky. It looked very small. The opening, probably built up more than a man's height above the ground for reasons of safety, like the chimneys of the Underground, had been crisscrossed with iron bars.

At least it cast a little light. Jack saw a niche in the wall. He lifted her into it. The nook was just clear of the surface. She tucked in her feet beneath her and huddled into the coat, shivering. The brickwork was arched at the top, tight against her shoulders but leaving a perfect space for her head.

There wasn't room for him too.

'Uh-uh—' she said, then screwed up her face with her effort to speak.

Jack bobbed in the water, his grimy shirt sticking to his shoulders. 'All the time in the world.' He waited patiently. He knew what she was going to say. She had spoken so easily to him in her sleep.

'You'll have to take me back h-home,' Joy said. Her eyes filled at the thought of home. 'You know you will.'

'Whatever I do,' Jack said, 'I'll do on my own terms. That's who I am.' He reached out to touch her, but she shrank away. 'This is all I know,' he said simply. 'I never was a child.'

Jack Riddles looked up at her with his brutish face. He was almost exhausted, immersed to his neck in ice-water, shuddering with cold. His long black hair floated around his shoulders, and the tendons stood out of his frozen hands like claws. His teeth chattered.

'I can't go no further,' he said. 'I'll throw 'em off the scent. I'll be back. Promise. Promise.'

VI

She waited, but he didn't come back.

She stared where his white shirt had disappeared, wading into the dark. The water pouring from the roof had hidden him at once, but still she stared at the place. The water seemed to pour down in slowed motion through the glow of the ventilation shaft.

She willed his white shirt and his head to reappear, thrusting through the cascade, but nothing happened.

She cried, but there was no one to listen. She clapped her hands, but they moved silently, their sound lost in the buzz of falling water. Anyway, she was not very good at clapping, yet.

She screamed, but she could not hear herself. She was not even sure she was making any noise, but her throat was sore.

She shivered under the long coat wrapped around her shoulders. The bottom half of the coat hung in the water, too heavy to move. At least she was dry, except for her feet.

Nanny would have made her take off her wet slippers. She pulled them off. Her feet were icy cold and she rubbed them, though she didn't have a towel.

The bricks pushed at her shoulders. She pulled up her knees to her chin and held onto her toes. She could not get comfortable on her haunches. She wriggled, but the bricks were very hard.

She stared, waiting.

She knew about hours and minutes, but it seemed she had been down here all her life.

The moonlight had changed its direction and the shaft no longer cast its glow on the falling water.

She wondered if Jack had done anything wrong and been caught and sent to prison. She imagined what it was like being him. It seemed much more important than being herself, and she imagined running through the streets all night and all day, the wind blowing in her hair.

The light faded from the ventilator as the moon went. It did not come back.

She stared at the dark and wondered about monsters.

Everyone knew monsters existed, except Papa and Mama. Nanny knew. Children had to be good, she whispered. There were goblins who crept into cots and stole a bad little girl's breath. Dragons lived in the fire who would bite her if she touched the flames. Fiends with golden eyes and sharp silver teeth came to devour children who told tales. There were monsters who could turn into huge birds and lift up a little girl in their claws, and fly her back to the deserts of Arabia and eat her. Ugly witches could pretend to be beautiful women, and there were even monsters who could take the shape of men.

But there were no monsters who actually were men.

Something trickled loudly in her ear, and she put up her hand. Her hair was wet. A grey glow from the shaft showed mist rising from the splashing water, and the wet trickled into her ears. She ducked her head under the coat and crouched there with only her eyes peeping out, her breath warm and comforting as it flowed over her cheeks and chin. Shivers gripped her, then she felt hot. She dozed.

Her eyes flashed open. The shaft showed daylight. It made a circle on the water below her, and the reflections sent ripples of light dancing over the dark walls curved around her.

The water-pattern was the most beautiful thing she had ever seen. The shapes flickered and flashed around her, darting like a flock of tiny animals.

She smiled. She held out her hands to them. One of her feet splashed in the water and the dancing ripples redoubled their shimmering around her as she teetered on the edge.

She drew back, and they faded away.

She imagined what Mama was doing. The light said seven-thirty, so she knew Mama was sitting in bed having breakfast. Tom was at the table in the children's room and would not go to school because it was Saturday. Her friend Jack was running through the streets.

No, she realised. Jack was hiding. He had to hide from the policemen and then he would come back for her. She knew he would. She picked up his coat and huddled it again around her shoulders, but the pain in her ears and throat grew no less.

She cried because the pain felt like stones being forced into her ears, it was so bad.

She felt a cool draught on her cheeks. The air was moving.

She stared at the water. The tiny animals had returned, flocking around her, filling the tunnel with flickering light. The water rose, spilling into the niche.

Along the roof of the tunnel, a pair of boots came walking upside-down towards her. Two legs hung from them, dressed in trousers, and a white hand pushed wearily on each knee.

A voice she did not recognise shouted faintly, 'Oh, shiiit! Shower-bath!'

Joy sensed something huge and black sliding past her.

She launched herself into the dark.

Chapter Four

I

Detective Inspector Bowler studied his pocket watch. He observed that it was seven-thirty. Seven-thirty, a frosty Saturday morning, and the Pentonville Road as quiet he ever saw it. The hansom cab rattled noisily but progressed slowly along the slippery vista.

He banged on the roof. 'Hurry it up, Jarvis!'

Bowler hated hansoms. They smelt of dirty leather, dirty horse and dirt. They bobbed unmercifully in time with the horse's arse, which worked directly in front of his face. All the cabbies were called Jarvis. They were all thieves.

Bowler finished off his piece of toast.

He had been woken at home by one of the Yard's monkey-boys, a police messenger. Their news was always bad news. Crumpling the telegram in his hand, shrugging on his coat, Bowler had kissed his fighting children and young wife goodbye on the steps of number eleven.

He stepped on the pavement and changed, at a stroke, from a family man into a policeman.

Then Mary – she had been born Màiri, Irish – came running after him along Danbury Street, waving the slice of toast. 'Dearest,' he interrupted wearily before she could start. He knew what was coming. Knowing people was his job. He couldn't help working, even with his wife.

'The park—'

'This afternoon,' Bowler said precisely. 'All of them, and the kite.' A canal barge slid under the bridge beneath them, towed by a mule, the back of the boat swirling with steam where oats were being boiled up to feed the beast. 'Promise. You too.'

'Yesterday you promised this morning.'

He spread his hands. 'There's been a kidnapping. A little girl. Her parents are important people.'

She sounded emotional. 'And only the great you—'

'The same age as our own dear daughter was.'

'You do your job,' she said over her shoulder. 'But you did promise.'

Now he was angry. His wife was the only person who touched his anger, the rest of his life went by the three C's, cool, calm, collected. 'Are you trying to say something to me?'

She turned. 'We love you, Charlie,' she said, then blew him a kiss. 'Find her.'

He wished Mary wouldn't wear her dressing-gown in the street. It let the side down.

Bowler tried the County Court rank, but it was bare of cabs at this hour. His whistle summoned one on the City Road.

'St John's Wood, Jarvis, make it sharp.' He settled back onto the hard, split leather, and the black hansom rattled and squeaked through Pentonville onto the frosty New Road. Eventually it turned north into the Edgware Road and rumbled past the gaudy posters of the Metropolitan Theatre. Bowler took a deep breath and prepared himself for what lay ahead.

First, he brushed the last crumbs of toast from his brown plaid overcoat. Lifting his brown billycock hat by its tightly curled brim, he polished his sleeve across the hard curve of the crown to bring up the nap, and laid it neatly on the seat beside him. Finally he slicked back his palms on his macassar-oiled gingery hair, the parting central and immaculate, razored.

He replaced his billycock hat, tapped it straight with his fist, and studied his reflection in the window-glass.

Detective Inspector Bowler was in charge.

He was forty, a clean, solid-looking man, topping the necessary five feet seven inches by a head. His pale-blue eyes gazed steadily between gingery, light-coloured lashes. The men of G Division, where he had risen through the ranks, nicknamed him 'Looker', and he had refined The Look since those days. As one of the twenty-seven members of the Detective Force at Scotland Yard, he had learned that the criminal classes were as much creatures of habit as the police. The uniformed branch usually had it well conned who they were looking for but had no case. At Scotland Yard they understood the criminal mind. Bowler's Look was unflinching, both intimidating and conniving, and this push-pull procedure worked so powerfully on the guilty that often confession took the place of evidence.

The hansom cab turned right at the bus stop and rattled down Abercorn Place, paused to negotiate the road-gate. One of the newspaper stringers in a grubby suit called out loudly, 'Detective Inspector Bowler! Any news, sir?' Bowler ignored him. The hansom drew up in Abbey Place.

A uniformed constable with a long walrus moustache popped open the cab door. He stared. 'Cat got your tongue, Police Constable?' Bowler said quietly.

The constable's salute remained frozen at the sight of Bowler's unmarked plain clothes. Not even a number or insignia of rank.

Bowler stepped down slowly.

He showed his warrant. 'Do it proper or get off the earth, Police Constable.'

The man stiffened his salute by one notch. 'Sorry, sir, didn't get who you were.' Every man in uniform hated the plainclothes police.

Bowler observed the crowd pressing forward in the house gateway. 'These people are breathing the air, Constable.'

'Sir?' The man rounded off his salute stolidly, eyes front.

'Why?' Bowler said.

'Why, sir?'

'Trampling on the evidence, Constable.' Bowler pushed past him.

'Evidence, sir—'

'Selling hot chestnuts and playing barrel organs next, Constable.'

The man hurried after him. 'No, sir!'

'Move them on.'

'No orders, sir! I was told to knock at the next house but there's no one—'

Bowler stared coldly. 'Who's giving you no orders?'

By now the man looked thoroughly miserable. 'It's Inspector Pultney, D Division, sir.'

Bowler turned his cold eye on the cabbie perched high behind the hansom's roof. 'What are you waiting for, Jarvis? Send your bill to the Yard. One and sixpence authorised.'

The cabbie yanked his greasy muffler to uncover his mouth. 'Two bob, sah!' he complained.

'Try it.'

The cabbie threw down his cap on the roof. 'An' me bloody tip!'

'Foul language,' Bowler said. 'Smell that man's breath, Police Constable. If he's drunk I'll see his licence.'

Constable Nutting knew cabbies were always drunk, it kept the cold from their bones.

'But, sir—'

'Or I'll see your number,' Bowler murmured, and Nutting knew his sort would do it.

'Yes, sir,' Nutting said. He pointed at the house. 'In there, sir. The basement.'

Alfie Nutting and the cabbie watched Detective Inspector Bowler's measured tread across the gravel. 'What's nigging that bloke, sah?' the cabbie said, exhaling a ginny breath.

'There's a little girl been snatched.' Nutting pulled lugubriously at his moustache, which had long strands of grey in it. 'It's a bad do. It might turn out very bad. Policemen are human, y'know. Even detectives. Maybe he's got a little girl her age.'

'One law fer the rich,' the cabbie muttered. He spat over the wheel at the fine house. "Oo'd care, elsewise? My sister's girl took a walk—'

'I should take a walk down ter the cabbie's shelter if I was you, Jarvis,' Alfie advised tolerantly. He stamped his cold feet. 'A nice hot cup of tea, and eggs and bacon . . .' He flicked the hem of his cape at a kid climbing the fence for a better view of the tragedy, clipping the offending ear a bright smarting red. 'Get scarce,' he commanded without rancour. 'Private property.'

Detective Inspector Bowler trod carefully towards the house. He knew he would not be allowed in the front door. The house was redbrick, too imposing and too over-confident in style for something so new. Nouveau riche it was called, and the ivy being trained up the walls would soon play merry hell with the brickwork. He looked around him. There were footprints among the bushes by the gate. The lookout had stood there, wearing shoes not boots. He had broken none of the branches, nor even disturbed the leaves. A professional.

He looked up sharply, hearing a sound, but it was only the police constable he had spoken to knocking at the house next door. This early, a reply would be slow coming. A common police constable would be sent round the back to make his enquiries. He would not be allowed to disturb the master of the house.

Bowler continued his observations. He walked with his eyes fixed on the ground. Any footprints on the gravel or grass had been trampled by clodhopping police boots. He crouched, scrutinising the frost that still remained in the shadow of the trees. A man in size twelve leather-soled boots, a barefooted boy.

They'd used a loofer boy to get inside. Bowler

straightened with a grunt of satisfaction. The white-gloved policeman guarding the steps, watching him from the corners of his eyes, was shooed away by the butler. 'My master requests you gentlemen to comport yourselves where you cannot be seen.'

Bowler chuckled to himself. Coppers were never gentlemen and never would be. His chuckle hid his resentment of the butler's snobbery.

He examined the tradesmen's entrance with experienced sweeps of the eye. The gate hung open. It looked like fifty people had tramped back and forth along the passageway beyond. A maid throwing away brussels-sprout peelings tittered at him as he passed. Some dull tool in a cloth cap had been set to work sweeping up spilled coal. Bowler looked round the yard at the back. The garden gate was closed.

A search party returned empty-handed. They'd been looking for a girl's body in the boundary ditch. If she was still alive she could be anywhere in London by now. He watched them wait for orders on the steps down to the kitchen door, lifting their helmets and rubbing their hair, one or two taking catnaps in the manner of uniformed men everywhere. Half a dozen policemen always looked like a crowd, yet just a few years ago Bowler had been one of them. He had changed, but men in uniform probably never would. They ignored him, knowing a detective when they saw one.

Again Bowler chuckled to himself.

Detective work was unmanly. A crusher's truncheon kept people in their place, and as long as he was top dog and his white gloves were respected on the street, his job was done. A detective was different. A detective went inside people's houses. Detectives like Mr Bowler went prying and spying into the tawdry little secrets of people's private lives, turning over their souls like mossy stones, getting their hands dirty. A detective's job was to appear like an ordinary citizen. He was a secret policeman. No one could tell how much he knew.

Bowler saw there was nothing left for him outside. In his experience the solution to a crime rarely lay in the evidence. It lay inside the heads and hearts of people. It lay in what they had seen, what they thought they had seen, what they thought, what they felt. They themselves were the clues, and in them he would find the truth, perhaps even the solution. It was time he went inside the house.

The men parted in front of him. Bowler went down the steps between them. He walked with a steady, measured tread, moving as ponderously as a centre of gravity, as though made of something weightier and more massive than flesh and bone.

'Who's in charge here?'

He had learned that way of speaking quietly that made himself heard. He knocked loudly on the door and one man jumped.

'Who was in charge here?' Bowler repeated quietly.

The door opened and a sergeant stepped out. His defensive glower changed to an expression of relief. 'Thank God, it's you, Guv'nor.' He almost managed a smile, then winced at his black eye.

'Sergeant Steynes.' Bowler touched the silver 'G' above the number on Steynes's shoulder. 'Old times.'

'Pure chance I was passing, Guv'nor.' Steynes

was a blunt-looking individual with broken veins in his nose. His cheeks were scratched. There was dried mud on the shoulder of his uniform, and he was not wearing his duty band. He stood aside and followed Bowler into the kitchen, then closed the door behind them. 'My old ma's not well—'

'Still the life and soul of the Eyre Arms?'

'Lives upstairs now, sir.' The kitchen smelt of boiled haddock. Bowler sniffed. A kitchen maid bustled past them with a mop, all ears. 'Late last night,' Steynes commenced, 'I left my mother's house. I returned towards Watling Street to catch the omnibus to the Feathers Street nick, where I was due to go on duty. I—'

'Wait.' Bowler crossed to the corridor. A very angry-looking girl carried clean washing streaked with dirt into the washroom. He reached in and stopped her. 'Leave it.'

'But I was told,' she sulked. Bowler put his finger to his lips. The heavy door further along, invariably in such houses, led to the silver storeroom. He overheard the butler's voice, complete with snobbish accent, checking off a list. 'H'one sterling silver coffee pot, fluted, Queen Anne. Yes. Sterling silver salad bowl and helpers, yes. Claret jug, here we are. H'it's all here, h'Inspector, h'except for the one h'item that was on the table.'

Bowler knew the lady of the house would keep her jewellery upstairs, probably in a pretty box that shouted its precious contents to the criminal eye. A good safe was almost impossible for a criminal to get into, but women liked looking at and touching their possessions too much.

101

'At about half past ten p.m. I proceeded along Hill Road,' Steynes said. 'I ascertained a man astride this here back fence in a suspicious manner. When challenged he dropped on me. In the struggle he punched me' – he favoured his eye – 'and cleared off through the stables in the direction of Watling Street. He was accompanied by a lad who ran like this.' He demonstrated the gait.

'Rickets,' Bowler said.

'On coming out into Abbey Place I saw a man with a young child. Red hair, about five, it was the Briggs girl all right. When challenged he picked her up and ran like the devil.'

'Those scratches?'

'Brambles, sir,' Steynes grunted. 'Almost got the bastard.'

'Get a view?'

'Much the same as yourself, sorry, sir, from the back. Longer coat than yours, *long* hair, no hat.'

'Did she struggle?'

An angry shout interrupted him. 'Of course she struggled!' A red-faced inspector had emerged from the storeroom. He marched up the corridor and put his face in Bowler's. 'Who are you? Who let you in?' His voice rose. 'What are you doing here?'

'You are Inspector Pultney.' Bowler waited for affirmation.

'Yes, Pultney, I am. Who—'

'I am Detective Inspector Bowler, Scotland Yard.' Bowler showed his warrant. 'I have been summoned to the scene of this serious crime.'

'It's not necessary,' Pultney said. 'We'll find the man drunk in some pub in Lisson Grove.'

'And the girl?'

'Shush, man, have a little tact.' Pultney winced at the ceiling, as though afraid of being overheard by the grieving parents upstairs. 'You know we almost never find them.'

The eavesdropping maid gave a cry. She pressed the back of her hand to her mouth and rushed past them, her mop falling to the floor behind her. The door to the servants' quarters slammed. Bowler watched with interest, making a mental note for later, then dealt with Pultney. He knew the type, probably an ex-Army officer at the end of his luck to take police pay. Both Pultney and the interview board had been scraping the bottom of the barrel the day he joined the force. Gentlemen made bad policemen.

'Inspector Pultney.' Bowler laid down the law. 'You'll leave a man at the front door with his hand actually on the knob, a man on the back door ditto. No one will come in or go out without my say, not even the master. Never mind playing about with the other houses, I want the garden searched by officers on their knees. I want to know everything. How many servants, who, when, where. How many fleas on the dog's back. The rest of 'em can get back to breaking up fights outside pubs, and pie-shops, and gin-palaces, and finding lost dogs in butchers' shops, and let me get on with my job.'

Pultney had gone purple beneath the eyes. He swelled. 'Who d'you think you are? I won't have my orders countermanded by some jumped-up plain-clothes—'

Bowler examined the table, the floor. He took off

his glove and came up with a gleaming silver speck pressed on his fingertip.

'This is a criminal investigation by Scotland Yard and I am seconding Sergeant Steynes to my assistance,' he said.

'The hell you are! This is my show, my patch—'

'He's G Division, no loss to you, Inspector. What was knocked off this table?'

'How do you know there was anything—' Pultney watched the detective blow his fingertip clean. 'What does it matter?'

'Everything matters,' Bowler said patiently. 'Everything is important. Steynes, take notes.'

'It was a candlestick, I think—'

'One candlestick.' Steynes licked the tip of his pencil.

'Silver,' Bowler said.

'It'll be melted down by now.' Pultney spread his hands. 'Be reasonable, Mr Bowler. I have my own divisional detectives, good steady men who know the system—'

Bowler pulled the crumpled telegram from his pocket. He held it over his shoulder as he walked to the stairs. 'My authority.'

Pultney took it. 'I won't be top-officered—' His voice faded.

Bowler examined the iron railings, the scuffed concrete steps. 'You observe the name appended beneath my orders.'

Pultney swallowed. 'Williamson, Chief of Detective Force.'

'Superintendent Frederick Williamson, my Guv'nor,' Bowler amplified, now on the top step. He went into the dining room and Pultney scrambled after him. He found Bowler standing among the broken wineglasses, tapping the steel tip of his boot on a broken plate. 'Mr Briggs, owner of this house and father of the abducted girl, is a personal friend of Police Commissioner Henderson,' Bowler said. 'They belong to the same club, or one of them. Colonel Henderson is the Guv'nor of my Guv'nor. So it comes right from the top. Here I am and here I stay.'

'Why you?'

'I am the very best,' Bowler said.

Sergeant Steynes moved round the room taking notes in tiny capital letters as he had been trained, faster and more legible than any typewriter. Bowler always liked notes, the more the better. He would go through the little black books over and over, like a diver painfully opening a thousand oysters to find one pearl. Steynes cursed as a wineglass exploded loudly under his boot.

'Damn you!' Pultney burst out.

'Sorry, sir.' Steynes looked at Bowler. 'Sorry, sir.'

Bowler had picked up a stair-rod he had found lying on the carpet.

Pultney cleared his throat nervously. 'Mr Briggs had asked us not to come upstairs until the servants have had time to clear up all this mess. It's embarrassing for him.'

'Have you wondered, Inspector, why all the chairs are knocked over towards the kitchen door?'

'I have not.'

'Because someone knocked them over to get there.'

Pultney followed him to the tiled, echoing hall.

Bowler stopped at the bottom of the stairs, examining the heavily varnished newel-post, finding a scratch of fresh yellow wood. He peered up the stairwell, counting the floors.

'You can't go up there,' Pultney said, alarmed. 'This isn't one of your cheap lodging-houses, you know. Mr Briggs is on ten thousand a year. He is a man of substance, Bowler, and this is his *home*.'

Bowler went upstairs, following the scrawl of sooty footprints around the stairwell. On the top landing a maid knelt, scrubbing the carpet. She stood respectfully against the wall, head bowed. Bowler knew he would see a trail of soot leading from the fireplace in the mistress's bedroom beyond, and so it proved. He examined the narrow staircase to the attic, then returned to the hall.

'I suppose you know almost everything,' Pultney said.

'No,' Bowler said. 'But I've seen enough to know where to begin.'

'I've an appointment with Mr Briggs for ten o'clock. Mrs Briggs, naturally, is inconsolable. He did not see why it should be necessary to add to her grief and I agreed.'

'I'll see them now,' Bowler said, and the clock struck eight.

II

The father was calm, the mother was weeping. Both of them had fish on their breath. Bowler smelt it as soon as he was shown into the study.

'Detective Inspector Bowler, Detective Force, to

see you, sir,' the butler said.

'You, what's your name?' Bowler asked. He had taken off neither his hat nor his overcoat, and he stood with his hands stuck deep in the pockets. The butler's top lip lengthened. A gentleman wore a cape.

'My name h'is Worth, sir.'

'I'll talk to you later, Worth.' Bowler trod across the expensive carpet towards the girl's parents, who were waiting by the fireplace. Her mother was sitting in an upright chair, swaying slightly, her father standing two or three feet to one side. Briggs was in his late forties. He wore a maroon paisley smoking-jacket. The choice of colour made his hair seem less red than it was, and pointed up the penetrating blue of his eyes, which lent his features a little distinction. It was not expected that Bowler would shake hands.

Bowler stopped in front of Briggs. He held out his hand. There was no response.

Bowler said, 'Good morning, sir. You're Joy's father?'

The woman wept more loudly at the mention of her daughter's Christian name.

Darby Briggs stared at Bowler coldly. 'I asked for a little more time.'

'This is my assistant, Sergeant Steynes,' Bowler said.

'This business is quite bad enough without putting up with two of you.' At last Briggs felt obliged to give the proffered hand a quick shake.

'Wait outside, Steynes,' Bowler said.

'Oh, he can stay,' the woman cried, half rising

from her chair. 'Just get on with it! Why do you want to talk to us?'

'Lydia, Lydia –' Briggs patted his wife's shoulder. Bowler decided that she was one of the most beautiful women he had ever seen. Her complexion was pale of course, almost sunless. Her lustrous chestnut hair fell in big slow curls to her shoulders, and the black shawl she wore set off her lovely skin to perfection. She was almost undressed, wearing no layers of petticoats, no bustle, no hat. Bowler knew he was seeing her as only her husband did. In just that simple black dress, little more than a shift, her slim ankles revealed as pale lines pointing to heaven, she seemed almost naked. Bowler stared into her, taking in her deep brown eyes, knowing and set wide apart, her pupils made enormous and dark by grief and crying. She would have taken a little laudanum, but there was still something wild in her. Bowler, who knew he was attractive to women, could not help responding to her.

He realised she knew what he was thinking. She knew the effect she had on men. Bowler drew the appropriate conclusions. She'd have lovers, then. Did her husband know about them? Where did she meet them? How was it arranged? How had she kept it from the butler and her maid? Were they conspirators?

You're an unlucky man, Mr Briggs, thought Bowler, to be married to a woman who knows she is as beautiful as this. She'll have given you no peace.

He turned back to Briggs. Definitely Briggs didn't know about his wife's infidelities, he wasn't the sort. He hadn't looked at her once. Possibly they had eaten breakfast together for the first time in years, broiled haddock, taken the bones out without looking at each other, toast, marmalade. Not a word said.

Bowler started to speak, but a hand on his elbow pulled him round. Lydia was straining towards him, her hands at full stretch.

'My little girl is gone! Snatched by some foul beast! And you're just standing there!' She put her hands over her face. Sobbing, she bent forward until her elbows slipped between her knees and it seemed that in the extremity of her anguish she might topple forward from the chair.

Bowler observed her with his hands behind his back.

'We're doing everything we can—' he almost said her first name. 'All we can, Mrs Briggs.'

Her husband comforted her with pats on the shoulder. 'I'm afraid Mrs Briggs is distraught,' he apologised. 'You can imagine her feelings.'

'Yes,' Bowler said.

'No,' she wept. 'You cannot.'

'Any mother would feel for her child as I see you do,' Bowler said. 'And any father,' he added. 'Mrs Briggs, I beg you to save yourself the trouble of any further distress. Go to your room and try to rest. I suggest you take no more opium.'

She stood unsteadily. 'Why not?'

'Dreams,' Bowler said.

Briggs rang for his wife's maid, Gaby.

'We returned from the opera at about eleven and found – you know.' Briggs spoke distractedly. 'Tom had put up a terrific fight, of course. As had the nanny, Mrs M'Kenzy. God, what am I to do? I have important meetings this afternoon. Will the matter be resolved by then?'

'I'll want to speak to everyone,' Bowler said. 'Doesn't matter whether they were witnesses or not. Everyone.'

'Why? The guilty people aren't here, Mr Bowler,' Lydia said.

'You should be out chasing this monster and catching criminals,' Briggs said, 'not pestering innocent people like us with your questions.'

'We're all sinners, sir,' Bowler said. Indeed, the first lesson a detective policeman learnt was the truth of the Christian belief that there are no innocent people. For the first time Bowler smiled, as though robbing his insolent words of offence, but his eyes did not flicker in their ceaseless observation of the man and woman in front of him.

'Indeed we are, all sinners.' Briggs could hardly deny the truism. He added thoughtfully, 'My friend Commissioner Henderson was right about you.'

'I trust he spoke in the highest terms, sir,' Bowler said without subservience.

'You have my permission,' Briggs said. 'Get on with questioning everyone, damn you.'

'Perhaps Joy will return while I am asleep,' Lydia said. 'You will bring my baby back to me, won't you, Mr Bowler?'

'Tell her yes,' Briggs ordered in a low voice.

Bowler opened the door. The maid was waiting. Bowler said nothing.

'He seems intelligent for a man,' Lydia said as she passed her husband.

Bowler closed the door behind her.

He turned to Briggs.

'I'll take those particulars now, sir.'

'Nobody told me she was half deaf and dumb,' Bowler said.

'That one's daughter is a mental cripple is not exactly the sort of thing one can afford to have bruited about the place, Mr Bowler. A banker must be most careful, you understand. Personal fallibility reflects badly.' Briggs went to the bow window overlooking the garden, the rooflines beyond rising up Maida Hill. 'We have not kept her secret, of course. We have merely been discreet.'

'You're ashamed of her,' Bowler said.

'No, it's for her own good.' Briggs spoke to the window. 'Joy could not possibly have held her own in school, or in public. In the nature of things a father sees very little of his child these days, especially a girl-child. I'm a busy man.'

'Too busy to be ashamed of yourself,' Bowler said.

Briggs span on his heel. 'I trust that man of yours is not continuing to make notes,' he said with a small, tight smile.

'She let you down,' Bowler said. 'An imperfect child. Your own flesh and blood.'

'You are insolent to the point of insult.'

Bowler waited steadily.

Briggs sighed. 'It's not as if she was a mongoloid or anything very bad, though you can imagine the taunts that the low classes of urchin shout in the street, should she be taken out. She is merely – difficult. Wilful. Irritable. Strange.'

'Sounds like all children of that age, doesn't it, sir?'

'Yes. No! I don't know.'

'Do you love her?'

'You go too far, Mr Bowler. You intrude.'

Bowler soothed him. 'Perhaps it was Lyd— your wife's fault.'

Briggs calmed himself. 'You may be right. There is no sign of any such mental symptom in my own family, certainly.'

'Then *she* let you down.'

Briggs dropped onto the chair his wife had occupied. 'This isn't some popish confessional,' he said shakily. '*I* have committed no crime. Neither has my wife. You cannot persuade me that I have. That either of us—'

'The worst crimes are committed in families, by people we think love us.'

'Ridiculous.'

Bowler said quietly, 'How badly do you want your daughter back?'

'I'd give anything, naturally.'

'Anything?'

'You're a frightening man, Detective Inspector. Do you believe all men are criminals?'

'That's my job, sir,' Bowler said. 'To get at the truth.'

'You are a fanatic, Mr Bowler.' Briggs was deeply shaken. 'An English fanatic. That's almost a contradiction in terms.'

'A professional, sir.'

'Many people would hold that against you, but I do not.' Briggs talked openly. 'I myself started as a mere junior clerk on the front desk at Prideau's Bank in Cornhill, on a salary of £50 a year. For almost thirty years I have worked my way up, I have fought my way tooth and claw. I have married a handsome woman. I have bought this house with a large mortgage. I'm good for it. I hobnob with the patrician classes. I have a box at the opera, my cellar is full of fine wines, my cook is French. All this, mine by my own efforts.' He held out his arms around the room, the directoire desk on gilded legs, the gilded chairs, the marble fireplace and the Landseer painting above it in a huge gilt frame, the library of morocco-bound books, identical except for the titles.

Bowler said, 'Did you love her?'

Briggs collapsed. 'I love my wife and I love my children.' He looked up appealingly. 'I couldn't understand her. I gave her everything, but she looked at me as though *I* were the stupid one. That child lived in her own little world. The best doctors worked on her. We employed an elocutionist to make her speak properly. The most eminent doctor from Boston, Dr Warren, advised on the cure of her stammer, and taught her to talk with her teeth closed, and to tap her head with her finger on the pronounciation of each syllable until she could repeat perfectly, time after time, *I can speak with certainty of its utility. I can speak with certainty of its utility.*'

'I'll talk with Worth now,' Bowler said. 'Let's go down to the kitchen.'

III

'What were you up to last night, Worth?'

'H'up to, sir?' the butler drawled.

'You heard.' Bowler sat at the head of the kitchen

table. Steynes waited behind him with his notebook.

'Last night being the second Friday of the month, sir—'

'What does that mean?' Bowler interrupted.

'My h'evening free, sir.' Worth raised his eyebrows. 'I was not here.'

'Twelve days a year.' Steynes gave a low whistle. 'I only get a week. All right for some.'

'A week is seven days,' Worth corrected him. 'I am h'allowed twelve h'evenings.' He bowed his head at Briggs, who sat on a hard chair by the pantry. As his staff's moral guardian he had insisted on listening in to the interrogations. Everything in *my* house is my business, he was saying by his presence, nothing swept under the carpet here, nothing hidden, no secrets. 'Most generous terms, sir,' Worth added.

'Get on with it,' Bowler said.

Worth squinted against the sun streaming through the fanlight over Bowler's head. He squirmed nervously. He was in an impossible position, pinned between the policeman and his employer. He knew his place, and this, here, downstairs, was it. Down here he was the master and he had to be respected, even feared a little. Downstairs had more rules and class-consciousness than up, and down here he was top of the pecking order. He knew all the wrinkles, no one came the old soldier over Otto Worth, no one got away with anything without cutting him in on the choicest slice.

But with Mr Briggs here he had to wear his upstairs face, elegant, polished, every aitch in place. 'I passed yesterday h'afternoon in preparation for the company of some two dozen guests who were h'expected to dinner tonight.'

'They're still coming.' Briggs cleared his throat. 'Mr Prideau, chairman of the bank. His two sons, young Mr Ernest and young Mr Winston. Other high officials of the bank and men important in financial circles.' He looked at Bowler. 'It is necessary to keep up appearances.'

'Anyone come to the house during the day, Worth?'

'No, sir.'

'Tradesmen?'

'The h'usual callers, sir. The milk woman. The grocer's boy, the milliner's boy, the butcher's boy, h'all with dog-carts. A knife-grinder. The coal-heaver.'

'His would be a horse-drawn dray?' Bowler said.

'Barely fits down the side passage, sir.'

'So the passage was blocked and you had to take the goods in through the house.'

'Yes, sir.'

'But a knife-grinder has no goods, only his labour. Where did he sharpen the knives?'

'In the kitchen, sir.'

'So you brought him down here through the house.'

'I'm afraid so, sir.' He looked nervously at Briggs. 'I wasn't to know, sir.'

Briggs crossed his legs the other way.

'An unfortunate lapse,' Bowler said.

Steynes took notes. 'What did he look like?'

'Oh, I'm afraid they h'all look the same, h'officer. Dirty.'

Bowler made an impatient gesture of his hand. 'Get on with it.'

'I served Mr and Mrs Briggs with a light dinner,'

Worth went on. 'It being not necessary for me to set the fire in the drawing room as they were departing for the h'opera immediately, I summoned the carriage. Mrs Briggs wore her jewellery and looked very fine, may I say so. Upon their departure I h'extinguished the lights, checked the windows, locked and bolted the doors. My duties completed, I retired to my room by the steps at the front of the house, which has its own small door for which I have the key. I put on my hat and cape, locked my door behind me, and departed.'

Bowler said, 'Where did you go?'

'My duties were completed, sir.'

Bowler said, 'You still have a life when your duty is finished, don't you?'

'No, sir.' Worth set his face. 'No, sir, I do not. It's my business, sir. It's the h'only time I get. It's my private life.'

'So you just disappeared, like a trick bunny-rabbit.'

Worth said with dignity, 'I walked, sir.'

'Very respectable. Where did you walk to?'

'Nowhere, sir. I followed my nose.'

'You're a bachelor, aren't you?'

'Yes, sir. I have not been fortunate in the marriage stakes.'

'So you walked the streets for five hours thinking innocent thoughts. Who saw you?'

'Half London, I should think, sir.' He glanced at Briggs.

Bowler put his face in the light. 'No, who *saw* you?'

'No one I could put a name to, sir!'

'You walked for every single minute?'

'I believe I may have stopped for a tipple to keep out the cold, sir.'

'What was the name of the public house?'

'I don't quite recall if it had a name, sir.'

Bowler moved his lips. Liar.

'Man to man, sir,' Worth confessed. 'Word in your ear?'

Bowler stood. He went into the corridor and stopped where they could not be overheard. He took off his hat and murmured, 'All right.'

'I frequented an h'establishment, sir.'

'Drop your act,' Bowler said.

Worth shrugged. 'I went for a jammy bit of jam, it's only once a bleedin' month. Mrs Chulmleigh's.' He grinned, put his arm round Bowler's shoulder. 'Man ter man, all right? Lisson Grove, yer can see it from 'ere. Yer know the sort of place. A pound of raw minced beef an' a couple o' gins an' yer can keep it up all night. All the blokes go, put a bob or two on the dog-bait or the rat, then it's sally upstairs. They can't get enough of it, them girls. Some of 'em do it wiv vegetables when yer shagged out.' He winked.

'How many girls?'

'Wot, at one time?' He winked again.

'How old are the girls?'

Worth pouted his lips. He exhaled. 'Thirteen, twelve if yer lucky, but they're pricey. I 'eard one say she was eight but she couldn't count.'

'All right.'

'Enough fer yer?'

'All right.'

117

Bowler went back to the kitchen and sat down. 'Mr Worth has accounted for his movements. Let's talk to the maids.'

'Polly, sir, Mr Bowler. Oh, I can't believe she's gone, sir! She was the sweetest little darling, we all loved 'er. It's the cruellest thing wot ever 'appened. I wish I'd been took instead. I do, sir.'

'Where were you last night, Polly?'

'I really do, sir.' The girl pulled anxiously at the frill of her bonnet. 'Am I to be let go, sir?'

'Not at all, Polly,' Briggs reassured her. 'Just answer Mr Bowler's questions as fully and properly as you can.'

'We was in bed, sir, sleeping.'

'All evening?' Bowler said.

'We're tired out of our minds, we got ter be up two hours afore dawn!' Her lip trembled. 'Me an' Dottie, sir, it's the room right at the front of the basement. We didn't 'ear nuffink. Anyways, there's no way out but through this 'ere door. It's fer our own good, sir. The streets is awful dangerous.'

'So Dottie was with you all the time, was she?'

'Yes, we was in bed together, sir, in each other's arms all the time.'

'Good God, girl,' Briggs said. 'In each other's arms? Why?'

She looked at him as though he was mad. 'Ter keep warm, sir.'

'You are Gabrielle Daniells?'

'Yes, sir, and I am my lady's maid, and everyone calls me Gaby, and I do not care if you do get me

118

dismissed.' She turned her pinched, determined face towards Briggs.

'Calm yourself,' Bowler said.

'There's things that need to be said, sir, and I'm going to say them, I've decided on it, and no one's going to stop me.'

Bowler said, 'Would you rather speak to me alone? Mr Briggs, perhaps you should withdraw.'

'Gaby could not say anything that could possibly diminish my high opinion of her,' Briggs said.

Gaby drew in a deep breath. 'Very well, Mr Bowler, sir, this is the way it is. I've worked in Mrs Briggs's service night and day for ten nearly eleven years, since just after Master Tom was birthed. I was there when Miss Joy was born, I saw her head come into the world, and she was the prettiest little baby that ever was born. I'm loyal as can be, sir, but it's got to be said. They pretend mothers always love their children, but that's a lie. My mistress Lydia only loves herself, no one else. Lydia only thinks of herself, she only cares about how *she* looks, and she only cares about people who admire her. And that's the truth.'

'That's enough,' Briggs said. 'I will not have such things said aloud in this house. This is unforgivable. Bowler, for God's sake, man, stop her.'

'How can I?' Bowler said. He took out his clasp knife and opened it. He cleaned beneath his nails.

Gaby tightened her fists. 'Lydia's never loved her little girl, never had time for her, the breast came from the wet-nurse, the little thing's never known love.'

'Of course my wife and I love her,' Briggs said

through pressed lips. 'You are an ignorant woman. You understand nothing of people of class.'

Gaby wouldn't speak to him. 'Because Joy is deaf, Mr Bowler, no one has ever listened to her. She is the brightest spark that ever was, but she has not been heard. It's us who have been deaf. It is us!'

Bowler pared his nails. Steynes's pencil squeaked as he wrote. He finished.

'It's not us who are on trial,' Briggs said at last. Bowler folded his knife and dropped it back in his pocket. 'I'll speak to you later, Miss Daniells,' Briggs said.

'I've packed my things,' Gaby said defiantly. 'All the years it's needed to be told, and I've wanted to tell it, and now I've got it off my chest!' She sounded jubilant. 'You can keep your reference. I'm a good riddance gone!'

She slammed the door behind her.

Briggs wiped his forehead. He glanced at Bowler. 'I don't know about you, but I could do with a stiff malt whisky.'

'Too early in the day for me, sir,' Bowler said. 'Are you sure you wouldn't rather wait upstairs?'

'It has been a rather dreadful day, but at least it can't get any worse. In fact I'm rather proud of what Tom did, though I shouldn't say it of my own son.'

'Bring in the nanny and the boy,' Bowler said.

'So you're the boy who ran from the top to the bottom of the house,' Bowler said. 'Our hero, Tom Briggs.'

'Yes, sir.' Tom sounded embarrassed. 'It was nothing really.'

'No, no,' Bowler said persuasively, 'it was something. It was a big something. Sit down, Mrs M'Kenzy.' He brought forward a chair and personally, standing behind her, helped her onto it. 'Steynes, attend to that matter we discussed earlier, would you.' Steynes went out.

Bowler returned to the head of the table. The sun streamed past him from the fanlight. He studied the nanny in silence. She was a pathetic sight. Her swollen face was shiny with superficial bruises. The corner of her lip was split an inch into her cheek and the doctor had stitched it. She sniffed a blood-speckled handkerchief to her nostrils.

Bowler said, 'How old are you, Tom?'

'I'm eleven, sir, nearly twelve.'

'That's old enough to know what's what,' Bowler said approvingly. 'Now, tell me what happened, can you do that?'

'I woke up. I heard a suspicious noise and naturally I went to wake Mrs M'Kenzy in her room.'

'No,' said Bowler. 'You always have to tell a policeman exactly what happened.'

Tom glanced at his father. 'Go on,' Briggs said encouragingly.

'Joy was looking out of the window,' Tom said. 'She woke me. She was excited.'

'Why?'

'I don't know. I told her to get back into bed. But she wouldn't. Then I heard a noise, and that's when I went to wake Mrs M'Kenzy.'

The nanny said, 'But I was still awake, of course,

121

sir. I am not allowed to sleep until the children are asleep—'

Bowler said, 'What sort of noise was it, Mrs M'Kenzy?'

'I beg pardon, sir?' She buried her nostrils in her handkerchief.

'It was a bumping noise in the wall,' Tom said. 'That's right, isn't it, Mrs M'Kenzy?'

'Yes!' she said. 'Tom was very brave. He grabbed a stair-rod and chased the boy downstairs just like his papa would have done.'

'I certainly would,' Briggs said. 'Well done, my boy.'

'He thought I had a gun,' Tom said proudly. 'He thought I was going to shoot him, and I would have. He cried, *Monkey didn't mean nuffink!*'

'Monkey,' Bowler said.

Mrs M'Kenzy said, 'But then the girl slipped out of my grasp and ran after them! There was nothing I could do. She's always had a touch of wild, that one, sir.'

'Surely you are many times stronger than a girl of five,' Bowler said, standing. He scuffed the toe of his shoe on the stone floor, making a steely scraping noise.

'She pulled me over, sir, the little vixen.'

'Is that how you sustained your injuries?'

'No, sir!' Mrs M'Kenzy proclaimed. 'That was here in the kitchen, sir, when that fiend came bursting through the door—'

Tom said, 'He looked like a Neanderthal man—'

'The brute knocked poor Master Tom over—'

'Just here?' Bowler interrupted calmly.

'Yes, just exactly where you're standing, sir! And he grabbed that stupid girl and laid into me when I tried to stop him—'

'And there was another man looked in,' Tom said in a rush, 'he had sharp eyes that sort of took everything in at once, and he had smooth hands like a girl. It was him who took the candlestick and ran down the garden—'

'Born criminals, sir,' Mrs M'Kenzy said. She showed her face for Bowler's sympathy. 'You ought to be locking them up.'

Steynes came in. He caught Bowler's eye and gave a glimpse of the empty bottle of gin behind his back. He put his little finger in the corner of his mouth and pulled as if to split his lip. Self-inflicted injury.

Bowler scraped his shoe loudly on the cleaned patch on the floor. He looked at Tom's freshly pressed pyjamas, still showing the creases where they had been folded, and observed how well washed Tom was for a boy. His fingertip examined the thin red line on Tom's neck.

Bowler hummed to himself.

He settled himself comfortably on the corner of the table.

Mrs M'Kenzy's snorts into the handkerchief became sobs. Her shoulders shook.

'I – I was so, so frightened,' Tom burst out. His voice broke into an adolescent honk. 'I thought I – I would, would never see my Mama and Papa again . . .' He held out his hands to his father. 'I'm sorry, Papa. I'm sorry.'

'Now tell me the truth,' Bowler said.

* * *

Bowler came down the steps from the front door. He sunned his face with closed eyes, then rubbed his neck as he walked away from the house. Steynes followed him across the gravel. He put on his helmet and pulled the chinstrap over his chin. He did not speak until he was spoken to.

'It's the unhappiest family I've seen,' Bowler said. 'Why do some people think of families as all the same, all perfect in their way?'

'I don't know, sir.'

'*We* know that more children are hurt or deformed by their fathers and mothers than by anyone else. Look at this place, it should be a haven from a heartless world. Instead it's a kind of hell, Steynes.'

'Yes, sir.'

'The nanny dismissed for lying, Gaby Daniells for telling the truth. At least we know now why the little girl didn't struggle. Right from the start that was the one thing I wanted to know. You can't blame the boy.'

'Way of the world, sir, isn't it.'

They stopped by the gateway and looked back at the house. Briggs came out, saw them, and started over.

'What are you going to tell him, sir?' Steynes murmured.

'I won't tell him I have a dozen such cases on my desk,' Bowler said. 'Girls run away, or taken unlawfully, or fallen down a manhole. How many of them are heard of again?'

'You don't think there's a hope, sir?'

Bowler said, 'You know what happens to them.'

124

'Yes, sir, I do.'

'We'll keep an eye out but there's not much else, girls are too easy to turn into cash. Her clothes are sold by now, she's locked in some back room somewhere or dead, and in six months Briggs wouldn't recognise her if he hired her in the street. I'll say there's always hope.'

'Yes, sir!' Steynes made himself look busy in front of Briggs. 'We'll make enquiries, follow up leads—'

'Let's get away from here,' Bowler said, then raised his voice. 'There's always hope, Mr Briggs. A ransom demand, perhaps—'

Briggs stopped in front of him. 'I suppose this must seem very small beer to you, Mr Bowler,' he said. He looked five years older, hollow round the eyes. 'You must have seen much worse things.'

'Sir, you must not give up hope.'

'I do not believe in hope.'

There came the sound of a window being banged open. All three men turned, looking back at Briggs's house, but it was as it had been. Then Briggs pointed towards his neighbour's house, almost identical beside his own. A sash window on the third floor had been lifted. A policeman stuck his head through the gap.

The policeman vomited down the redbrick wall. He heaved for breath, still vomiting. His helmet fell from his head, tumbling into the bare flowerbed below, planting itself on its spike like a strange blue orchid.

IV

Police Constable Alfie Nutting had knocked again

at the next house. He went down a step and looked up at the windows. All quiet, he noted. Curtains drawn. Saturday morning, sleeping late. He returned to the front door and knocked for the third time.

Inspector Pultney's voice carried to him from Briggs's house. 'Leave it.'

Alfie put his hand to his ear. He didn't like starting, but he didn't like stopping once he'd started.

Pultney was called away.

Alfie sucked his moustache with his lower lip. It was a bad habit and Abigail had been at him about it for years, and now Beth and Becky were old enough to nag him it was three against one in his house. On his last birthday they had presented him with a curved device that had mystified him, and he had turned it over in his big hands, but he couldn't guess what it was. A spoon, he said, but they shook their heads. It wasn't that. A thing for scratching your back, but it wasn't that either. When he had to give up it gave his three women almost infinite pleasure, because he was not the sort of man ever to give up on anything, and the skirted victors had joined hands and danced around him in the tiny scullery. It's a thingummy, Gail told him. For keeping your moustache out of your gravy and your soup, Beth giggled. No more soup-sucking noises, Becky had warned, and given him a kiss on the forehead. She was like him, the serious one, and she'd made him try it out at once, because she understood that his moustache was very important to Dad. It was a moustache of stature, long and bristling, almost warrior-like in its impressiveness, though he was the gentlest of men. His moustache intimidated small naughty boys, reassured women and was respected by everyone else.

He raised his fist to knock again at the door, which had been very heavily constructed.

'Yer can knock 'til yer blue in the face,' the milkman called. He filled the two empty pitchers set by the tradesmen's entrance. "E won't answer. That's Sparklestein's, that is.'

Alfie went over. 'Who?'

'That's what we call 'im. The jeweller from 'Atton Garden. Supplier of sparklers to 'Er Majesty the Queen.'

'Oh yes?'

'God's truth, guv.'

'What's his real name then?'

'Fats Goldblum.' The milkman patted his belly. 'Mr Aaron Goldblum, that's Jewish, an' don't they know 'ow ter complain if the milk's a touch sour. A millionaire, an' counts 'is change ter the last farthing.' He shook his head in disgust. 'Just 'im an' 'is missus, no kids.' He knocked open the tradesmen's gate. 'Fussy britches, 'e is, but cow-juice keeps 'til evening this time of year.'

'He'll open up to Her Majesty's constabulary, or else,' Alfie said.

'Nah, Saturday's their Sabbath. They don't do no work, not even go ter the door, they just lie about in the shadows.' The milkman brightened. "Ere, yer could take these pitchers down fer me. Them dogs give me gip.'

'You do your own dirty work,' Alfie said, then looked again at the silent house. With a sigh he

127

hefted both pitchers in one hand and went down the passageway.

'Wolfounds!' the milkman called cheerfully. He gave the horse a slap on the reins. 'Gee-up!'

Alfie trod carefully. 'Anyone home?' The coal-heaver had delivered yesterday and he stepped over the lumps which had not been swept up. In a fenced corner of the yard he saw a kennel large enough for wolfhounds, but no sign of the dogs. He wondered where they were.

He went down the area steps and banged on the kitchen door. No reply.

'Come on, come on.' It was his job to be suspicious, but he could see no sign of a break-in. The kitchen door was very heavy. He tried the handle but it hardly rattled, still locked on the inside.

Just as he was about to give up he heard the lock turn. The door opened ponderously. A little maid, hardly more than a child, looked out. She wore a night-shift, and shivered at the cold air.

'Police. You haven't done anything wrong,' Alfie reassured her frightened face. 'It's just routine.'

'Why aren't the dogs barking?' she said. 'The bolts were open, and the door was only held by the new lock.'

'Can I come in?' Alfie pushed past her into the kitchen.

He sniffed. It smelt musty.

'It's my day off,' the maid said dully. 'I've been asleep. I make Mr and Mrs Goldblum a little something to eat after sunset.'

Alfie dropped the pitchers by the table. One of them wobbled softly on the stone floor. There was something soft under his boot too. He examined the sole. A cube of meat was stuck to it, flattened. He bent down and pulled it off. Best steak.

One of the dogs lay under the table, its mouth open in a snarl. 'Christ!' Alfie shouted. He jumped back, but the dog did not move or breathe.

Alfie crouched. He touched its head and a piece of meat fell from between its teeth.

'Oh no,' Alfie said. He liked dogs. He had a Jack Russell dog called Splodge because he had a brown splodge on his back. Splodge was getting on now, and he slept most of the day, but he still fetched slippers downstairs at coming-home time. It would be quicker for Alfie to do it himself, but Splodge had his pride.

Alfie dropped the piece of meat on the table. Other pieces had been scattered on the floor. He wiped his hands and went forward. The sun streamed past him.

The other wolfhound had climbed halfway up the stone steps at the far end of the kitchen, then collapsed against the iron railings. It looked like a grey astrakhan coat thrown away.

Alfie stepped over the foam by its mouth. 'Oh dear,' he said. 'Oh dear me.' He remembered the maid. 'You'd better go back to your room,' he called down. 'Lock the door after you and don't come out.'

The top door opened onto a dining room. The table was long and shiny and the chairs had tall backs. Alfie's boots made no sound on the expensive carpet. He opened the double doors into the tiled hall.

Nothing. Very faintly he could hear a horse

clopping by on the road outside, and the hiss of blood in his ears.

'This is the police!' he shouted. 'I think you ought to come here right now, sir or madam! Something's happened!' His voice echoed up the stairwell and came back again, shockingly loud. He cupped his hand on the newel post and craned his head up the staircases rising away from him. No one looked down.

'I am a police officer. I am coming upstairs.'

He drew his truncheon and held it at the ready going up, but nothing went wrong. The drawing room and the parlour were full of silent furniture, dark and ornate, foreign-looking.

There's nobody here, Alfie thought. I can feel it. This place is empty.

He ran up the next flight of stairs.

Bedroom doors.

He leant on one with his shoulder. It was the wife's bedroom.

Mrs Goldblum stared at him, tied in an upright chair. Her face was a huge scream. Her mouth gaped enormously at him, like a snake's about to swallow its prey. For a moment he really thought she was alive, but when he touched her hand she was so cold and hard with death that he broke out in a sweat.

Here, Alfie realised. Those bastards committed the real crime in here last night, not next door.

She wore a dark brown dress, very full, but her feet stuck stiffly out beneath the hem, one shoe on, one shoe off. At her throat gleamed a silver brooch, rather showy, proclaiming her husband's wealth and love. Her hair was pulled back in a bun which stuck up clumsily, like some ridiculous new fashion, forced by the rope encircling her head. The rope held the balled handkerchief in her mouth, gagging her. It had been tightened with her shoe, breaking her teeth and dislocating her lower jaw, then tightened until her spine cracked.

Alfie took a step backwards, then turned in case there was someone behind him.

The landing was empty. He took deep breaths.

'Steady now,' he told himself. 'You've seen worse than this, my lad.'

Her room was large, of course, larger than Alfie's whole house. On her dressing-table, large enough for Alfie's family to sit round, her jewellery box stood in front of the mirror. The design was very beautiful, inlaid with precious woods. The box alone would have fetched enough to keep Beth and Becky in clothes and shoes for a year. Its many drawers had been opened and they glittered, full.

Alfie stared in the mirror.

Behind his reflection he saw that her big double bed had been pushed aside. A man's feet stuck up over the counterpane. He wore black patent leather shoes.

'Mr Goldblum, sir?' Alfie croaked. He turned slowly. 'Are you all right, sir?'

Goldblum was dead. He was tied to an upright chair that had been pushed over backwards. There was the most terrible expression of suffering on his face. He had died with his hands clamped over his chest. He looked as though he was trying to hold himself together. His eyes were still fixed on his wife.

131

Beside him the moved bed revealed a floor-safe.

Alfie thought, where does a man whose life is jewellery hide his most precious pieces? With his most precious possession.

The safe below her bed was almost full of jewellery. It had been opened by a key. Such jewellers' keys were almost impossible to duplicate.

The key in the lock was covered with blood.

Alfie swallowed. His stomach rose in his throat.

He knelt and touched the dead Jew's hands. They flopped aside.

Goldblum's clothes were scarlet with blood. His jacket and shirt had been sawn open with a knife. The wound was large enough for a man to get his hand inside.

Alfie went to the window. He could see Detective Inspector Bowler standing next door with two other men. Alfie banged the window open and leaned out. He tried to hold the helmet on his head.

V

Bowler came out of Goldblum's house into the soft evening light. It had been a long day and he was exhausted. He took a breather in the porch with his hands stuck in his overcoat pockets. Police Constable Nutting was adamant that the house had not been broken into. The sky over the roofs of Watling Street was red and gold, fading. Bowler watched the lamp-lighter trot along the road with his long flare-tipped pole, his little dog yipping beside him in the dusk. Beyond Briggs's house the moon was rising serenely above Regent's Park. The smoke from Briggs's

132

chimneys drifted across the moon's face.

Bowler stiffened.

He remembered the loofer boy. Briggs's chimneys were in plain view to him, so, equally, a boy climbing on the chimney could have looked into Goldblum's porch.

Bowler took a step, staring, as a light came on in one of the attic windows. He could see the window plainly now it was lit. The nanny packing her things to go and live with her mother in Waterloo. Or perhaps it was Tom's room.

Bowler didn't have to look at Steynes's notes to remember Tom's statement. He remembered it as clearly as though hearing it.

Joy was looking out of the window.

'Steynes!' Bowler shouted. He ran into Goldblum's house and dragged Steynes out by the arm.

'The girl was kneeling on the windowsill looking straight down into the porch here. The boy said so. *Joy was looking out of the window. She woke me. She was excited.*'

'I remember,' Steynes said. 'I've got it written down in black and white.'

Bowler gazed up at the lighted window.

'She saw the murderer,' he said. 'That little girl's more than a victim. She's the key.'

Part Two

The Painted Boat

Chapter Five

I

Joy launched herself into the dark. She fell forward.

Don't cry, little one, she remembered Jack's voice echoing. *We're safe in here.*

Almost at once she struck something soft, sloping. She slid back down the slope. She rolled, flopping. Her hair tangled around her face. She caught her ankle a ringing blow on something made of iron. All she could think of was the black water below, opening beneath her, dragging her down. 'Jack!' she shouted.

Something flat and hard caught her. She banged her head and her ears felt lanced by a skewer of pain.

Water roared and spray came from ahead, poured over her, disappeared behind her.

She covered her ears with the palms of her hands and lay dazed, remembering.

I will never hurt you, I promised. I promised that worthless brother of yours. I promise you.

Jack's voice began to shrink. *This is all I know,* he said with such sadness that she reached out to him. *I never was a child.*

He was gone. His voice faded until she couldn't

hear him any more, only the slow tramping sound of boots. The tramping boots neither approached her nor receded.

A dot of light appeared ahead of her. It broadened to a circle of daylight that rushed closer, widening around her. Incredibly, the sky was downwards. She gazed dizzily down into the sky rippling, growing brighter beneath her, and thought she had never seen anything so beautiful.

Now she saw roofs hanging down into the sky. She saw a mule standing upside down. Three upside-down boys of different sizes waited beside it. One of the boys stood on tiptoe, pulling the mule's long ears affectionately.

Sunlight exploded around her. The rays of sun streamed down a steep grassy slope. She was sliding from a huge black hole at increasing speed, the bricks flying past her as red as blood. She tried to crawl back into the dark but she was carried outwards without effort.

The daylight struck so bright and sudden on her night-adjusted sight that she could not open her eyes. She put out her hands and crawled blindly.

Suddenly there was nothing under her.

Joy fell head-first, landing with a bang of wood and a crash of things falling after her. She opened one eye and saw a Red Indian girl wearing feathers in her hair. She saw a vase of flowers lying on its side, the water miraculously not falling but remaining still and placid. Then something moved, and she realised her head was lying between two enormous feet.

'Strewth!' a woman's voice muttered, very deep.

"Ow long've *you* been wiv us then?'

Joy was pulled up by a gigantic horny hand.

She looked into the face of a baby.

The baby's ruby-red cheek, flushed with its exertions, was nestled into the ponderous white curve of a breast. Its lips puckered around the jutting nipple. It sucked calmly, returning her look without any change in the contented expression of its baby-blue eyes. It had not learned fear. Its head was a pale cloud of curls as fluffy as cotton, frizzing uncut to the shoulders. A girl, then.

The baby grinned. The grin spilt drops of milk over Joy's face, her lips. She tasted its thin sweetness, and her weakness and hunger washed over her. She reached up, sucked the nipple like a strawberry into her mouth. She heard the woman's surprised laugh. Her last memory was of the baby surveying her seriously from the other breast, its chubby fist now kneading its mother's bosom possessively, drinking as deep as she.

'Gawd save us!' Dad Wampsett said, waving his hand through the steam. 'Wot yer gone an' got up ter an' done now, Eleanor?'

II

'No!' Kes Wampsett said. 'No, no, no.' He drew back, gripped the rope roving of the tiller under his right armpit ready for the sharp turn. 'We're not even going ter talk about it, Eleanor. Right, that's the end of it.'

But still, he couldn't get the sight of the girl out of his mind. There was something obscene about her,

139

wearing that long coat, drinking from his woman's breast. A girl of four or five who should have been able to look after herself, obscene because so pitiable. Such pitiable need that he had seen exposed in the girl's instinctive, groping form. Her filthy face and clawed hands blue with cold, her body still shivering convulsively, slimy stuff and bits of blood leaking from her ears. Maybe she'd been beat and given the chuck.

'Look-it, Dad!' one of the boys called up. 'She's drinking our Ma's tit!' They sounded revolted, jealous. 'It's disgusting!'

Kes knew you saw worse things around here, if you looked. Most girls in London were under fifteen, and most of them looked little different from that child. Kes kept his eyes on the towpath.

'She's nothing ter do wiv us,' he called down without looking.

Eleanor wiped the girl's ears with a rag. 'Wot was that 'Is Reverend the vicar of St Peter Vee said 'bout the travellers 'oo crossed ter the other side of the road?'

'But this is the Regent's Canal,' Kes said. 'This is real life, not the blooming Bible.' He crossed himself for blasphemy. 'I got me schedule ter keep ahead—'

'The Good Samaritan came along an' got 'is 'ands dirty 'an 'elped.'

'But 'e was a man,' Kes said. 'Yer only a woman.'

'Get on wiv yer job,' Eleanor said contemptuously, and blew her nose on the rag.

Kes was weary to his bones, too weary to fight her. With his foot he righted the water-can painted like a vase of flowers by Grandma Pebble, propping it against the Red Indian girl whose portrait adorned the locker. He had just time to crouch and rub his stiff legs before the bridge and he groaned, favouring his aching back. For nearly half an hour he had been lying flat on his back on top of the cargo. The tippet-cloth had not softened the top planks much, or maybe he was getting old. He had planted his feet on the tunnel roof, walking the boat forward. Legging a monkey boat loaded with twenty-five tons of horse manure through the Maida Hill tunnel was hard labour, even with momentum built up and the water taking the weight. Kes's greying hair was matted with soot and brickdust that had dropped on him from the roof, his eyes red-rimmed and inflamed. He gripped the tiller once more and it took all his strength to push on enough port hellum for the *Poca* to follow the canal's curve beyond the Chapel bridge. Thirty yards ahead, Ham dragged on the tug-hook, then drove the mule, Ramses, forward along the cutting. The mule was older than the boy. Kes watched the tow-strap pull taut on the bend, water wringing out of its creaking cotton strands, and towpath ash puffed around the mule's hooves as it took the strain.

And there was this nonsense going on below.

'Look 'ow she's got Cottontop going, that's all I can say.' Eleanor's voice came muttering from down in, busy with her own mysterious thoughts not his masculine concerns. "E wouldn't touch a drop o' Mum's yesterday, yer know wot 'e's been like, 'e was a real fret. Now look at 'im.'

'Now then, Mrs, I've no time fer yer wiles,' Kes said, half-threat, half-plea. He knew, as she did, that she would get her way if he really looked at the girl. When it came down to it he was as soft-hearted as Eleanor. They were a team.

The *Poca* slipped beneath the aqueduct carrying the Tyburn river over Kes's head.

"E's guzzling fit ter bust, Dad,' Shane piped up unhelpfully.

'Shut it, by Jiminy, both yer young sprogs!' Kes shouted down. He rubbed his grimy face with his grimy hand, but he still wouldn't look. Regent's Park passed on his right, out of sight so that people like he should not be seen. His greasy clothes itched and he scratched. Mum was on about Cottontop again. She'd let his curly cottony cloud of hair grow as long as a girl's, and they called him Cottontop because there wasn't a boy's fourth name. Ham, Shane and Jaffrey were named after Noah's three sons in the Ark. 'Me an' yer Ma often 'ad forty days an' nights of solid rain on the Mon & Breck canal,' Dad would tease the boys when he was in a jocular mood, which he often was. 'The *Poca* is our Ark, lads, an' we sink or swim together.' Until last autumn such simple truths handed down the family were sufficient education for boys, and natural cunning would make men of them, but now they must be registered with the education department until the age of fourteen, and must learn reading and writing. Kes supposed such skills would make the boys useful in dealings with the dock offices, but he was afraid the School Boards would take his children away and teach them to look down on him. Kes had started his family late in life, just when he and Eleanor thought maybe it wouldn't happen after all, and now there were the four. But Noah had stopped at three apparently.

But now there was the girl.

'She's got lovely soft clothes on underneath,' Jaffrey winked. 'I can see 'er bum.'

'That's naughty,' Shane hissed, looking. 'She 'asn't got a doodle!' They stared, amazed. "Ow does she pee then?'

'She don't pee,' Jaffrey said. 'She's perfect.' The boys watched the girl with respectful looks. She was now doubly mysterious to them, and so doubly to be admired. 'I bet she don't do the other, neither,' Jaffrey whispered.

'D'yer want ter feel the back of me arm, yer two?' Mum growled. 'She's a poor lost creature. Look at 'er coat. Stolen! An' where d'yer think she got satin like that? Stolen! She's a needful creature. Let 'er nap.'

'Stole! She ought ter be in prison,' Jaffrey said, awed. 'She's a crinimal.'

'Criminal,' Shane said.

'She's too young ter be a criminal,' Mum said, looking down quietly. 'Yer got ter be eight ter be a criminal.'

'I reckon she got in before the tunnel!' Shane said, wondering what sort of eight Mum was talking about. He could already count much better than either of his parents, but he was interested in meanings, and much of what Mum said was rather difficult. He hoped eight was about food. He never ate enough of anything, except cod-liver oil.

'P'raps she's come all the way from Paddington docks,' Jaffrey said. 'Sneaked aboard in the dark, chased by the police, 'id under the cloths—'

'Or from somewhere deep in the countryside—'

'She's a stowaway!' both boys exclaimed excitedly. 'Whooooo!' The Macclesfield bridge swept overhead and their shouts echoed back off the iron pillars, frightening them.

Eleanor let their bragging wash over her. Boys would be boys. A private expression had come over her face. She kept her head down so that what she was feeling should not be seen.

'Yer can't 'ave stowaways on a little monkey boat like our *Poca*,' Shane pointed out sensibly, the older twin by thirty-two hours. He'd popped into the world just before the middle of the night, Mum said, so Jaffrey's birthday came after his own by two calendar days. Mum knew how to say such things because she had a little reading and a few numbers from her own mother, Grandma Pebble. Shane went on, 'Yer only get stowaways on wool clippers an' pirate schooners—' His eyes lit up, realising what he had said.

'Pirate schooners!' both boys shouted.

Grandma Pebble started snoring like a pig and they put on her hat more comfortably, turned her so that she was quiet, then returned their attention to the girl without a break in their concentration.

'Let's make 'er walk the plank,' they whispered.

Kes kept his gaze resolutely above the cabin top. The mule's breakfast of steaming corn mash was boiling in its ornate nose-tin on the *Poca*'s equally ornate back end, and again he waved away the steam blowing over him. He cupped his hands and roared over the fore end to Ham, 'Gee-up!' Long-skirted ladies chattering on the Charlbert bridge above, carrying bags of bread to feed the ducks on the ornamental lakes of the park, glanced down their noses at the dirty-faced folk in their dirty boat sliding below them along the scummy industrial waters of the canal. Then the ladies hurried onward with their little paper bags and shrill laughter, having noticed nothing.

When none of his family was watching Kes opened the hatch between the well and back post where the food and odds-and-ends were kept. He slipped his fingers behind the backing and pulled out tobacco. He bit off a quid defiantly. Chewing baccy was a disgusting habit and Eleanor loathed it, which added to his relish. He squirted a stream of black saliva into the muddy water.

Kes was worried. He was always worried. Worry and work were his life. The *Poca* was laden so low in the water with street-manure that sparrows could have drunk off the top guard, and gauging the cargo's weight at the toll-house had taken longer than expected. A Number One never had a second of schedule to spare. A Number One owned his own boat and held himself a cut above the other boatmen, but sometimes it suited Eleanor not to realise that time was money. A Number One's schedule was writ in stone or his customers wouldn't trust him next time. He had only himself to blame when things went wrong. That meant Eleanor could be a very difficult woman, if she chose. Kes worried until his stomach hurt, but he didn't let Eleanor know.

He heard the lions roaring in the Zoo twenty-five feet above their heads. The mule twitched its ears. 'Gee 'im on, 'Am, boy!' he hailed.

'Yer kept the smacking whip, Dad,' Ham called.

'Then use sharp talk!' Ramses was their livelihood, and a boy's harsh words never hurt an animal, but the whip could. Ham, who had been miles away thinking of the girl, looked delighted to receive licence, and let rip. God knew where a good lad not old enough to shave learned such effing and blinding, but this was London. London was Sodom and Gomorrah rolled into one, in Kes's view, having been born in sound of Limehouse Dock. The sooner the boys had green grass under their feet again the better. They were growing up too fast.

He snatched a moment to squint through the door-hole into the tiny dark cabin-space of the *Poca*. 'I'm *not* going ter talk ter yer, Eleanor,' he repeated, hardening his heart, 'that's the end of it.'

'She's a girl, see, Christopher,' Eleanor grunted comfortably from the shadows.

Kes knew her calling him by his full name, Christopher, meant that wasn't the end of it, not for her, and so not for him. Eleanor was going to talk about her feelings to him, and she was going to go on for hours, and he was going to listen to her. He slipped his sixpennyworth in first. 'She stinks, Eleanor! God knows what she's like. She's a Londoner. She's an orphan, or a runaway. Or a thief, yer said so yerself! Yer could be clasping a viper ter yer bosom, Eleanor, no end of trouble. Bring 'er up out,' he suggested reasonably, 'see she's all right, leave 'er on the towpath. Show some sense, woman.'

'She's a girl,' Eleanor repeated.

'But she's not a baby, Eleanor.'

'But look at 'er, Dad,' Eleanor said. 'She's got a stripe on 'er wrist, where it don't show. She's been striped by a switch or a riding crop—'

'Or a smacking whip,' Kes said, looking at last. 'Poor little thing.'

'I got four boys,' Eleanor said solidly. 'But boys ain't the same as a girl, Kes. Look at 'er!'

Kes threw up his arms. 'They're all kids!' he said. He glared impotently at her massive shadowed figure below him. 'They'll be falling from the blooming clouds next if it's up ter yer, Eleanor.' His cabin was full of his family. He brimmed to the gunwales with family, the dog getting between everyone's feet, the cats, the brightly coloured parrot leering from its stick. The two in-between boys, the twins Shane and Jaffrey, were squeezed into the corner between the ornamentals now that the bed had been lifted up and the drop-table pulled down, eyeing the new girl like they'd never seen a girl in their lives before. There was not an inch available for more life. Grandma Pebble started snoring again where she had been put next to the bottle-stove, blowing out her moustache of white hairs, her blue-veined ancient hands and face still splotched with yesterday's paint. And in the middle of this squeezed mass of humanity and mess and smelly fug sat Eleanor in her barely respectable state, the baby and the girl clinging to her bosoms. The baby started to kick when Eleanor's shawl covered his face and cut off his air. ''Ware Cottontop!' Dad called nervously.

'Mind yer own work!' Eleanor shot straight back. She was getting angry now. 'It's nuffink ter do wiv yer, Kes! It's my business down 'ere!' That was true. Down in was Eleanor's home. Kes was only captain on deck, up out. On boat-handling matters she submitted to him instantly, but down in she wore the skirts and made sure he knew it.

Kes wrenched his attention from the scene below, busy with straps and sluices as they started the descent through the first of the Hampstead Road locks. Water swirled around them, the stone walls rose above them. Lining the canal now were big villas with servants and views where parents need hardly see their children, or each other for that matter, he supposed. Heaven it would be to be a gentleman. But the fact of it was he lived rubbed against Eleanor twenty-four hours of the day. She knew him inside out, for better or worse, and he knew her.

Kes slowly realised this situation with the stowaway girl required careful handling. Above all was the schedule. Eleanor was a big woman of big feelings, God bless her, but he was convinced she had never worked anything out for herself in her whole life. She needed him as much as he needed her. Her face had a beautiful strength, but her emotions blew over her like storms, and a wise man battened the hatches and kept his head down until sunshine. Her storms were darker but her sunshine was warmer than any other. The problem was, she just didn't think things through like a man. She had him for that.

They passed the Bass warehouse. There were said to be a hundred thousand barrels of beer stored inside. The warehouse was no longer supplied by boat but had its own railway line bridging the canal. A locomotive clanked overhead, showering sparks from its tall funnel, and Kes sighed glumly. Railway bridges crisscrossed the canal in every direction nowadays. He looked round as cinders from the Midland Railway were dumped with a roar from the St Pancras sidings into waiting barges. But all his thoughts were on Eleanor.

She was a one for her sons, Eleanor was. No one got between Mum and her sons, not even Dad. She was even happy to see him off to the pub, so long as he was walked back, not carried, for her time alone with them. Kes was the father of all her four boys and they were the most married couple he knew, though not in the eyes of the Church, but love was the best marriage licence. Eleanor had changed her name from Pebble when they got in tow to make them sound wed. She'd felt it was right and that was that. They were inseparable.

But now there was the girl.

Kes wondered how he could best be kind to his wife.

The mouth of the Islington tunnel gushed smoke as the steam-tug broke into the light. It waited with impatient panting noises as the *Poca* was strapped to another boat. Ham untied the tow-strap from the looby on the mast and led the mule up the hill over the tunnel. Kes jerked his thumb at Shane and Jaffrey. 'Yer both. 'Op it. I'm going ter 'ave a confab wiv yer Ma.'

'But Dad,' they said, then got his look and ran obediently up the granite setts after their elder brother. For once, Kes thought, Ham looked pleased to see them, wanting to know all about the girl no doubt. The dog jumped ashore and ran with them, barking. 'Come on, Lily,' the boys called. 'Come on, Lilypad!'

The boats were shafted forward, ropes were thrown, and the tug seized them. A few pale figures swarmed over its deck, blinking nervously in the light of day, then disappeared below. The tug backed towards the hole, a huge, antiquated machine as broad as the waterway and almost as old. Its upperworks of squealing brass pipes and clanking, whirling flywheels barely fitted beneath the arch. Pulling itself with loud groans along a chain laid on the canal bed, it dragged the *Poca* into the darkness, and there was nothing more for Kes to do.

The air was black and foul, trembling with the racket of thundering machinery. Kes held his hands over his ears. He ducked below and closed the little double doors behind him, everything arranged to save space. Water drummed on the deckhead, they were passing beneath a river. It was pitch dark in the cabin but he laid his hand on everything by touch, missing nothing. The lucifer match flared between his fingers, illuminating Eleanor watching him. He lit the wick of the brass oil lamp, then tossed the match out through the top hatch, which he slid closed. Suddenly it was almost silent in the cabin.

The flame came up slowly between him and Eleanor, glowing on the well-worn but lovingly polished brass fittings that surrounded them. Kes shook his head, admiring her even after all these years. Eleanor was a busy woman but she made time, *forced* time, to keep her strange little home on the water perfect, absolutely perfect. Not one thing out of place. The cupboards, the sliding door to the sidebed hole, the hatches, even the papier-mâché tea-tray, were all painted in brilliant colours, intricate visions of castles and flowers. The sidebed door was a scene of misty mountains and a castle, the coal-box a riot of dog roses entwined with bumble bees. Brass door handles, brass hooks, mule brasses, all were burnished to a perfect gloss. They speckled the bulkheads like brilliant eyes. *We are your home*, they said. *Look at us, see how cared for we are, how much time and effort is put into keeping us. We are your home*. Even the battered, cranky bottle-stove, an old enemy, gleamed with black lead as though it was forgiven. Then Kes saw his worried expression reflected in half a dozen pots and pans, and he couldn't help smile.

'That's better,' Eleanor said.

'Wherever I look, I always see me and yer both.' He sat and nodded at the pans. She never used them, cooking was done in the old iron stockpot, always simmering, never empty. Something bumped in the dark outside, was gone. They sat with the lamp glowing on their faces like an oil painting.

'It's the way we've always been,' she said. 'Yer not changing me now.'

'I wouldn't change yer fer the world, Eleanor,' he said sincerely, since the boys weren't there to snigger at them being lovey-dovey.

'Don't try an' get round me that way, yer sly old fox,' she warned, and he laughed. Then Eleanor shifted on the stool, and for the first time he realised how uncomfortable she was. Her back must be breaking. He reached to take the baby but she clasped them both protectively in her arms. 'They're sleeping.'

Kes studied the red-haired girl unsentimentally.

151

She was about four or five, and he lifted her hand and rubbed it. Her skin was clean beneath the dirt, not greasy with years of ill-use. Her fingers were soft, her nails trimmed not bitten. 'She's never worked,' he said.

'I'm not saying anything, Kes.'

The girl's face glowed like a coal. Her long black eyelashes fluttered on her cheeks. She snatched breaths through her open mouth with small hiccuping noises.

Kes's worry returned. 'We can't afford a doctor and we can't turn back.'

'I know,' Eleanor said sympathetically. Kes had endless faith in doctors, and the police too. Really he just wanted matters taken out of his hands. 'We'll find out 'er name when she wakes up, an' then yer'll know wot ter do.' She meant that *she* would have decided by then. Decided how to get her way.

'We'll be back here in a couple of days,' Kes said. 'I can't stop, it's money. It can't do no harm, can it?' He worked it out. 'We'll carry on to Duckett's Canal and cut through to the River Lee navigation. First thing Monday it's Jeavons' Hundred Acre farm near Broxbourne, an' manure off an' turnips on fer back 'ere.'

'Then wot?' Eleanor said, swallowing a lump in her throat.

'Then yer got ter tell the police.'

He opened the slide and stuck his head out into the noise and dark. They were coming to the end of the tunnel. The boys were waiting and the mule was hitched on without a break so that the *Poca* didn't lose way. Under the Danbury Street bridge a fleet of barges passed them on the other side, towed by a steamer. A man and a woman stood on the bridge above them, arguing.

'Yer got ter tell the police,' Kes said, nodding. 'They'll know wot ter do. Yer'll do it. Yes.'

'Yes, I will, Dad,' Mum promised.

III

I've been here before. Joy wondered if her brother Tom was here, and her friend Jack too, and hoped they were.

She slept, drifting in and out of insensibility. She felt as hot as a fire, but she was shivering.

The pain in her ears and throat was awful. She could not swallow. But dimly she recognised this pain as a familiar wicked friend, as much a part of her as her hands or her feet. She had endured these poorly bouts from before she could remember, from when she was a baby probably, and she knew she would feel the pain swell inside her head until it was almost too much to bear. And then slowly, slowly, it would fade away.

Until next time.

She had learned not to scream. That never helped. It only made the pain worse. So did crying. You mustn't be a noisy girl.

'Crying doesn't make it any better,' she remembered them saying. 'It doesn't help. Stop it.'

Now Joy neither screamed nor cried.

She pressed her lips together and lay silently. The fever raged in her, taking her thoughts. She could no longer remember which was a dream, and which was memory. She was hardly aware of herself, only of her pain.

'Why don't she say nothing?' mumbled a man's worried voice calling down. 'Don't she feel nothing?'

Joy bit her lips until they bled.

She was given some oil to ease her throat. The oil tasted horribly of rotten fish. She struggled.

'She's fighting for her life,' came the woman's voice, rough-edged but kindly. She was the mother. Vaguely Joy saw the pale curve of a sunbonnet, the woman's face beneath it looking as broad and weatherbeaten as a working man's.

'She's yer responsibility, Eleanor,' the man's voice mumbled, though really he must have been talking quite loud. 'Wot if she dies, and she's yer responsibility?'

Gentle hands held her. Eleanor's dress was the thickest and coarsest ever seen, as though she must do a man's work. The rough material smelt of wood and coal and rancid milk, but her big enfolding arms were warm and comfortable, and very feminine.

Eleanor's soft breaths played over her hair as the fever rose.

Suddenly the baby was no longer looking into her eyes but lay asleep on its back on a shelf, held in by a piece of wood. Time had passed. It held its pink milky hands clutched beside its face. It had not been swaddled properly, because its hands should have been clamped tight to its sides. Sometimes the winter sun moved, slanted across its face. That was bad too. Everyone knew babies must be protected from the sun and air.

The old woman by the stove was waking. She

wiped her lips on the back of her hand. Her seamed and withered face leaned forward towards Joy, noticing her for the first time. She laughed like a child, clapping her hands in approval. Her lips moved.

A girl! Yer've struck it right at last, Eleanor.

Her old face had been transformed into the kindest, most guileless, simplest smile that Joy had ever seen.

That beautiful smile was not only for Joy. It was above all for the old woman's own daughter.

'Yer struck it right at last, Eleanor!' the old woman cackled in a voice so high and hard that Joy heard her clearly through her dreams, over and over.

Then there was the man's voice again, speaking almost a different language, this language of adults.

She's yer responsibility, Eleanor. Wot if she dies, and she's yer responsibility?

Joy blinked. She must have been asleep, because she had been laid in a sort of cupboard with sliding doors. It was very comfortable, and at first she thought she was floating in the air, because she saw a blue river winding into the distance. She saw faraway mountains and castles and tiny brightly coloured birds, and dreamt of them.

It was dark outside. She heard an owl hoot, and the sound of wind in trees.

Her eyes flickered as she slept, close to death.

Chapter Six

I

Lydia leaned towards the mirror over her dressing-table. With her own hands she dragged off the brilliant purple dress over her head.

'Awful!' she said. 'Take it away. I won't wear it.'

Polly, the thin, worried-looking creature who had replaced Gaby as her ladies maid, burst into tears. Lydia dropped the dress on the floor.

'Get out,' she said.

'But ma'am—' Polly looked frantic. She picked up the dress and clutched it to her, trying to think of something right to say. 'But ma'am, this shade is so fashionable.'

'That's why I mustn't wear it tonight,' Lydia said. 'Something sad. Old-fashioned. Reliable.' She went down the row and seized a dress of a colour she really did not like, bottle green. Green did not generally suit her eyes, it made them look too dark, and her hair would seem merely brown instead of chestnut. The room would be lit by candles tonight, kinder than gas but not so bright. It would do no harm to appear a little bruised beneath her eyes, valiant even. 'This one will have to do.' She

157

threw the gown on the couch to be made ready for her.

But Polly, dismissed, had already gone. The silly girl had no idea how to handle her mistress. She would not do.

Lydia stood in her petticoats. Seeing herself, she raised herself up on tiptoe and pressed her midriff. She admired herself in the mirror, turning a little. Her neck was still smooth, her eyes sparkled from drops of belladonna. She was forty years old and her confidence in herself was complete. She knew she was beautiful. She knew she could summon and dismiss, bewitch and leave bereft. The City was a hard world, hardest of all for a woman. Tonight she must be soft, deferential, and less intelligent than the men around her, though they were fools away from their desks. Rich fools. Making money was their life just as being beautiful was hers. Her wit would flatter them, not cut, her femininity would please and never threaten them. Each man would envy her husband for possessing her. She must glow in the reflected light of his coming success, yet stand in his shadow.

It would be hard. Very hard.

And Darby Briggs, almost three decades of loyal service man and boy at Prideau's Bank and still only General Manager, and with no hope of further promotion because the Bank was privately owned, would think he did it all. Lydia's dream was as real to her as though already made of stone, with Corinthian columns, built on Cornhill. Across the portico 'Briggs Bank & Co' was written in big gilt letters. But first the money must be raised.

There were the distressing events of the morning to consider.

Other wives would be here, and they would see through Lydia if she were not careful. To cry off the dinner would be unthinkably suburban. On the other hand not to show grief would be considered cold-hearted. But to go too far and be overwhelmed by snivelling would be taken as weakness and would be embarrassing for everyone.

Lydia decided that tonight's dinner party, so long arranged, was an opportunity for grace. She must suffer gracefully. Old Prideau would go early, after the oranges, he always did. He'd take his sons with him. Then the real business would begin.

The Briggs Bank & Co would be founded on the telegraph and the typewriter. Male clerks did not have the patience or dexterity for typewriters, so women would be employed. Women were cheaper, half the price or less. On these economies of speed, scale and sex would the Briggs fortune be built. The rewards for success were simply enormous, Lydia knew. Hambros Bank paid their clerks less than three hundred pounds a year. Each partner made about six thousand pounds. However, Mr Everard Hambro, whose name was over the door, who would be here tonight, would receive over fifty thousand pounds personally in remuneration.

The top was the only place to be.

Lydia bent towards the mirror, examining her lips. They would need a little pomatum.

There was a knock on the door. Eventually Darby came in. Nothing infuriated her more than his habit of knocking and waiting. She wished he would just

159

burst in, lift her petticoats, grip her breasts, and enter her from behind.

'One can't help thinking about her,' he said.

Nothing would happen. Lydia stood up. 'Are you just going to stand there on this night of all nights?' She clicked her fingers for her dress.

'Where's your girl?' Worth had dressed him, Lydia saw. Darby shot his cuffs uneasily. He was wearing the gold cufflinks she had bought him with his money. Then he actually obeyed her command and fetched her dress! But he said nothing about how beautiful she was.

'Oh, you mean Polly,' she said. 'No good.' She let some of her intense displeasure break through. 'I can't believe you let Gaby say those dreadful things in front of everybody!'

'How could I stop her?'

Lydia's anger flashed into flame. 'Now your Detective Inspector Bowler knows more about us than we knew ourselves, thanks to you. You let her blab! You just sat there limp as a rope—'

Few men could have resisted Lydia half-naked and as furious as she was, but Darby just stood there looking shaken. 'What a terrible business,' he said miserably. 'I'll never forgive myself for being out.'

Lydia faced him squarely. 'My dear, it is tragic. But I want you to keep your mind on what is important tonight. Have you got that quite clear? When we're successful, you can grieve all you like. These things happen.'

'I wonder if I'm right to go ahead with this evening,' Darby said. Lydia realised that he was losing heart. 'I don't suppose old John would be too pleased if he found out I was planning to set up on my own,' he added.

She stated the obvious. 'If you succeed, Prideau and the clan can think what they like.' She kissed his forehead to buck him up. 'Stop thinking like a clerk and start thinking for yourself. Thinking of us,' she said. Thinking of *me*, she meant.

He looked at her earnestly but did not respond to her. 'All right.'

'You've got to forgive yourself, Darby,' she whispered. She let him breathe the scent of her. 'You know who is really to blame.'

'Blame?' He looked towards the window. It was already getting dark.

'Tom was such a coward, wasn't he?'

'But he's my son. Our son. You can't blame him.'

'That's what I mean. Can't I?'

'Lydia, don't.'

'He let you down. Will you punish him?' She pulled away. 'Well, we won't think of it now. I expect Tom blames himself as much as anyone. I would, wouldn't you?'

Darby closed his eyes.

'We've got to think of ourselves,' Lydia said. She shushed him to the door. 'Now, send Dottie up, or do you expect me to dress myself?'

II

When it was dark Jack stood up. Darkness meant safety. He flicked a match across his thumbnail, lit a cheroot. His tangled black hair touched the roof-beams as he looked round the back room of the

Lisson Grove pub where he had spent the day. The costermonger was saying goodbye to his friends, shrugging on his coat. 'Zo I zold her the sheep's head with the eyes in, to zee her through the week.'

Someone called, 'Night, Zolly.' Zolly clapped the shoulders of his laughing friends, then headed for the door. Still in his shirtsleeves, Jack slipped after the coster through the crowd of drinkers, followed him outside. The door banged closed.

Zolly stopped at once in the alleyway, lifted his coat, and relieved his bladder. He squirted merrily, humming to himself, unaware of Jack standing behind him in the gloom.

Jack reached into his belt for his knife.

He remembered that his knife was gone.

Zolly looked round, still spraying. His eyes widened. He opened his mouth to shout.

Jack punched him in the belly. He hooked his leg behind Zolly's knees and pulled, dropping him on the cobbles.

'Yer lucky,' he said. He put his foot on the coster's head and stripped off the coat. 'A little girl just saved yer life, Zolly.'

He put his fingers to his lips. He nodded, smiling, then bunched his fist in warning.

Zolly nodded frantically. Not a sound would he make.

There was money in the pockets too. Jack whistled softly as he took to the backstreets. The arms were too tight and the buttons wouldn't do up over the muscles of his chest, but he was warm enough. He could hear the coster screaming now he was safe. It was a cold foggy night, clear moonlight above. Jack could tell where the water was by the silence below him, and the fog thickened to a real soup. He came to the bridge. This time he knew where to find the steps.

Before going down he looked around him carefully, taking the cheroot from his mouth and sniffing for a trap.

What a fool he was to himself, coming back for her. Putting himself in danger for her.

But he had promised her, and Jack kept his promises.

He took off the coat and folded it behind the bench. This time he knew how cold the water would be, and he shivered even before he felt its touch. He dangled his feet below the icy surface, then swung himself down.

It touched his nipples and felt a bloody sight colder this time.

The bricks rose around him as he plodded into the tunnel mouth. There were foul slimy things on the canal bottom. He clamped the cheroot between his teeth, puffing it for the red glow of illumination. He kept it dry beneath his hand where water poured from the roof.

He smiled as he came to the niche.

The niche was empty.

He reached up into the niche as deep as he could, but there was nothing.

He moved his feet on the canal bottom, feeling for the weight of her drowned body. Nothing. The current had carried her away.

'Yer bastard,' Jack said of himself. 'Oh, I'm a bloody bastard. I've killed her.'

He had killed her as surely as sticking the knife in her. She wasn't as strong as a man. It seemed so obvious now. He hadn't thought.

The impossible happened. Tears streamed down his cheeks.

For as long as he had lived, he'd had only himself to care about, and he simply hadn't thought of anyone else. He had never cared for anyone. He had never loved anyone. Now it was too late. Jack felt how vulnerable he was, how close to dying.

He shook himself. There was nothing he could do about anything.

By tomorrow he'd probably have forgotten about her.

He turned, startled, shielding his eyes.

A brilliant star of light had come into the far end of the tunnel. The water began to tremble with the thrash of a propeller. Smoke swirled around the acetylene lamp as it approached. Jack struggled back the way he had come, trying to get away from it, but the water held him back like treacle. The cheroot dropped from his mouth. He heaved himself forward, paddling with his arms. He heard the hiss of steam. The water built up behind him, pushing him ahead with long slow strides. His head was ducked under as the wave caught him.

Then he was in the entrance, blue moonlight, misty waters. He pulled himself around the corner and clung to the bricks. The steamer swept out of the tunnel past him. Machinery clanked. It towed barge after barge, like a train. He had never imagined that things so large could move so fast in the dark. Huge seventy-ton butties with cargoes piled high, nitrates for Waltham or gunpowder from there, coal, flour, all locked down by heavy iron bars to protect them from needy folk.

The undertow dragged at Jack, the water rushing to fill in behind the barges sucking him forward. He pulled himself, shaken, onto the canal bank.

He unfolded the coat, wrapped his arms around him, stamped his feet, shivered life into his cold limbs.

He didn't think about the girl.

It was time he got back to St Luke's and Mrs Oilick's and the only life he knew.

He set off running.

III

It was dark in the attic.

Tom was afraid to light the lantern because he would see her playthings, her comb, her mirror. His little sister's bed waiting for her, turned down ready. He had laid her favourite toy on her pillow. He imagined her coming back and cuddling herself into the pillow the way she did. If only she would come back.

Mama and Papa had not been up. The last he had seen of Nanny M'Kenzy was her walking away down the road, sewing bag in hand, her portmanteau to be sent for no doubt.

Tom went to the window.

At first everything was black night. He saw his pale face looking back from the glass. Then his image dissolved and he saw out as Joy had. The moon shone down. Fog drifted through the rooftops and treetops of London. The streets were laid out below like a map made of mist. On his right Tom saw number seventeen, where old Captain Summers's widow lived alone. She was estranged from her surviving children, Eugenie and Henry, who was a medical student somewhere. Some dispute over the will. Once, Tom knew, the Summerses had owned all this land along the road, but it had been sold and these new houses built. Now most of the furniture had been removed from the old house, and not a light showed.

How strange all this must have seemed to Joy. She had not even known their names.

Tom looked to the left. Men had been coming and going from Goldblum's house all day, and he wondered why. A policeman still guarded the porch. The moonlight gleamed on his helmet and long moustache. It was the same man Tom had seen keeping back the crowd. His relief arrived, and the policeman saluted and left.

There was a knock on the attic door. Light flooded in, but it was only Dottie bringing supper. It was fish and chips. She left the lamp on the table and handed him the tray with her eyes down.

'Have they found her?' Tom asked.

'Oh young Master Tom, sir,' she whispered breathlessly, 'yer don't know? They've found Mr Goldblum next door! That's where the real crime was, bang under our noses, an' we never knew it!'

Tom said, 'Mr Goldblum?'

'Gutted like a fish, sir.' She slipped to the door, looked back, then left before she was overheard talking to him.

Tom put down the tray. He let the lamp go out and sat in the dark.

Nanny gone. Mama and Papa in their separate rooms. Tom knew he would be unforgiven as long as Joy was unfound.

He did not think she would be found.

He slipped from the bed to the floor. He shuddered to think what that monster was doing to her. Perhaps right now. This minute. This second.

He imagined her screaming.

Tom drew up his legs until his head was between his knees. No one could punish him as hard as he punished himself.

Chapter Seven

I

Yer got ter tell the police. They'll know wot ter do.

Eleanor Wampsett had not the slightest intention of telling the police anything. She'd done her duty, said 'Yes, Dad' loyally and submissively, but she'd kept her fingers crossed behind her back. Grandma Pebble had thought she was hiding a biscuit there, and peeped behind her hopefully.

'Oh, Eleanor,' she'd tutted reprovingly.

Eleanor got herself respectable to go ashore in Paddington. Going ashore with nothing to do was an almost unheard-of treat, or would have been if she hadn't felt guilty about disobeying Kes's order.

Kes was the best man she had ever known, and she loved him truly. He was a considerate husband. The boys could not have had a better father. He was hardworking and honest. He did not get drunk too often, and he was kind and often made her laugh. She would have cut off her fingers rather than let him down.

But this was not the first time she had lied to him.

A man liked to feel he was in charge. That was all right by Eleanor, as long as she got her way.

It's all for the best in the end, she told herself.

She remembered young Jaffrey's christening. In his sermon His Reverend the vicar of St Peter ad Vincula had lectured them, 'The road to damnation is paved with good intentions,' and he had looked directly at Eleanor Wampsett as he said it. She had swallowed with an audible click. How much did His Reverend know? She had put sixpence into the collection, more than she could afford.

There was almost no space in the tiny cabin of the *Poca*. Eleanor moved her elbows and knees with the skill of years of practice as she took off her dirty apron and faded sunbonnet. She dropped a cloth over the parrot so that he should not watch her change and say the things the boys had taught him. The cats were out mousing and Lilypad the dog was somewhere with the boys. Eleanor put on her black dress and a black coal-scuttle bonnet that came down to her eyebrows. 'Fat old sow,' the parrot said in a muffled voice.

'I'll kill 'em,' Eleanor muttered.

The girl lay curled just as she had been left in the sidebed, Cottontop beside her. At first Eleanor had been reluctant to put them together, but there was an affinity between the baby and the girl, and they looked nice sleeping together. The girl had put her arms around Cottontop, she was not always completely unconscious. 'Now, Gran, if she wakes—'

'I won't let her pinch anything,' Grandma Pebble said at once. The lesson had been long. 'Kes. I'll call Kes if she wakes?'

'Don't let 'er run.'

'I won't let 'er run. Did I ever tell yer, years ago—'

'I'm leaving the boys ter look after yer.'

'Don't worry, I'll look after 'em,' Grandma Pebble said blithely. 'Yer enjoy yerself.' She put back her face to be kissed. It was a strange, not-adult gesture, as if in her old brain Eleanor was still a child. 'Don't eat all yer biscuits at once, Eleanor,' she scolded, 'or it's a smacked bottom fer yer.'

'I won't,' Eleanor said sadly. 'Mind yer don't sit too close ter the stove, dear. Turn yerself round from time ter time, toast the other side.'

Grandma laughed her high laugh. 'Yer my Eleanor! Yer'll never grow up, an' I'll never grow old.'

'Oh Gran, I've growed up,' Eleanor said, calling her Gran because the boys did, hugging her. 'I love yer, Mum,' she said quietly.

The old woman looked her straight in the eye. 'Best get on wiv it quick now, girl, an' do wot yer've decided, like yer always do.'

Eleanor went up out. The *Poca* shook as the hold was emptied. The frost-encrusted turnips were being shovelled into wheelbarrows on the dockside. The sweating wharfies were as shirtless as though it was summer, and their muscles were brown. Their trousers looked very baggy. One turnip in ten, Eleanor knew, slipped off the shovels and rolled out of sight somewhere, as often as not up a trouser-leg, which was how men on the Lump kept their families. Pay was for beer. Stealing and pilfering supported the whole vast dockside industry, she knew, everyone did it. Each ton of cargo the *Poca* carried weighed twenty-two hundredweight, not twenty, to account neatly for theft. The wharfies called to Eleanor

171

cheerfully and weaved around her with their barrows. Sheep unloaded from double-decked boats were herded towards the abattoirs. One man stopped work for long enough to help her up the steps to the road. 'Real gent!' she joshed him, liking her effect on men.

'No bother,' he grinned, 'just getting yer out our way. Safety,' he grinned again, and she knew theft would go double the rate now her back was turned. She didn't worry, because she knew these men were scrupulously honest where it mattered, and her little home and its knick-knacks would be respected and perfectly safe. The cabin-slide didn't even have a lock on it.

She saw Kes watching her. He had told her to ask everyone if they had seen a little girl who was lost. 'Yes, Dad, I will.' She went in an obedient manner to a man in a flat cloth-cap and spoke to him. 'Yer wouldn't know the time, would yer?' He pointed at the chapel clock, and she hoped Kes had not noticed this peculiar reply to the question she was supposed to have asked. There was a woman hanging out washing between one of the spikes on top of the dock wall and an outhouse, and Eleanor hurried gratefully out of sight behind the wall.

She walked the streets for an hour.

Boats were all she knew. Streets were strange to her, and buildings even stranger. The rooms inside looked huge to her eyes, and she saw wasted space everywhere. She jumped aside as carts went careering past her at a terrifying speed, and people pushed around her from every direction. 'Right country cousin yer are, my girl,' she told herself.

Usually she was so busy she never looked about her, it was all a rush. Before a trip she usually bought twenty pounds of beef and boiled up a lobscouse stew in the stockpot, adding a layer of carrots and potatoes one day, turnips and potatoes the next, and so on until they worked through the beef in the end. And there was flour to buy, if they hadn't been carrying any as cargo for a while, to make bread and biscuits. Kes had worked all-male boats in his youth, living in bare board cabins on a fare of boiled-up beefbones for weeks on end, and he regarded the family life he had now as a luxury.

What a wonderful life we have, Eleanor thought as she looked around her, and realised it was true. She imagined the little girl wandering streets like these. The children staring at her from doorways seemed so small for their age. Their skin was pale and greasy, the alleyways were too narrow to let in the sun. Their teeth were rotten and discoloured, even the infants' milk-teeth. Eleanor's heart went out to them, but there were so many of them that their faces were all the same. There was nothing she could do. She did not know how to cope with what she felt.

She turned the corner into a different street. Eleanor began to enjoy herself. It was like a foreign country. The roadway was for people and the pavements were lined with brightly coloured stalls. Behind them men hung about in the doorways and yards, Greeks and Jews doing business with glances and shrugs. The stallholders shouted their wares in different languages, some hard and throaty, others sounding like songs. The stalls were hung with all breeds of food, odd-looking sausages, rabbit, horse, cheeses the size of cannonballs like no cheeses she had seen before, floury white outside, and one of them was cut open to show the soft yellow inside. She hesitated, tempted by a ludicrous desire to buy something so unusual, so useless. Kes would never eat it. The boys would turn their noses up at it. It would probably taste horrible. At the next stall a woman wearing a headdress cupped Muscatel raisins in her hands and held them out like a supplication. Eleanor was doubly tempted. Loose like that, they cost barely more than ordinary raisins. But Muscatel were special. They weren't for people like her.

Eleanor lost her nerve and walked away, but she kept looking over her shoulder.

Here the air swirled with spicy smoke, and meat and frying fish of shapes she did not recognise hissed and spat in wide pans. A dark-eyed, toothless man held up balls of minced meat to her on a skewer, and when she recoiled he laughed. 'Foreign muck!' she said, not taking any nonsense. But another man was selling rugs, they did look quite nice, and she imagined how good a rug would feel under her toes on a frosty morning. The next stall was stacked with brass plates, beautifully patterned, and one would have looked lovely hung next to the cabin mirror.

Eleanor began to linger. The more she lingered, the more she enjoyed herself. So this was what shopping was like!

Spanish costers hawked oranges and lemons from straw trays, Portuguese fishermen set up creaky barrows heaped with herring, fresh yesterday. French onion-sellers and Italian ice-cream sellers

174

jabbered at her. Children gathered around the hot-chestnut man. His oven roared as though about to explode. Women wearing heavy gold earrings carried trays laden with Southend oysters, winkles, mussels, swimming in as much Sarson's vinegar as you could drink. But then Eleanor's magpie eye was captivated by a stall piled high with electro-plated silverware, cheap bits and bobs, secondhand candlesticks and bits of garish jewellery. Her fingers were bare except for her lying wedding band, but she imagined what she would look like wearing one of those rings. 'Don't be shy,' yawned the stallholder, and she realised he was a Cockney. He dealt with another customer, knowing better than to hurry a woman making up her mind, but he didn't take his beady eye off her. "Allo, Arthur, 'ow are yer?' The two men talked in low voices.

Just holding the ring gave Eleanor pleasure. The other customer was not buying but selling, it seemed. She glimpsed a silver candlestick in the front of his coat. 'Give yer a couple o' bob fer old times sake, chum,' the stallholder shrugged.

'It's worth five bob, Matt,' whined the man in the plum-coloured coat.

'It's broke.'

'Sod yer,' the smart man said, but hesitated.

Eleanor plucked up her courage. She held up the ring. 'Ay, shop, 'ow much yer asking?'

Matt told her. It was about what she had expected. 'But 'alf price to yer, love,' he added carelessly.

That was cheap. The gold ring seemed awfully inexpensive for the weight. It was respectable for a woman of Eleanor's class to wear gold, as a way of putting something by. She slipped it on her finger and enjoyed dreaming for a moment. It seemed you could get stuff very cheap in these markets.

The two men talked again. 'Someone came by asking fer a candlestick very like that 'un, Arthur.'

Arthur sounded instantly worried and suspicious. 'Wot sort o' someone?'

'Someone wearing blue, if yer know wot I mean,' Matt said. Arthur knew. 'One bloomin' candlestick, yer'd think the bluebottles 'ad better things to do—' He stopped. Arthur was gone, flitting along the alley like a shadow. 'I know yer sort,' the stallholder told Eleanor, 'yer'd take all day looking a gift 'orse in the mouth, yer sort would.' He clicked his finger for the ring, and Eleanor gave it up.

She walked on, attracted by the heavenly aroma to a stall festooned with fresh herbs tied in bunches, and spices in jars. This time she was not to be put off. She held out a penny, pointing at a jar, any jar. It contained olive oil.

Eleanor had never spent money on olive oil in her life.

It was a wonderful feeling.

Kes would grumble. She didn't care what he said, she'd sort him out in bed. She turned back through the crowd, pushing her way confidently. The ring would be going too far, but she had something else in mind. She pushed past a thin man selling trinkets from a barrow. She could see the cheeses ahead of her.

Two policemen stood in front of her. They looked angry. '*Will* you get out of the way?' demanded one. 'Will you, or won't you?'

'I wasn't doing anything wrong, sir,' she said.

They glanced at one another. They were young enough to be her own children, but they were so tall that she had to look up to them. Their eyes were deliberately shadowed by their helmets, which were so high that they made the policemen seem even taller, and their shoes were raised on thick heels. Chin-straps pulled their faces up sternly. Their shoulders were made even broader by heavy capes. She realised that they had come deliberately to the street market. Their shoes were spotless, their gloves perfectly white. They did no work. The working people of the market looked at them out of the corners of their eyes.

The police weren't for these people, Eleanor realised. They were against them.

She was so frightened that she could not move. These policemen were nothing like the elderly, reliable parish constables she and Kes saw from time to time in the country. These lads had joined the Metropolitan Police as a career, as a means of getting on.

'She didn't mean no harm, sir,' a butcher called, resting from his labours on a doorstep.

'Can't see you with that hat on,' said the policeman on the left. 'Take it off, then we can all know you.'

'Yes, sir.' The butcher lifted off his straw boater and held it in front of his belly. 'We're honest men and women 'ere, sir.'

Other people came forward, very jolly and submissive, all watching the policemen, all seeking to appease them so that trade could continue, but still the two young policemen would not move.

'Come on, luv.' A costerwoman tugged Eleanor gently by the elbow. 'Stand aside, why don't yer, yer making 'em nervous. We don't want no fuss 'ere.'

'Off the barges, are you?' The policeman on the right had noticed Eleanor's flat-soled boots at last. He decided she was harmless. 'Cut it, mother, and watch where you're going next time.' He put out his hand, stopping the thin man slipping past them with his barrow of trinkets. 'I'll talk to you, though. What *do* we have here . . .?'

Eleanor thanked the costerwoman, who shook her heavy ringlets in disgust. 'Them rozzers is always 'ere, that's why business is down. We 'ate 'em! We 'ate 'aving ter suck up ter them pipsqueaks!' She pointed as the thin man was taken in charge and marched away. 'They're drivin' us off the streets, the police don't want no more open markets. They want everyone in shops, see, 'cos it makes their job easier.' She spat. 'Shops is private property. They don't fly by night, like us costers. They 'as walls an' doorways. Walls is 'ard ter get through, an' doorways is easy ter police.'

'I never thought—' Eleanor swallowed her words. She had always trusted the police, and had never realised they were deliberately making such great changes to the way people lived. Like Kes she had been born in London, but in those days the police force had been in its infancy. She didn't remember seeing a policeman from one year to the next.

'Everyfink's a crime these days.' The costerwoman spat again. 'Even that, it's against the byelaw. It's so they can arrest yer if they don't like yer face, that's all.'

She hobbled away. Eleanor stared after her until she was gone. The bottle of olive oil felt hard in her hand, and she remembered the girl. *Yer got ter tell the police.*

Eleanor was glad she hadn't told them.

There, it was said. She was glad.

'An' there's another thing,' she said aloud. Through the crowd she saw the woman wearing a headdress. Eleanor strode to her and bought two pounds of the Muscatel raisins. Then she bought one of the round floury cheeses, just because she wanted to.

Right from the start, she hadn't felt guilty about what she intended to do. Now she felt justified.

It was afternoon by the time she got back to the dock. The *Poca* was being shafted across by Rat Island to the Joshua Fellows, Morton & Clayton wharf. She walked round by the bridge. Kes had arranged a general cargo from Joshers, mostly industrial vinegar for the Black Country, and the poor old *Poca* was laden so deep that she looked to be bending in the middle. Water lapped at the cloth-hooks that secured the tarpaulins. Along the top planks Eleanor's three elder boys sat dangling their legs glumly, obviously chucked out of the cabin to do work. They clutched their jackets around them and shivered pathetically for her benefit. Ham wore the stovepipe hat that was his proudest possession. It would have dropped over his ears had he not padded his head with felt.

'They're sleeping again,' he said, jerking his thumb at the cabin. 'Yer aren't really bringing the police ter the dockyard, are yer, Ma?'

'Where did yer get that 'at from?' she snapped.

179

'Found it,' he said defensively.

She slapped him. 'I'm not saying yer done anything naughty, mind. But that was fer just in case yer were thinking of it.'

'Ow, Ma! A couple of lousy turnips, honest.'

Kes came out of the ganger's office. He looked so anxious that he infuriated her.

'Well?' he said. 'Wot 'appened?'

She went below and he followed her. 'Well? Eleanor?'

Eleanor thought the girl's sleep seemed easier. Her eyes no longer twitched beneath her eyelids, following feverish dreams, and her complexion had lost its heat. Eleanor opened the stove, stoked it and made sure Grandma Pebble wasn't taking her nap too close, once she had woken with a large hole burnt in her skirt. Eleanor sat herself down on the three-legged stool, keeping her back to her husband, opened her dress and showed Cottontop the breast. He gave hicking cries of desire and latched on with his mouth and both hands. He kicked his left leg in time to the suck, and she gave a sigh of relief to be back home.

'Yer still watching?' she told Kes impatiently. 'Why don't yer go an' cast off or something?'

'Wot's this, Eleanor?' He prodded the cheese in its string bag.

'Wot does it look like? It's a cheese.'

'It doesn't look like cheese,' he said suspiciously.

'Don't eat it then!' she snapped. 'An' I bought some Muscatels.'

''Strewth, I'll just go an' stick my 'ead in the canal while yer busy, shall I?' Kes said without moving. 'I don't deserve the way yer treating me, Eleanor. I don't know wot's got into yer, that's God's truth.'

'Wot do yer know? Yer never did understand me. Yer don't understand the first thing, yer blind deaf an' dumb, yer wouldn't know wot ter do wiv yer 'ead if it wasn't tied on. Yer a good man, Kes, none better, but yer make me feel wanting.'

He watched her feed. 'I love yer so much, Ma.' He closed the cabin-slide and knelt beside her in the shadows. 'Our own little lad,' he murmured, stroking Cottontop's hair fondly. His hand slipped to Eleanor's breast, still stroking.

'Don't start that,' she said, shifting Cottontop to the other side, but leaving herself hanging bare.

'I'm the only one round 'ere who doesn't get a drink,' Kes said. Her nipple hardened between his fingertips. He blew gently, making the milk still clinging to it feel icy cold, then licked it with his hot tongue.

'Not in front of Granny,' Eleanor moaned.

'She's out for the count! We'll be arguing later, she can listen to us then.' He nipped her lightly with his teeth.

'Ouch!' she said. 'Yer as bad as Cottontop.'

'Men are just little boys at 'eart.' He put his other hand on her ankle and raised his hand to caress her knee, lifting her skirt. He took deep breaths. She knew the signs. Now was the time.

'I talked ter yer precious police,' she said. That was true.

He slid the sidebed door almost closed so that the girl should not see them. 'Wot about it?' But Eleanor knew that all he was thinking about was her legs.

He knelt between them. 'This isn't proper,' she murmured, rocking the stool.

'Yes it is!'

'They said they'd do wot they could.'

He stopped, horrified. 'But wot about that place in 'Atton Garden, the Foundling 'Ostpital?'

'They won't take ill children or orphans.' Eleanor knew this was true from when Nan Tubbs got in trouble for her second sickly child, and her husband put it on the street. 'An' the child 'as ter be left by its mother, it's got ter be 'er first child, an' she 'as ter be of good reputation.'

'Can't we stop talking?' Kes begged.

'That's a good idea,' Eleanor agreed, leaning back. One way or another, she always got her way.

II

'Four Whitehall Place. Here we are.' Charlie Bowler walked beneath the pale stone arch into the cramped courtyard beyond. Only a polished brass plaque revealed this dingy collection of cottages knocked together to be Scotland Yard, the headquarters of the Metropolitan Police. He knocked on the door and spoke to a policeman standing at the desk. 'Detective Inspector Bowler to see Superintendent Williamson.'

'Very good, sir.'

'I know the way,' Bowler said.

Little had changed at the Yard since the days of 'King' Mayne, and probably never would. The rooms still smelt of old, waxed wood and the floors still creaked. Steynes, wearing plain clothes, took off his pillbox hat and held it awkwardly. He sneezed as dust got up his nose. 'Sorry, sir.' They passed tiny offices where inspectors worked two to a desk. Sergeants were packed like warehouse clerks on the next floor, Bowler knew, and constables had standing room only in the ledger-rooms on the third storey and along the attics. The most senior officers were accommodated here on the ground floor. The corridor was almost completely dark, except when an opened door admitted daylight from the office beyond. They passed the telegraph room manned by a florid-faced sergeant, who glanced up. Someone closed the door and Steynes cursed as he tripped over saddles, harness, discarded uniforms, books and reports stacked in the gloom. 'You'll get used to this place, George,' Bowler told him. Out of earshot they talked like friends.

'You should never have left G Div, Guv'nor,' Steynes said. They stood aside as a bevy of young uniformed men jostled past them. Their shift had ended. It was a strict rule that they wore uniform even off duty, to reduce public suspicion that the police were everywhere in secret. A policeman wore his full uniform at all times, except in bed and in the bath, seven days a week. He was a policeman in blue even sitting down to breakfast with his family.

Bowler said, 'I'll tell you a secret, George.'

'Yes, sir,' Steynes said.

'It was my ambition to be the first copper to rise through the ranks. Ordinary constable to Police Commissioner.'

'I'm sure you'll do it, sir,' Steynes said loyally.

'You and I both know it doesn't work that way. But once I thought this was—' Bowler hesitated.

'The future. I thought Scotland Yard was the future, George. A central police agency with money spent on it, and a job to do, a job done properly. Look at this mess.' Scotland Yard was starved of funds. Books were piled on the staircases, and constables climbed between them to reach the next floor. 'I think the politicians are as bad as the criminals, don't you?'

'I wouldn't know about that, Guv'nor,' Steynes said. They came to a door with WILLIAMSON on the frosted glass. The Superintendent's clerk showed them through the uncomfortable ante-room into the broad chamber beyond.

'Detective Inspector Bowler, sir.'

The window behind Williamson showed sunlit Whitehall busy with carriages. The light changed his face for a moment as he came round his desk. 'Charlie,' he said, using Bowler's first name in the lower-class way he affected with all his officers, the band of brothers under his paternal control. The chief of the Detective Force looked like a cunning bulldog, with formidable dark eyes and sagacious jowls. He had a fondness for plaid suits and shooting parties, and cultivated the air of a country farmer. But his accent was roughest London when he wanted. He was no gentleman, and his bite was very much worse than his bark. As a junior officer Bowler had held Williamson in awe, and he still wore the plaid in imitation of him, the ghost of his youthful admiration that had done his career no harm.

But now Bowler knew Freddie Williamson kept a mistress. It was a detective's job to know such things.

Williamson kept her in style in a corner room on the fifth floor of the gigantic new Charing Cross Railway Hotel, a minute's walk from the office on the way home. Her name was Maisy. She was not cheap, neither were her tastes, nor was her room.

Where did a man with no private income and a family to support get the money?

Bowler had looked round the smooth professional faces of his colleagues, the band of brothers. How much did they know? The man who blew the whistle on Williamson would find himself an outcast, his career stopped dead in its tracks. He would get the worst jobs, treated without honour, without loyalty, for he had shown none. Gradually his life would become impossible.

'Give me the gist on the Goldblum business while we go up,' Williamson grunted. He took Bowler's elbow.

'Sir?'

'Commissioner insists on hearing your report. Who's this man?'

'Steynes is my right hand, sir. We worked together for many years in the past. I've asked for him to assist me.'

'Always the best choice, the man you know,' Williamson affirmed. He put on his hat as though they were going outside. The ante-room was now full of waiting people, the measure of Williamson's influence and reputation. 'Back in ten minutes!' he barked at his clerk, barging through them.

Bowler opened the door and followed Williamson's broad back down the narrow corridor. 'The Goldblum business,' Williamson flung over his shoulder.

Bowler stuck to his guns. 'I think the Briggs case is more significant, sir.'

'Significant? What sort of word is that? More significant than a dead millionaire jeweller By Appointment to Her Majesty?'

'Goldblum is dead. But there is a chance the Briggs girl is still alive.'

Williamson took the stairs. 'You know what happens to them as well as I do.'

'I believe that while there is still a chance of finding her alive I should concentrate my enquiries—'

'Believe, believe,' Williamson scoffed. 'You always were a believer, Charlie.'

'Yes, sir, I am,' Bowler said.

Williamson grunted as he climbed. A constable coming down stopped and ran backwards in front of them as they came up. He tucked his helmet under his armpit and stood to attention. They squeezed past him on the landing. 'She's dead, Charlie,' Williamson puffed. He tackled the next flight. 'Or if she isn't dead she'll turn up one fine day, but I've never known it happen. Or the family will get a ransom demand, *if* the kidnapper can write, or else he'll post pieces of her like that Whitechapel business. Then you can do something, but until then you're strapped.'

'We do have some leads, sir.'

'You have a hundred cases falling off your desk with a higher chance of success. Don't waste your time.' Williamson pushed on his knees to reach the final landing. He paused to catch his breath. The Commissioner was the one policeman to break the floor-by-floor reverse hierarchy of Scotland Yard, having his office at the very top. 'Charlie, I want all your attention on this Goldblum business. The man was a Jew, but he was a rich one.'

'Yes, sir.' Bowler took a deep breath. 'Mr Goldblum's guard dogs were poisoned. Mr Goldblum was struck on the forehead to immobilise him. He and his wife were tied up and tortured to reveal the exact location of the floor-safe. The thief left Mrs Goldblum's jewellery box intact. He was after something very special.'

'And prepared to go to any length to get it, I understand.' Williamson shuddered.

'Perhaps he did not realise that Goldblum was prepared to go to almost any length to keep the key. Perhaps the situation simply got out of hand, sir.'

'Never be merciful on the man you are hunting,' Williamson said.

'Goldblum's wife was strangled in front of him,' Bowler said. 'Goldblum then swallowed the key rather than give it up to her murderer. The murderer then cut open Goldblum and removed the key from his living stomach.'

Williamson swallowed. 'My God, man.' He raised his hand to knock on the door in front of them.

Bowler said, 'Goldblum's chief diamond-cutter, Dr Lukas Meulenhoff, is returning from Amsterdam where he's been all last week. He's known as "the Doctor of Diamonds", cutting is a great skill apparently. His steamer docks in an hour. He'll know what it was in the safe that was so special.'

The door was opened by a servant and they went in. The Commissioner's carpeted apartment commanded a view of the Admiralty on one side, the

Embankment and the river Thames on the other. The panelled walls were lined with books, and exotic Indian shrubbery flowered in enormous pots. The desk was covered with papers, a rack of pigeonholes was stuffed with more papers. The Commissioner was kept busy by his subordinates. 'I've brought Detective Inspector Bowler, sir,' Williamson said. 'As you asked.' His tone implied disapproval.

'Ah. Bowler.' Colonel Edmund Henderson had pale eyes and wore jackboots. He was a military man of the new breed, having purchased his commission but not his rank, which he had earned through family, friends, and some merit. He was not a policeman and never would be. In the English tradition he was an amateur appointed over the professionals, a safe pair of hands.

'I trust you have not let me down, Bowler,' Colonel Henderson said in his high military voice. He left them standing. The servant poured him a small glass of port. 'I promised Darby Briggs and that charming wife of his my best man.' He snapped his fingers, forgetting her name, and Bowler almost blurted out, *Lydia*.

He cleared his throat instead. 'I'm putting all my energies into the Briggs case, sir.'

'My own instinct exactly. But Williamson here disagrees.'

Bowler seized his opportunity. 'I have leads, sir.'

'Good man! Excellent. Told you, Williamson. Bearing fruit.'

Williamson looked irritable. 'The Goldblum case has more disturbing features and is more important, with respect, sir.'

'A dead Jew.' Colonel Henderson sipped his port. 'Mr Briggs is a member of White's Club.'

'Yes, sir,' Bowler said.

'General Manager of Prideau's Bank. Confidant of old John Prideau. Prideau's loans funded the Embankment.' Henderson nodded at the broad new thoroughfare reclaimed from the river. 'In lieu of interest, payment was made in kind to Prideau's. Land, Mr Bowler. Thirty acres of prime building land created in the centre of London. Land for a new police headquarters.'

Bowler understood how it was done. Henderson would go through the old boys' network to get his way. That was how the really big decisions were taken by the government. 'There's talk in the Clubs, Mr Bowler, of acquiring the site for a Grand National Opera House or some such white elephant. I believe London would be better served by a new Scotland Yard. A landmark against crime.'

Williamson said, 'But there is a murderer out there, sir, right now, walking the streets—'

Bowler said quickly, 'Commissioner, I believe that Joy Briggs saw the murderer.'

'Hypothesis!' Williamson said.

'I believe that she can lead us to him,' Bowler said.

'There you are!' Henderson told Williamson. 'Two birds with one stone, eh? Pursue your enquiries with vigour, Mr Bowler. Williamson, he is to have every assistance.'

'He's already appropriated one valuable sergeant to his team, badly needed elsewhere.' Williamson was white with anger. 'Mr Bowler is a fine detective, sir, but I warn you he is quite obsessive on the

189

subject of catching criminals.'

'I take that as a compliment, sir,' Bowler said.

'You'll need extra shoe leather.' Henderson tinkled the little bell on his desk. 'What was the name of the constable I asked for?' he called to the clerk. 'The man who found Goldblum's body.'

'Sergeant Steynes is sufficient for my purposes, sir,' Bowler said.

'I never underestimate the value of luck in a man,' Henderson said. 'Send him in.'

'I'm sure I can find a use for him, sir,' Bowler said smoothly.

'What drives you on, Charlie?' Williamson asked in a low, mean voice. 'What gives you your push?'

A civilian marched into the room. He stood to attention. Dressed in plain clothes, in which he looked supremely uncomfortable, for a moment no one recognised him. He was no longer young, and his moustache was long, lugubrious, and grey. His belly was bigger than his chest despite his tight belt. His trousers were too short, with a faintly moth-eaten air.

The new man looked one by one at the three senior officers ranged around the desk. All three wore plain clothes, and even Sergeant Steynes in the corner was similarly attired.

'Detective Constable Nutting reporting for special duty, sir,' said Alfie Nutting, and saluted as stiffly as though he still wore a uniform.

'Nutting, get to St Katherine's Dock straight away,' Bowler ordered as they emerged from the Scotland Yard archway. 'Meet Dr Lukas Meulenhoff off the

Frieslander arriving from Holland. Bring him by hansom cab to Goldblum's premises at fifty-two Hatton Garden.'

'Yes, sir,' Alfie said. 'Hansom cab.' He had never ridden by hansom. He had only tuppence in his pocket.

'And stop standing like a policeman.'

'I was a policeman before my two girls were born, sir,' Alfie said with simple dignity. 'Now they're old enough to marry. For ten years I wore the old top hat and swallow-tail coat. I *am* a policeman.'

Bowler stood on the kerb. The sun was hazing over and he put up his collar. 'You don't like me, do you?'

'I'll do my job, sir,' Alfie said.

'We got off on the wrong foot,' Bowler said. A hansom approached. He whistled and the driver lowered his whip. Alfie got in. He caught his baggy overcoat, borrowed from his neighbour, on the latch and had to get out again to free it. Bowler watched as he was driven away.

'What about him, sir?' Steynes asked.

Bowler shrugged. 'Like the commissioner said, he's just shoe leather.'

From Trafalgar Square they caught a cab to Hatton Garden and warmed themselves at Diego's Italian coffee shop on the corner near the gold refinery. Sheep from the country milled from the Farringdon Station railway goods yard and were driven along Cowcross Street towards the Smithfield meat markets. Hatton Garden, Saffron Hill and St Luke's were all in G Division and both men knew this area well. The massive gate-tower of Pentonville Prison, showing its grand Venetian clock, jutted above the rooftops sloping away below them. Some of the Italian street traders toiling uphill recognised Steynes in the bow window. They pulled their sleeves in appreciation of his clothes and called that he was a very fine gentleman now.

'Bloody Dagoes,' Steynes said.

'There's ten million in diamonds in this street,' Bowler said. Hatton Garden, surrounded by poverty, was the centre of London's jewellery trade. The buildings were well looked after, solid and substantial, many of them with heavy bars across the windows. 'Here we are.'

A cab drew up and Nutting got out. He carried a suitcase that was obviously heavy. He helped down a skinny, precise man wearing silver-rimmed spectacles. Lukas Meulenhoff was in his seventies and he looked cold. 'Shnow,' he greeted them in a plummy Dutch accent. 'It is shnowing in Amsterdam, it is shnowing in the Channel, and soon it will be shnowing here.'

'I'm Detective Inspector Bowler,' Bowler said.

'Of course you do not remember me, do you,' the old man said fussily. 'I have spent my life in Mr Goldblum's service. You did not notice me. I remember when you were a sergeant here.'

'One night some thugs tried to break down the door with sledgehammers,' Bowler said.

'Ya, is right. Ever afterwards Mr Goldblum has great faith in the British police. Come in.' The building was whitewashed, one storey high, windowless. Meulenhoff unlocked the heavy outer door with two keys. They went in and he locked it behind them. When he knocked on the inner door a small hatch was opened. Suspicious eyes squinted at them. "Allo, Dr Meulenhoff. Detective Inspector Bowler. 'Oo's them other two?'

'I vouch for them, Max,' Meulenhoff said. 'Hallo, Griff, are you there too? Terrible business.'

'Right-o,' Griff yawned. He opened the door. 'We're paid till the end of the week. We'll keep this up till then.'

'Business will continue as usual,' Meulenhoff said. In a low voice he added to Bowler, 'As you know, Mr Goldblum had no children. The firm will have to be sold.'

They went down a short windowless corridor lit by hissing gas-jets. 'Griff and Max often rode home with Mr Goldblum,' Meulenhoff said. 'That was the time of danger, gentlemen. In here is safe. At home is safe.' He realised what he had said. 'I am so sorry. What a terrible end. As a man Mr Goldblum had his faults, but he knew the value of jewellery.'

They came to a room. Alfie put down the heavy suitcase with a sigh of relief. Meulenhoff took off his coat and gloves and brushed them meticulously. 'It is good to be home,' he said.

'This is your office?' Bowler asked.

'My surgery.' Meulenhoff went to the bench along one wall and one by one removed the black velvet covers from microscopes, lenses, clamps, pieces of precision machinery formed of finely turned steel or brass. 'My operating table,' he said.

'The Doctor of Diamonds,' Bowler nodded, 'the Surgeon of Stones.'

'So said the *London Illustrated News*.' Meulenhoff

bowed modestly, delighted. 'For thirty years I have been Mr Goldblum's most valuable asset. We have had jewels and settings through here whose cost and rarity would make you gasp.' He spread his fingers. 'These hands, these eyes, have been more valuable to Mr Goldblum than any of them.'

Steynes knocked a microscope with his elbow. 'Sorry.'

'Was Mr Goldblum grateful?' Bowler asked the Dutchman. 'All this skill of yours that he used for his own benefit. Ever get under your skin, did it, that you'd made him rich, and not you?'

'I don't expect you'd understand, Inspector,' Meulenhoff said. 'Mr Goldblum was a gentleman.'

'How much did he pay?' Steynes asked.

'Excuse me, sir.' Alfie drew Bowler aside. 'While I was waiting, sir, I took the liberty of enquiring about Mr Meulenhoff at the shipping agent. The *Frieslander* sailed last Monday week with him aboard. The gangway officer remembered him. There were no sailings around last Friday or Saturday.'

Bowler stared at him, surprised. 'You thought of that off your own bat?' he said.

'I think the Dutchman is in the clear, sir.'

Bowler glanced at Steynes, then turned away and talked to Meulenhoff.

Steynes put his face by Alfie's head. He spoke in a low voice. 'We know how to do our job, you.'

'Yes, sir.'

'Keep your nose clean, and when we need your help we'll get on our knees and beg for it, right?'

'Yes, sir.'

'In the meantime keep your mouth shut.'

Alfie stood to attention. When no one was watching him he pulled at his moustache. It was his habit.

Bowler asked Meulenhoff, 'What piece of jewellery was so valuable that Mr Goldblum died rather than give it up?'

'Obviously it would not be merely a matter of money.'

'What, then?' Steynes said bluntly.

'Beauty,' Meulenhoff said. 'Beauty which cannot be bought, only possessed.' He lit the jewellers' acetylene magnifying lamp and opened a drawer. He chose something which he laid in the palm of his hand, then held it under the light, and the men gasped.

The setting was silver, too plain for the fashion of the day. The silvery starburst drew the eye to the single diamond at the centre. The diamond concentrated the light in its shimmer. They seemed to gaze inside the stone as though it had no surface.

'No sparkle,' Meulenhoff said. 'Smooth cut and polish, no facets. Very old-fashioned. A jeweller today could make it glitter and flash to blind your eyes.' He flexed his fingers as though longing to unleash his skill. 'A water diamond of exceptional size and purity.' He waited, savouring the moment.

'What's that in it?' Bowler asked. 'A flash of something.'

'A drop of blood,' Meulenhoff said.

Alfie touched it with his fingertip. He wondered how it had got inside.

'In the thirteenth century the Kings of Spain knew it as the Bloodstone, and believed it contained the blood of the Virgin,' Meulenhoff said. 'The Moors of the ninth century called it the Rage of Bethlehem. It has been lost and found many times. Always lost, always found. Chemical analysis shows it was mined in India. Perhaps brought back to Persia with the body of Alexander the Great, around the neck of Roxanne. I like to think so.' He sighed. 'The stone could be cut along the red flaw into two perfect gems, but each would be worth very much less than the whole. Perfection is simple, a flaw is complex. Mr Goldblum understood this. The stone was his obsession. Beautiful in its purity, beautiful in its flaw.' He sighed again. 'A gift fit for the Empress of India, Her Majesty the Queen.'

'This is out of my depth,' Steynes said.

'The stone was to be purchased by the Lord Mayor and Corporation of the City of London, as a gift to be presented at the Mansion House banquet in Queen Victoria's honour on the tenth of February, the anniversary of her marriage to the Prince Consort.'

'But Albert's been dead and buried for nearly ten years,' Bowler said.

'Not to the Queen. She still wears black. The gift is not for its purity but for its flaw. Her life without him.'

'What's all this got to do with us?' Steynes said.

But Bowler understood. 'These are trying times for the monarchy. The Queen's ill, living in seclusion. She's been the target of assassination attempts. Many people think she gets too much money. Sir Charles Dilke has called for her to be deposed and a republic established, and even *The Times* is against her.'

'No better time for a grand gesture of loyalty from the patriotic burghers of London,' Meulenhoff said.

He shrugged. 'Now they'll have to think of something else. One big diamond, perhaps.'

Steynes said, 'But if the thing was stolen from Goldblum's safe, then what's this?'

The Dutchman took a chisel and scratched it across the diamond, shattering it. 'It is not the real thing, you were looking only at a copy made of paste,' he said. 'Imagine the real one.'

Alfie sucked his moustache with his lower lip. Bowler knew the signs by now. 'What is it, Constable?'

'I'd like to ask Mr Meulenhoff a question, if I may, sir.'

'Fill your boots.'

Alfie said, 'Why did Mr Goldblum let the thief into his house?'

'Friday night is *Shabat*,' Meulenhoff said, 'but Mr Goldblum was not as devout as his donations to the synagogue pretended.'

'We don't know he let the thief in,' Bowler said.

'Pardon me, sir,' Alfie said, 'we do. When I found the body, all the doors and windows were barred and locked. All chimneys were secured by locked iron gratings. Nobody could have got in without being invited in by Mr Goldblum.'

Bowler frowned. 'Are you saying the thief was a spirit, because he somehow locked and bolted the house from the outside when he left?'

'No, sir. The kitchen door was not bolted. It was held closed only by one of those new Linus Yale cylinder locks from America, the very best. Self-locking. The thief had only to close the door quietly behind him when he left.'

'That's impressive,' Bowler said, then shook his

head. 'But it's too neat. I still won't believe it was not the thieves next door. Even if not guilty themselves, they may be witnesses.' He got ready to go. 'Thank you for your help, Mr Meulenhoff.'

'Always a pleasure to help Scotland Yard,' bowed the Dutchman.

Bowler and Steynes left Alfie Nutting to take a full description of the missing jewel. They put up their collars and walked towards the Pentonville Road. The pavements were slippery with a dusting of snow. As usual there were no cabs. The air grew thick with snowflakes. All around them they heard churches that they could not see tolling three o'clock.

'Alfie Nutting's a good man,' Bowler said. 'He knew what questions to ask. He's been wasted pounding a beat all these years.'

'I think he'd be happier back there, sir.'

'I'm afraid we're saddled with him. Listen!' Both men stopped, recognising the noise. It was the distant rumble of an explosion.

'Bloody Irish Fenian bastards,' Steynes said.

But this time, he was wrong.

A steamer was towing six butties westward along the Regent's Canal towards Paddington. Among them was the barge *Gravesend* with a cargo of sugar, nuts, straw-boards, coffee, petrol, and five tons of gunpowder. With the Maida Hill tunnel just coming into sight beyond the bridge, the *Gravesend* exploded.

The bridge was destroyed and three crewmen lost their lives. The canal was closed for repairs. No one knew how long they would take.

Chapter Eight

I

Don't cry, little one. We're safe in here.

Joy's eyes flickered open.

As always, she smiled at the baby lying beside her. She knew he was a boy because she had seen him changed. The hazy sun that glowed through the hatchway made his cheeks seem as red and rosy as summer apples, though she knew it was cold midwinter. The baby boy looked at her then opened his toothless mouth and grinned for all he was worth. She had discovered she could make him smile just by smiling. If she frowned, he cried. They were old friends by now. This cupboard with sliding doors was the whole world to them both.

"Strewth!" came the man's muffled voice from above. 'It's them Germans invading France! Wot was *that*?'

Dimly she heard a thunder like falling water.

'It was a bomb, Kes,' came the woman's voice. 'It's not the Germans, it's them Irish bombing us at 'ome. Nothing's safe nowadays.'

Joy blinked, and when she woke again the woman was stumping down the steps. She still wore her sunbonnet, but there was snow on it, and snow across her shoulders, and snow speckling her gloves too. She pulled off her gloves with her teeth and warmed her white hands by the stove. After a while she opened the little door with tongs and lumped more coal on the fire. Her hands were red now. She stamped her feet, blowing on her hands and cursing, squeezing the pain out of them under her armpits.

She turned and grabbed the baby. 'C'mere, Cottontop, yer little devil.' She fed him at the breast then sniffed him underneath. 'Never fails.' She changed him on her knee, wrapped him up in the swaddling again, and plonked him back in the bed. 'Now yer.' She heaved Joy out of the bed and held her over the pot. Joy struggled. She wanted to do it herself. But the woman's strength was much greater than her own.

'Eleanor, up out,' called the man's voice. Joy had heard Eleanor call him Kes. Eleanor and Kes and Cottontop. Eleanor went up out. Joy sat on the pot by herself and realised she had got her way. She was doing it herself.

She had won a victory.

The little room banged from side to side. This often happened, and Joy began to wonder why. All she had thought of until now were these strange, strong, kind people. She was still helpless enough to know she needed them utterly. When she finished she put the pot back in the cupboard where it was kept. It took all her strength to climb back into the bed.

She lay beside the baby. 'Cottontop,' she murmured happily, and brushed a cottony strand of hair from

200

his eye. He stared at her seriously, and she slept.

When Joy woke the same old stuff was being poured into her ears again. The drops that splashed out made her neck slippery. Her hearing popped gloopily and the voices again receded, mixed up in the noises of her own heart beating and her breaths in and out. When she moved her hand on the blanket it sounded up the bones of her arm as loud as a train.

She was fed the rotten fish again. She choked and gagged.

'She's on the mend,' she heard Eleanor call up the steps.

'Yer be careful,' Kes called down. 'S'ppose it's something medical wiv 'er? Doctorish.'

'Don't talk ter me 'bout doctors!' Eleanor shot back robustly. 'Wot do doctors know? Only good doctor's an 'orse-doctor. Don't 'ave no faith in 'uman doctors meself. All talk an' no dirty 'ands.'

It was night. The radiant castles and mountains that Joy knew lay everywhere around her were invisible in the dark, though she knew each of them by touch under her fingertips, by their raised outline. She knew where each brightly coloured bird was painted. She heard Grandma Pebble snoring somewhere below, in her cot on the floor perhaps. The stove made a very faint glow, barely revealing Grandma's shock of white hair down there. Joy closed her eyes. Grandma Pebble muttered as she turned over.

I can hear you, Joy realised. I can hear everything about you. Her brother Tom had a word for something that was very clear. The word was crystal.

I can hear you as clear as crystal, Joy thought.

She could hear water lapping around her, as though they were surrounded by the sea, a vast peaceful sea. When she moved an arm fell across her shoulder. She cuddled into the warmth beside her, the smell of warm boy.

Joy sat up.

She counted the shapes under her blanket.

She was sleeping with three boys. Four if she included the baby. The eldest was the one with the funny name, Ham. He slept a little higher in the bed, his arm thrown along the bolster above his brothers' heads, as though protecting them from her.

She lay down. His hand touched the top of her head. She pushed it away. Tom had told her girls were poison. She thought the same about boys.

'Dad,' Jaffrey said.

Joy pretended to be asleep.

'Dad,' Jaffrey burst out in a frightened voice. 'Dad!'

'Sssh,' came a sleepy mutter from the crossbed. At night it was pulled down across the back part of the tiny room. The beds were on different levels to make the most of what little space there was.

'Dad, I got ter go,' Jaffrey said, panicking.

There came the slap of bare feet. Jaffrey was plucked out of bed and Dad pushed open the slide with his head. The light outside was white but very dim. Holding Jaffrey under the armpits, Dad went up the steps and held him out. There came a tinkling sound.

'Finished!' said Jaffrey through chattering teeth. He was brought back down, asleep as soon as he was put between his brothers. Dad closed the slide and Joy felt him pick up the baby and take it back to Mum in bed. Cottontop sucked busily at his night feed.

Joy was woken by the boys scrambling over her. Thin grey light showed around the slide where it didn't quite fit the roof, and she realised it was morning. The boys shivered, cursing the slap of their bare feet on the wood, trying to keep on the rug. They had pulled their down-at-heels boots off to sleep but they were dressed in no time. They banged open the slide, showing the dim sky. It was barely dawn. Their flying figures jumped out blowing steam from their mouths, rubbing their hands on their arms. 'It's f-f-*freezing*!' they shouted. 'Oh-oh-oh blooming *freezing*!'

'Collect twigs an' any old bits of tree branch going begging,' Kes yawned from the outside of the crossbed. He rolled over so as not to wake Cottontop. The baby lay asleep like a little limpet on Eleanor's tummy, instinctively hanging on to her with his curled feet as well as his hands. 'By hook or crook only, sprogs, no cutting, remember.' Sprog was his word for a boy, Joy realised. 'Make a fire an' start the mule's mash boiling.' Kes pulled on his trousers in bed. He tucked in his nightshirt so that it was now a shirt, then pulled on the working coat that he had previously laid over the blankets for extra warmth. Sounds of bickering came from above. 'Ham, yer in charge!' he bellowed, waking the baby.

'Aye, Dad,' Ham said.

'Why can't I be in charge?' came Shane's voice from outside, then, 'Ow!'

Jaffrey submitted quickly. 'Yer the one in charge, Ham.'

'Yer bet I is,' came Ham's voice cockily. 'Dad said so, didn't 'e?'

Joy smiled to hear them argue. Arguing meant they were friends.

'I'm coming,' Kes said warningly. He pulled on his boots and went up out, where he spread his arms cheerfully. 'Snow, yer sprogs! But no snowballs until after work.' A snowball socked him behind the ear. 'Which one of yer was that?' The room rocked and the boys' high-pitched giggles dwindled in the distance, and silence returned.

The bed creaked.

'Welcome ter the land of the living, girl,' Eleanor said. She wore only a linen shift, and clasped Cottontop to her bosom as she swung her legs out of bed. Joy thought what shapely nice legs Eleanor had, quite at odds with the way she looked concealed by baggy skirts. She realised that Eleanor's breasts were so large because of the baby, not because she was fat. The light caught her blue, watchful eyes prettily. She really was quite pretty. 'Been right poorly, yer 'ave,' Eleanor said. She sat companionably on the edge of the bed.

Joy nodded.

'Better now?' Eleanor asked.

Joy nodded.

'Yer got a tongue,' Eleanor said, returning the baby to her breast without taking her gaze from Joy's eyes. 'We know one another quite well, yer an' me.'

Joy nodded.

'Yer not a nodding dog, are yer?'

Joy shook her head.

'There's nothing ter be frighted of, darlin',' Eleanor said gently. She realised the baby had been quietly feeding while she slept, and transferred him to her other breast. 'We folk might look rough, but we're not 'ard. We aren't going ter eat yer, I mean.'

Joy bit her lip.

'Yer a shy one,' Eleanor grinned comfortably. She sat closer, so that their arms and knees touched, warm and close. 'I was shy meself. No, I was! An' I wasn't always this big, grown-up. Once I was a little girl like yer. Wish I'd 'ad yer 'air, though,' she said longingly.

Joy touched her flame-red hair. It felt sticky and horrid. She blushed.

Eleanor laughed. It was a very jolly sound. 'Yer face is as red as yer 'air, little one!'

Joy pursed her lips. She made her face go pale again.

'Am I talking ter yer right?' Eleanor asked. 'I'm used ter boys, see. All mine is boys, I'm not used ter girls. Tell yer a secret.'

Joy nodded eagerly.

''Ere's me secret. I always wanted a little girl. It was so I could see meself in 'er, so I'd always remember what I felt like when I was that age. Well, I really think yer do understand me, don't yer? Boys is diff'rent. They just sum yer up an' get as much as they can out of yer, yer got to keep one step ahead of 'em all the time. I reckon yer four years old.' Eleanor waited. 'Five?'

Joy nodded.

'Yer don't miss much,' Eleanor said. 'I think yer seen into me quick as an arrow. Wot's yer name?'

Joy looked at her knees. She was wearing the pink satin dressing-gown. It was blotched with dirt but there was no one to wash it. Her eyes burned. A tear trickled down her cheek.

Eleanor held Joy's face against her own. 'Yer don't 'ave to tell me.'

'T—' Joy said. The right letter would not come. She put her fists to her mouth. 'T-T-*TOM!*'

'Tom? Well, I didn't know that's a girl's name, dearie.'

'J—' Joy struggled to squeeze the word past her tongue.

'Something starting wiv a J?' Eleanor said tenderly. 'Take yer time.'

'*JACK!*'

No, no, she shook her head frantically.

Not Jack. Eleanor watched the little girl's body racked by sobs. 'Oh dear,' she sympathised, 'my poor darlin', oh my dear. Yer all right, they didn't do nothing ter yer. I've looked.' She hugged her again.

She watched the girl open the soiled pink dressing-gown and feel around her neck. Inside her white silk nightdress, by now as grey and greasy as a second skin, the foundling wore a necklace of coins.

She lifted her hair and took off the necklace over her head.

Eleanor bent forward, interested. But they were just a child's toys, coppers, sixpences, a threepenny bit, threaded on a string. The largest was at the centre, a silver coin bigger than the palm of a child's hand. Eleanor's face flashed in its shine.

'Where'd yer get that thing from!' she said, shaking her head. 'Stole that, I bet, or 'ad it stole fer yer.'

The little girl took a knife. Her tongue worked between her teeth with concentration. She used the knife-point to scratch three ragged letters on the coin. Then she added a full stop.

JOY.

'Joy,' Eleanor said. She called up out, 'Kes, c'mere, look at this!' There was no reply. He was fetching the mule from the pub stable where they had berthed it overnight.

Eleanor turned back to the girl and spoke softly.

'Joy, my friend Vera 'ad yer trouble when she was yer age. Everyone tagged 'er VerVera, an' still do, she can be difficult, see. She was a stammerer. 'Er adopted Ma used ter beat 'er rotten fer it, an' the worse it got, the more she beat 'er. It's only 'uman nature, innit, VerVera made the 'ole fam'ly look one apple short of a picnic. But listen ter me. VerVera isn't stupid, an' she isn't nervy. I'm close to 'er now I'm older an' she tells me things when we're laying up at Cody's Bend. She told me 'er trouble was 'cos she 'eard the words in 'er mind afore she spoke 'em. 'Er tongue got confused wot wiv the orders getting mixed up 'twixt captain an' engine-room, like. Is that wot it's like fer yer, Joy?'

Joy nodded.

'Relax. Do it like VerVera. Don't listen ter yerself.'

'Yes.' Joy stopped, unsure if she had spoken.

'Wot did yer say?'

'Yes.'

'On the boat we say aye.'

'Aye.'

207

'There! It's easy, innit!'

'Innit,' Joy said. Her face was transformed by excitement. 'Listen! It's me!'

'Take it easy, or I can't understand yer. Move yer tongue an' yer lips big, like yer was singing. Don't mumble. Slow down.'

'It's me!'

'There was nothing wrong wiv yer, Joy. Nothing that kindness an' olive oil couldn't cure.' Eleanor tousled the girl's hair.

'You tricked me,' Joy said. 'I don't mind,' she added. 'Can you still hear me?'

'We won't stop yer now yer've started,' Eleanor said. 'Chattering nineteen ter the dozen yer'll be, if I know anything about little girls. Where'd yer come from, Joy?'

Joy thought of the trees reaching up towards her window in the moonlight. She could not explain.

'Where am I?'

'Same place we always are,' Eleanor said, surprised. 'Aboard the *Poca*.'

'What's the *Poca*?'

Eleanor pointed at a japanned flower vase. Around it sailed, in brilliant colours, a long boat with its name scrolled along the cabin. 'The *Pocahontas* for long, but not for short.' She frowned, wondering what she had said that was so marvellous, as the child giggled and clapped her hands.

'Pocahontas! But that's me! I'm a Red Indian princess!'

'Yer a strange one,' Eleanor said. 'But I s'pose all children is strange. It's like being in another country, being a child. 'Aven't yer got a proper last name?'

Eleanor tried to put it in a way the girl would understand, because very likely her parents were not married. 'I mean, is it the same as yer Mum's, or yer Dad's? Or didn't yer know either one of 'em?'

Joy looked at her, confused.

Eleanor decided. 'Pocahontas of the *Poca* it is. I'll buy yer story. Yer were on the run, weren't yer?' she asked kindly. 'I don't mind, darlin'. Yer age can't do nothing wrong.' Grandma Pebble was still asleep, and Eleanor began to worry where to put the wakeful baby. He had learned to roll, and she must go up out and be busy any minute now. 'Joy, there's one thing I truly 'ave ter know. Yer must answer me truthfully. Will yer do that?'

'Yes,' said the girl in her self-confident, assertive way. She folded her arms and waited for the question.

'Joy, listen ter me. Does anyone love yer?'

There came the sound of footsteps outside, the jangle of harness. 'Eleanor, up out,' came Kes's order. 'It's a short day, an' a long way ter go.'

'I don't know,' Joy said. She looked at her bare, grubby feet. 'I don't know.' No one had ever spoken to her about love.

'Eleanor, up out, now!' Kes shouted.

Joy held out her arms for the baby.

So she was on a boat. She had never been on a boat before, only the rowboat with Tom in the park, him doing all the rowing because he was the boy. When he pulled the oars Tom slipped off the seat, which he called a thwart because proper sailors did. He landed on his back in the bottom of the boat with his legs in the air, which was called catching a crab.

This was a bigger boat, with a cabin, and Joy was inside it.

She knew what she was supposed to do. She must look after the baby, just as Tom had looked after her. She was the elder one now. She was responsible.

Cottontop gazed up at her with his big blue eyes. He blinked.

She smiled, so he smiled.

'You haven't got any teeth,' she reprimanded him. She stepped over Grandma Pebble who was still asleep on the floor, and wrapped him up more tightly to make him proper. 'Not one.'

'Neither've I,' Grandma Pebble said. She looked up with a broad smile, all gums.

'You've been watching me.'

'Aye, fer long enough.' The old lady stretched in her blankets. 'It's just the same, the beginning of life and the ending of it. 'E's got 'is teeth ter come an' I've 'ad mine, that's all. 'Elp me up.' She held out her gnarly hand. Joy didn't want to touch such withered, frightening skin. Grandma Pebble clicked impatiently and heaved herself up on Joy's arm with surprising strength. 'There, that wasn't so bad, was it?'

Joy was ashamed of her bad manners. 'I didn't mean to be rude.'

'There's worse things in life than being rude. Much worse things! Awful things.'

Joy laughed.

The old lady scratched her hair, stretched her back. 'Like being old, fer instance. I can't bend down. Pull the po out fer me, would yer, love?'

Joy hugged Cottontop to her chest and bent down,

pulled out the decorated pot from the drawer. The old woman swept up her skirt and sat. She looked at Joy with beady eyes, impeccably keeping her balance on the pot as the boat jerked, but Joy tottered. Cottontop complained sleepily and tried to get his hands out of the swaddling, then lay still against her. The boat jerked again and this time Joy's stagger woke him.

'So yer Eleanor's girl. Yer got a lot ter learn,' Grandma Pebble said. 'I don't think yer know the first thing about anything. But there's something about yer. Yer got the touch wiv Cottontop, fer sure.'

The boat bumped for the third time. 'I'm sorry—'

'Don't say sorry, ever. An' don't use this po no more, it's mine.'

'I won't, Grandma Pebble.'

'Grandma'll do. Use the outside, not the navigation, do it rural in the bushes. Yer'll 'ave ter learn yerself wot leaves ter use, comes by experience. Laburnum'll teach yer a lesson, make yer bum into one gynormous blister. Yer won't try that twice,' she said comfortably.

'Eleanor's girl? You said I'm Eleanor's girl.'

'I know wot I said! It's not news Eleanor never wanted boys, she kept Ham in skirts 'til 'e was eight, an' Jaffrey's only just out of 'em, 'e was seven afore Kes put 'is foot down. But boys is boys, my dear, an' ever will be so. But yer diff'rent.' Grandma Pebble gave a beautiful smile, chilling because there was something mindless behind it, an old lady chatting on a pot which made her about the same height as the child she was talking to. Joy supposed this situation was normal. She glanced at Cottontop from

211

the corner of her eye. He was asleep again on her shoulder. She laid him quietly in the sidebed and slid the door almost closed so that he should not roll himself out somehow.

Grandma Pebble put out her hand to be pulled up. 'Wait 'til we're out of the lock afore yer empty the po.'

'Lock?'

'We're in a lock. 'Strewth, girl, don't yer *know*?' She remembered. 'No, yer don't know nothing. Well, it's not the sort of lock yer thinking of. This is a lock with a quay, not a key!' She chuckled at Joy's confusion because the words sounded the same. 'I'm working well today, aren't I?' She sat down on the stool, puffed. 'That's it, dear, make yerself useful. Now *that's* something a boy won't do.' She watched Joy fold the blankets neatly and hinge the crossbed into the wall out of the way. 'A bulk'ead, that's wot we call a wall. The floor's a sole, that's a Norfolk word, Mr Pebble being a Fenland man, though Eleanor was borned in Commercial Road lock so she's a Londoner. An' the ceiling's the deck'ead.'

'Bulkhead, sole, deckhead,' Joy said. Something thumped outside and the cabin shook.

'Now we're held 'gainst the bumping-pieces. The ropes are called straps.' Metal rattled and squeaked. ''Ear the windlass? Ham's strong enough ter use it 'imself now, or Shane an' Jaffrey both. 'E's raising the paddle—' The old lady listened as water roared. 'There's a gate afore us an' a gate behind, see, an' the raised paddle lets water flood into the lock from upstream. We're going uphill. Eleven foot this time. We'll go up an' up the levels till we get ter the

Cowroast, four 'undred feet or more in the top o' the 'ills.'

'What happens when the lock is full?'

'Then the top gate is opened an' out we go into the next pound.' She explained. 'A pound's the stretch of water ter the next lock. Might be a few yards sometimes, might be miles. The canals were dug deliberate, by Irish navvies mostly, they're not natural rivers. The mule pulls us, Ramses 'e is.'

'Ramses must be so strong!'

'Yer can move a boat wiv yer little finger, girl. An' once it's going, it don't want ter stop. The water takes the weight. But sometimes the flow's against yer, or the wind, an' then it's an 'ard, 'ard slog.' She slid the kettle on the stove and pointed at the shape folded against the bulkhead. 'Let the cross-table down, girl.' Joy unlatched it and squeezed herself aside. The table almost filled the cabin. 'Yer'll get used ter backing an' filling in 'ere.' Grandma Pebble opened a drawer and put out a piece of oiled tarpaulin as a tablecloth. 'We got lace fer best,' she apologised. She pointed at a cubbyhole Joy had not seen. 'Now the teapot. Not that knobbly Church Gresley one, it's fer best. I mean the big 'un.'

Joy fetched down a big metal teapot with both hands. On it was painted, in letters made of entwined flowers and naked cherubs that looked distinctly like Cottontop, the motto HUG ME SQUEEZE ME KEEP ME WARM.

It sounded low and vulgar, and Joy knew what to think about that. Grandma Pebble laughed. 'Yer a funny one! Didn't yer never live, before? Didn't yer 'ave a life? Yer got such a lovely serious little face,

213

an' then yer break through like the sun!' She warmed the pot on the stove and filled it with boiling water. There was a bang from outside. Something creaked like a huge door opening.

'Don't worry. That's the upper gate swinging out. We'll be under way again in two shakes of a bee's knee.' She reached up and pulled the cover off the parrot, which woke and shuffled on its rod.

'Breakfast,' Grandma Pebble prompted, taking two loaves from a box.

'Blooming starvin'!' the parrot swore.

'Won't be a minute,' Kes called down.

The old lady fed the bird a morsel. 'This 'ere's Rainbow. Everything 'ere 'as a name, Joy. The tabby cat's 'Arriet an' the kittens is 'Arrikin, Larrikin, 'Ooligan an' Barrel, 'cos 'e's the fattest.' The cats mewled around her ankles. 'Lilypad's the dog, but she's best chums wiv 'Arriet 'cos they was babies together. During the day Lily walks wiv Ham an' the mule, mostly. She's Ham's dog, 'e found 'er.'

'Why did he call her Lilypad?'

''Cos that's where 'e found 'er, a tiny little puppy curled up asleep on a lilypad. Someone'd chucked 'er in the canal as excess ter requirements, like, an' there she was. 'E brought 'er 'ome in 'is pocket.'

'I like animals,' Joy said.

Grandma Pebble laughed. 'Oh, yer'll like this family then!' She sniffed, showing that she was really proud of her daughter and grandchildren. 'Better than some on the navigation, I'll tell yer. Eleanor's got 'er 'ead screwed on straight, she's never done nothing dishonest, and she's got a good man in Kes. She's a boatwoman an' a mother an' as good as a wife, Eleanor is, an' she keeps the sprogs in trim as tight as a schoolmistress though she's 'ad no schooling, an' she's doctor an' seamstress too. She did all this crochet work, an' she keeps this cabin 'ole neat an' tidy, an' makes all the clothes. That's why she an' I wear skirts, mostly, 'cos we ain't got a space long enough in 'ere ter pattern a full-length dress.' The old lady sighed as if imagining such a luxury, then dosed milk from a pitcher into fireclay mugs. 'Yesterday's, but we ain't passed a dairy farm yet.'

'Grandma,' Joy said.

'Yes, dear?'

'Why don't you treat me like a child?'

'Bless me, darlin', yer don't be'ave like one. Yer like a little grown-up, yer is.'

'I wish I knew how to behave,' Joy said.

Grandma Pebble filled the pot with boiling tea then stuck her head out through the slide. 'Tea up!'

Eleanor took over steering and the boys came piling down. Elbowing each other aside, they shoved themselves round the table and drank from the mugs with both hands, then spread jam on doorsteps of bread that Ham cut with his knife. He continued to wear his stovepipe hat indoors, though even now he was sitting the top bumped the deckhead. 'That's enough jam!' Grandma Pebble leant over their heads and slapped Jaffrey's hand. 'Got ter last till summer, that jam 'as.'

'There's more kept in the 'atches,' Shane said through his mouthful. 'I saw it, big stone jars.'

'I remember 'er boiling it,' Jaffrey said piningly. 'It smelt *gee-orgeeous*.'

'All right, yer can 'ave one slick more,' Grandma

Pebble relented, and Joy saw how pleased she was by the compliment. With Eleanor steering up out and Kes walking beside the mule, Grandma was in charge down in. Joy could see the boys thought Grandma was a soft touch, but she was sure Jaffrey had told the truth about the jam.

Ham pointed his knife at Joy. 'Why don't she stop looking at me?'

'She's never seen anyone eat like yer do!' Shane giggled.

'I always eat like this,' Ham said. He pushed bread in his mouth with the heel of his hand, looking at Joy insolently. 'I'm not going ter change fer 'er.'

'She's 'ungry,' Grandma Pebble remembered. 'Yer must be starving, dear.'

'I'm not *very* hungry,' Joy said. But the jam did smell good, and the bread was still soft and fluffy. It was bakers' bread, not Cook's. Probably they didn't have room for Cook on the boat.

'We've put 'er off 'er food,' Ham said, snatching another piece. 'All the more fer us.'

Joy's tummy squeaked and the boys roared with laughter. She took a slice of bread. 'May I have a little jam, please?'

'A little jam!' Shane clutched his sides with laughing. Eleanor's arm reached down through the slide and clouted him round the head.

'Watch yer manners!' came her voice. Shane looked for his cap. He rubbed his head.

The bread and jam was delicious. Joy thought it was the most delicious food she had ever eaten. She felt the warmth come back into her tummy. She glanced round politely then helped herself to another slice, but Ham grabbed it from her hand.

'I got my bright eyes on yer, Ham,' Eleanor said through the slide. 'Come on, yer know the rule. Share an' share alike.' A look of pure rebelliousness crossed Ham's face.

'But she ain't like us,' he said. 'She ain't one of us.'

Then he broke the bread in half and held out a piece to Joy.

'The crusty 'alf,' Eleanor said inexorably.

'But Ma, yer know I like the crusty!' Ham complained. He caved in and handed Joy the crusty piece. Joy watched him, fascinated. His lower lip trembled, but he didn't cry.

'After making all that kerfuffle, girl,' Eleanor said irritably, 'fer Gawd's sake eat it.'

'I didn't make a kerfuffle,' Joy said.

'Yer did!' Ham said.

'She did!' said Shane and Jaffrey together. Those two always did things together, Joy thought, except when they were fighting. And even fighting, she realised, was being together as far as this family was concerned.

Eleanor swung the tiller out of the way and came below. 'We're at the lock,' she said, clearing herself a space at table with her broad hips. 'There's a Samuel Barlow coming down, we'll 'ave ter wait our turn.'

'What's a Samuel Barlow?' Joy asked.

'A boat carrying coal,' Ham said. 'Don't yer know *anything*?'

'By the bye,' Eleanor said, jamming a doorstep generously on the palm of her hand, 'this is Joy. She'll be wiv us fer a while.' Eleanor sat among them grinning and stuffing the jammy bread in her mouth, slurping tea from the mug in her other hand, as hungry and thirsty as any of her children.

II

The two men waited in Turnham's Alley. They stood together as if talking, shivering in the side door to the Metropolitan Music Hall. A church bell tolled six o'clock, but the iron-shod evening traffic streaming past their hiding place overwhelmed almost every other sound with its continuous roar.

Steynes put his mouth close to Bowler's ear. 'I'm stone cold, Guv'nor. I could do with a good strong cuppa.' There was no reply. Steynes could see a stallholder in the Edgware Road selling tea from a steaming urn.

'Wait,' Bowler said. Snow covered his hat, his shoulders, the toes of his steel-tipped shoes.

Steynes waited. He stamped his cold feet. 'What exactly are we looking for, sir?'

A slant of gaslight caught Bowler's face. The boys were still working in the road, weaving expertly between the vehicles, sweeping away snow and slush with their long-handled brooms. They worked as hard and constantly as tiny machines for the farthings and halfpennies that were tossed their way.

Bowler grunted. 'You remember what the boy Tom Briggs said?'

'I have it written down, sir.'

'There were three of them,' Bowler said. 'A man with sharp eyes and smooth hands like a girl. He called the other man Jack. Jack who? There must be thousands of Jacks in London, millions of 'em probably. But there's only one Monkey.' Bowler pointed. 'And there he is.'

The two men crossed the road quickly, but the child's pale face turned towards them, saw them. 'Get him!' Bowler said.

The urchin dropped his broom. He dodged to the left, then ran to the right, and Steynes was wrong-footed. The boy darted away. His bare feet clung to the snow and he shouldered himself into an alleyway as quick as a flash. "'Elp! 'Elp!' he cried. Steynes ran after him heavily, then stopped.

Menacing shapes poured into the entrance, tearaways and gonophs in tall hats and waisted coats. They blocked his way. Nothing was said. They leaned against the walls, waiting. Their mouths chewed pieces of straw casually, but their hands and eyes were ready for trouble. They wanted him to come in. They could smell a policeman a mile off.

'Clear the way,' Steynes said. Nobody moved.

'Leave it,' Bowler said. He pulled Steynes's shoulder. 'Leave it. Now I know where I'll find him.'

Chapter Nine

I

'A pint of 'ot tea each ter warm 'em, 'alf a loaf of bread ter fill 'em up, an' a good lick o' jam ter keep 'em strong. A busy day's work ter make 'em sleep. An' last but not least, cod-liver oil ter keep 'em regular. Me own recipe fer 'appy families, this is.' Eleanor filled the teaspoon from the dark brown bottle. 'Ham first.' Ham pinched his nose and swallowed his medicine. 'Yer, Shane. No faces. Now Jaffrey.' Eleanor went down the line of her sons, who stood to attention like little soldiers. 'Now yer can all 'ave yer spoonful of sugar ter take away the taste, an' get up out, an' I want a good day's work, an' no argifying. There!' she beamed.

The boys dug spoons into the sugar drawer and their disgusted expressions were replaced by angelic looks. They rushed up the steps pushing one another, Ham reaching back to grab his stovepipe hat, then were gone. A few snowflakes drifted through the open slide. Joy looked up, longing to go out. In London the snow was sooty in a few hours, but here even the sky was white, and there was no sound of traffic.

'Now yer turn,' Eleanor said, holding out the teaspoon. Joy took her medicine. It tasted of rotten fish but she was used to it and she knew it did her good. However, she dug a spoon into the sugar drawer because the boys had, and Eleanor seemed to expect it.

'Warned yer,' Grandma Pebble whispered in Eleanor's ear. 'Girls is diff'rent.'

'No, boys is,' Eleanor said.

'Yer'll see,' the old lady winked. Then she shivered and sat down, exhausted by her talking. 'Bitter, it is! Winters was never this cold when I was a girl.'

'You still are a girl,' Joy said sensibly, and both older women exchanged looks.

'If yer feeling so much better, it's time yer pulled yer weight,' Eleanor said. 'Yer can't go out like that, yer look like a sweet. Take that pink thing off. That other thing' – she meant the grimy silk nightdress – 'well, I s'pose yer'd better keep that on fer a shift.' She rummaged under one of the beds. ''Ere's one of Ham's old shirts, just fold the wrists up. Jaffrey's trousers wot I was saving for Cottontop, they'll do. Shane's old high-laced boots, stuff a bit of paper in the toes an' they'll fit. Do 'em up tighter.'

'I can't do bows,' Joy admitted. They had always been done for her.

'Useless, yer is.' Eleanor did double bows so that they wouldn't come undone, and tied up the trousers with string as well. She took a pair of scissors that looked as big as shears and cut the bottom half, still damp, from the coat Joy had been found in. 'That's an Army coat.' As she folded back the arms, pulled in

222

the waist with string, again she exchanged a look with the old lady.

'Ask 'er no questions, hear no lies,' Grandma Pebble said.

'Yer a sight, girl!' Eleanor clapped Joy's shoulder. 'Yer look like a little pepperpot. Off yer go. An' don't trip over an' run back crying ter me fer sympathy, 'cos yer won't get none!' The baby gave his wet cry and she groaned. 'No rest fer the wicked, eh?'

'I'll change him,' Joy offered.

'Yer must be off yer rocker,' Eleanor said.

'I've watched you. I know how to do it.'

Eleanor spread her hands. 'Be me guest, darlin'. Show me.'

Joy put Cottontop on her lap and unwrapped his clothes and roller, the bandage which stopped him moving too much. She unpinned the wet towel and handed it seriously to Eleanor, then took a dab of petroleum jelly on her fingertip and worked it round the baby's bottom. She followed it with a fresh rag which she pinned with difficulty, holding Cottontop down with her elbow, because the spring on the safety pin was strong. Then she rolled him up good and tight.

'Not bad,' Eleanor said.

'Told yer,' Grandma Pebble said, and pushed Eleanor's shoulder with her knuckles. Eleanor grunted non-committally and held out her hands for her son. She loosened his arms a little.

'All right, off wiv yer, girl. Watch yerself an' don't get drowned.'

'Don't forget me po,' Grandma Pebble said.

Joy took it and went up out.

Light flooded around her. She shielded her eyes with one hand. Everything was pure white as far as she could see, white fields, white hedges, white trees. Across the snowy landscape the canal waters went winding ahead of them like a gleaming black ribbon. The mule was jet black on the white towpath, Ham deliberately slipping and sliding alongside for the fun of it, his dog barking round him excitedly, but the mule just plodded steadily. Its brasses gleamed, and even its dark leather harness was polished like brown metal.

'Don't just stand there holding that under our noses!' Shane said, revolted.

'Empty it!' Jaffrey said.

Joy emptied the pot over the back end of the boat.

'Yer all but splashed the paint,' Jaffrey said.

'Close one,' Shane said. The boys stood on each side of the tiller, one pushing, one pulling, as the bends came up. It took all their strength, and Joy couldn't help smiling at them because they looked so funny with the tiller as high as their chins. 'Just put the pot down on the 'atches,' Shane puffed, 'I'll rinse it fer yer when we get on a straight.' Despite the cold the boys' cheeks were red and shiny from their heavy work. 'Close the slide, quick, keep some warmth in the cabin 'ole afore Gran bellyaches.'

Joy shut the slide and watched them with her hands behind her back. 'I know you two. You're Shane and Jaffrey. You're twins.'

'We're older than yer. We're nine,' Jaffrey said.

'I'm older than 'im,' Shane grinned. "E's two days be'ind.'

'Ham's older than both of you,' Joy said.

'Two's better than one,' Shane said. 'We'll look after yer.'

'Then tell me where we are.'

They looked at her blankly. Shane yelled forward, 'Ham! Oy!' Ham looked back. 'She wants ter know whereabouts!'

Ham scratched his head. 'Grand Junction.'

'Grand Junction,' Shane said.

'Is that a place?'

'No, it's *where we are*.'Undreds of miles of it.'

Joy looked at the trudging figure. 'Why doesn't Ham like me?'

'Can't imagine!' the twins said together. The front of the boat had come to a bend. They grunted. Shane pushed at the tiller and Jaffrey pulled. Water gurgled behind the rudder, trying to force it straight. Then slowly the boat began to turn, all the tons of it, from the strength of two small boys.

'I'll go and talk to Ham and I'll make friends with him,' Joy decided. As the back end of the boat swung round she jumped ashore. It was further than she had thought. Ice crackled as she slipped back down the bank, then she pulled herself up on a tussock and walked on the towpath beside the boat.

'Idiot!' Shane called across. The boys didn't like her leaving them for Ham, she realised. 'Yer nearly fell in.'

She smiled and skipped unconcernedly.

'There's sharks in the canal!' Jaffrey called. He scraped together a snowball from the cabin roof and threw it at her. It went wide and Joy stuck out her tongue.

She ran ahead a little and walked beside the front

end of the boat. Water swished under the curved stem, which was painted tarry black. Sometimes it knocked ice aside like pieces of broken glass. On each side of the front the name *Pocahontas* was painted all flowery in bright dandelion yellow, snow white, speedwell blue. The top of the stem, like the tiller, was decorated with beautifully knotted ropes in all sorts of shapes. She wished she had a skipping rope. The cargo took up most of the *Poca*'s long length, and was covered by sloping tarpaulins. The boxmast was painted with diamonds and tiny Union Jack flags. There was a walkway along the top, but she saw no railings to stop anyone falling off if they lost their balance. The side decks were thinner than a footstep, almost overflowed by the rippling black water. The cabin at the back was so brilliantly painted that it looked like another world, she thought, magical and mysterious with palaces and swooping birds. There was a smoking chimney supported by a bright brass chain, and a drinking-can painted like a vase of flowers, and another showing a Red Indian girl with feathers in her hair. The heads of the twins peeped round the sides to steer, not tall enough to look over the top, and they looked so funny with their caps and earnest expressions that she laughed. They took their duties very seriously. She walked backwards, waving at them, then bumped into something.

'Watch where yer going,' Ham said. 'Yer almost walked into the tow-strap.'

'I nearly fell in the canal.'

'Yer mean the navigation.' He lifted the rope over her head, then shook her hand off his arm. 'I said it

226

would be trouble, a girl on our *Poca*.'

She was silent for a moment, then asked, 'Why?'

"Cos girls is bad luck, stupid. Everybody knows that.'

'Your mother and grandmother are bad luck, are they?'

Ham fell silent. The canal crossed an embankment. Joy pointed at a thatched village in the fields below. 'Where's that?'

Ham shrugged. Joy gave a little skip. That meant he didn't know. She was getting to learn him better, and the more she irritated him, the more he revealed. She knew much more about boys than he knew about girls. She walked beside him looking up at him brightly. Ham tried to ignore her. He blew as much white breath as the mule.

'The name sounds something like a bell ringing,' he said, giving in reluctantly. He was much older than her and he didn't want to look silly. 'Tring or something. I don't care.'

'Thank you, Ham. I like your hat.'

'It's mine,' he said. He glanced at her and touched it proudly. 'Me very own.'

She smiled to herself.

A wooden bridge swung into view round the bend. Kes had gone ahead. He saw them coming and wound vigorously. One end of the bridge rose up in the air and they passed beneath. A cart had to wait. Kes let the bridge down and tossed his brass windlass to Ham. 'I'll take me breakfuss now, boy.' He jumped aboard the boat, took off his cap, and disappeared below.

A few flakes of snow whirled down. Joy put back

227

her face and tried to catch them on her tongue. 'I love snow, don't you?'

'No.'

'Why not?'

'Yer won't either when yer've 'ad ter walk in it all day,' Ham said tersely. He blew on his hands. His gloves were ragged.

'You should have got gloves instead of a hat,' Joy said.

'Shut it, will yer?'

'What?'

'Yip yap, yap yip.'

Joy walked in silence for a while, then showed him her tearful face. She had been crying. 'You don't know how lucky you are,' she said.

'Me lucky!' Ham looked at her incredulously.

'Because I can talk, you're the first friend I've ever made,' Joy said.

'I 'ave loads o' friends,' Ham bragged. 'I don't 'ave no friends 'oo are girls.'

She pointed. 'What's that?'

A big bird flapped away from the canal bank at their approach. Its long legs trailed below it. 'She's an 'eron,' Ham said. 'Lives on fish.' They were entering a cutting. Steep snowy banks rose above them. 'I've seen queues of kingfishers along 'ere in the summer, Joy. Cor, an' wild flowers everywhere, like a painting. An' the smell o' them.'

'Scent.'

Ham pushed her suddenly, hard, so that Joy almost slipped in the water. 'Watch it,' he said.

She caught up. 'Why did you do that?'

'Why shouldn't I?' he demanded. 'I'm not soft.'

'I thought what you said was lovely.'

'Oh, shut it.'

She tried to talk about something a boy would be interested in. 'Are there really sharks in the canal?'

He realised how frightened he could make her. 'Big ones, there are. Mouths full of teeth pointing backwards, so yer can't get out once yer in. They 'ave ter roll over on their backs ter bite yer, though.' He was disappointed when she did not look as terrified as he secretly was.

'Do the herons catch them?'

Ham thought about it, interested. She looked at things in such a different way. 'They might do. I've never seen it.'

'What do the sharks live on?'

'Boat people's children wot fall in the water! Mum an' Dad both say so. That's why yer got ter be so careful not ter fall in. I can't swim, can yer?' Ham shuddered. They both walked a little further from the water. It was snowing steadily now. Slow veils of white hid the hill and drifted around them. The mule's hooves made no sound in the deepening snow and even their voices were muffled.

'Ham, what's your name short for?'

'It's short fer Ham,' Ham said. He whistled as Lily barked at a rat-hole. Joy whistled too. 'Oy, she's *my* dog, not yers. She does wot I tell 'er, no one else. 'Sides, yer can't whistle proper. Through yer teeth, like this.' He mocked her efforts. 'Pathetic. Try again.' He grinned, then covered his ears as her squeak became a piercing whistle. 'Ssssh!' he said.

She stopped. Ham stared at her, uncomprehending.

229

She seemed to turn in on herself. She wrapped her arms around her body as though squeezing herself shut.

He hesitated, then abandoned the mule and ran back to her. 'Wot did I say?'

She shook her head.

'Whistle as loud as yer like,' he encouraged her. 'Yer was just getting it right!'

'Hey, wot about the mule?' Shane called. The boat was overtaking them.

"E's a good backerer, 'e knows the way, 'e'll come ter no 'arm!' Ham shouted furiously.

'Yer'll come ter 'arm if Dad sees yer,' Shane advised. The boat slid past. Water bubbled quietly under the back end. The ripples died away and left the canal as smooth as black glass.

'Yer not soft,' Ham told Joy quietly. 'Yer little, an' yer a girl, but yer like me. Yer 'ard as metal inside.' He touched her chin. 'Come on, little girl.' He grinned, trying to make her laugh. 'Iron girl.'

'I'm not made of iron,' she said.

"Ard as nails!' he said. 'Yer can whistle! Go on, whistle as loud as yer like!' He put his fingers to his teeth and shrilled piercing blasts, then covered his ears as she did the same. 'Louder! Wake the dead! *Louder!*' They ran along the canal bank as fast as she could go, overtaking the boat. Joy whistled and shrieked as loud as she could. The dog barked and jumped joyfully at her waist as she ran.

Ham caught up the mule. He was laughing so hard he had to hang from the bobbins.

Kes stuck his head through the slide. 'Now then, wot's all this noise?'

'Noise?' Ham said. 'Wot noise?' The twins, who had been whistling too, were almost bursting.

'Children,' Kes grumbled. 'Yer all as mad as otters.'

Ham doubled up with delight. 'Yer mean adders, Dad!'

'Hatters!' Joy said, and gave a piercing whistle that echoed from the hills hidden on each side of the canal.

Kes pointed at her. 'I looked ter yer ter bring some sense into their thick 'eads, girl.' He frowned and shook his head at them one by one, then slowly his face broke into a broad grin. 'I'm 'appy yer 'appy!' he said, and went below.

II

It was night in London. Snow whirled from the rooftops and filled the narrow streets, piling into the doorways. The three men walked on the cobbles down the middle of the road, swept clear by the wind. Their capes and overcoats flapped around them as they came down the steps into Playhouse Yard, Cripplegate.

'That's the place,' Bowler said. 'The Beggar's Hotel. Steynes, show your light there.' Steynes lifted the bull's-eye lantern through the front of his cape, where it had been keeping his belly warm in the manner known to policemen everywhere, and uncovered the lens. Its harsh glare revealed the wooden building in front of them, all peeling paint and icicles, its broken windows patched with strawboard. Encased in thick wire mesh was a gas-lamp, but it was broken. Above the door a faded sign proclaimed HAT MANUFACTORY. Over it had been painted in large black letters HOUSELESS POOR ASYLUM.

'The temperature, as you have noticed, gentlemen, is below freezing,' Bowler said, 'and the Asylum for the Houseless Poor has opened its doors.'

'And closed them again, by the looks of it,' Alfie Nutting said. He rubbed his hands and wished he had some gloves, but he did not know how much longer he must remain a plainclothesman and he could not afford unnecessary expense. He had Beth and Becky growing up and dowries to face in the future, no doubt, and there was the funeral club, and coal bills, and Christmas coming. Christmas always cost more than he planned. This year Gail had set her heart on a turkey because Mrs Merridew was having one. The butcher was putting the final plump on them in the pen behind his premises. Nearer Christmas he would hook the carcasses all over the outside of his shop to advertise them and draw the women in.

'What's that smell?' Alfie said.

'People,' said Bowler.

'You don't see people like this in St John's Wood, eh, Constable?' Steynes joked. He dug Alfie in the ribs. 'Sheltered life you lads live in D Division. Painters and effetes.'

'I live in Southwark, sir,' Alfie said. 'Wellington Street, sir. I walk to work and back again, sir. I see quite a bit.'

'Not enough,' Steynes bragged. 'This is the real stuff.'

They walked towards the building. The snow piled

232

against it stirred and rose up.

'Christ,' Alfie said. 'Look at these poor folk!'

The children slept on, but the snow clung to their mothers and fathers like cobwebby shrouds. 'Keeping busy tonight, ladies and gentlemen?' Bowler said. They nodded, grinning, shivering. One man slipped back down again. 'Why aren't you people inside?' Bowler asked.

'No room inside, sah,' said one man, holding his hands over his ears against the cold.

'Full, is it?'

'Yes, sah.'

'Late, were you?'

'Not quite early enough, sah. Terrible weather.'

"E's 'ad 'is three free nights' worth!' one blowsy girl said.

'An' yer too, Molly Cochran,' called the man with the ears, not hearing how loud he spoke. 'Three nights wiv a baby wot she stole ter get the double ration of bread, sah. Double rations!'

'Not that the babe got a bite,' groaned the man who had slipped down.

"Twas sickly, any road,' Molly said. 'No teef.'

'Give me a penny, sirs,' begged the man, looking up, 'for the sake of Jesus's sweet blood.'

'Well-known screever, that one,' Bowler told Alfie. 'Paints with chalks on the pavement outside the National Gallery.'

'Bugger-all good in this weather,' the screever groaned.

'Christ's head in haloes, style of Rembrandt,' Bowler said. 'Beautiful.'

'What about him now, sir?' Alfie said.

233

'You'll have to move on, all of you,' Bowler said. 'Police.'

'Come on, hook it!' Steynes said when the vagrants grumbled. He knocked his boots against their feet. 'Police officers! You're impeding the highway.'

The women picked up the children, holding them beneath their bosoms as if to shelter them from the snow, or give them warmth. They shuffled across the yard and looked back through the snowy gloom. Since the three men were still watching them, they shuffled out of sight.

'They'll try anything, that lot,' Steynes said. 'I'll just make sure they've done as ordered.'

'I'll do it,' Alfie said. He crossed the yard and put his hand in his pocket. He had a silver sixpence for his supper.

'Don't be stupid,' Steynes called. 'You'll just make 'em worse.'

Alfie turned the corner and found the shapes had dropped down where they stood. They saw him and moved weakly, still grinning. Alfie flicked the sixpence onto the screever's coat. 'Make sure everyone gets some.' The old man popped it in his mouth.

'Bastards,' he said. 'Bastard rozzers, all of yer, sir.'

Alfie went back. Bowler banged on the door with his stick. It was opened by the sleepy Deputy. 'Full, thick-ears,' the Deputy yawned. Steynes pushed in and Bowler showed his badge. 'Police.'

'Sorry, Mr Bowler, didn't recognise yer.' The man held up his lamp, blinking.

'Go back to your pit, Master Deputy,' Bowler said.

'We can amuse ourselves. Name of Monkey?'

'Wouldn't know 'im, Mr Bowler.' The Deputy closed the door behind them to stop the snow. 'There's five 'undred in the Refuge tonight an' they don't 'ave names.' Bowler opened a thick ledger on the pulpit. Inside were five columns painstakingly filled in by the clerk. Name, age, trade, place of birth, place where applicant slept last night. 'Believe them names an' yer'll believe anything,' the Deputy said. 'Two Lord Palmerstons tonight. I'm back ter bed.'

'We'll start in the Boys' Ward,' Bowler said, knowing the place.

Steynes's bull's-eye lamp illuminated a long chilly room. Two braziers had been set in the middle. Railings around them kept people away from the heat. By now everyone was asleep. They slept in rows along each wall, about sixty of them in all, one sleeper fitted in each box. The boxes were about a foot high and looked like rows of open coffins, as if this were a Christian catacomb. 'Shine your light, Steynes.' Though it was still called the Boys' Ward the boys had obviously been found too noisy by themselves, and there were many men to be found sleeping among them or pretending to be asleep. Alfie covered his mouth.

'Cover your nose, not your mouth,' Steynes advised. 'It won't smell so bad.'

'I think I'm going to be sick, sir.'

'You'll get used to it,' Steynes said.

'I never have,' Bowler said. 'I never have. Light here, man.' But it was only some scrawny boy sleeping with his mouth open as though he were dead. 'You find the worst and most experienced thieves in these

235

places.' Bowler moved on. 'They horde together in these disgusting multitudes. The worst thing is that they talk to one another. Here they devise and concoct plans of robbery and mayhem, each one's experience adding to that of another.' The light shone on sleeper after sleeper. Some woke, shielding their eyes.

'Lookit!' someone said. 'It's spies.'

'You fellows seen Monkey?' Bowler asked amiably.

'No, sah, Mr Bowler,' the men replied respectfully, with glowering faces.

The plainclothes policemen came to the last box, which contained only the waterproof mattress and piece of tawdry sheepskin. 'Two to a berth somewhere,' Bowler said. '*Inter Christianos non nominandum.*'

'Beg pardon, sir?'

Bowler turned to Alfie. 'The sin of sodomy.' He raised his voice. 'Thank you, gentlemen. Don't do anything I wouldn't, and a very good night to you.'

They turned aside from the Lower Ward and the women's wards and went upstairs past the Chapel Ward. 'Straw Loft next,' Bowler said. He ducked beneath the pitch of the roof, following the narrow walk between the boxes. 'Here we are,' he murmured, beckoning. 'Here's your little nemesis, Steynes.' Steynes shielded the light to allow them to get close, then revealed the beam at full brightness. Bowler prodded the sleeping figure of Monkey with his stick. 'Rise and shine, young fellow.'

'Don't 'urt me!' Monkey cried. He rubbed his eyes. 'Monkey didn't do nuffink, honest.'

Steynes pulled him up and shone the light in his

face. 'I want a word in your ear,' he said. 'Nowhere to run now, have you.' Monkey shuddered and wrapped his twisted limbs around himself. His coat was taped together and his canvas trousers tied with string around the ankles. Steynes said over his shoulder to Alfie, 'This one gave me the sneak in the mews behind the Briggs house. Then the other day he did it again in the Edgware Road. You won't do it three times, no sir. You'll be down the nick, son.'

'Not yet,' Bowler said, and Steynes drew back. The light shone past Bowler. He crouched reassuringly in the shadows. 'Monkey, I'll ask you questions, and if you tell me the right answers, we'll let you sleep.'

'I dunno,' Monkey said anxiously. 'I got a right ter be 'ere.' He looked fearfully at Steynes.

Bowler said, 'Do you know me?'

'I don't rightly 'spect so, sir, less'n yer tip regular. I don't look at their faces, sir. I just sweep the crossing.'

'I am Detective Inspector Bowler.'

'I ain't never talked ter no 'tective afore, sir.' Monkey looked interested. 'Is that a policeman?'

'It's definitely him, sir!' Steynes said. He tore open the coat. 'Nice pyjamas, son.'

'I didn't steal 'em,' Monkey snivelled. 'They was given. Well, almost given.' He wiped the back of his hand across his nose without moving his arm. 'Jack made me take 'em! 'E did, sir.'

Bowler's eyes gleamed, alert. 'Jack who?'

'I dunno Jack who. Wiv the knife.'

'So you admit you were in the Briggs house,' Alfie said.

'Jack put me down the wrong bleedin' loofer ter the wrong bleedin' room!' Monkey burst out. 'Not Monkey's fault! Then the boy come down—'

'Young Tom,' Bowler said. 'The girl kept telling him she saw something outside but he didn't believe her.'

'He bared his arse, but I just wanted 'is lovely stripey 'jamas!' Monkey cried. Someone muttered in their sleep. Monkey dropped his head in his hands and put his fingers in his hair.

'Let's get him down to the station,' Alfie said.

'I want more,' Bowler said.

'So it was you who stole the pyjamas. Boys have been sent to prison for much less.' Steynes lifted Monkey's head to the light. 'Then you stole the candlestick.'

Monkey looked frantic. 'I never did! That was Arthur!'

'That's right.' Bowler clicked his fingers as though trying to remember the name. 'Arthur . . .'

'Smart Arthur,' Monkey said. ''E was the lookout.'

Bowler and Steynes turned to one another. 'I should have known,' Bowler said. 'He's always in and out of trouble. It was him by the Met. It was him who said Jack. Arthur Albert Simmonds with his shaved pickpocket hands.'

''E lives Putney way,' Monkey said helpfully.

'I know where he lives,' Bowler said. 'Come on, lads.' He ducked beneath the rafters and Steynes lumbered after him, his bulk silhouetted by the light he shone ahead of him. Monkey settled down to sleep. Alfie paused, stroking his moustache, then turned back. There was only the yellow glow of the brazier now.

'Monkey?'

Monkey sat up sleepily.

'So you didn't go in the Goldblum house next door,' Alfie said.

'Next door, no, sir. One job's enough in a night. None of us went next door.'

'Up there in the moonlight by the chimneys, though, a boy would have a pretty good view, wouldn't he?'

'I don't look, sir. I don't 'ave an 'ead for 'eights, if it was up ter me.'

'You didn't see anything?'

'No, sir, not nuffink.'

'But you could have done.'

'All I 'eard was a scream, sir. Somebody giving the wife wot fer, I 'spect, or 'er giving 'im some lip back. I don't think people in them big 'ouses is much different from us, when yer come down ter it.' Monkey yawned. 'Please, sir, can I go ter sleep now, sir?'

'That's all.' Alfie stood. 'Keep out of trouble, Monkey.'

Chapter Ten

I

'Dad,' came Jaffrey's voice. 'Dad, I got ter go.'

A groan came from the crossbed in the dark. The bed creaked as Kes swung his legs out, then they heard the cold slap of his bare feet on the bare wood. He always got the one place the rug didn't stretch, and he always cursed under his breath as he padded across and fumbled for Jaffrey.

'That's me,' Joy whispered. 'There's Jaffrey. Jaffrey, sit up so he can find you.'

'I'm c-cold,' Jaffrey shivered.

'You're waking us all up,' Joy said. On the crossbed she heard Cottontop start muttering, then his contented sucking noises. She knew he was kicking his left leg. He always did.

'Q-quick, Dad,' Jaffrey said.

'Someone's farted,' Shane said.

'That's my fart,' Ham said proudly.

'We know wot it is,' Kes grunted, and the blanket fell off all the children as he plucked Jaffrey up. Kes pushed the slide open with his head, went up the steps over the coal-box, and held Jaffrey out by the armpits.

'Dad,' Jaffrey said, 'there's no tinkle.'

It was the time of day called blue o' the morning. The sky was still full of stars but the horizon was showing a faint violet line. The canal reflected its glow without a ripple.

'I am doing it, Dad,' Jaffrey said in a panicky voice, 'but I'm not tinkling.'

"Is doodle's dropped off,' Ham said.

Shane sat up, horrified, and the blanket slipped off again.

'If you two don't stop it I shall get very angry,' Joy said.

Kes stood Jaffrey on the water. 'Oh my Jesus,' he said, 'come an' 'ave a butcher's at this, Ma. The navigation's solid.'

'I'm standing on the water!' Jaffrey squeaked.

Eleanor sat up on the crossbed.

"Ow will our Cottontop get churched now?' she said.

'It's ice!' squealed Jaffrey, excited. 'The navigation's set 'ard as a rock!' There came a bump against the side of the boat as he skidded and sat down. 'Ooh, ow,' he yelped.

The other children, undeterred, fumbled for their clothes and raced up the steps outside. Ham was first, trying to get one leg into his trousers over his boot. Joy followed and watched. She pulled on her trousers and buttoned up her coat, which reached almost to the deck. The boys jumped down onto the ice and slid on their backs. The light was growing and they looked like laughing shadows. They leapt up and ran standing still, putting on a show to try and make her giggle. Shane was a natural comedian.

He slid past the boat balanced on one leg, his cap raised. 'May I 'ave the pleasure of a dance, madam?' he called.

Joy put one foot nervously on the ice. Ham pulled her off the boat. 'She'll dance wiv me,' he said.

'I asked first!' Shane said hotly.

'Boys, boys,' Dad called.

The ice was snowy near the banks and not too slippery, but in the middle of the navigation the surface was clear and dark, holding the reflection of the stars. Joy's boots slid this way and that but Ham held her up. 'Yer'll get the 'ang of it,' he said, sliding easily. He held her up then gave her a push, and Joy slid along without walking her feet.

'Yer look like a sliding pepper-pot on a table in yer long coat!' Ham called. He ran then slid alongside her. ''Old on me belt, I'll push yer faster.' They were going much too fast.

She gasped, 'It's Shane's turn now.'

'Proper little madam!' he said, and pushed her into the reeds. The ice was thin between the stalks and one of her feet broke through into mud. Joy sat down with a soft crunch. She held her foot and cried. Ham had gone on but Shane slithered over and helped her up. 'Ham didn't mean no 'arm,' he said. 'It's only a bit of dirt.'

'He pushed me,' she said.

'Well, Ham's older.' Shane offered eagerly, 'I'll 'elp yer! Let's get away from the side an' do a waltz like foreigners do.' The stars had faded and the sheen of hard ice in the centre of the canal was shiny with the colours of the dawn. Shane was not nearly as tall or heavy as Ham but he was more graceful.

'La-da di-di da-da,' he shouted at the top of his voice, bending down to hold her round her shoulders, her hand clinging onto his with her arm outstretched. 'We're dancing on the dawn!'

'Shane, come an' 'elp yer mother,' Kes called. Joy held breathlessly onto the side of the boat. Kes hadn't bothered to start a fire to boil up the mule's mash. 'We're frozen in fer today,' he told her glumly, 'that's fer sure.' He took the boathook and went along cracking the ice between the *Poca*'s hull and the canal bank. 'Ice can squeeze a boat,' he explained, 'that's why she's fitted with these iron strips along the side.'

'Hasn't the ice made you happy at all?' she called.

'It's all right fer kids,' Kes muttered, 'but the old *Poca* don't earn 'er keep in a freeze. That means no cash coming in.'

'Will we starve?'

'No,' Kes said, 'no, we won't starve, not while we can, y'know, *eat* each other. We'll start off eating the little ones—' He laughed at her round eyes. 'I was joking, girl.'

'Dad's always joking,' Shane said. Probably that's where Shane gets being funny from, Joy thought.

'Yer'll taste of sugar an' spice an' all things nice, Joy,' Jaffrey said shyly. 'But I'll taste of puppy-dogs' tails.' He rubbed himself behind where he'd taken a fall, then his face changed, remembering. 'Wot about the church?' he said.

Eleanor stuck her head out of the slide. 'Yes, an' it's no joking matter, Kes. 'Ow are we going ter get Cottontop ter 'is churching?'

Kes threw up his arms. 'Well, I can't make the ice

disappear, love, can I? The *Poca*'s 'ere fer the duration. And unless yer want ter walk thirteen mile along the towpath ter St Peter Vee and thirteen mile back again carrying a baby, we're stuck too.'

'But it's arranged last time with Reverend,' Eleanor said. Her big tough face was close to tears, and Kes looked away. 'There's yer mum an' dad'll be there at Cody's Bend, Kes, an' they might not get another chance. The Wampsetts an' the Pebbles 'ave been christened at St Peter Vee since Great-Grandpa's day—'

'Longer,' Kes said.

'All the boys 'ad their 'eads wetted there—'

'I know, I know,' Kes said. 'We're stuck. Wot would yer 'ave me do, Ma? Abracadabra?'

They looked at each other miserably.

Joy said, 'Can't we slide the *Poca* over the ice?'

Kes shook his head. 'All seventy foot of 'er? Do yer know 'ow much twenty tons of vinegar weighs?'

Jaffrey said quickly, 'Twenty tons.' Kes pushed him with the blunt end of the boathook and Jaffrey slid slowly across the navigation. 'Clever lad, that one,' Kes said. "E's got application, that Jaffrey of ours. 'E's so sharp 'e'll cut 'imself one day.' Jaffrey ran to get back, then coasted slowly over to them.

'Wot about the road?' Eleanor asked. Her face fell. 'Three foot deep in mud this time o' year, no doubt.' She bobbed Cottontop against her to keep him quiet. She'd washed him and his face looked very pink. Ham slid across and ran up the embankment.

'Yes, the mud's frozen,' he called down. Shane had scrambled up beside him. 'The road's 'ard as iron an'

245

sharp as razors,' Shane called.

'Rutted,' Kes grunted. 'Even the Royal Mail wouldn't get through.'

'The Mail goes by train anyway,' Ham said.

Joy said, 'We could walk along the canal.'

'Wot, on the water?' Kes banged the heel of his hand on his head, realising.

Jaffrey clicked his fingers. 'Skates!'

'Ice-skates!' Ham whistled. He pushed through the group with his face both eager and angry, obviously wishing he'd thought of the skates himself. The boys jumped aboard the *Poca* and rummaged in the hatches. Only their feet showed. Jaffrey backed out and held up something by its laces.

'Last year's,' he said, rubbing the mould off on his sleeve. Joy saw an old pair of boots with yellowed bones tied underneath.

'We'll need more,' Kes said.

Shane and Ham had pushed their heads right to the back of the hatches, searching. 'Look,' Shane whispered in Ham's ear, pointing at a small package.

'Dad's back on chewing baccy,' Ham said. 'It's 'is secret!' Both boys stared at one another. They grinned their heads off. 'Not a word,' Ham winked.

''Ope ter die.'

Ham backed out and held up a handful of boots and bones. 'Beefbones!'

Kes examined them eagerly. 'Muttonbones an' porkbones, no good,' he told Joy. 'They split. But beefbones! 'Ere's the ticket.'

'But I can't skate,' Joy said.

Shane laughed. 'Neither can Cottontop!'

'I'm not ice-skating 'olding a baby,' Eleanor said.

246

She laughed. 'We're all totally bonkers, aren't we, even thinking o' this?'

'It was 'er idea really,' Jaffrey said, nodding at Joy. 'She thought of it.'

'I don't care whose idea it was,' Kes said, 'it's a good idea, an' we are going ter do it. Can't 'ave Cottontop miss 'is christening.'

'I can't skate neither!' Grandma Pebble quavered, sticking her head through the slide. 'Yer'll 'ave to do it without me.' There was a sudden silence.

'All or none,' Kes said. 'I won't break the family up. This is our significant day.'

They all looked at Joy, the shortest of them. She stood in her cut-off pepper-pot coat that touched the ice. She clasped her hands behind her back and her hair looked very red in the rising sun.

'We need a sleigh,' she said.

'The coal-box,' Jaffrey shouted. 'Bits of iron – the ice-plates – fer runners. An' a length of rope!'

'I am not accustomed, at my age, ter travelling in a coal-box,' Grandma Pebble said.

'Ah,' Shane said, 'but it's a *painted* coal-box, Gran.'

The boys brought the box up, emptied it, then unbolted the lid. Joy cleaned the inside and laid down a straw mattress for a seat. Kes screwed ice-plates underneath the box then bored two holes in the front. He pushed each end of a long knotted rope through and tied them off. 'Like leading reins,' he told Grandma Pebble. 'We'll bow-haul yer.'

While the women were getting themselves spruced Kes walked to the next boat moored along the bank. The *Lurcher* looked as though it was made of tar. There were no wooden disks on the mooring ropes to stop rats getting aboard. Ezra Jones, grimy as a coal-miner, sat in the smoke from the chimney to keep warm, a greasy sack wrapped around his shoulders. His two daughters stared at Kes out of slack, smudgy faces. They looked as plain as pudding basins but they were growing strong arms and big hips. The Jones clan always said they could muscle a trip faster than anyone else from end to end, but none of them was bright. In summer they worked from four in the morning until ten at night, water levels permitting, with hardly time for food or sleep or anything else. Eleanor wouldn't sit next to them in a pub because she said their smell spoiled the beer.

Kes stopped. 'Mr Jones,' he said, not stepping aboard.

'Mr Wampsett,' Ezra said, not inviting him.

Kes coughed as the smoke blew over him, brown sea-coal, the cheapest, hardly worth stealing. He said, 'It's about our getting Cottontop churched, Mr Jones.'

Ezra Jones coughed and hunched lower. One of his daughters stroked his hair with a hand like a ham, yet the gesture was strangely tender. Kes thought her name was Morwenna. The other was Blodwen and stood with her arms crossed.

'Wot's a churching ter me?' Ezra muttered to his knees, then squinted up out of the side of his face. 'It's only that Shane of yer's wot's mad on churches, I thought.'

Kes said, 'If yer'd keep a weather eye on the old *Poca*, would yer mind?' There was no answer. He added, 'If yer please, Mr Jones.'

'Now yer need us it's please, Mr Wampsett.'

'Please.'

'Wot yer carryin'?'

'Stuff, nothing ter interest yer. I'm leaving the dog on guard too, she'll bark if anyone comes close.'

'I might keep me eye out, I might not,' Ezra grunted. 'Yer a dozy lot, yer Wampsetts. We'll pull except on the Sabbath, rain or shine. Us'll be at Jam 'Ole an' on the return two days afore yer. That mule of yers is not a patch on our 'orse.'

Kes didn't argue. 'Well, we're 'appy, that's all. Please an' thank yer an' goodbye, Mr Jones.' He tipped his hat to the girls and walked back to the *Poca*. Then he kicked one of the big rope fenders.

'Feel better?' Eleanor said. She had dressed Cottontop in his christening robe and brushed his hair as straight as she could. She folded the robe carefully around him then wrapped him in a sheet, then a brown blanket.

''E looks like a little parcel ready for posting,' Kes said. 'Wot's this about yer being potty on churches, Shane? First I've 'eard of it.'

Shane shrugged.

'I've made the boys spit-an'-polish,' Eleanor said. 'Yer too, Kes, wash yer face, an' yer not wearing them trousers.'

The coal-box, its shiny black painted with red and yellow roses, had been put on the ice. Everyone was calling it the sleigh. The boys, with improbably pink faces still sparkling with drops of washing water, their hair parted in the middle and slicked flat, lowered Grandma Pebble over the side of the *Poca*. She hung from her arms like a rather skinny, wrinkly

249

doll. Her boots, made shiny with lacquer, stuck down below her long black skirt and her white apron. She wore her black best top and frilly coal-scuttle bonnet, which was strapped down with a big black bow tied beneath her chin, and the flouncing reached halfway down her back. Ham stood on the ice and took her weight from below. "Ave yer got me?' Gran quavered. 'Yer such strong boys,' she added admiringly, and their faces set with concentration. She knows how to make them work hard at looking after her, Joy thought. Ham guided Gran's feet into the sleigh, and she sat down on the mattress with a sigh of relief. 'Arrived safely!' she said.

Joy was handed down and sat between Grandma's knees. 'Comfy, girl?'

'Comfy!' Joy said. She braced her feet against the front of the box and rested her chin on her knees.

'Lean back a bit if yer like, keep me warm.' Grandma Pebble touched Joy's hair longingly. 'Look like fire, yer does. I wish I could toast me 'ands on yer.'

'You can if you like, but my hair's horrid and dirty because I haven't washed it,' Joy said, and behind her Grandma Pebble's lips twitched in a smile to hear such a decided tone in a child's voice. 'I tried to comb it but I couldn't, and when Eleanor tried she tugged and I wouldn't let her.'

'Well, if yer wash yer 'air once,' Grandma Pebble advised, 'yer got ter wash it ever after.'

She laughed aloud when Joy said, 'You're quite right of course, but I will wash it.'

Joy held up her arms for the baby. Cottontop was

handed down to her. She smiled at him and he smiled back as always, then lay looking peacefully up at her face. While Eleanor strapped on her skates the boys picked up the leading rope. They tugged the sleigh gently onto the centre of the ice.

'They're our mules, them boys,' Grandma Pebble said.

But Joy was looking back at the boat, and Gran followed her eyes. 'The *Pocahontas*,' she murmured. 'Ain't she a sight? On the navigation everyone calls 'er the painted boat.'

'Why?' Joy said.

'Look at 'er!'

Golden early rays of sunlight streamed along the canal. Now that the tarred black covers over the cargo were white with snow, the *Poca*'s gaudy colours and sparkling brasswork were almost too bright to look at. Each painted picture along the side of the cabin seemed to reach inside the boat as though it was real. 'Who painted her?' Joy asked.

'Why, I did it in me 'ead,' Grandma Pebble said.

Joy twisted round.

'Everyone's born good at something,' the old lady sighed. 'They used ter say it was in me fingers, yer age. Now I got arthritis, but I can still do it. It's in me 'ead, *I* say. That's never changed.' She looked back longingly as the boys began to tug them forward over the ice. 'That's where it matters.' She tapped her head. 'I've been the same all me life. I've never grown old inside.'

Joy, like the old lady, watched the boat shrink behind them, then they both turned with the same movement to the front.

They passed the *Lurcher*. The blank, strong faces of the Jones girls turned to follow the extraordinary sight of the skating Wampsetts without interest. There was no waving. 'Look at those fat idiots,' Ham said. Eleanor ignored them too, although it was said the girls were good to their father. She moved in, skating a little behind Kes. Kes put one arm behind his back, leaning forward with long strokes of his legs. By now the Jones girls had fallen far behind. They still had not moved when the first bend came up and the canal bank rose to hide them from view.

Two swans swam in a circle, keeping their patch of water clear of ice. Ducks flew down, slipping and slithering ludicrously. A moorhen peered anxiously from the reeds.

'Everyone all right?' Kes called. He skated backwards with long strokes to look at his family. He must be a very good skater, Joy thought.

'Gee-up!' Joy shouted at the boys pulling the sleigh. Ham was leading, Shane and Jaffrey on each side behind him. Her shout made them put their heads down and they tugged with a will. Flecks of ice flew from their skates. The skids beneath the sleigh began to rumble. Grandma Pebble hung onto the sides. 'Not too fast,' she called. Ham pretended not to hear her. The air blew in the boys' faces, pulling their hair out behind them.

'Faster!' Joy called. 'Giddyup!'

The boys had almost caught up with Eleanor and Kes. 'That's quite fast enough, yer lot,' Eleanor said. She skated beside them with a big swaying rhythm, white breath curling over her shoulder, the tail of her best black bonnet flapping. 'Isn't it a lovely day?

252

We're 'aving a day out!' Kes slid back and skated alongside. His cheeks were red and he smiled without lines in his face as though he had lost years.

Joy looked silently round their beaming, happy faces. It seemed to her that there would be nothing else but this moment going on for ever, the skaters moving across the ice, the sunlight flashing around them. She felt her whole life stretching ahead of her, the baby held tight in her arms, the iron runners thrumming on the ice beneath her, her hair blowing and everything rushing backwards. On the bends the sleigh swung wide and the reeds whipped alongside with a thin swishing sound, then a new straight would open up like a white arrow, maybe with a little stone packhorse bridge set somewhere in the distance, its arch echoing briefly as they swept beneath in no time at all. As for the low wooden cock-up bridges, rather than waste time raising them the skaters ducked their heads and bent double, coasting with their knees and knuckles almost brushing the ice as the bridgework flashed overhead, then they straightened and their skates took up the rhythm again.

'Giddyup! Giddyup!' Joy cried.

'Yer'll wake the baby,' Grandma Pebble said.

'He's awake! Giddyup!'

'Us mules is doing our best,' Ham said. He wouldn't admit that he wasn't as strong as iron. They passed a pub with boats moored in front of it. The boat people waved and someone who recognised them called out, 'Mornin' to ye, Christopher! Eleanor! And ye, young Hamlet.'

Ham blushed beetroot red to the tips of his ears,

and skated harder than ever.

Eleanor clapped her hands to her cheeks. 'My God, I'd forgot! Wot on earth are we going to call Cottontop?'

'Don't you *know*?' Kes yelled. He swept around a couple of skaters, wobbling as they set off, then angled smoothly back.

It was the first time Joy had seen Eleanor flustered. 'We can't christen 'im Cottontop, the Reverend wouldn't wear it, Cottontop's not a Christian name any more than Kes is.'

'I'm as Christian as yer is!' Kes said hotly.

'Christopher yer was christened, an' that's the only name wot the Church an' God care about, Kes. As Christopher yer'll be buried an' 'ave it writ on yer 'eadstone, even though no one calls yer it, except me when I'm peeved wiv yer. But *Cottontop!*'

'I like it,' Joy said.

'I like it too,' Grandma Pebble said.

'Yer keep yer oar out of it, Gran,' Eleanor said.

'We ought ter choose a good boatie name,' Ham said.

'Fishface!' said Jaffrey.

'I name this baby the *SS Great Eastern*,' Shane intoned, 'an' God bless all who sail in 'im.'

'Yer'll get a smack round the 'ead in a minute,' Eleanor said. 'This is serious.'

'Damian,' Shane said seriously.

Seriousness was so unlike Shane that they all stared at him, coasting, and the sleigh's velocity slackened.

'Damian? Wot sort o' name's that?' Kes said.

'It's a good name,' Joy said.

'There are four saints called Damian,' said Shane. 'It is a worthy an' distinguished name.'

'I like it,' Eleanor said.

'Wot does our Shane know about saints?' Kes demanded.

'That's settled, then,' Eleanor said. She took up her swaying rhythm again. 'Damian 'e is.' Kes was shaking his head. 'Shut up, Christopher,' she called back. 'Catch me if yer can.'

Kes hunkered down. The bones thrummed on the ice as the boys strained to keep up with him. The canal curved around the edge of a village and some village kids threw stones at them from a bridge, but none came near. Beyond a small coal-pit and gasworks they passed the usual jumble of warehouses, wharves and moorings that grew up outside any village, then came into open country again. But now the blue sky ahead of them had faded to brown and yellow. Beneath the mass of drifting smoke the factory chimneys looked like little gleaming steeples. Coming closer, the children realised that each chimney was made of a million bricks. The chimneys trailed plumes of solid black and vivid yellow into the huge pall above. Grandma Pebble pointed. 'Even the butterflies are black in this part of the world.' The canal was lined with tall warehouses and endless rows of houses, each tiny house beneath its tiny smoking chimney-pot with its front door and step onto its cobbled street, and thousands of women out there hanging out the washing in the sun and smoke. Kids crowded onto the canal to slide on the ice, knocking each other over, fighting, forming into gangs. As soon as they saw strangers they shouted. They wore wooden clogs and caps of a shape Joy had never seen before, and some of their faces were so thin and pale that she thought they ought to be eating instead of playing at fighting.

'Some of 'em don't get enough ter eat,' Grandma Pebble said.

Joy couldn't imagine it. 'Why don't they ask for more?'

'They dunno 'ow,' said the old lady. 'Whoa!' A chemical factory spilled boiling fumes into the canal and the ice was rotten. Ham, Shane and Jaffrey took off their boots and carried the sleigh along the towpath barefoot. Past the place they strapped their boots on and the family took to the good ice again, picking up speed. A gentleman skating past them going the other way with flapping coat tails raised his top hat to them. 'Good day!' The light was a strange lurid colour because of the sun gleaming oddly through the billows of smoke, now faint, now strong, but here no one else seemed to notice. Joy realised that this strange place was completely normal.

But instead of following the navigation into the heart of the city, Kes held out his arm as formally as a bicyclist and swooped to the right at a junction of the waterways. Brick factories rose over them, modern gantries and cranes squealing steam and smoke, broad iron barges being loaded from horse-drawn gangways, four horses to haul each queue of rusty chaldron wagons from the pit. Ice-breaker boats, half a dozen men throwing their weight from side to side, worked clear lanes for the barges to be moved out of the way. Gangs of wharfies worked in sullen teams beneath the new machinery. The noise died away. The buildings fell back. The skaters glided past the ramshackle clapboard warehouses which lined the navigation, family businesses worked by older men and kids, a plodding donkey or two to swing the heavy stuff up by gable-crane. A low shanty town of huts and rubbish-tips spread along the canal banks, then within moments they were deep in the countryside again. It was as though the city had never been. The only roads were farm tracks. The only houses were farm houses.

'Not far to Cody's Bend now,' Eleanor called.

'Why's it called Cody's Bend?' Joy asked.

'An old man called Cody lived there,' Kes said. 'That's what everyone called 'im, any road.'

St Peter ad Vincula, the church at Cody's Bend, was dwarfed by the railway viaduct. The ancient stone tower peeped through the modern brick columns soaring upward to the arches. The children shouted with excitement as a train curved out of the treetops on their right. It crossed above the canal on the viaduct, rumbled high over their heads sending its sparks and cinders showering down, and disappeared into the hill beyond. A newspaper curled down from the sky, thrown by some passenger for the pleasure of seeing the long fluttering drop. The children skated past various items strewn on the ice that would normally have sunk without trace, the brown glass of a burst beer bottle, an old hat, expired tickets.

'The Manchester, Sheffield and Lincolnshire Railway Company,' Jaffrey said. He blushed when

257

everyone looked at him, impressed.

'Clever clogs,' Kes said.

'The good old M,S & L,' Ham said, determined not to let Jaffrey be too clever.

'Look at St Peter ad Vincula,' Shane said.

The church had been built long ago, on the dry mound where the water-meadow rose into the woods. Once its square tower had been the centre of a village, but the village had moved to be nearer the railway halt. Only a row of cottages under rotting thatch remained along the old track that was now the towpath. The cottages were falling-down old and had been taken over by the boat people. 'In my grandad's day the women didn't come aboard the boats,' Kes said. He turned in to the bank and sat down with a sigh of relief, favouring his stiff legs. The skating had tired him more than he admitted.

'And the men lived like pigs,' Eleanor said. She sat on the towpath and unstrapped her skates, then brushed the snow from her dress. Now that they had arrived she was too excited to be tired. 'Back then the boats 'ad crews, not families. Ham, slow it! Watch out fer yer grandma.' Jaffrey slid round behind the sleigh, slowing it. The reeds clicked as the sleigh approached the bank.

'Men and women were meant ter live together,' Grandma Pebble said definitely, putting out her arm to be helped ashore. 'All men or all women together make trouble, that's all. The women left at 'ome used ter bicker an' bitch terrible after a week, an' the men came back not washed nor eaten, only drunk.'

Joy climbed out of the sleigh. She held the baby

258

and saw faces peer through the windows of the cottages. The boys took off their skates and Eleanor fussed around them, making them wear high starched collars with the proper studs, looking smart. The doors of the cottages opened, but no children ran out. A little terrier rushed round the back of the tumbledown sheds and barked. Then a man with a stick came slowly out. He walked down the garden path.

'Dad!' Kes said. "Ow are yer, Dad?'

'Mustn't grumble,' old Clem said, leaning his stick against the fence. He embraced Kes. 'Thought yer was never coming back, boy.' Tears shone in his eyes.

'Well,' Kes said. He cleared his throat. 'Got ter follow where the cargo goes.'

'Oh, I know 'ow it goes, boy. Yer mother's missed yer.'

Kes put his arms round his mother, a plump jolly woman who looked a little like Eleanor with white hair, almost blind. She hugged Kes with her eyes closed, squeezing him tight. 'Knew yer'd make it, son,' Constance said. 'Just knew. Got me Sunday best on 'cos I knew yer would. Skates, that's a new one.' They exchanged family news.

'Got an orange fer each of yer, fer Christmas,' Clem told Ham, Shane and Jaffrey, 'if yer stay.'

Joy noticed other people, retired to this peaceful place after a life working on the water, gathering round. They pushed each other forward. They all seemed to be part of the family too. One of them was carried in a chair by two men as old as she. 'Yer 'aven't seen our new baby,' Eleanor said, taking command. Joy hung on to Cottontop as she was pulled forward. 'Now then, this is Aunt Aggie, say 'allo, an this 'ere's Uncle Nat.' She raised her voice as though he was deaf. ''Allo, Nunc! 'Ere's Eth an' Eli, they're two of a pair, those two, Joy, an' yer got ter treat 'em with respect 'cos they ran the old *Londinium* from Moira fer near on 'alf a century.' Joy bobbed respectfully, but the withered faces around her were only interested in the baby she held. 'That one up there,' Eleanor waved to a man working on a ladder by a derelict, roofless cottage, 'that's Peter Pebble. Grandma's 'usband's youngest brother, if yer follow.' The man raised his cap and retreated slowly down the wobbling ladder. 'Thinks 'e's a practical man. 'E's getting ready ter lay thatch on in the spring, 'is cousin'll boat 'im proper Norfolk reed along the navigation . . .' To Joy her voice seemed to fade away. Joy stared at the lady at the back of the crowd.

'You're VerVera,' Joy said. There was a silence. Everyone looked round.

'She's the one I told you about,' Eleanor said.

'Yes, I am,' the lady said. She came forward. She wore nothing but black. 'And you, little lady, are like me.'

'Don't start that second sight nonsense,' Peter Pebble called, stepping off the ladder with obvious relief to be on solid ground again. He had round red cheeks, a bright apple of a face.

'Don't listen to 'im, Joy,' Grandma Pebble whispered. 'Vera was found wandering on the towpath. I mind the day though Eleanor was 'ardly older 'erself. Vera was three or four years old, abandoned like a dog.'

'Perhaps she fell from the sky,' Joy said.

'No, that don't 'appen in real life. Everything comes down ter people. There are wicked people in the world, Joy, an' there are people the world makes wicked.'

'And there is us,' VerVera said, leaning down. Alone of all the people here, she ignored the baby. She peered into Joy's face. 'And there is us, Joy.'

'It's time fer everyone who's coming ter get ter the church,' Eleanor said. 'After all this trouble I won't 'ave us late fer Cottontop's churching.' She unwrapped the plain brown blanket and pulled Cottontop out of it like a present. 'Ah,' the women cooed, pressing round. Eleanor nestled him proudly in her elbow. He wore her own long christening robe of Honiton lace, but the fluffy woollen shawl had been patiently crocheted by her own grown-up, work-worn fingers. Eleanor pulled it up around his ears to keep him warm, and the look in her eyes was purest love.

Walking as fast as the slowest of them, exchanging news as they went, the group followed the raised gravel path across the water-meadow. The church rose out of the trees ahead of them. Joy walked beside VerVera. Neither of them needed to say anything.

II

'Method,' Bowler said. 'That's the half of it with police work, gentlemen.'

It was midday in London and the low winter sun struck along Putney High Street towards the marshes of Barn Elms, illuminating the Thames like a dull steel blade among the snowy rooftops. Bowler leaned back on the creaking leather seat. He cleaned beneath his fingernails with the point of his clasp knife. 'Prevention, detection, administration. Charge books neatly kept. Don't forget observation, most necessary. Criminals must *know* they are going to be caught. The police keeping an eye on everyone for their own good. See anything, Steynes?'

'Not since the woman went out to the public baths and came back.'

'Mrs Elsie Simmonds,' Bowler said.

'What's the other half of detective work, sir?' Alfie asked.

'Waiting,' Bowler said. He stretched his legs. 'Get me some cocoa, Detective Constable Nutting.'

Alfie climbed down from the 'growler' cab and went to the nearby barrow-stall. Navvies swarmed on Fulham Bridge, working to preserve the ageing wooden spans. Pedestrians hurrying across the Chelsea Water Company's aqueduct, open as a footbridge, were rooked of tuppence for the privilege. The whistle blew, the red flag went up, hammers rattled, and again road traffic was backed up solid for half a mile on each side of the river. Alfie carried the steaming mug back to the growler. The mass of carriage roofs, cabs, wains driven by yokels coming from the country overloaded with hay as high as the telegraph wires, made the High Street almost unbearably busy.

Such concealment suited the men in the four-wheeled growler very well.

It was dark inside the growler, and there was condensation on the window. Steynes wiped it with his glove. A woman plainly but neatly dressed, her skirt brushed, came out of the doorway across the High Street. 'Different woman,' Steynes said. The three men watched her through the cleared circle in the glass, knowing they could not be seen.

'Miss Edna Hawkins,' Bowler said. They discerned stairs going up the hallway behind her. 'They're in the first-floor room, like the landlord said.' Miss Hawkins waited impatiently on the step, fiddling with the wicker basket over her arm, then a youngster of about ten came out. She twisted his ear and walked away, then came back and kissed the top of his head. 'Peter Aloysius Lucan Hawkins. She's his aunt.' The aunt put her arm through the boy's elbow as though he was quite the little man, and together they walked away along the pavement. 'Off to the shops,' Bowler said.

'How are you so sure, Guv?' Steynes asked. Both men were irritable and tense this morning, Alfie thought.

'The shopping basket over her arm,' he said. Alfie was taking to detective work. Now that he looked into ordinary people and examined how they lived instead of merely keeping them in order, he saw that there was more to policing than he had thought possible. Everything about people was a clue. Everything they did revealed something about them. It was exciting, but exhausting. For the first time since he joined the force, Gail had accused him of bringing his work home.

'Miss Edna's the elder sister. She's the one with the money,' Bowler said. He finished the cocoa and handed the mug to Alfie, who put it on the floor. 'It's all there in Chancery records. The boy's legally her ward.'

Alfie had been amazed how much could be learned from looking at public records and talking to friends, relatives, neighbours. A detective could build up a whole picture of a person without even seeing them. 'Here goes someone else,' he said.

A boy came out. His trousers were ragged but he carried a towel. A pretty woman in a shabby third-hand dress followed him. She held a chipped, enamelled pitcher. They shivered. 'Bert Simmonds and his mother Elsie,' Bowler said. 'She's fetching milk. The boy's been sent off to the baths. That's their routine.'

Elsie crossed the road. The three men craned their necks, looking up at the bow window on the first floor.

'He's inside,' Bowler said decisively.

Elsie came back. The pitcher was full now, its weight leaning her to one side. 'And the *other* half of detective work,' Bowler said, 'is timing.'

Alfie worked it out. 'But that's three halves, sir,' he muttered.

Bowler gauged his moment. 'Come on, men.' They jumped down from the cab, Alfie last. They ran across the road and arrived at the exact moment Elsie unlatched the door. 'Detective Inspector Bowler, ma'am,' Bowler said politely. He pushed past and held the door wide for her, like an invitation into her own premises. 'May I come in?'

'Of course,' she said unthinkingly. The woman was an amateur. 'Is something the matter, officer?'

'Upstairs, lads!' The detectives knocked her aside

and pounded upstairs. Alfie leaned his arm across the stairway as the woman tried to come up. Elsie was left in the downstairs hall with the pitcher hanging from her hand, staring up.

There was only one upstairs door. 'Steynes,' Bowler beckoned. He stood back. Steynes hit the door with his shoulder. The wood splintered from the frame at the first blow, hanging from one hinge. Steynes gave it a kick and the door fell in. Bowler walked over it into the room.

He took off his hat and lifted the curtain by the patterned side.

'Mr Arthur Albert Simmonds,' he said, dragging off the bedclothes.

Arthur, blinking the sleep from his eyes, considered denying it, but the man had addressed him by his two Christian names like a magistrate. He knew he was rumbled. 'Police, are yer?' Arthur pulled a sheet over his private parts. He stood up on the mattress with all the dignity he could muster for Elsie's sake. He could hear her downstairs. She was crying. 'Yer got the drop on me, sir.'

'That's right, Arthur, I do.' Bowler looked around the gloomy corner that had been curtained off from the rest of the room. 'What a hole. You let your women push you around like this, do you?'

'Necessity is a 'arsh taskmistress, sir,' Arthur said.

'Detective Inspector Bowler.'

'I won't make no fuss.' Arthur reached for his trousers with one hand. 'Down at the station, sir?'

Bowler frowned. 'Quite the eager beaver, ain't you.'

'Don't want ter worry the wife about nothing, do we, Mr Bowler, sir.' Arthur grinned, fawning. He was seriously alarmed by all this attention, the Metropolitan Police taking the trouble to invade his little castle. It never would have happened in the old days. He pulled up his trousers by one leg. The candlestick he had been unable to sell was standing in the corner, only partly hidden by a pile of washing. The cream plate painted with a blue cat, another gift from Captain Combuskle, meaning nicked in Piccadilly, stood in plain view by the washing bowl. Elsie was going to find out the truth about him. Arthur wept inside.

He picked up his father's plum-coloured coat and felt some strength flow into him. He wasn't beaten yet. He threw the coat casually over the candlestick behind him and stepped onto the floor.

'I'm sure there's been a mistake, officer. Anything I can do ter 'elp yer get it sorted out, sir? I know my duty as a citizen, sir.'

'I'll talk to you right here, since it means so much to you,' Bowler said nastily. 'I'll talk to your wife right here too, Smart Arthur.'

'She doesn't know,' Arthur said miserably. 'Don't tell 'er, sir. I'll come quiet. No switches,' he begged. The thought of being dragged out handcuffed in front of Elsie and the neighbours was more than he could bear.

'Detective Constable Nutting,' Bowler called. 'Let Mrs Simmonds come up.'

'Don't, sir.' Arthur tried to grab the curtain as Bowler pulled it down. The pegs clattered onto the bare boards. Daylight flooded in from the other part of the room with its bow window, box-room, proper bed, a table and chairs. Arthur stood blinking. He stepped from one bare foot to the other, then remembered to tuck in his shirt.

'I'll tell yer everything yer want ter know, sir,' he said.

'You are Arthur Albert Simmonds, a jobbing clerk, and you have a string of petty convictions as long as my arm. You aren't even good at being bad, Smart Arthur.'

'Yes, sir,' Arthur whispered, cowed. He turned his eyes appealingly to the doorway. 'Don't let 'er in.'

'Number fifteen, Abbey Place, the fourth of December,' Bowler said. 'Where were you?'

'It was my birthday, yes, sir.'

'*Where were you?*'

'I was there, sir.'

'And Monkey, the loofer boy.'

'Yes, sir, it was me brought that little scalawag there,' Arthur confessed in a whisper.

'You were the lookout.'

'There was nothing ter see, sir.'

'Do you expect me to believe that?'

'I don't know, sir.'

'A kidnapped child and a horrible murder. That's nothing, is it?'

Arthur shook. 'I don't know nothing, sir.' Bowler strolled around the daylit side of the room. He came to the table and knocked over the chairs one by one. 'I think yer must mean Jack, sir,' Arthur whispered.

'The child and the murder, both Jack?'

'I don't know about no murder, sir.'

Bowler clicked his fingers. 'Jack who, he slips my memory?'

"'E'd split me if I told yer, sir.'

Bowler grinned in Arthur's face. 'Better keep quiet then.' He twisted his heavy boot on Arthur's bare foot. Arthur's lips trembled. His face screwed up. Bowler used his heel. Then he stepped back. Both men were breathing heavily. Steynes, by the doorway, looked away as though he had seen nothing.

'Ask Mrs Simmonds to come up,' Bowler said abruptly. 'Do it, this time!'

Steynes went onto the top landing and called over the rail to Alfie below. 'Send the woman up.'

They heard Elsie's voice. 'What is going on?' Her footsteps tapped upstairs. 'What are you men doing here?'

'Just routine, ma'am,' came Alfie's reassurance.

Arthur swallowed. 'It's a deal. It's Jack Riddles yer looking fer. Yer'll find 'im at Mrs Oilick's in St Luke's.' He gave Bowler a peculiar, savage look. 'Yer part o' the world, ain't it? Go in there an' get 'im if yer dare. 'E's not easy meat like me.'

Elsie ran to him and hugged him. 'Arthur,' she said, 'the man downstairs said they're policemen.'

'They are.' Behind her back, Arthur held out his wrist for the cuffs. 'Take me quiet.'

'I won't need to ask you any further questions for the moment, sir,' Bowler said. He put on his hat and touched his finger to the brim in salutation of Elsie. 'Your husband has been most helpful in our enquiries. Good morning, Mrs Simmonds.' He nodded at Arthur and left. Their footsteps clumped on the stairs then the outer door slammed.

'You're shaking!' Elsie said.

Arthur realised he was shaking all over. 'Yer crying,' he shuddered. 'Yer crying without showing it.'

'Yes,' she said, 'I am. Those men really were policemen, weren't they. They weren't criminals.'

'Oh, Elsie, I'm so sorry!' Arthur clasped her to him and hugged her so tightly that she arched her back in the way she did when they made love. 'All these years I've lied ter yer an' played yer along. Now yer know the truth.'

She laughed, then kissed his eyelashes. 'Arthur, I've always known. You've never had any secrets from me.'

'Yer don't understand. I'm no good.'

'No one's good. All I understand is that you are the man I love.' She folded his shirt collar properly along the crease.

'I love yer, Els!' he cried.

'I know,' she murmured, cuddling him, 'but I could never make you believe how much I love you. You've never believed it, Arthur. You never have.'

'I believe yer now.'

'Then believe in yourself,' she said.

He kissed her fiercely. 'No, I believe in us!' he said. He stepped back from her, suddenly uncertain. 'But if yer know everything—'

'I do know about you,' she laughed. 'I'm a woman in love, not an idiot. You've always tried to do your best.'

Arthur drew a deep breath. 'I'll tell yer wot 'appened,' he said. He sat on the mattress, then rested his forehead in his hands. 'See, that night, I was waiting fer Jack in the doorway of Turnham's—'

While he talked Elsie moved slowly around the room. She looked mostly at Arthur, listening, but from time to time she bent down and set one of her sister's overturned chairs right, or put Edna's table back exactly as it should be. The rug had been knocked crooked and she put it straight. Then she watched from the window for a little while. 'The growler's gone, Arthur. But the man with the long moustache is still by the hot-cocoa stall, watching. He was nicer than the other two.'

'Softer,' Arthur said.

When he finished she came back to him and sat on the mattress. She held his bruised, swollen feet in her lap. 'That horrid Mr Bowler stood on your toes. Can't we report him?'

'You must be joking!' Arthur jumped up. 'We're going. They've left me ter stew in me juices fer now, that's 'ow the bluebottles work. But they're going ter come back an' knock us up at some odd hour o' the night, an' when they do, we're not going ter be 'ere.'

'But where else is there?'

'Els, me Dad 'ad a word fer it. We got ter shingle-split.'

'Shingle-split?'

'Go anywhere, don't matter where, as long as it's not 'ere. Yer got a cousin in Manchester, ain't yer? 'E'll put us up fer a day or two, till we find our feet.' Arthur dragged his coat over his shoulders. 'Build a new life.' He put on his socks and shoes with little hisses of pain. 'We're going ter need money.'

'But this is our home.'

'No it ain't, Els,' he said seriously. 'This never was

ours. It's yer sister's. Let 'er 'ave it, it's wot she's always wanted.' He pulled Elsie to her feet. 'We'll find a place of our very own, promise yer. Listen, yer got something put by fer a rainy day, ain't yer?'

'Only for a real emergency, Arthur.'

He pointed out of the sunny window. 'It's raining, Els! It's pouring!'

She shivered. 'You really are frightened.'

'Els,' he said, 'I am absolutely bloody terrified. I'll tell yer about it in the train.' He looked into her eyes, hiding nothing of what he felt. 'Trust me.'

She knelt and lifted the loose floorboard by the fireplace. It was such an obvious place that Arthur had never thought to look. She reached in and fished out a knotted handkerchief. She undid it and spilt out a couple of sovereigns and a handful of smaller coins, whatever she had managed to scrimp and save over the years. 'I never guessed there was so much,' Arthur said, humbled. He knew it would all be gone by evening.

There was little enough to pack. Most of it fitted into Elsie's embroidered sewing bag. They were almost finished when the door opened. Arthur gave a shout of fear. But it was only their son Bert standing there with his towel over his arm, smelling of coal-tar soap. They looked at him guiltily. He knew at once what was happening.

'But I can't go,' Bert wailed. His face reddened. 'Wot about all my friends?'

'Yer'll make new friends,' Arthur grunted. ''Ere, carry this bag.' He opened the rear window. The roof sloping down over the scullery halved the drop into the back yard. The heat of the stove had melted the

271

snow. Arthur forced the painted plate into the bag and grabbed the silver candlestick. He squeezed through the window and backed crabwise down the slates. He got his foot on top of the fence and swung himself down, then held up his arms. "Urry up!' Bert slid the bag down and jumped after it so nimbly that Arthur reckoned he'd gone this way before.

'Me, Dad?' Bert said innocently.

Elsie slipped down. For a moment she wouldn't let go of the windowsill. This home had been as proper as any they'd had.

"Urry!' Arthur begged. Her fingers released their grip and he caught her.

He wrapped the candlestick in Bert's towel so as not to attract attention. He led them along the marshy banks of the river Wandle, then they cut through the back-doubles to the Thames. Workmen were knocking down old houses, making way for a new bridge to be built over the mudflats. Arthur kept looking behind them. They walked as far as Battersea, then crossed the Thames on the rickety wooden bridge and waited for an omnibus to King's Cross. When it came they climbed up the back and sat on the empty top deck. Bert went to the front where he could sit behind the driver. Arthur sat with Elsie at the rear. He glanced over his shoulder. There was no sign of the policeman with the long moustache.

'Stop it!' she said. 'You keep looking behind you. It's making me nervous.'

'*You* nervous,' he said with a shaky laugh.

'What's got into you, Arthur?'

Arthur blurted, 'I'm almost sure Bowler is the man I saw outside Turnham's Music Hall.'

'So? So what?'

'Els, 'e 'ad me bang ter rights today. 'E saw this candlestick. 'E's got enough on me ter throw away the key. So why didn't 'e arrest me?'

Elsie smiled. She didn't understand crime. 'Should he have done?'

'Yes,' Arthur said. 'But 'e didn't. That's wot worries me.'

'I should be grateful for small mercies, dear.' Elsie covered his hand with her own, then rested her head on his shoulder. In a way she was pleased that the truth about her husband was acknowledged between them, that they did not have to lie to each other any more. Today, by bringing matters between them into the open, Detective Inspector Bowler had accomplished more for her marriage than she had dared. She closed her eyes and let the rhythm of the horses' hooves and the rumble of the iron wheels soothe her. Arthur's shout woke her.

He was leaning over the side of the vehicle. The traffic had stopped and someone called that there had been an accident ahead. Elsie did not know this part of London well, but she recognised the Edgware Road by the Marble Arch, which was behind her, and Turnham's Music Hall ahead. Near there, someone had been run over in the road. A crowd had gathered. The omnibus, turning right into the New Road, inched past. Arthur stared over the rail. His knuckles were white.

'Terrible! Terrible!' One old man was holding his hands to his ears as though still hearing the sound. 'People, people rushing everywhere, he must have slipped—'

'It's Monkey,' Arthur said.

The boy lay outstretched in the roadway. He had been cut almost in two by the wheels that had run over him. His face had been crushed into the back of his head by a horse's hoof.

Chapter Eleven

I

Alfie Nutting was surprised by the knock on his door so early. He finished polishing his boots as Gail slid his breakfast plate in front of him. 'Who's that at this hour!' she said crossly. 'Start buttering that bread, you girls.' She wiped her hands on her apron and bustled down the hall. Alfie looked at his plate of bacon, black pudding, fried potatoes, and fried bread with a rich yellow duck egg on top, sent by Gail's cousin in Croydon who had a farm. He added salt and pepper liberally and raised his knife and fork.

'Oh, it's you, Mr Bowler,' came Gail's voice. Alfie groaned. She called. 'It's your Mr Bowler, dear!' Alfie dropped his cutlery and stood.

Through the doorway he saw it was still dark in Waterloo Street. Behind Bowler's outline the first gleam of dawn glowed off the huge new Phoenix Works gasometers that towered over the little houses. 'I won't come in, Mrs Nutting,' Bowler said. But he did.

'This awful mess!' Gail said, drawing attention to it by trying to conceal it, flustered. She elbowed Alfie aside and he retreated with his hands up. There was washing in the hall and the dog's basket smelt of old dog. Fortunately Splodge was in the yard for his morning penny. 'At least have a cup of tea in the front parlour, Mr Bowler,' she said.

'Don't mind if I do,' Bowler said. But he came into the kitchen.

He looked around him, missing nothing. 'These are your two girls. How did something as ugly as you make something so pretty, Alfie?' He's very jocular for so early in the day, Alfie thought. Bowler's mood changed. 'Don't they grow up quickly,' he said sadly. 'Beth, aren't you? And you must be Becky. No, don't let me disturb you.' But Gail caught their eye. She shushed them along the hall and the girls rushed upstairs.

He even knows about my family, Alfie realised. He hated being caught big-bellied in his vest and dangling braces. 'Look, sir, I'm sorry about yesterday,' he said stiffly. He closed the kitchen door because he could see the girls' long hair hanging over the banister and knew they were eavesdropping. He snapped the braces over his shoulders. 'I know I was a right fool, waiting out the front while the Simmonds family did a bunk the back way—'

'You couldn't watch both sides of the house at once,' Bowler said reasonably. His temper had not been so reasonable yesterday. Bowler and Steynes had arrived as darkness fell, found the footprints crossing the back yard, and only then had Alfie realised that Smart Arthur and his family had flown the coop. The light at the window was the sister moving around. Bowler had been furious, knocking-down furious. He had raised his gloved fist in Alfie's face and called him a stupid effing copper. No other officer had ever spoken to Alfie like that. Alfie had thrown down his hat and squared up. There was almost a fight on the stairs. 'How was I to know Smart Arthur was so important?' Alfie had shouted as they argued.

'He's important to me,' Bowler had said. 'He's important *because they never tell you all they know*.'

A detective knew instinctively that he couldn't trust anybody. No one ever told the whole truth. Everyone had something to hide.

No sign of the Simmonds family had been found. A man like Smart Arthur could hide himself anywhere.

Alfie had failed. He knew Bowler had come here this morning to tell him he was back in blue, and he sighed. He had enjoyed the challenge of detective work, becoming a man blending anonymously among a million others in this teeming city, no longer standing out as a helmeted object of suspicion and respect. Gail was happiest married to a uniform though. She bustled back in and poured the tea, leaving the door swinging. 'I'm sorry about the smell, Mr Bowler,' she sniffed, opening the window. 'Alfie likes his breakfast fried in beef dripping. You caught us unawares.'

'I suppose I'm back on the beat, sir,' Alfie said. 'Well, the wife won't be sorry. I don't suppose the kids will either, will you, girls?' Giggles from upstairs.

'Back on the beat?' Bowler said. 'No, I need you too much this morning.' He pushed Alfie's breakfast away. 'No time for that. Get your hat and coat on.

Ah, thank you, Mrs Nutting.' He took the mug of tea from Gail and gulped it, though Alfie knew her tea was always red-hot. 'Been up half the night!' Bowler said. Alfie looked at him like a detective. Bowler's manner was jovial, with the recklessness of a man who has taken a big step and can't turn back now. He wouldn't sit down, he was like a cat on hot bricks. He's becoming obsessed by this case, Alfie thought. He's like that French policeman who got his teeth into a case in France and just couldn't let go. Alfie sat down and tied his shoelaces steadily.

'What's this?' Bowler said. He rattled something on the table.

Alfie was fearsomely embarrassed. 'It's a thingummy, sir.'

'What's it for?'

At least there was something Bowler did not know. 'It's a device for keeping your moustache out of your soup, of course, sir.' Alfie heard Beth and Becky splitting themselves with laughter on the stairs. He stood up and pulled on his overcoat with dignity. He still had no gloves.

He looked round. Bowler was gone.

'Ah,' came Bowler's voice from the front parlour. 'Christmas cards.' Alfie followed him in. Gail threw him a wild look, Bowler would be examining the whole house next. Bowler peered at the cards on the mantelshelf. '*And let us die, when death shall come, on Christmas in the morning*,' he read sentimentally. Mr Ward's Christmas cards were the latest thing, some of them with spaces for family photographs to be stuck to them. Last year Alfie and Gail had received half a dozen cards through the penny post, which obliged them to send half a dozen of their own, and they had received twice that number already this year. They would have to buy more.

Bowler said without turning round, 'We're going into St Luke's.'

Alfie stared at his back. 'But we don't do that,' he said. He knew police patrols had shown their faces along Field Lane for the last twenty years, but only in groups, and he had heard that officers who left the road were pelted with stones and human manure. Four policemen who'd lost their way in St Luke's were savagely beaten, lucky to get out alive. Last year most of the three thousand assaults on police, nearly half the men in the force, had been near rookeries. No wonder so many men were handing in their numbers.

'We're going in,' Bowler said. 'We've got to, sooner or later, so it may as well be now.' He was speaking with such determination that Alfie knew this was the big decision that had been taken. How had Bowler swung it with Williamson and the Commissioner? 'We can't have places that policemen can't go,' Bowler said. He showed his teeth in a smile.

He went to the front door. 'Thanks for the tea, Mrs Nutting,' he called over his shoulder.

In the street Bowler stood in the snow. Alfie came out and closed the door, shivering. There was not a sound round them, and only a few lighted upstairs windows whirling with snowflakes. Bowler put up his collar and spoke to Alfie in a low voice. 'We're going in, and we're going to bring Jack Riddles out. Every able-bodied man is on duty. I'll issue cutlasses if necessary.'

Alfie followed him down the street. Bowler walked fast on silent footsteps through the snow. 'We'll meet Steynes on London Bridge.'

Alfie ran to catch up. 'Cutlasses, sir? Against our own people?'

'You dare call them our own people,' Bowler said quietly. 'They're criminals, garrotters who seize ladies from behind and cut their throats, baby-farmers, kidnappers, sodomists, housebreakers, murderers. If you call them our own people you're as bad as them.' Suddenly he smiled and clapped Alfie's shoulder. 'Don't worry! The Commissioner is a military man. With these Fenians about we have the perfect excuse, if one should be needed.'

London Bridge rose ahead of them. Snow swirled through the gas-lamps into the depths of the river. 'No cabs this weather, sir,' Steynes said.

'We'll walk. Plenty of time.' They crossed into the City and puffed uphill past the Globe Insurance building. On top of Cornhill stood the banks and discount houses, vast and grey in the snow, the hub on which world trade turned. 'Briggs's territory,' Bowler said. Two burly men slithered past them pushing a barrow laden with skins, still bloody and steaming, bound for the tanneries of Bermondsey. The Smithfield abattoirs worked all night. 'Going to be a cold winter,' Bowler said. 'The farmers are killing what they can to save on forage.' The detectives turned north along Moorgate. 'By the bye,' Bowler said, 'the boy called Monkey.'

'I remember him,' Alfie said.

'Tragic accident. The traffic always goes too fast.'

Alfie said, 'The last thing I said to him was to keep

out of trouble. Poor Monkey. He wasn't a bad'un really.'

'We'll never know that now,' Bowler said.

'All them boys is bad,' Steynes said. 'Believe me, we see it in G Division.'

'No homes, no family life,' Alfie said.

'Well,' Bowler said, 'that's the trouble with making a living running in and out of traffic.'

They turned left into Featherstone Street. Black Marias and covered vans were parked everywhere, or trying to park. Horses whinnied. Policemen were being formed up in ranks. 'Eyes right! Dress to the right!' shouted a parade-ground voice. A blue lamp glimmered through the snowflakes. The steps to number fifty-five, the police station, had been swept clean. The bars over the windows were painted dark blue. It was a very constabulary kind of building, almost forty years old, dating from the earliest days of the police. From the imposing pulpit in the bridewell a sergeant administered a ticking-off to two shivering youngsters in the grip of a large, red-faced, puffing constable. 'Now off you go, lads, and fer 'eaven's sake don't do it next time.' The sergeant noticed the visitors and pointed above their heads. 'Straight through. Mr Briggs is waiting for you.'

'I thought Briggs would like to see this,' Bowler said. 'Purely as an observer.'

He led the way down a busy corridor. Everything was tiled as white as a public urinal. There were so many policemen waiting that the cells had been opened and pressed into use. One constable complained his boots had been stolen. Other men smoked or yawned into their beards, resting like

281

soldiers before a battle. Many of them could remember the Chartist riots.

'Just like the good old days,' Bowler said, and a cheer went up.

'This had better be worth getting me out of bed,' Darby Briggs said ungraciously. He wore a long herringbone cape and top hat. A muffler kept his ears warm, and he carried a silver-topped cane.

'Scotland Yard always gets its man,' Bowler assured him. 'We'll get your daughter out, too, if she's there.'

'She'd better be,' Briggs said. A couple of men shook their heads. They didn't like having a civilian along.

Bowler called the sergeants round him and Briggs was pushed aside. Alfie counted twenty-eight heads, mostly grey-whiskered men in their fifties and sixties. As always, young constables would do the running today. There was a large wall map showing the area. Bowler rapped it with a truncheon. 'Seven hundred acres in G Division, three hundred and twelve lads,' he said breezily. 'Every single man jack of you's on the hop this morning. I have a hundred and fifty special constables – ratepayers, that is – patching in on the regular rounds, and I can call on half of them if I have to.' His truncheon banged the map. 'I want these streets blocked off. I want at least one man on every alleyway. Method, gentlemen. System. We'll go in near the church and drive the scum of St Luke's out in front of us. The women are as bad as the men. I want every woman taken into custody.'

'On what charge?' someone asked.

'Contagious Diseases Act,' Bowler said. 'By law

282

any woman, any woman at all, can be forcibly taken from the street and inspected for disease. Of course, that might take a little while. As for the men, if there's any trouble I'll have the Riot Act read.' The men grinned in their whiskers. The Riot Act meant truncheons, and many of them had old scores to settle with the public. 'And remember, lads, no whistles until you hear *my* whistle blow.' They filed out noisily. The sound of their boots faded.

'All for one little girl,' Alfie said.

'One is enough,' Bowler shrugged. 'I have no choice.'

Freddie Williamson, chief of the Detective Force, passed the doorway. He saw Bowler and came back. Snow clung to his bulldog jowls. 'What's this nonsense about cutlasses?'

Bowler said, 'Only for the lads' own protection, sir.'

'I'd better not see them.'

'No, sir.'

'Is that clear, Bowler? Not without my special order.'

Bowler looked at him. I know you're on the take, Mr Freddie, sir, his eyes said. I don't know what your racket is, but I do know that you're washing your fingers in the till somehow or other. Those bags under your eyes come from sleeping with Maisy, not your wife. And not sleeping much, by the look of you.

'Yes, sir,' Bowler said. 'Absolutely clear.'

Briggs came in. Williamson said disagreeably, 'Well, you've still got the Commissioner on your side. But I hear you've set up in business on your own account, Mr Briggs.'

'That's true.' Briggs was surprised by Williamson's knowledge. Williamson waited, so Briggs volunteered more information. 'I leave Prideau's employ on the last day of this year. Briggs Bank and Company is inaugurated on the first day of the new year, fully capitalised.' He smiled, but no one else did.

'I should be very successful if I were you,' Williamson said. 'Maybe you needed old Prideau's influence more than you thought. Good morning, sir.' He pulled on his deerstalker cap and left. Briggs stared after him.

Bowler clapped Briggs on the shoulder. 'Come with me, Mr Briggs. Don't stray. You men, stick close on me.' Half a dozen constables, each of them tall and fit, fell into step behind him. 'Steynes, Nutting, keep your eyes peeled.'

They went down the steps. Alfie was surprised by how little dawn had come forward. The street was a grey glow, every building softened by snow and gloom. It was bitterly cold. After a few minutes' walk Alfie squeezed a snowflake between his fingertips. It did not melt. He plunged his hands in his pockets. More policemen joined them, their heavy tread muffled by the snow. Steynes had acquired a truncheon. Near the church he crouched and propped the business end on the pavement, his ear to the handle. From the distance came a faint rattle. It was loud and clear to Steynes. 'Old Street is ready, sir.'

'On a quiet morning like this sound travels for miles under the pavements,' Bowler told Briggs. 'Perfect conditions.'

The men gathered around them, listening. More signals came.

'GS,' Steynes murmured. 'Goswell Street ready.'

'Long-long-short, three shorts,' Bowler said. 'Mr Samuel Morse's code.'

'Incredible,' Briggs said. The streets seemed deserted and silent. 'I would never have guessed that all this police activity was going on under our noses.'

'It's hardly started,' Bowler said.

'AG,' Steynes said. 'Aldersgate ready and waiting, sir.'

Bowler looked at the jumble of worn-out buildings stretching in front of him. 'Still asleep in their beds,' he said. 'Now, Mr Jack Riddles, I'll have a word with you.' He walked forward. 'Give the signal, Steynes. Quiet as mice behind me, gentlemen, if you please.'

Almost at once the buildings closed around them. They stumbled in the snow and shadows. Alfie walked close behind Bowler, shoulder to shoulder with Briggs. The banker was breathing short, sharp breaths of excitement. Briggs knocked his top hat on a low brick arch across the alley. He took his hat off and walked with it swinging from one hand. He looked alert and vengeful. 'Steady, sir,' Alfie said. Briggs hardly glanced at him.

A plume of snow drifted down from a rooftop and Bowler stopped, but nothing happened. They had not been discovered. 'All asleep on a morning like this,' he murmured. He walked forward, deep into a maze of courtyards and alleyways. Walls rose high above them on every side. Briggs looked up, trying to see the sky.

'I've seen Charlie Bowler come in here in full uniform,' Steynes said.

'Brave,' Briggs said.

'Young. Didn't know no better,' Steynes said. 'He got me out, though.' He nodded. 'That's the way it was. Hooligans from Field Lane, yours truly in hot pursuit, then in here it was the boot on the other foot and *me* in hot water, I'll tell you.'

'Then you owe our Mr Bowler your life,' Briggs said.

'I wouldn't put it so high,' Steynes said. 'I owe him my balls, though.'

'You must be grateful.'

'Look at him,' Steynes said. A wall blocked the path. Bowler beckoned, his finger to his lips, and a constable ran forward with a ladder. 'He never backs down,' Steynes said, 'not once he's set his mind on something. Look.' Bowler had climbed the ladder and was peering over the wall. 'It's a one-way street at least.' He rapped the paving with his truncheon, giving their position. Bowler motioned and a second ladder was brought. 'It's a no-way street.' Bowler swung the ladder over the wall and climbed down the other side. 'The bastards keep steps hidden in the houses,' Steynes said. The men filed after Bowler with a steady tread. Some stayed to guard the wall. More came after them. Briggs and Alfie hurried to catch up.

Bowler crossed St Thomas's burial ground. Briggs had lost his hat. They turned downhill past a bitter-smelling dye house. As Alfie passed the door a woman came out and emptied a pot of its foul yellow contents. 'Watch it,' he said.

She stared at Alfie. Her eye travelled along the file of policemen behind him.

She screamed.

'Get her,' Bowler said. Two burly policemen pushed through the rotten door after her. The men outside heard her screams running upstairs through the house.

'That's done it,' Bowler said. He blew piercing blasts on his whistle and rushed forward down the alley. Whistles took up the refrain all around them, sounding like a giant flock of birds. Footsteps pounded. 'She soaked you,' Briggs told Alfie as they ran.

Alfie decided to worry about it later. He was almost sure that Briggs's stick contained a sword. A sword-stick was illegal but difficult to detect. He stuck close to Briggs. Bowler's coat flapped in front of them. A man came out of a doorway pulling on his shirt and Bowler knocked him down. He rushed on. The man was lifted up, pushed against the wall, arrested.

Two men came out of the Blue Anchor. They ran away, shouting. Bowler jerked his hand and two young constables sprinted ahead. The men split up and were gone. The policemen raced back. Their helmets were crooked.

'Chin-straps,' Bowler said. 'Steady, lads, steady.' He turned left past the Shears pub. Suddenly the windows opened and stuff was thrown down, pots, stones, bits of furniture. They heard the strange, frightening keening of women screaming with anger. 'Eyes front, lads,' Bowler said. 'Keep it steady.' The police formed up and advanced with a steady tramp over the cobbles. The snow had not reached into here. Along Twister's Alley children with hard faces dodged out here and there and chucked bricks, turds, bottles, lumps of ice broken from buckets, anything they could find. The youngest tossed snowballs from Chequer Yard, their feet sometimes flying from under them with the effort of the throw. Toddlers patiently scraped together small earnest handfuls of snow.

'Devils,' Briggs said, breathing fast. His knuckles were clenched white on his stick.

People came out of doorways. The police knocked them back with truncheons. They could hear back doors opening and a babble of movement starting everywhere. 'We've got them on the run,' Bowler said.

'They're cutting round behind us!' someone called in a high, panicky voice. 'They're surrounding us!'

'Let 'em,' Bowler said. 'Look out!' A woman dropped a full bucket of water from a roof and it exploded like a bomb, showering the police. There was a chase and a fall. She was dragged out in her apron and arrested. 'Take her to the Black Maria in White Cross Street, and any others like her,' Bowler said grimly. A policeman screamed and dropped his truncheon, clapped his hands to his neck. He had been hit by broken bottle-glass from a child's catapult. Another kid grabbed the dropped truncheon and was gone before anyone could move.

'Baton-thongs secure on your wrists, lads.' The sergeants passed the word. 'Check them now.'

An inspector came over. 'Good enough for you, Bowler? It seems that any man who wants excitement today can get it at a very cheap rate.'

'Clear this street,' Bowler said irritably. 'Remember the Clerkenwell riots? If there isn't room in the vehicles, hold 'em in the yard of the old debtors' prison.' He turned to Briggs. 'I'm going to get demolition orders on this whole area, if I can.'

Behind them the police charged with truncheons raised. Bowler turned away impatiently. 'We're wasting time. Come on.'

They slithered down the steps into a sunken street. It was empty and quiet, nothing moved. The sounds of running and shouting faded behind them. 'Rookery Row,' Bowler said. 'Quick now!' He dashed forward. Briggs drew his sword. Alfie ran after him but Briggs kept ahead. Bowler ducked into a low doorway. Briggs was five seconds behind him, Alfie ten. That was plenty of time for a man to lose his life. Bowler put his hand in his overcoat pocket. The doorway was so narrow that he turned sideways to get through. 'Sir!' Alfie called.

Bowler went into Mrs Oilick's dolly-shop alone. It was the bravest thing Alfie had ever seen.

There were no sounds of violence. Alfie shouldered his way inside. 'Gone!' Bowler said.

Their heads almost touched the ceiling. Bowler confronted a woman who blocked his way by the table. Short and plump as a bird, she surveyed them with beady black eyes. Briggs stood panting by the fireplace. His unsheathed sword glinted. He was in a fine state of excitement. 'He was here?' he panted. 'That fiend Jack Riddles was here?'

'This is a respectable public 'ouse,' Mrs Oilick said, crossing her arms. 'I know my rights.'

'Shut it, Agnes,' Bowler said. A cat twined round his ankle and he kicked it.

'There's no fooling yer, Mr Bowler,' she simpered.

289

'Of course, yer was born 'ere, wasn't yer? Within the border of St Luke's, I've 'eard. Like yer was one of us.'

Bowler slapped her. She screamed and put up her fists. He looked into the slaughter room, empty, but the fire was bright, playing cards scattered on the table. He checked the door on the far side, came back. 'Upstairs!' he told Alfie. Alfie went up but found nothing, only small rooms with the doors hanging open, the smell of cats, cheap perfume, rancid flesh. Whatever had happened here was over. A girl of about eleven sat composedly brushing her hair. 'There's one girl but it's not her,' Alfie reported.

'She's my daughter,' Mrs Oilick said.

Bowler said, 'Where is he?' He kicked the cupboard by the fireplace. Bottles fell out. 'I'll tear the place apart if I have to.'

'The dear chap 'ain't done anything naughty now, 'as 'e?' Mrs Oilick backed away in front of him as Bowler's face darkened.

'She's trying to keep you from the back room,' Alfie said.

They looked round as a constable half fell down the step from outside. Sounds of fighting, whistles, yells, carried from the street, then the pursuit moved on. 'Arrest her,' Bowler told the constable. He knocked Mrs Oilick across the table and her skirts flew up. 'Resisting arrest.'

She scrambled after him in a blind fury. 'I 'ate yer! I 'ate the bloomin' lot of yer!' Bowler pushed her away and the constable caught her. She bit his arm. He lifted her up and dropped her, then dragged her out by her hair, but it came off. She screamed and clapped her hands to her bald skull. She wriggled away from him. The constable put his foot in the small of Mrs Oilick's back and dragged her out by her clothes.

Briggs said in an appalled voice, 'Suppose we find my daughter?'

The detectives stared at him. Bowler kicked open the door to the back room and went through.

'You'll still love her,' Alfie said.

Bowler stepped over piles of clothes, feather hats, dresses. He pulled the sheets off the bed and laid his hand inside. 'Still warm.' There were cats everywhere. The charcoal brazier beneath the crucible had been pushed over and pale flames ran up the curtain that concealed the back door. 'He's a clever bastard, this one.' Bowler had to waste precious seconds beating down the curtain with a broom handle. He stamped on the flames. Then he put his hand in his pocket and went out.

Alfie and Briggs followed him outside.

They were in a deep snowy alley. Two figures crouched at the end, a man and a woman in a long red dress. The man held her by the wrist as if fearing she would run away. He wore only trousers and a white shirt. Already falling snow bulked out his shoulders broader than ever, and dripped half-melted from his matted hair. He knelt with his ear to the handle of a knife. Its point rested on the paving stones.

Briggs hissed, 'What's he doing?' Alfie saw he held his sword as though his life depended on it.

'He's listening,' Bowler said. He moved forward without a sound.

Briggs's eyes were very bright. He breathed through his mouth. He followed Bowler like a man pulled by a wire. Alfie kept close beside him.

The girl saw them and squeaked. Everyone stopped.

Jack saw Bowler. His body stiffened.

'Give it up, Jack,' Bowler called. He held out one hand. 'Where else can you go?'

Briggs raised the sword. 'I'll kill him,' he said. He tried to shake off Alfie's hand. 'I promised Lydia I would.'

'Honour's satisfied, sir.' Alfie held him with a firm grip. 'Let's put that thing away now, easy now. Don't want to cut ourselves, do we. Let Mr Bowler handle this, he's the professional.'

'Damn you all,' Darby Briggs said. His lips trembled, then he handed over the sword-stick. 'I did try . . .'

Bowler called, 'Put down the knife, Jack.'

Only twenty paces separated the two men. Jack stood slowly. He was as tall as Bowler. His eyes narrowed as whistles shrilled somewhere between the buildings.

'All this trouble fer one man,' Jack called. 'Flattered, I am. Mr Bowler, ain't it? 'Eard tell of yer.'

Bowler said, 'Don't run, Jack.'

Jack ran. The girl hitched up her skirt and rushed after him, shouting. Bowler drew his hand from his pocket. Alfie saw the gun.

'Sir!' Alfie shouted. 'Don't—'

Bowler released the safety catch. He drew back the hammer with both thumbs. He swept the gun up smoothly and sighted on the fleeing figures.

The shot crashed out.

Then another, and another, and another.

II

'This is fun!' the girl said.

Jack leaned back against the wall. 'Off yer nut, Maggy, yer are.' He risked a glimpse round the corner. Running footsteps echoed, but he saw nothing. 'They're off the wrong way. Chasing shadows down Salmon and Ball Alley, I reckon.'

'Anyway,' Maggy said, turning up her filthy, once-pretty face to the snow, 'it's better than being indoors, isn't it, Jack?' He supposed she was still young enough to be excited by the snow. She was fourteen but he had taken trouble to make her look younger. He jerked back as another shot crashed out, then tugged her, and they ran again.

'Christ,' he said, 'those aren't warnings.' He twisted and turned through the maze, then skidded down some steps. They could go either way. 'Better split,' he said, giving her a push.

'No,' Maggy said.

He showed his fist to her face.

'I'd be frightened without you, Jack,' Maggy said. She began to cry.

He looked at her wonderingly. 'Strange bitch,' he said.

'You made me one,' Maggy told him. She looked him square in the eye.

'Well, now I'm freeing yer.' Jack pushed her away and knelt, listening to the knife. 'We shook 'em, I reckon.' Her dress rustled and he looked round. 'Yer still 'ere?'

'Are they close?'

He grunted. 'They're everywhere, girl, an' that's no lie.' He listened. 'More rozzers called in from Old Street.' His lips moved as he counted the dots and dashes.

'Jack,' she interrupted.

He glared at her.

'Jack,' Maggy said, 'you know, you should've pushed me on the gun.'

'Right enough,' he grunted.

'You know you should. It was common sense. I would've taken the bullet and you would've got clean away. But you didn't, Jack. Why didn't you?'

He grunted.

'You aren't such a hard case,' she grinned.

'Ain't I, Maggy?'

'You wanted me to come with you,' she said. 'A bit of you did, anyway.'

'Bugger me!' he said. He shook his head. 'Stay wiv me an' yer'll swing wiv me, I reckon.'

She knelt beside him. 'I wouldn't mind swinging with you, Jack. You've got a lovely mouth, when you smile.'

He stared at her, completely baffled.

'Not that you smile often,' she said. They heard the tramp of marching men.

Jack grabbed her. 'There's more coming through from White Cross Street. The bastards are cutting us off. They really mean it this time.' He looked around him frantically, then backed into a corner.

'You're clever when you use your head,' she said

complacently. She knew he'd think of something. Jack never gave up, and he was resourceful.

He held the knife blade upwards in his fist, ready to kill. Snow sifted down between them from above. They both looked up.

'The rooftops!' Jack said. 'The bastards 'aven't got me yet.' He crouched and ran back up the steps. The alley was clear. He slipped across, held the knife in his teeth, and scrambled up on the wall. Maggy held out her arms to be pulled up. Jack waved down. 'Every man for 'imself,' he said. 'Cheerybye.'

'The police are coming!' She shook her fingers at him. 'Quick!'

Jack cursed and snatched her up. She kissed him as she came over the top. He'd been had.

Jack hunched down on the ledge and wiped his lips. 'I s'pose I could always use yer,' he admitted grudgingly. The sound of marching boots came closer. 'Blimey,' he said. 'Yer weren't lying.' The two of them froze as still as ice statues as a police squad tramped steadily below. Maggy grinned and picked up a brick to drop on them. Jack grabbed it and made a face. She pouted. The marching sound faded, blending into the general ruckus of shrieks and shouts that beat and echoed round the courtyards below.

'It 'ad ter 'appen one day,' Jack said. 'I got it sorted out ready. I'm Jerry Lynch o' the Ratcliff 'Ighway.'

'And I'm Mrs Lynch.'

'Bugger me if yer is,' Jack said.

Jack and Maggy slipped silently away across the snowy rooftops. Forty feet below them, Alfie came to the corner of White Cross Street. A policeman was carried past him with blood streaming down his face. Alfie leaned back in a shop doorway. He closed his eyes.

'All this and twenty-five bob a week,' he said.

Chapter Twelve

I

At Cody's Bend the fun of making Christmas Christmassy began in earnest. Life in the little row of cottages alongside the canal seemed wonderfully spacious after living on a boat. Earlier the children had been set to work cutting up bits of paper and painting them for decoration, making an incredible mess and clutter. Now they had been turfed out.

'It's always a relief when they're christened,' Eleanor said, ducking under the paper chains that crisscrossed Vera's front room. She tried to sound cheerful now she had everything that as a youngster she had ever wanted out of life, a man as good as a husband, family, happiness. 'Now if our Cottontop – I mean Damian – should die, God forbid, at least 'e'll go ter 'Eaven.' She packed away Damian's christening robe and baby shawl with a sigh. Her tongue was always wanting to call him Cottontop, but the time for that was past.

'What's wrong, Eleanor?' Vera said.

Eleanor watched from the window as Joy went outside. The girl carried Damian in her arms, their faces close. The sun was bright on the snow and

Damian was grinning. His eyes, looking up at Joy adoringly, were the colour of the blue sky. Joy looked after him more than Eleanor, washing him in cold water to toughen him, and when she changed him she set him upright to dance from her fingers. Nothing would make her give him to his brothers. Eleanor grinned to see her so protective. Joy wore a long skirt cut from one of Grandma Pebble's leather gardening aprons, kicking the hem ahead of her as she walked. She still wore the top part of the Army coat, no more to be parted from that than from Cottontop. Damian, Eleanor corrected herself. She looked towards the woods as Joy waved to someone there. Shane and Jaffrey had been sent to find holly. 'Nothing makes Christmas as Christmassy as holly and red, red berries,' Kes had said. Jaffrey had added, 'And oranges.' The boys had not forgotten Grandad Clem's promise of an orange for Christmas. 'An' chopping plenty o' firewood,' Kes said meaningfully just before he left. The roly-poly ice-breaker had come groaning down the navigation past the cottages this morning, dragged by a dozen dusty pit-ponies blinking and bewildered by the dazzling snow. The man wielding the iron flail onto the ice from the front end waved. The channel was clear for today but this clear sky would freeze it solid again tonight, Kes reckoned. He and Ham had set off ahead of the boat to skate back to the *Poca* and fetch her up while they could.

Eleanor turned away from the bright window.

'Oh, it's nothing, Vera,' she sighed. 'I've 'ad my bellyful of kids now, I'm finished. I'm old. It don't matter if I die now. I wonder which baby will wear

298

the robe next, that's all. Some little feller not thought of yet. Maybe I'll never know. It's sad.'

'Or little girl,' Vera said.

'Boys run in our family,' Eleanor said gloomily. 'Ham'll have kids first, I 'spect, him being the eldest. I mean, 'e's just a kid 'imself, but they grow up so quick once they start. An' I think 'e's started, if yer know wot I mean. Seen 'is upper lip? Fluff! An' 'e's started *looking*.' She perked up. 'A little girl?'

Vera prodded the smoky fire. 'Well, I reckon I have a good half-chance of being right, don't you?'

Eleanor didn't believe in chance. Life didn't go like a dice rolling. Things happened because they were meant to. 'Vera, is it true?'

Vera wouldn't look at her. 'Christmas,' she said, 'the season of snows and sins.'

'Is it true yer got the gift o' second sight?'

'I think the only nice gifts,' Vera said, with a grunt of satisfaction as the flames caught, 'are Christmas gifts. Christmas gifts, and children's laughter, Eleanor. That's all I care about. All other gifts, talents, intelligences, imagination, I believe they all have a dark side to them. Do you really want to know the future?' She shook her head. 'I don't think so.'

It wasn't in Eleanor's nature to let something go once she'd got hold of it. 'Still, it'd be nice to know, wouldn't it?'

'Would it be nice to imagine yourself dying of a cancer?'

Eleanor was alarmed. 'I wouldn't want that! I meant something nice.'

'The brightest gifts have the darkest side.' There

was something implacable and alarming about Aunt Vera. She always dressed in black bombazine, black bonnet, even indoors. 'The world ends with us. We shall soon be dust.'

'I'll 'ave another cup of tea,' Eleanor said, and turned again to the window. She tutted affectionately. 'Look at those two! Where's she off to?'

Joy went through the garden gate. She ran as though she were flying. It seemed the whole world opened up in front of her, snowy fields stretching to the horizon, the glittering white curve of the canal, the viaduct arching overhead, the church below. Damian giggled as she bounced him. He was old enough to cling on to her lapels with his tiny fists and he showed all his pink gums. His pale curly hair blew against her lips as she ran.

'Careful yer don't fall!' Grandad Clem called. He looked up from his garden where he was kneeling, sowing small salad vegetables in frames, sweeping snow from the glass with his sleeve. 'Now, girl, why do I do this once a week?'

Joy thought he was tricking her, the answer was so obvious. 'So that you've always got them coming up fresh later in the year.'

'Clever girl!' He watched her face light up with pleasure. 'Yer almost give me my faith back in town folk,' he said.

'Your son Kes was born in London,' she said. 'So were you.'

'Can't be all bad then,' Clem grinned. 'But we got out.'

The upstairs window of the cottage, set close under the deep thatch, opened. 'Clement Wampsett,'

Constance called, 'are you still there?' From her black hands Joy could tell she was cleaning the lamp-wicks with vinegar to stop the smoke. It was a task she could do by touch.

'He's planting his salads,' Joy called up. Damian pulled her lip to get her attention. She nipped his nose and he chortled, wriggling inside himself, then looked at her appealingly.

Constance called, 'Tell that old fool ter come inside afore 'is knees fix.'

'He's coming,' Joy said. She nipped Damian's nose again, rewarded by a squeal of glee. Clem stood. His knees creaked, but he grinned at her.

'Yer wot we needed round 'ere. Young folk keep us all young.' He waved after her as she ran on, always in such a hurry. 'Where yer off ter now?' he murmured.

Joy heard Grandma arguing with Peter Pebble as usual inside her little house. This time the roof he had repaired had let snow inside and it had melted on the bed, and Grandma was telling him off that she was more comfy living on the boat. Joy didn't mind them arguing. Eleanor said they were never happier than when arguing. 'Don't worry, yer should've 'eard 'ow she used ter go fer 'er 'usband, my dad. Cor!' Joy understood. Grandma really was good with her hands, whereas Peter Pebble just thought he was.

Next door Aunt Aggie was cleaning gold Christmas lace with roche alum, burnt and powdered, doing it outside because the dust was sifted so fine and made her cough. Damian waved to her for the first time. 'Good boy!' Joy said. Damian pointed to Uncle Nat sitting on a three-legged stool on the towpath, fishing with a rod and line through a hole in the ice.

'He pointed,' Uncle Nat said.

'Yes. He can point and wave now.'

'Then he'll do it all the time now he's started.' Uncle Nat held up a wicker basket and Damian inspected it seriously. 'Fish.' Uncle Nat's long white hair was pony-tailed with a spotted red handkerchief and he had tied a copper hot-water bottle to his tummy. 'The Canal Company stocks its reservoirs with fish. Roach, perch, tench, bream, and carp,' he said as though teaching the names to the baby.

'Fsshh!' Damian bubbled.

'Carp are best, five pounds heavy when they're put in, and don't they grow! During floods some fish escape into the canal. Good news for us. And for herons and otters too.'

'Isn't it stealing?' Joy said.

'Aye, the Company defines anglers as predators and charges for a fishing licence.' The shadow of the viaduct was swinging over him. He moved his stool back into the sun.

'But they don't charge herons and otters,' Joy said.

Uncle Nat reeled in and cast. 'Or me.' He followed her with his eyes. 'First rule of catching' – he called after her – 'don't get caught.' He wondered where the child was going. Then he saw the church beyond her, and understood.

Damian waved over Joy's shoulder. She found the path between the snowy reeds and grasses of the water-meadow. Ahead of her rose St Peter's in its net of bare trees. She heard a gunshot and old Eli, carrying a blunderbuss almost as long as himself, stood up in the ditch. He crossed the meadow and picked up a rabbit by the back legs. Two more hung from his belt.

'Not lived till you've tasted Eth's rabbit pie,' he grunted as he went past. 'Can't talk, busy. See all tomorrow. Merry Christmas.'

'Merry Christmas,' Joy said. Damian waved. She wrapped his hand in a mitten but he pulled it off again. She put it on again and went through the lych gate. Rather than come all the way round to the gate Shane and Jaffrey were scrambling over the wall. 'Hallo!' Joy said. Both boys jumped with surprise.

'Thought yer was old Soames!' Jaffrey exclaimed. The twins were festooned with every bit of greenery they had come upon in the winter wood. They went ahead of her into the church. 'It's Shane's idea, an' 'e asked 'Is Reverend, an' old Soames said yes.' They dropped bits of bark and leaf behind them.

'What's Shane's idea?' Joy asked.

'Greening the church,' Jaffrey said.

Shane took off his cap and bobbed respectfully towards the altar. The Reverend Soames was tall and grey, with close-set eyes and a large hook nose. He looked down at the boys and snatched off Jaffrey's cap with his long bony fingers. 'No hats in church.' The boys scuttled past him. 'No mistletoe! No, no! *Never* any mistletoe in church, Shane, I would have thought you of all people knew that.' Shane threw out the mistletoe as though it were red hot. 'Mistletoe is a parasite,' Soames said. 'Those sinister white berries, Shane. Pagan ritual.'

'I'm sorry, sir,' Shane said.

'What else do we have?' Soames grinned indulgently. 'Laurel, that's all right. Bay, holm ivy, holly, good. And you've found some rhododendron leaves, the latest thing. Good, excellent. Pray place them up!'

Joy came into the nave and gasped with wonder. The twins had transformed the inside of the church into a miniature forest. Sprigs of holly and yew had already been stuck into the high pews. While the twins continued their work hanging laurel from the lanterns, anywhere they could find a place, their voices echoed cheerfully. The Reverend Soames turned to Joy with an avuncular smile. 'So you are Joy, Eleanor's little find.'

'Yes, sir,' Joy said. Damian threw the mitten on the floor.

'Eleanor has a weakness for strays.'

'Yes, sir.' Joy wondered what a stray was.

'She always has,' Soames mused. 'That awful foundling Vera would not have been taken in but for Eleanor, you know. Even as a child Eleanor was . . . wayward. Determined.'

'Vera would have drowned in the navigation,' Joy said.

'Their friendship has continued. The boat people are a strange folk. Now Vera lives in my parish, but she is not what I would call a parishioner.' He crinkled his face into a smile and bent down to what he thought was the child's level. 'But you are not a wicked girl I trust?'

'Yes, sir, I am very wicked.'

'Oh!' Soames picked up the mitten. He looked at it helplessly.

Joy pushed the mitten back over Damian's fist. 'I am very wicked, sir, otherwise I should not have been beaten.'

Soames was startled by the revelation, but eager to believe it. 'Not beaten by Eleanor, surely?'

'No, sir.'

Soames murmured, 'That woman is no stranger to sin. All that Pebble family have a selfish streak in them. They make up their own minds.' He patted Joy's head. 'Well, I trust you are sorry for your wickedness?'

'No, sir, I don't think I am sorry,' Joy said. 'I don't know what I did that was wicked.'

But Soames's mind was still on Eleanor. 'All women are full of sin. After all, 'twas Eve introduced Adam to the apple.' Damian threw his mitten on the floor. 'I wish you'd stop doing that!' Soames said. Joy wondered what he knew about Eleanor. She knew if she asked him he would not tell her because he was grown up and she was just a kid, but that merely increased her curiosity. She thought about Eleanor in a new light, sensing her as a real person as well as everyone's Mum.

The Reverend liked to appear busy and mysterious, and had arranged to be called away. Joy helped the boys hang up the shrubbery as well as she could. She had a bottle of milk kept warm in her pocket and she sat in a pew to feed Damian. He was hungry and did not object to his change of diet after the first few puckers and whimpers. Jaffrey lay down beside her on the wooden bench, folded his cap under his head, and went to sleep. Shane sat across the aisle, his head bowed, and Joy knew he was praying. Damian slept with his hands wrapped around the bottle, giving warning grunts if she tried to pull it away.

'Are you praying for oranges?' Joy called.

Shane looked up. 'No.' He hoped the oranges would come without the need for prayer.

'What for?'

'Yer wouldn't understand.'

'I like oranges,' Joy said confidently.

'No, not blooming oranges.' Shane was embarrassed. 'Promise yer won't laugh?'

'Cross my heart!' Joy crossed her heart as well as she could holding the baby. She didn't take her eyes from Shane's.

He looked surprised. 'Yer mean it. Yer diff'rent, aren't yer.'

'Yes,' she said.

'I was praying for yer.' Shane blushed bright red. He slipped onto the bench beside her and made sure Jaffrey was asleep. 'It's supposed ter be private. I was praying fer 'appiness. 'Appiness fer yer, an' fer us, an' fer everyone in the 'ole world.' He worried, 'D'yer think it's too much?'

'No,' Joy said.

Shane whispered in her ear. 'When I grow up I want ter be a vicar an' 'elp people. That's all I want ter do.' He looked at her eagerly. 'D'yer think I could be serious enough?'

'Shane, what does wicked mean?' she asked.

'I dunno.' He scratched his head. 'Knowing that wot yer doing's wrong an' still sailing ahead, I s'pose.'

Jaffrey woke up. He yawned and squinted through

306

the doorway. 'The *Poca*'s coming back.' The children ran outside. The light was failing already. Shane turned back and closed the door carefully behind Joy. Then he winked at her. Suddenly he was a young boy again, racing ahead throwing snowballs at his brother. But it had happened. He had shared his secret with her.

Joy followed them as fast as she could. Sunset glared brightly, gleaming on the painted cabin of the boat, throwing deep shadows across the land. The channel was icing over and Ham stood on the front end using the pounder, a sort of sledgehammer, to break the thick ice near the bank. The mule, lathered, hung its head wearily. The boys yelled greetings at their father, but Kes was tired. He jumped ashore with the mooring strap and skidded wearily on the ice. 'There,' he said. He hammered the dogleg anchor into the bank to hold the boat. 'That's the sound of no money coming in.' Then he tried to grin, because it was almost Christmas.

'Come on,' – Eleanor hugged him – 'yer've 'ad a long cold day. I got a nip o' malt British brandy fer yer, wot's fer the plum pudding really, but we'll make an exception this once. Yer too, Ham.'

Kes must have imbibed a lot more than a nip, because he was still asleep at four in the morning when the children woke.

They lay whispering excitedly for a while then Ham, elected, swung his legs out of the bed. Damian was sleeping upstairs with Eleanor. She'd slipped him a good slug of gin in his milk so that he would not wake her until dawn. 'An' then they'll kiss an' cuddle all the time, that's wot they always do when they got time off,' Ham said. He looked towards the ceiling. 'We won't see 'em till church.' The fire was almost black and Ham's pale naked figure crept across, avoiding the squeaking board and the sleeping dog, and prodded the flames to life. A row of Christmas stockings was illuminated above the mantelshelf. The other children watched Ham from their knees on the bed. The suspense was almost unbearable. He got a chair and stood on it, leaning on tiptoe across the holly, reaching out.

'Ham,' Jaffrey said, 'yer 'ave got a big doodle.'

Ham said proudly, 'That's 'cos I'm growing up.'

'Mind the holly,' Joy said. She tucked her feet up inside her nightdress, shivering, then held out her hands to the fire. Ham unpegged the stocking on the left.

''Urry up!' Jaffrey said. He had gone through the night and was dying for his tinkle, but he knew how cold it was outside. When he woke earlier and called for help, his father's snores had sounded very distant. The cottage, though it was tiny, was very large and strange to children whose home was on the water.

'It's got funny writing on it,' Ham said. He could read a few words, awkwardly, from mornings here and there at school when the boat was loaded or unloaded, but these letters were very ornate. Holly was twined around them. A robin redbreast stood on the first letter. 'I think it's an H,' Ham said.

'Funny writing means it's done by Grandma Pebble,' Shane told Joy. 'She can't write, but she got a toll-keeper on one of the locks ter write the letters down fer 'er last year, an' she copies 'em.'

Joy skipped the squeaking board and stood beside

308

Ham. 'If it's an H it must be you,' she said.

'Why's that?'

'You're the only one whose name starts with an H,' she said. Ham couldn't resist peeping eagerly into his stocking but she poked him. Impatiently he reached up and handed down the next one. 'S for Shane,' he said.

'It's got a blackbird on it, wearing a clerical collar!' Shane said. 'Grandma knows!' He sounded so excited that Joy was excited too. It *was* very exciting being a boy. They had such dreams for themselves and what they would do, as if anything were possible for them when they grew up.

Jaffrey's name had ice-skates hanging from it. 'That's because they were my idea,' Jaffrey said. The bed squeaked under his excited bouncing. 'She remembered!'

Joy wondered if their dreams would come true.

'Look,' Ham whispered. 'Look, Joy.' He pointed at the fourth stocking. 'It's *you*.'

'She didn't know 'ow to write yer name,' Jaffrey said, awed.

Instead, Grandma Pebble had made a drawing of Joy's face. It was perfect as a mirror. Joy actually turned her head as if the drawing would turn with her.

'I'd rather 'ave that than words!' the boys said. They sat on the floor and rifled through their stockings, pulling out oranges, nuts, sweets and licorice strips.

'It's beautiful,' Joy murmured.

'I got a pot o' strawberry jam o' me very own!' Jaffrey was ecstatic. 'Mum must've made it in the garden 'ere and kept it fer me, special.' He dug his fingers into the jam luxuriously and sat sucking them by firelight.

Shane had been given a small Pan's pipes, lovingly carved. 'Dad did that,' he showed them off, "e's great at it.'

Ham had a tin whistle. 'It's the sort where it sounds 'igher the 'arder yer puff,' he said, longing to try it out. 'Wot yer got, Joy?'

'Girl stuff,' Jaffrey said. Joy pulled out a hair ribbon embroidered with flowers. She gathered back her hair and Ham knotted the ribbon expertly. Each of them had a little wooden animal, a mule for Ham, an elephant for Shane, a rhinoceros for Jaffrey, a giraffe for Joy. She found a little trumpet in the stocking.

'That's 'cos yer always blowing yer own trumpet,' Ham said.

"E means yer stand up fer yerself when 'e bullies yer,' Shane said. 'Ow!' Ham had boxed his ear.

'Don't yer never say nothing against 'er,' Ham warned.

Shane rubbed his ear. He pulled a little tin man from his stocking. 'Wot's this fer?' Joy found one too. The other two had goalposts, and each of them had a straw to blow through. 'It's a game of blow-football!' they decided. They set up the goalies and knocked them over by blowing at the little wooden ball through the straws, almost strangling themselves trying to laugh quietly. After the game they lay on their elbows cracking the walnuts carefully, so that they could use the shells as boats later, with matches for masts and paper sails, and hold races. Jaffrey fell asleep over his jam.

At dawn Eleanor came thumping down and dumped Damian with Joy. 'Merry Christmas,' she said, then went thumping back upstairs. The ceiling creaked like a ship in a gale. Joy took down Damian's stocking. There was a little wooden *Poca* inside for him to play with, a doll that looked like a harmless sort of furry bear, and cotton reels looped together with string that fascinated him.

Dressing for church, getting together, and going there took up most of the morning. The boat people filed into their cold pews at the back, Constance guided by Clem, Uncle Nat steaming because his hot-water bottle was leaking and the children had not told him. The other parishioners, well dressed, living conveniently close to the railway halt, sat away from them. The boat people were not part of the place the village now was, and they never would be.

Joy leant across to Grandma Pebble, who was talking to herself. 'Thank you,' Joy whispered.

The old lady smiled.

Kes sat nursing his headache. 'Richly deserved!' Eleanor said, then gave him a kiss.

Kes groaned. 'Too loud,' he said. He tapped Uncle Nat's shoulder. 'Nat, yer steamin' like yer in 'Ell already.' Nat untied his bottle while the Reverend Soames sermonised. Some of the knots had shrunk, wet. The children enjoyed themselves too much to listen to a word. But afterwards Soames thanked them in front of everyone for their work greening the church. Shane swelled with pride.

They walked back through the snow. At Peter

Pebble's a hot punch was waiting, seasoned with British brandy, ginger, and herbs and spices preserved from his autumn garden. The atmosphere became rather convivial. Kes set out to amuse the children, playing musical chairs with Shane's flute, knocking Peter's furniture over. 'Look at 'im playing the fool,' Eleanor told the other women. Peter handed round paper crowns. 'Still, let 'em 'ave their fun once a year, I s'pose.' Next door at Aggie and Nat's the fish course had been set out, including a carp with a lemon in its mouth, and there was elderflower cordial to drink. Eleanor cuffed Ham, who had both hands full. 'FHB.'

'Family 'old back,' Ham sulked. He didn't like fish anyway. The party moved to Eli and Eth's cottage. Several grown-up guests tripped on the step and had to try again. A single huge puff-pie had been set on the table. 'Rabbit and hard-boiled eggs,' Eli bragged. 'Tasted nothing till you've tasted Eth's rabbit pie.' He checked each guest's chomping jaws. 'Good, eh? Best you've ever tasted.' Eleanor tapped Kes's shoulder. 'Put yer crown on straight.' He gave her a benign grin. She helped him next door. 'Yer behave proper in yer Mum an' Dad's 'ouse,' she warned him.

Clem and Connie had killed and roasted one of their geese. As everyone gathered round the table Jaffrey came in from feeding grain to the little flock. 'I didn't see Daisy,' he said. Everyone looked at the roast. 'Oh,' Jaffrey said.

At Vera's there were cheeses, most of which she had made herself, except the floury foreign cheese the size of a cannonball that Eleanor had bought in

Paddington market. Kes and the boys had refused to eat it, but now they devoured it having forgotten where it came from. Eleanor went ahead to her own house to check that the plum pudding was boiling. Moving very slowly now, everyone started to arrive. They staggered over the doorstep, ducked beneath the mistletoe, groaned when they saw the size of the pudding. But the children whooped with delight, showing off. 'Bottomless pits, yer bellies,' Clem said. 'Yer was the same, Kes.' Today was the one day of the year when the children were allowed to be seen and heard among adults. They assembled round the pudding, gazing, and Joy held Damian up to see.

Eleanor's pudding was as large and black as a bomb. She had used sixteen eggs and more than two pounds of sugar, and decorated the top with white sauce and holly. Everyone sat down round it to eat although they didn't think they could eat any more. Then their elbows moved faster.

'Blooming delicious!' Kes said.

'Now yer know wot I wanted them special Muscatel raisins fer,' Eleanor said, and he chuckled because she had got her revenge at last.

'Yer win, Eleanor.' Kes went outside and played snowballs with the children. Clouds had come up and a thaw was setting in. The snow turned to slush. Water rippled over the ice covering the navigation. 'Good thing it didn't 'appen earlier,' Kes yawned. 'We'll be under way in the morning, an' yer'll be working, an' this'll be no more than a memory.'

The children sat on the canal bank watching it get dark. The gleaming wet snow made the earth shine up under the black sky. They huddled together for warmth. A train curved above their heads, puffing sparks. They hardly glanced up to see the marvel.

'The perfectest Christmassy Christmas ever,' Ham said. 'That's all.'

II

Arthur groaned. He sat with his elbows on the three-legged table. It was three-legged so that it would not rock on the uneven floor, but one of the legs was broken, so he had to hold it up with his knees or it fell over. Rain rattled down the tar-paper windows. A train rumbled beyond the wooden wall.

'End of the line,' Arthur cried. 'End of the line!'

'Don't go on so,' Elsie said busily. She was coping, as usual. Her mother's cousin Gabriel Paz, the sailor on whom they had pinned their hopes, had turned out to be in as bad a case as they. He lived with his seven-year-old daughter in a railway shack behind the Manchester Piccadilly station. He had pointed Elsie to a similar abode even closer to the line. They had not seen or spoken to him since.

Here in this strange, foreign place, Arthur was the foreigner. Worse, he was a southerner. Here in Manchester his face didn't fit. His London accent and cunning manner, and aversion to work, marked him out as a newcomer, a know-nowt, a victim.

Water trickled down the walls and dripped from the roof. He listened as Elsie, holding a blanket over her head, dropped newspapers in the puddles then threw them onto the sodden heap in the corner. The usefully absorbent *Manchester Evening News* was the one thing they had in plenty. Arthur had hawked them on the corner by the station. They'd all got wet and couldn't be sold, but he'd had to pay for them. They got wet because it turned out he was touting them on someone else's pitch. Arthur didn't know the unwritten rules and regulations here. Half a dozen beefy blokes set on him, knocked over his stock, trampled it into the gutter with their clogs, then did the same to him. A policeman had seen what it was about and looked the other way. Arthur was lucky to have escaped with nothing worse than a black eye.

Elsie refused to be downhearted. They would try again. Neither would she let him sell the candlestick, which stood in the corner. She had hung the plate with the blue cat on the wall as though that made this dreadful place home.

Arthur hunched his plum-coloured coat round his shoulders. Elsie sat beside him and shared the blanket. They sat with their heads together in the gloom beneath the blanket listening to the rain. A train began to racket and roar. Arthur cringed. He put his hands over his ears.

He looked so miserable that Elsie laughed. 'Better and better!' she said, hugging him. 'Things can only get better! Are we happy yet?'

III

Lydia said, 'You still haven't talked to him.'

'Not yet,' Darby Briggs admitted. He stood as she crossed the Persian rug to his desk. Lydia always had that effect on him, even though he, not his wife, was the one in charge. As usual she had not knocked.

315

Only servants knocked on doors. Among people of her own class Lydia considered it a bourgeois habit. She looked divine as usual. She wore a complicated and obviously very expensive evening dress in one of the latest brilliant dyes, set off by a simple chain of pearls as perfect as her complexion. The effect was, well, exciting. Darby cleared his throat, overwhelmed by her vitality. He wanted to tell her how beautiful she was. Instead he heard himself say, 'How much did that dress cost?'

'You're tired,' Lydia said instantly. She laid her hand lightly on his arm. 'All your meetings with those boring joint-stock money men—'

'They aren't boring, Lydia.'

'And your heavy responsibility, Darby. Raising a paid-up capital of fifty thousand pounds. All your plans coming to fruition.' Lydia sighed admiringly. Three times she had said *your*. She meant *our*, of course. Without her push Darby would have hung on at Prideau's for ever and ever. Without her he would not have had the guts to borrow to the hilt, as he had. She gave him a smile of admiration, patting his hand.

Darby inhaled the scent of her, grateful that she understood the huge gamble he was taking. Neither of them had been born into wealthy families, but Lydia had acquired class with a passion. He was meticulous in his work, but she had learned to sparkle. 'Darby, you're going to succeed,' Lydia said definitely. He was surprised his questioning the cost of her dress had not angered her, and wondered what she wanted. 'You're going to succeed hugely, Darby,' she said. 'I can feel it. We'll have a house in

316

the country and a park and lots of sturdy tenant farmers tugging their caps, and you'll invite clerks down for the weekend and have your own cricket eleven, like Lord Hillingdon at Glyn's Bank.'

Darby brought her down to earth. 'A country house on that scale would cost two hundred thousand pounds.'

'Small change! You'll be Lord Mayor one day.' She raised her eyebrows when he laughed. 'It will come true, mark my words. I shall insist upon it.'

He squeezed her hand, buoyed by her determination. Lydia slipped onto the couch. She patted the cushion for him to sit beside her. 'You really must speak seriously to Tom,' she said, getting down to business.

'I shall have to beat him, of course.'

'Naturally one loves one's children. I want what's best for my child, what mother wouldn't? But he just mopes in his room all day. I can't stand it.' Confining their son to his room had been Lydia's idea but Darby didn't like to say so. As the head of the household everything flowed from him, not Lydia. 'I will have no more nannies or governesses or tutors in the house!' she said fiercely.

'Yet Tom must receive an education. As a day pupil—'

Lydia took her handkerchief from her left sleeve and dabbed her eyes, making herself tearful. 'What worries me is the harm to your reputation should his cowardice become public knowledge. Your own son.'

'Our son.'

'He is your reflection. What will people think of you? People who matter.' She meant City gossips,

Darby knew. Worse, as a matter of course all bankers kept written character files on each other, like a self-regulating secret society. In a fraternity where a man's word was often literally his bond, tens of thousands of pounds rode on a nod or shake of his head. Trust ranked supreme. In the City it was a truism that a man of known wealth, known integrity, and known ability was trusted with the money of his neighbours. The confidence was strictly personal. Without trust, the Bank of England might not allow him a drawing account. The London Clearing House might not grant him use of its facilities. A single whisper of doubt, magnified, could cause a run on his bank. Without the oxygen of confidence his doors would close and investors would clamour on his steps. Many banks, many men, did fail.

And then there was Society to consider. Lydia was right.

'It's the first thing that occurred to me,' Darby said.

'You've hidden your anger,' Lydia purred. When Darby did not respond she added, alarmed, 'To some people it looks like weakness, no doubt.'

Yet still Darby hesitated. 'Sparing the rod may have made him suffer even more, in anticipation.'

'So Tom's got away with it. He sold his little sister's life to save his own – pushed her into the arms of a monster – *take her*, the little swine confessed to Mr Bowler, *take her*—'

Lydia's voice had risen. Darby stopped her. 'My dear, you cannot imagine what it was like in St Luke's. You simply cannot. You would not believe such conditions as I saw, inevitably breeding such horror. Naturally Tom was terrified by the brute.'

'Thank God for the police, that's all I can say!' she exclaimed.

But Darby had come back from his day in St Luke's with something changed inside him. 'We cannot entirely blame Tom for the way he behaved.'

'Then you are blaming yourself. Perhaps you should! How can you live with that?' Lydia was infuriated. 'You are his father. You have the authority. Use it.' Real tears filled her eyes, tears of rage. 'I'm so ashamed. It's not Joy I care about. Children aren't everything. They take your figure, take over your life. We cannot become slaves to our children, to Tom and the memory of our poor lost little girl, and give ourselves up to grieving for ever.' She said earnestly, 'You know that I am right.'

Darby said quietly, 'Did you love her?'

'You're starting to sound exactly like our Mr Bowler.' Then Lydia said, 'Yes, of course, because she was yours.' She kissed his lips, allowing herself to soften. 'Darby, you must not brood or become trapped by the past.'

'Then I am trapped by the future, Lydia.' He paused. 'By your dreams and aspirations.'

'They're yours too,' she said quickly.

'It doesn't seem to matter so jolly much any more.' Then he pushed her caressing hand away. 'God damn it, Lydia,' he swore. 'We've been married for fourteen years and you still aren't in it with me. I love you. I want more than your caresses. Tom means more than anything in the world to me now, he's all I've got—'

'*Anything?*' she burst out.

'Except you. You know I love you, Lydia, and you do not care.'

She stood, then patted him on the cheek and turned away.

He jumped up and grabbed her shoulder, then let her go.

'All right, I'll do it for you,' Darby said. 'I'll deal with him.'

Lydia took a piece of paper from her right sleeve and dropped it on the couch. 'Don't forget we are dining with Baron Grant and the Sampsons tonight. The Bischoffsheims will be there.' She went to the door without looking back.

Darby picked up the piece of newspaper. It was an advertisement cut, he saw by the print and quality of the paper, from *The Times*.

NO VACATIONS

Dr Thaddeus Gregory's Private Boarding Academy
A Particular Education for Sons of Gentle Folk
Infants to the Age of 18 Years a Speciality
Confidentiality Respected
Discretion Guaranteed
Apply: Dr T Gregory, Headmaster
Green Hill Hall, Wootton Bassett, Wiltshire.

Darby sat at his desk and rang for his butler. After a couple of minutes the servants' door concealed in the panelling opened. 'Good h'evening, sir,' Worth said when his master was silent. Darby had felt uncomfortable with his butler since Mr Bowler had revealed Worth's coarseness and secret life. Now

Worth's airs and laboured aitches grated on his nerves. Not until Mr Bowler exposed it had he known Worth's first name to be Otto, which was unpleasantly foreign. He would have to be let go, although he had given good service.

'White tie and tails as h'usual, sir?'

'Worth, give Master Tom my compliments and ask him to step downstairs.'

'Yes, sir.'

Darby Briggs waited.

There was a tap on the door.

Tom came in. He was thinner and so looked taller, but he was very pale. His hair was long and lank. He closed the door carefully and came across to the desk.

'You sent for me, Papa.'

Darby decided to be jovial. 'I'll wager you've padded the backside of your trousers before coming down, eh, my boy?'

He struck exactly the wrong note. Tom's awful expression did not change.

Darby laid his hands flat on the desk, as though they were cards. 'You didn't look after your sister, Tom. We'll say no more about it.'

Tom did not look relieved. He shivered as though the room were cold. 'Please let me apologise, Papa. Mama has not spoken to me since—'

'I've been thinking about what's best for your future, Tom.'

'Yes, sir.'

'What you need is stiffening up at a good boarding school.' Darby touched the advertisement with his fingertip, turning it round to show Tom.

'No vacations!' Tom said. 'But that means no holidays. I'll never see you again, sir.' He drew a trembling breath, terrified of crying in front of his father. 'I'd rather you beat me, sir.' He stopped. 'Forgive me, Papa. Forgive me.'

'I shall write forthwith to Mr Gregory.'

IV

'You haven't lost your nerve, have you, Jack?' Maggy said, coming in. He didn't go out often, and he was getting rather dull. She leaned petulantly against the door.

He struck her across the face. 'I won't tell yer again.'

She rubbed her face and cried. 'Mr Jerry Lynch.'

'Getting better,' Jack said.

She dried her tears on her skirt, lifted the hem above her waist. He looked at her long adolescent legs, then helped her to remove the contents of the pouches strapped to her thighs. There was a small, vicious-looking herring knife stuck through her garter. She was learning fast how to handle trouble. 'Am I bad enough for you, Mr Lynch?' she smirked winningly, then flounced her skirt and preened herself in his lap. She kissed his chin, then nipped him. Jack stared at her. Her dark eyes had wicked lights, and she was full of fun. The Ratcliff Highway had transformed Maggy.

'Yer don't need ter be so bad,' Jack said. 'Where's that knife come from? I'll let yer off, if yer want.'

'Where would I go?' she said, tearful again, or maybe, he thought suspiciously, she had learned to pretend. 'There's nowhere without you, Jack. I mean Jerry.' She kissed him, pulling his lower lip with her teeth. 'Jerry.'

'Yer'll manage,' he said briefly. 'It's sink or swim in this life, an' by God, girl, yer a swimmer.'

'I got you to thank for it,' she said earnestly, wriggling her bottom in his lap. He hadn't used her, not even for bilking, and they had become lovers.

'Leave off,' he said tiredly.

He rubbed cobwebs from the window and looked into the street. God, how those sailors rolled. The slate-grey Thames was a forest of masts. Jack wished he'd thought of this place years ago. The whole length of Ratcliff was nothing but easy pickings, almost too easy. Sailors paid off from the boats rolled from pub to pub, their pockets burning with pay. Every other house was a tavern, often two standing together. Upstairs was usually a brothel or a dance hall. Every fifty yards some grimy passage led away, full of drunks snoring off last night, the whites of their eyes still blue with gin as they woke. The roadway was a bedlam of sailors with kitbags, beggars, drunkards, oyster stalls and baked potato cans, and queues of gaudy women with crimped, oiled hair buying breakfast. Every meal was breakfast. Negro music drifted up from the cellars, and Chinamen in petticoats hurried on their own inscrutable business between the opium dens.

Jack had let Maggy out, and she had taken to the life like a duck to water. She'd acquired a taste for lifting purses, kerchiefs, watches, loose coins, and by now she craved the excitement. And she was the best he had seen, fast and light with her fingers. Her fearlessness could have taught Smart Arthur a thing or two. She had a slit hidden in the folds of her skirt and always returned with something worthwhile squirrelled inside her leg-pouches. He checked over the pickings on the table.

'I'll see wot I can get for this,' Jack said, impressed. He held up a gold ring. "Ow'd yer get this off 'is finger?'

'Oh, he tried to be a naughty boy,' she said coyly. 'I would've cut it off him if I'd had to.'

'Why?'

'For you, Jack.' He raised his fist and she grinned. 'Jerry.' She threw herself back on the bed and parted her thighs.

'No time,' Jack said. 'I'll nip these up ter 'Oxton. I can 'ave this watch re-christened. Yer a clever girl.'

She yawned. 'I'm your girl.'

Jack shrugged a sailor's pilot-coat over his grey shirt. He'd had his hair razored so short his skull showed through the fuzz. He pulled a nautical cap over his eyes. Flat-soled boots made him look shorter than he was, and he walked like a sailor. He shoved the stuff in his pockets. She was already asleep.

He slipped into the street and put up his collar against the Thames wind. The Ratcliff Highway stank of fish, tarry ropes, rum and mud. He walked with his shoulder almost brushing against the front of the houses, pushing past the people. Seagulls whirled, screaming. Someone held out a potato smoking-hot from an oven. In a knife shop he saw a dagger with the blade engraved, 'Never draw me without cause, Never sheathe me without honour.' Near the Seamen's Mission Jack pushed forward past rows of more shops, bow windows full of sou'westers, shops selling nothing but seaboots, pawnshops showing rows of sextants and bo'sun's pipes, bow windows crowded with ship-models, and ships in bottles, seashells, albatross heads, and swordfish swords. Pub signs clanked and swung above his head. There was an extra commotion in front of him.

It was too late to turn back. Jack pulled down his cap brim as a whistle shrilled, then blue uniforms appeared and the police hauled a man out of a beer-shop. A crowd gathered. Under the new law beer-shops must be licensed, Jack knew. The licences were issued by magistrates, and so were impossible for all but the most upright rate-paying Christians to obtain. Everyone knew the pubs would be next to be licensed, and the hostile crowd swelled to yell support for the beer-seller and his right to freedom. Jack elbowed his way through, and a dirty-faced man in rags bumped him. Jack had seen him here and there.

'Wotchit!' Jack said.

The man followed him, threading through the crowd, trying to sell him something. Jack pushed past a Negro in a black coat with red satin facings and a fiery tie, then a group of Spaniards in red shirts and blue trousers.

The ragged man was still behind him.

Jack dodged into a passageway, but his feet were tripped from under him. A knee was pushed into the back of his neck, his wrists handcuffed. Jack struggled to reach his knife. 'Detective Sergeant Spavins, H Division,' the ragged man identified himself. 'I've been watching you.' He helped himself to the knife.

A uniformed constable rolled Jack over with his foot.

'Bloody spies,' Jack cursed them. He kicked and spat.

Spavins warned him to be still, then booted him in the belly. He patted Jack's pockets. 'What do we have here, Mr Lynch?' He pulled out the gold ring, but through his pain Jack's immediate reaction was relief. He hid his elation behind groans. Spavins did not know his real name.

'I'm looking after it fer a friend,' Jack grunted.

Spavins pulled out the watch, half a crown, a gold chain, sailors' earrings, a piece of fine jewellery.

'Very generous friends,' Spavins said. He nodded for Jack to be taken away. 'You're coming with me, Mr Jerry Lynch. Receiving stolen goods. Possession of an offensive weapon with intent. Resisting arrest. See you in five years.'

He'd said nothing about Maggy. Perhaps Spavins didn't know as much as he claimed.

Five years! Jack knew he'd never see her again.

Chapter Thirteen

I

To Joy, Kes realised, watching her, their time at Cody's Bend was already as far away as life on another planet. To her Christmas was a distant memory. Children were totally ruthless about what happened to them. They thought only of the future, raced forward, living for tomorrow. Tomorrow was their time, he thought sadly. At his time of life much of Kes's pleasure came in recalling the past. What might happen tomorrow to her and to his sons, and to the world they were growing up in, frightened him. Mule-drawn boats could not compete for ever against steam railways, always more of them, always newer, always faster.

Life on a boat could be very hard, he knew. Accidents and drownings were commonplace, especially among women and children. Ropes could snatch taut with the whole weight of a boat, amputating hands or legs. George Scarter had been strangled that way, on a peaceful Sunday afternoon lockside. There was danger everywhere. It was easy to miss a step, fall between boat and lock chamber, and be crushed. Windlasses and pinion gear were not always well maintained. Martha Priggins had been knocked into the water by a swinging balance beam and never came up.

Like nearly all boat people, Kes couldn't swim.

'Bend coming up,' he said, and reached for the tiller.

'I can do it!' Joy exclaimed, white-hot. He blew on his fingers, chuckling.

She scratched her hair as though it revolted her. She wore only a skimpy hat and the sun was very strong. Kes supposed she was itching. Watching her scratch made him itch too.

'Yer got me at it now,' he told her, scratching.

'Why can't I have a bath?' she said.

She was a fierce, determined, different creature, this girl. He couldn't make her out. She didn't let the boys walk over her, they knew better than to step out of line with her, or to go too far in their pranks. Apart from Damian she was the youngest, but with her flaming hair – and her temper could flame, too, if she didn't get her way – Joy's willingness to attempt any task, and her refusal to be put down, meant that Shane and Jaffrey respected her. But she was all girl too. She wanted her own way too much, and she could be spiteful if she didn't get it. Once, provoked by Ham, who snatched Damian when she was teaching the infant to toddle, Kes had seen her dark brown eyes literally flash with fury and revenge. Scrambling out of bed the next morning, Ham had stuck his bare feet into boots that had been filled with canal water. Kes had hoped it was canal water. Ham swore it was piss poured from the po, and he had still not forgiven her.

But Kes hadn't punished her. You couldn't larrup a girl, and words didn't hurt her. Besides, Eleanor had taken Joy under her wing.

Not that she needed looking after, in Kes's opinion. Joy could look after herself. He wondered where she had learned it. Some very tough street, he reckoned.

'Oh, draw my bath,' he said prissily, 'give me my scented soap.'

She just glanced at him, as briefly as a dismissal. Either she didn't know what soap was, or she thought scented soap was the only sort. Yet he didn't think she was putting him on. There was something very genuine about her.

Kes chuckled, watching with growing admiration her battle with the huge ashwood arm of the tiller. The toecaps of her Blucher boots jutted beneath the hem of her leather skirt. The hobnails scuffed the deck as she pushed with all her strength. 'Good,' he said approvingly, 'good lass. That's it—'

'Don't talk,' she instructed through clenched teeth. Kes grinned. The rudder angled into the flow of water, quivering, and slowly the *Poca* began to turn.

'Easy on the hellum now,' Kes said. 'The old bitch'll keep turning of 'erself, now she's started.'

Joy let the rudder straighten. Kes was right. The front end was still swinging. Trees, the towpath, Ham and the mule, swept past in front of the towing mast. 'Why d'you call her *old bitch*, Kes?'

'The *Poca*? Can't live with 'er, can't live without 'er, me darlin'. Just like me missus, she is.'

Joy said, 'Why do you talk stupidly like that about Eleanor?'

Kes was taken aback. 'Everyone talks about their

329

missus the same way, don't we?'

'But you love Eleanor and you'd do anything for her.'

'Yes course I would, she's me best mate an' always will be, but—'

'Then why did you say it?'

Kes gave up. All children were impossible, but he reckoned girls were worse. Boys were naughty, but girls were conscientious, and they were always in the right, and that was hard to live with. 'The *Poca*, bless 'er, is old, me dear. Built at Braunston afore Nurser's Yard were there, she was. Took six of us three weeks, elm bottom, oak sides.' He reached for the tiller. 'Steady 'er,' he warned.

'I know! Don't you dare touch!' Joy was already pulling on the tiller where she had pushed, catching the *Poca*'s turn, lining up the boxmast on the new stretch of pound. The navigation ran straight as a shining arrow into the distance, seeming motionless. Ham and the mule plodded sleepily. It was the first very hot day of spring, and the trees along the towpath were vivid green. Clouds of gnats and midges swarmed in the reedbeds. Ham slapped his neck. Heat and smuts boiled out of the chimney when Eleanor put on coal, cooking up a new batch of lobby. The smell of stewing meat was mouthwatering. Joy and Kes ducked, pulling down the chimney with a rod as the *Poca* passed beneath a packhorse bridge. They coughed in the smoke. Coming from the far side of the arch Kes tightened the chain and the chimney rose up again. Both their faces were smudged with soot.

Joy knelt and dug her hands into the rippling

water, splashed her face clean. That was another way she was different from the boys, Kes mused. Maybe Eleanor had been right to want a girl after all. The differences that made Joy special made all the whole family stand out and realise that they, too, were special.

They had hardly thought of themselves before, taking everything for granted. Grandma Pebble with her paintbrush, Jaffrey working beside her with increasing skill. Shane wandering along the towpath with his nose buried in *The Children's Friend* or *The Cottager*, published by the Religious Tract Society. Ham with his energy and strength, proud as a cock-of-the-walk of his silly stovepipe hat and spotted red silk neckerchief. Kes himself, kindly and more patient than many a Number One behind schedule.

'Why are you laughing?' Joy said. She had such a serious way of asking questions, her eyes fixed resolutely on Kes's eyes, his lips, as though every detail of his response was important, that he laughed louder.

'Why d'yer always ask why?' he said.

'Because then I'll know everything,' she said fiercely.

She saw everything as though seeing it for the first time, he realised. Those eyes!

'No one knows everything. The more yer know, girl, the less it makes sense, in my opinion.' Kes wiped his lips with the back of his hand, tasting soot. He wiped his hand on his guernsey top.

'It makes sense to me,' she said.

'That's 'cause yer don't know nothing.'

'Now you've smudged your guernsey,' she said,

in a tone that said it served him right. A pint-sized girl telling him off!

'Wot's that? Wot's that silly bugger doing still wearing 'is guernsey?' Eleanor poked her head up out and handed round mugs of tea. 'Don't yer know it's a 'ot day, Kes?'

'This is my Jiminy,' Kes said. He patted the guernsey affectionately, as if that were sufficient explanation. He called any old and worn-in piece of clothing his Jiminy, and the more comfortably ancient and lived-in the item was, the more of a treasured friend it became. He was almost inseparable from his patched corduroy trousers, also called Jiminy. His battered leather sailor's hat and his greasiest sou'wester were both Jiminies.

'You've worn your guernsey every day since Christmas,' Joy said. 'And those trousers.' Kes had the uncomfortable thought that, if she had noticed this much about him, how much more had she noticed that he did not know? 'Don't go nagging on at me, yer two bossy women, yer as bad as each other!' he snapped grumpily. Eleanor snorted, winked at Joy, and pulled her head back into the cabin. Kes squirted black baccy-juice guiltily from the corner of his mouth over the side. That was another thing, his chewbaccy didn't last as long as it used to.

'And you really ought to change your hat,' Joy said.

Kes sighed.

They saw a lock in the distance. Ham left the mule plodding and ran ahead with the gleaming brass windlass-crank to 'set' the lock – Joy nodded as Kes explained the words – closing the upstream top gates, winding up the downstream paddle sluices to let the water out. He pushed open the bottom gate and they saw the slimy green rectangle of the lock chamber. 'Trust the mule,' Kes said, picking up a loop of strap and coiling it loosely, 'it knows wot's wot better'n us, girl.' He cocked his hand to his ear as Ham shouted. Ham pointed and jumped up and down.

They looked behind them, warned by a busy wheezing, puffing sound. 'It's Ezra Jones an' the *Lurcher*, by buggery,' Kes swore. Going at least three miles an hour faster than the *Poca*, piling a swell of water in front of her blunt stem, the *Lurcher* swept past them on the left. There was no horse. Instead, a dirty iron chimney now stuck from the cabin roof. It poured smoke and sparks along the towpath. Ezra Jones and his two filthy, broad-beamed daughters stood at the back end of the counter, which had been rounded out. Foam from the propeller thrashed white spray beneath their feet.

'Lookathat!' Eleanor said, outraged. "'E's 'ad 'er converted!' She braced her hands on her hips, still holding the gravy ladle. Joy, hungry as always, slipped her finger round the rim and licked it luxuriously.

'Brentford ter Braunston three times a fortnight!' Ezra Jones yelled. The excitement of steam seemed to have given him extra energy. 'Fifty mile a day! Suck on that, Wampsett!' He waved, and Kes's reply was drowned by the thrashing propeller. The back end of the *Poca* was swept towards the other boat, pulled in by the rush of water, but Joy tugged on the hellum and kept them straight.

'Yer did well,' Kes told her. Then he burst out, 'Look! The bastard's pipped us ter the post!'

It was true. The *Lurcher* would be at the lock several minutes before the *Poca* could arrive. Kes threw down his hat.

'Now then,' Eleanor said, 'that's enough of that language. If it wasn't that bastard Ezra Jones, yer wouldn't mind so much.' She clouted Joy with the ladle for licking.

'Getting our Ham ter set the lock fer 'im!' Kes said, enraged. Joy rubbed her head. She picked up his hat and he calmed down, muttering. 'Thanks, girl.'

'Got ter pay the toll 'ere,' Eleanor said. 'I'll get the papers.' She reached down in and pulled them from the straps that held odds and ends to the deckhead, umbrellas, wood saw, the smacking whip. 'Shane! Stop dozing in them books!' she called along the towpath. 'Need yer fer proper work. It's papers!'

Shane leapt aboard and dumped his books in the cabin. 'These are proper work, Ma.'

'I just want ter be sure the 'keeper don't bilk yer father,' Eleanor said. Sometimes she thought her sons couldn't count much better than she, but she wanted to show she had faith in them.

'Did yer see that engine?' Shane's eyes glowed.

'Don't talk ter yer Dad 'bout it, 'e's already fit ter be tied,' Eleanor said. She turned to Joy. 'Damian's 'aving 'is afternoon kip. Fetch 'im ter me if 'e wakes.' She waddled along the top planks to the front end, getting ready for the lock. 'Them stinkin' Joneses is going ter stink more'n ever now.'

Ham seemed happy enough to help them, though. The *Lurcher* moved through in no time, a fading billow of smoke drifting between the trees. Ramses plodded even more slowly up the slope onto the lock wall, flapping its ears against the pestering flies and thinking of its feed, no doubt. 'Seen its nose-tin on the cabin roof,' Kes grunted, 'knows I always feed it 'ere. Port yer hellum a touch, lass.' He flicked a loop of rope over the bottom gate and took a turn on a cleat. The rope creaked, taking up the strain. As the rope pulled the gate closed behind them the *Poca*'s way was checked. The mule stood still on the lock-side, looking down at its nose-tin some ten feet below it, now the *Poca* was in the lock chamber, then yawned. The tow-strap hung limp. The *Poca* slid forward very slowly now. Ham opened the top paddles a few inches and the swirl of water coming in stopped the boat, holding it against the cool, dripping wall.

Ham grunted at the windlass. The mechanism had gone stiff. 'Lost yer strength, sprog?' Kes called. He climbed up the steps set in the wall, disappearing from sight, then his head reappeared against the sky. ''And me up the nose-tin, girl.' Joy heard him unstrap the wicker muzzle that stopped the mule grazing. She caught it as he threw it down. He tied on the nose-tin, the mule's third feed of the day, fed dry with water to follow. Ramses ate and drank while he worked.

Joy stayed where she was. Down here, in the gloom of the lock-chamber, the air felt deliciously cool. Eleanor's voice came from above, calling Shane over, then she heard Kes's boots on the gravel. It fell quiet. They had all gone into the office.

Ham tugged at the windlass. Joy yawned sleepily. Damian's cheerful grin appeared in the cabin-slide. 'Ook!' he said. He must have woken quietly and got himself on the coal-box somehow, teetering with all his strength.

'Oh, you're so proud of yourself,' Joy said. She caught him and rubbed noses. He jumped his legs around her waist as she lifted him out.

'Ook!' he said, pointing at the sky. Apart from Mama and Pa-pa, ook was his only word. He used it a lot.

'Yes, look!' Joy said. 'Sky. Clouds. Boat.' The water was not rising as it should. She went up the steps, lifting the hem of her dress to keep it dry, and came up into the sunlight and heat. The lock-keeper's cottage was whitewashed, surrounded by shimmering gravel. The office must be round the back. An empty barge was moored by the upstream gate, no one in sight, only Ham cursing the windlass. 'It's stuck,' he said. He doffed his hat and rubbed his arm across his brow, showing off a little.

Joy went over. Ham struggled with the crank. 'Gears need more grease,' he said. This time his hat fell off, and she picked it up.

'I wish I was as strong as you,' she said.

'I bet yer do!' Ham said. Damian took the hat and dropped it completely over his own head.

'Peep-bo,' Joy said. She peeped under the brim. Damian squealed with excitement.

'Ham . . .' Joy said.

'Can't yer see I'm busy?' Ham heaved at the crank with sweat running down his face, then looked round for help. He looked straight through Joy, the girl was no good. Jaffrey and Grandma Pebble in her black skirt were a long way ahead on the towpath. They had stopped to paint or sketch a bird. Shane was busy in the office.

Ham battled with the crank.

Joy said, 'Ham, is it really true there are sharks in the canal?'

'Yes. Why?'

'I want to wash my hair.' She held out a matted length with an expression of distaste, then looked at him hopefully. 'It's a warm day.'

'They'll *get* yer,' Ham said. 'Serve yer right.'

'Not if you keep watch.'

'I'm not keeping *cave* on no silly girl washing 'er 'air!' Ham said, alarmed. 'All teeth an' eyes, they are. Not afraid, are yer?'

'Yes.'

'Well, I'm not,' Ham said. He gave the crank a final bash then stepped back. 'Wash it in the bucket.'

'No.' Joy lifted the hat. 'Peep-bo!' Damian nearly exploded with delight. His face had gone bright red from the heat in there. She waved the hat by its brim to cool him.

''Ere we are.' Ham leant over the lock-gate, looking into the water. A piece of driftwood had jammed the long-toothed bar that led down from the windlass into the water. Only the top of the sluice-gate showed above the surface, partly raised. It could go neither up nor down.

Joy watched the current rise in sullen swirls from below, lapping over the driftwood. Soon the place would be deep below the water as the lock chamber filled.

337

'Quick!' Ham rolled over the railing.

'Don't,' she said, but that just made him more eager.

'Don't tell me don't!' Ham bragged. 'Watch me!' He hung over the edge by his arms, feeling for one of the big oak cross-beams with his feet. Then he stood up and leaned back, hanging onto the toothed bar with one hand, and reached down into the water. 'Give the crank a twist.'

Joy heaved at the handle with one hand. It moved. Damian cried because she had dropped the hat. He reached out for it and she nearly dropped him.

'Stop it!' she said. 'Ham, come out of there.'

She looked around for someone to take Damian. There was no one. She couldn't leave an infant crawling on the edge of the lock. She settled him again on her hip, bouncing him when he cried. He arched for the hat with both hands. 'Shut up!' she said. 'Shut up, or I'll give you a stripe.'

'Almost free,' Ham said. The water had risen to his armpit. He looked up, grinning with the strain. 'Give it another half-go, would yer?'
The crank spun easily for a full half-turn, then jammed again.

'Sorry,' Joy called down anxiously. She didn't understand the mechanism. Black water foamed into the lock-chamber. Yellowish foam rose to the surface.

'Not yer fault,' Ham grinned cheerfully.

His face changed. 'Joy, me 'and's caught!'

'Don't,' she said. 'I know you, Ham.'

'It really is!' Ham panicked, tugging and jerking

his arm. 'I'm caught between the bar and the gate! Turn it off! Turn it off—'

She struggled with the crank with one arm. It wouldn't budge.

She leaned over the edge. The water bubbled around Ham's hair. His face was frantic. He called out but water filled his mouth. It rose over his face. He jerked up like a fish then went down again.

She saw his eyes looking up at her through the water.

She thought of the sharks.

Joy screamed.

No one came.

There was a train in the distance. She heard clankety-clack, clankety-clack, crossing some points. She always remembered the sound.

Ham splashed. He whooped a deep breath.

'Choo-choo!' Damian said, pointing.

Joy gave her shrillest whistle. Jaffrey looked up from his drawing. He looked the wrong way, at the train, then straight towards her. Joy waved her arm, beckoning. He jumped up. He ran in slow motion, miles away.

Joy dropped Damian in the empty barge.

Joy ran onto the lock-gate. Ham had gone over the railing, but she was small enough to duck underneath. The water foamed below her. She swung herself down, standing in a ringbolt. Ham's boots had been too large to fit it. She saw his boots below her now, his legs trailing up through the water, his white ankles.

Kes shouted at her from the lock-side.

Eleanor screamed, 'Where's my baby?'

Joy dropped from the ringbolt. Her hands slid down the greased bar. She plunged into the water. Her skirt flew up round her face underwater.

She went down. Nothing held her.

The water felt icy cold. It pushed into her ears and nose. Her hair floated upward. Yellow bubbles poured past her eyes, then cleared.

She imagined the sharks gathering round her. She imagined them with all the darting vividness of child's imagination.

She was looking into Ham's distorted face. He was terrified. Bubbles snorted from his nostrils.

A feeling of intense relief washed over Joy. No great mouth had seized her.

She reached down, pulling on Ham's clothing. Her feet floated past her, drifting higher than her head. Ham was frantic with terror. His eyes stared like yellow orbs.

His wrist was caught behind the bar.

She pulled, but his fist caught.

His hand was clenched round the bulky piece of driftwood.

She tugged, but he would not, could not let go.

She bit his hand.

Ham shrieked a stream of bubbles. He kicked, and was gone.

The water following him swept Joy up. She floundered on the surface, gulping water, choking. Ham lay on the steps. Kes held out a boathook. He overstretched towards her and almost fell in the water.

He hauled her in.

He and Jaffrey dragged her up the steps.

She choked canal water over the gravel.

'Yer threw my baby in the barge!' Eleanor screamed at her. 'I trusted yer ter care fer 'im—'

Kes punched the lock-keeper. The man fell down. Kes kicked him. 'Saving on yer maintenance, yer bloody skinflint, I ought ter skin yer . . .' His cursing faded away through the boiling air.

Ham came up the steps. He was very pale. He crossed the gravel to Joy and knelt beside her.

'There are no sharks,' she whispered.

Ham put his arms around her, shivering.

'It could've been worse,' Kes said quietly. They were sitting around the lantern on the towpath. Its glow reflected in their eyes. Their faces and hands were pale blurs in the dark. 'It could have been a lot worse.'

'It nearly was,' Eleanor said. 'Suppose we were sitting 'ere, an' Ham 'ad been drowned?'

They could hear cows moving in the field beyond the ditch. A water-rat splashed by the canal bank.

''Oo would've believed it,' Eleanor whispered, turning to Joy. 'If we 'adn't looked after 'er an' taken 'er in like one of our own, our son Ham would be drowned dead in a terrible accident by now.'

'Well I'm not drowned,' Ham asserted vigorously. His courage ran stronger than ever after a couple of hot gins and a plate of stew. 'An' I won't be, neither.'

'That's enough of that talk.' Kes crossed himself superstitiously.

'Saved by a girl,' Joy said, huddling the blanket closer around her. 'I wish I had a bandage on my hand like him,' she said enviously.

'It's time yer was abed,' said Eleanor briskly. 'An' the twins. An' yer, Ham. My Christ, yer might've been lying dead now.' She put her arms around him, but six hours had passed since his near escape, and now he wriggled and looked embarrassed.

'She didn't 'alf bite 'ard,' he said, favouring his bandaged hand.

'We 'aven't told 'er thanks,' Shane said. He put into words what none of the others had spoken. 'Yer saved Ham's life, Joy.'

'Thanks,' Ham said gruffly. 'If I 'adn't frightened yer about the sharks, I wouldn't've been frightened so much meself. I'm sorry.'

Joy stuck out her tongue at him.

She still wore the blanket around her shoulders, not letting them forget. 'Can I have another plate of stew?' she piped up.

'I reckon we could all do with some,' Kes said. There was a rattle as everyone held out their tin plates, forks upstanding. 'Just this once,' he added quickly.

'I'm sorry wot I said earlier, 'bout yer not looking after Damian,' Eleanor told Joy, digging the ladle into the pot for an extra deep portion. 'I admit it. I was wrong.'

'The empty barge was a good place ter bung 'im,' Jaffrey said. ''E couldn't 'urt imself in there, 'e couldn't get out, an' there was nowhere ter fall off.'

'I see that now,' Eleanor said, 'but I didn't in the 'eat of the moment.'

'*She* did,' Kes said.

'Don't go on about it all night,' Ham said, 'yer'll give 'er a swollen 'ead.'

'As fer yer, Ham, I ought ter give yer a thick ear,'
Kes said. 'Stupid thing yer did, that was.' He watched
Joy eat. 'I don't think we've been feeding 'er enough,
Ma.'

'Yer mind yer own plate,' Eleanor said.

Kes helped himself from the ladle. Insects had
gathered around the lantern and he waved them
away. 'Least said soonest mended, I reckon.'

'I'll never forget,' Ham told Joy simply. 'I never
will.'

'It's the fault of them Joneses,' Kes said. 'But fer
them, nothing would've 'appened. But did yer see
the rate they went!' he went on longingly. 'Eleanor,
I'd give me nuts fer steam.'

'Christopher,' Eleanor said warningly.

Kes was unrepentant. 'I would, though.'

'Not that much,' she said coyly. '*I* wouldn't.'

'Just thinking 'ow bad today could've gone gives
me the shivers,' Kes said. He pulled her against his
shoulder. 'We got ter get on, 'aven't we, darlin'? We
got ter do better.'

He stopped chewing, realising the children were
asleep.

He pulled something out of his mouth. 'That's the
same bit of gristle I chewed last week,' he said.

'Waste not want not,' Eleanor said sleepily.

He looked around him fondly at the children's
faces sleeping in the circle of light. 'My,' he said,
'don't all our kids snore.'

II

'Jack Riddles,' Jack whispered to himself. Himself

was all he could think of. He sat on the bench. The bench was six feet long. The cell was thirteen feet long, by seven feet wide, by nine feet high. He sat with his hands over his ears. The walls were of heavy engineering brick, soundproof. There were no pipes to tap messages along. Jack had no idea how long he had been inside, or how long he had been sitting here. St Luke's slipped through his fingers. He could hardly remember Maggy or the bad things he had done, or the good things, if there were any. He jumped to his feet and walked up and down. He wrapped his arms around himself and clung to his name like a drowning man. 'I'm Jack. That's 'oo I am. I'm famous Jack Riddles.' No, that was wrong. 'I'm Jerry Lynch,' he said aloud. The false name boomed in his ears, but no one answered him. 'I'm Jerry Lynch,' he shouted. No one could hear him. Jack had never heard another prisoner.

Jack had never spoken to another prisoner.

Jack had never seen the face of another prisoner.

He was alone, like everyone else, in solitary confinement.

With a policeman for every street and crime rising, public interest in prisons and punishment was intense. Hanging, whipping, transportation, long sentences of hard labour, all had failed to punish, deter or reform criminals.

Mr Jerry Lynch was a model prisoner in a model prison.

In the Pentonville National Penitentiary five hundred and twenty criminals were locked in five hundred and twenty cells, each of them continuously observed. The five great corridors of the prison radiated from the Central Inspection Hall like the spokes of a wheel. A model prison required model warders, men exhaustively trained to swear by the System without thinking about it. The System required no thought of either warders or prisoners, only obedience. Here in Pentonville Mr Jerry Lynch would serve the first eighteen months of his sentence, all that human nature could bear in such a place, soundproofed, heated, well fed, in a solitude designed to instil permanent terror.

The drawback of the Separate System, apart from its great expense, and the impression of softness and good treatment it gave the public, was that it could not be continued for a sufficient length of time to redeem an offender without causing insanity.

Mr Jerry Lynch had been sent down for handling stolen goods. It was his first offence and he was thought capable of redemption. Had his real identity been known, he would have been hanged in Newgate by now.

Many men would have preferred that fate. At least death was quick.

Jack stopped pacing. He stood with his face in the corner, whispering to himself. He hated crying. It made his nose run.

A quiet knock came on the heavy iron door. The warders wore woollen overshoes so that their approach could not be heard. Quickly Jack pulled the brown beak over his face. He was no one. He peeped through the eye-slits, knowing he was being examined through the spy hole. His behaviour was satisfactory. The door opened.

He saw a line of men masked outside. They filed

patiently along a length of rope. Every fifteen feet in the rope there was a knot, by which each man knew his place. Jack, the number clipped to his chest being D23, took his position between D22 and D24. The knot felt warm and familiar. Each man wore the leather beak to hide his shameful face, and held a knot. Each man felt a deep, clinging sense of contentment at being allowed that small comfort.

The line moved off in step, in silence. A word was punished by flogging. They trudged around the cobbled yard like brown ghosts. Surrounded by massive walls, some men held back their heads. They were trying to see the sky. Jack's eye fastened on the campaign medal that the Head Warder wore on his chest, the only vivid flash of colour. Jack could not remember what colour green was.

'Jack Riddles,' he whispered to himself, not moving his lips. 'Green is the colour of grass.' His criminality was being replaced by the System. He could no longer tell what was false and what was true, but he knew he must believe what he was told. He was a miserable sinner. 'Green is the colour of grass,' he whispered to himself. 'The sky is blue.'

After a good meal with white bread the men were led to the treadwheel. Each man was locked in a separate compartment, facing a wooden wall. They climbed up the steps as the steps came down, and another step. The treadmill creaked as it revolved, grinding air. Isolated in their compartments, the men were allowed to put back their beaks. And step. The sweat slid down their faces. After five minutes the effort of climbing the wheel was heartbreaking. After fifteen minutes they were led away to pick oakum. Fifteen minutes later they were led back to the treadmill. The routine lasted for six and a half hours, more time than Jack could count.

Jack thought a lot while he climbed the treadwheel. He thought of himself running through the streets, pursued by policemen. Whistles. Shouts. It wasn't Maggy with him, he carried a little girl on his shoulders. He heard her whispering in his ear as though she were speaking to him now – as if anyone spoke in this dreadful place.

You'll have to take me back h-home, she said.

Jack rubbed his snotty nose with the back of his wrist.

And step. The treadmill turned, rattling.

His own voice saying, *This is all I know. I never was a child. I'll be back. Promise.*

Promise.

Jack knew he wouldn't come back, any more than Maggy would come back. Jack knew he was finished up. The handbar shook under his fingers with the turning of the treadmill. How terrible he had been to that little girl! He would never have realised how evil he was if he had not got caught.

The handbar shook fast and slow.

A message was being tapped along it, from where or to whom Jack could not tell. He picked out the letters IDAY, then only the random vibrations of the bar again.

Jack could hardly contain his excitement.

He walked the knot back to his cell. Iday. Friday. For the first time he had hope. He looked eagerly at the beaked heads around him, but nothing happened.

Whatever happens is next Friday, he thought.

347

But what was it today? Jack did not know. In a model prison, every day was the same. The food was the same, a quarter-pound of meat, bread and a pound of spuds, cocoa, milk, molasses as a sweetener for good conduct. It never varied. Day or night warders punched time-clocks to make sure that their rounds were exactly regular and the solitude of the prisoners kept entirely featureless of variety. Except on Sunday, Jack thought excitedly. Even Pentonville could not ignore the Sabbath. On a Sunday there was no treadmill, no hand crank, no shot drill passing a cannonball up and down a line of men. On Sunday the men stayed in their cells.

Except for chapel. Instead of the usual two divine services of half an hour each, on a Sunday the prisoners were harangued by the chaplain for their sins for nearly two hours. After a few months under the System a chaplain could make brawny navvies cry like children, and work on the men's feelings any way he pleased. A persistent chaplain photographed his thoughts, wishes and opinions on the prisoner's mind. He could fill the man's mouth with his own phrases and language. He was all they had.

But the System could not harm men already made strong by belief. It would not work on fanatics with a cause. They remained defiant.

In the morning Jack waited impatiently, already wearing his beak. He took his place on the knotted rope. The line of men shuffled forward. Instead of turning right to work, they were led to the left, to the chapel. It must be Sunday.

The rows of pews ascended steeply, almost to the

ceiling. Each man sat hidden in his own compartment, a gaslight illuminating him, able to look only to the front like a blinkered horse. The chaplain stood facing them on a three-decker pulpit, warders sitting below him and on each side, holding their pillbox hats on their knees. They looked like alert dolls. No prisoner could smuggle a note or tap a message without the certainty of observation and punishment.

The organ pipes at the top of the room boomed, and Jack sang hymns with the others. This time he listened alertly to the voices around him. Most were from London, mumbling drearily. One or two from Manchester. Then he picked out an Irishman's lilt. The Irishman was singing with a will, broad and clear. An educated man. Now that Jack listened, he could hear other such defiant voices.

Fenians, he realised. There are Fenians in the prison. Before he was sent down, everyone had heard of the Irish Republican Brotherhood's attempt to seize Chester Castle and its arsenal. The Metropolitan Police Commissioner, Colonel Henderson, had informed the *Pall Mall Gazette* that there were ten thousand armed Fenians in London. It was said plainclothes policemen often went armed in response to the threat.

Jack thought, so this is where Burke and Casey are held.

Perhaps it was their voices he heard now.

He was sure of it.

In other prisons, as in the pubs, he knew such men often spoke Gaelic to avoid being understood. That would not work in Pentonville. Jack listened to them sing. He began to grin.

During the responses, their words did not sound quite right. They were passing messages. Their canted response Mercy of the Lord Our God sounded, through the middle of a cough, like *Etty Elob*.

They were using a form of backtalk. Jack was sure of it. Backtalk, born in the pubs, was designed to be used in noisy surroundings. A chapel was equally suitable. In Shears Inn backtalk, *Etty Elab* meant white ball. Jack thought *Elob* might be a variation from another pub, the Angel in Clerkenwell perhaps, or *lob* might mean throw.

Jack closed his eyes. He knew enough. It would happen on Friday, and the signal was a white ball.

He counted the days.

III

At six o'clock on Friday morning, as on every other morning thirteen days out of fourteen – the fourteenth being his day off – Police Constable Alfie Nutting set off for work. It was still dark, for the nights were growing longer. Despite the clouds of rain blowing past the Phoenix Gas Works he scorned the horse omnibus, often slower than a man on foot, and despised the filthy cattle-trucks of the new Undergrounds for the smuts they sometimes deposited on his spotless blue cape. From Waterloo Street to St John's Wood was a considerable hike, but it was a relaxing furlough which he enjoyed at the beginning and end of the day. Gail's brother walked from Hampstead Hill to his cobbler's shop in Burlington Arcade, which was at least as far, and back again in the evening, uphill. He had cobbled

Alfie's boots, and they were very comfortable.

Now that Becky was to marry Edward Farebrother, who lived across the road, thirty-two Waterloo Street was more like a meeting house than a home, with people dashing in and out at every hour of the day, Beth moping for Alex Cox, the puppy soiling the stair-carpet, and no place for Alfie to read his newspaper in peace.

Alfie was back in uniform. The Briggs case was long dead. His face had never fitted between Bowler and Steynes, he reckoned. It happened that way sometimes. Take one copper and you had a policeman, went the old saying, take two and you had a clique. Alfie had applied for the Detective Force, divisional work if he couldn't get Scotland Yard, but someone blocked him at every turn. He supposed that letting Smart Arthur Simmonds and his family slip out the back way would always be held against him. He had taken his return to beat constable hard, as a demotion, but Gail had been delighted to see him back in blue. 'And you can start smiling again, too,' she said, 'like you used to.' She patted his belly. 'And I'll get the man I married back.'

Alfie had put on weight as a detective. It was a pleasure to walk it off. He strode along the middle of Webb Street. Corner-shop owners washing the pavement called out greetings to him as he passed. The terrace houses stretched away in every direction until they were no larger than toys, merging into the pall of London. Smoke was already starting from the chimney of the japan factory, yawning costers were setting out their wares in The Cut market. Alfie knew that half the stuff was pilfered of course, but under the ancient laws of *market ouvert* it could still be purchased innocently. He took care here, keeping wide of alleys and corners. He wasn't wearing his duty armband, but young costers were always keen to prove their pluck by 'serving out' a policeman with a stone or a kick. Rather than cut down past the Necropolis Station he took the broad thoroughfare of the Waterloo Road towards the bridge. The South Eastern Railway curved above his head.

The Thames was dismal, flecked with foam around the landing stages and anchored barges as the tide fell. He crossed onto the broad expanse of Waterloo Bridge turning a halfpenny in his pocket, ready to pay. He could see the toll-gate and toll-taker's hut on the Middlesex side. The gate was already open to pass traffic from the country. Pedestrians were not permitted to walk on the roadway, but must push through clicking turnstiles. But this morning a small crowd had collected on the pavement near the middle of the bridge. Alfie knew it was trouble. He could smell it running as strong and dark as the river.

A policeman couldn't turn back or cross the road on the other side. Alfie walked forward steadily.

Above each buttress supporting the bridge was a bay with a seat in it. The men peered over the stone parapet, the rain dripping from their hats. One man clambered on the seat, his apron and pockets identifying him as the toll-taker. He saw Alfie's uniform and beckoned. 'Ossifer! Shocking!' he cried.

Alfie walked over calmly and stopped. There was a form of words which was always used. 'What has happened here, sir, please?'

'Look, ossifer,' the toll-taker pointed. 'Shocking!'

A City gent pulled back from the parapet. 'Some poor suicide, obviously.' He shook the water from his umbrella and walked on. The others were already drifting away, not wanting to have to make statements, except for two excited little boys in cloth caps. The elder held his little brother up so he could peer over the parapet. The youngster squealed with joyful disgust. 'I can see 'er, the wicked devil! Killed 'erself!'

'Now, then,' Alfie said.

'It's a woman,' the toll-taker said. He had been 'Waterloo' all his life. His father had been toll-taker before him, and nothing that happened on his bridge surprised him. 'Bad 'usband, I 'spect. Usually is. Or bad wife. Bad kids, sometimes. Drives 'em ter it.'

Alfie jerked his head at the kids. They scattered. He took off his white gloves so they wouldn't get dirty, held his helmet on, and looked over the edge.

It was dark. Drains trailed pale spray beneath the bridge. The Thames slid far below. The woman had not fallen as far as the water but had struck the buttress and slid down. 'Always 'appens when they jumps from a bay,' the toll-taker said gloomily. 'Ter make an 'ole in the water yer got ter jump from 'twixt the arches, but they don't think o' that in their state o' mind.' Her legs trailed in the water, held against the buttress by the tide. Her head was twisted horribly, staring upwards, her chin pressed against the weedy stone.

Alfie swallowed. He never forgot a face.

The woman staring up at him was Nanny M'Kenzy.

That business was long ago, Alfie thought. This didn't make sense to him. It can't still be going on,

353

he thought. Monkey killed in an accident, and now the nanny dead. It was as if an invisible cloud hung over those who had been at the Briggs house on that night.

The last he had heard of Miss M'Kenzy she was living with her mother on the Surrey side, not comfortable but not destitute. Yet as a detective, he'd learned that people sometimes killed themselves for the most insignificant reasons, or no reason at all that anyone could find. Sometimes suicides took their secrets to the grave, even from detectives.

'She's a goner,' he said briefly. He pulled back and settled his helmet on his head. Water had trickled up the back of his neck. A Thames River Police landing stage was close by the north end of the bridge. 'You'd better fetch an officer on duty.'

'I sent a boy ter get the ossifer,' the toll-taker said, evaporating. 'I'll get back ter work now . . .'

'Hold it a minute. Did you see what happened?'

'Suicides.' The toll-taker shook his head gloomily – 'I seen every sort of suicide. Yer talk ter me about suicides, ossifer. Why, three quiet types went through one day, paid their halfpence each an' walks on calmly, then the tall one in the middle, 'e takes off 'is shoes an' cries out, Cheerio lads! An' 'e's over in a trice, an' gone. Never found 'is body.'

'But this woman was alone?'

'No, ossifer, that's why I told yer the story. She 'ad two bulky gennelmen with 'er, see. 'Er brothers, I 'spect. They often like ter keep it in families.'

'Did she struggle?'

'Ossifer, she did not struggle.'

'Did she look frightened?'

'She looked nervous but composed. Resigned ter it, I'd say.'

'Resigned to what?'

'I mean ter being with 'em. She looked surprised when they stopped an' 'eaved 'er up. She opened 'er mouth. They always scream when they goes down, in my experience.'

Alfie looked over the edge. A four-oar galley of the Thames Police manoeuvred below. They got a rope round the neck of the woman and dragged her in. Her arms and legs stuck up as though she still clasped the bridge. They put a blanket over her and pulled for the shore. Alfie watched the young officer on duty come through the gate. He obviously knew the toll-taker. 'Hallo, Joe. Usual business?'

'The usual,' Joe shrugged. The two men walked into the shelter of the toll-booth's broad overhang, talking, and the young bobby got out his notebook.

'It wasn't suicide,' Alfie said. 'It was murder.'

They didn't hear him. Alfie returned to the edge. The parapet was a good four and a half feet high, and Miss M'Kenzy had been neither young nor slim. Alfie could not have lifted her. Two strong men, then. She had gone with them, if not willingly, at least obediently. Had she known them? Possibly.

One thing Alfie did know. She had no brothers. Miss M'Kenzy was an only child.

Alfie went to the toll-booth and paid his halfpenny in the hatch. He pushed through the turnstile, which clicked. The bobby looked up. He raised his pencil. 'You see anything?'

'No,' Alfie said, 'I didn't see it.' He turned his shoulder, showing his divisional letter and his number. 'You know where to find me.'

The bobby shrugged. 'Shouldn't be any need. It's obvious what happened.'

'I think—'

'Happens all the time here,' the bobby said. He put away his pencil and accepted a cup of cocoa from the toll-taker.

Alfie walked along the Embankment. It looked all wrong, a broad thoroughfare along here where all his life there had been mudflats. The buildings behind the Embankment Gardens were the old shoreline. The turf laid in front of them was still so new it was patchy, and the tiny trees were tied to wooden stakes. Alfie's footsteps slowed. On impulse – and he was not a man given to impulse – he took the track by the old water gate and went into Scotland Yard.

Bowler was in the front office. The cramped rooms were as busy and crowded as always, there was always something going on here, some operation being planned. Bowler leaned over the desk. His finger stabbed a sheaf of posters with faces on them, he was giving orders to three plainclothes men. 'Villains all. This man's Burke. The Irish Republican Brotherhood tried to spring him from the Middlesex House of Correction in Clerkenwell, and he was moved quick-sharp. Now we've had a tip-off from Dublin Castle.' Dublin Castle was the centre of British intelligence in Ireland. 'Ranger, Spavins, Knowles, you'll draw pistols and ammunition from the armoury.' Steynes stood by the window loading a gun. Men pushed in and out through the narrow doorway. Alfie took off his helmet and went in. Bowler looked straight across at him. Those unmerciful eyes, ice-blue. Alfie stood to attention and saluted.

Bowler said, 'Are you reporting, Constable?'

It was as if they had never met.

Alfie said, 'The nanny's dead, sir.'

'The nanny?'

'Off Waterloo Bridge. Miss M'Kenzy, sir.'

'I remember her,' Bowler said impatiently. 'I'm busy. A woman and three men are loitering near the wall of the Pentonville Penitentiary, acting suspiciously—' The telegraph chattered busily.

'It looks like suicide,' Alfie said.

Bowler stopped. 'Do you know how many bodies there are in this river?' he said wearily.

Alfie shook his head. Bowler did not speak, only looked at him.

'No, sir,' Alfie responded finally.

Bowler sighed. 'I'm not surprised she's dead, frankly. She was unreliable. She had no hope of another responsible position after the references Briggs gave her. She lied, you know. She claimed she was awake on the night in question. She was drunk. But she might have been lying about that too.' He stepped back as men jostled between them, sending the posters fluttering to the floor. One of the plainclothes men bent to pick them up. The florid-faced sergeant called out the telegraphed report. Children had witnessed a man pushing a barrow along a street by the prison wall.

'I don't think she jumped, sir,' Alfie said.

'She was probably drunk when she went over,' Bowler said. He patted Alfie's shoulder. 'Once a detective, always a detective somewhere inside, eh? Can't stop playing.'

'Sir, I—'

'Mr Bowler, sir!' someone called. Bowler ignored the excited shout.

'Alfie, forget it,' he advised. 'Leave it to us.'

The man who had called pushed forward. He brandished the sheaf of posters he had picked from the floor. 'What is it, Mr Spavins?' Bowler said.

'This face, sir. I arrested this man.'

Bowler glanced at the poster. His look changed. He seized it. 'You *arrested*—'

'Yes, sir. Before I was seconded here. But the name—'

Bowler called Steynes over. 'It's Jack Riddles.'

'His hair was cut short and he rolled like a sailor,' Spavins said. He looked from one man's face to the other, then tapped the *Wanted* heading and shook his head. 'His name's Jerry Lynch, though.'

It could happen, Bowler knew. Just recently Horrocks, who had murdered a policeman a year ago, had been found in Coldbath Fields prison. He had been sent down for shoplifting. Without a national identity system – the British would never follow a lead given by the French – it was easy for a criminal to change his name and disappear. But once a criminal, always a criminal, and the police carried out regular sweeps through the prisons on that basis.

'It's him,' Bowler acknowledged. 'He's clever.'

Steynes handed over the pistol.

Bowler went to the door. 'We'll be there in fifteen minutes!' he threw over his shoulder. The room emptied rapidly.

'Sir—' Alfie called. 'Won't you at least investigate—'

'No,' said Bowler.

Alfie walked to work. His sergeant tore him off a strip for being ten minutes late.

IV

'Green is the colour of grass,' Jack whispered. The line of hooded men swayed rhythmically as they trudged the exercise yard. The cobbles were hard through their soft shoes. No concession was allowed for the rain, and their brown prison clothes were black with wet. The jacket did not cover the hips, and each man shivered as he clung to his knot, head bowed. Except the two men a little ahead of Jack, whose beaks moved alertly from side to side. They were looking around them.

Burke and Casey, Jack thought.

It seemed that they had been walking for hours. The line would be marched back inside soon.

Just as the door was opened, a white ball sailed over the prison wall. The white ball landed in the yard with a loud smacking sound, so that everyone looked at it. The men ahead turned around, the line faltered. The ball bounced high, every man's eye following it instinctively. Their beaks bobbed up and down in time with the bouncing of the ball. Everyone watched the ball career off a wall and bounce again. One of the warders tried to catch it.

But Jack watched Burke and Casey.

Their two figures dropped the rope and scampered to the wall. They crouched behind one of the massive brick supports.

Jack dropped his knot. He ran over and fell to his

knees like the Fenian men, with his hands over his ears. A masked face turned towards him.

'Mother of God,' protested an Irish voice.

The wall blew inwards. Jack heard an enormous rush of sound then everything went silent. The wall disintegrated. Bricks flew upward in flames and smoke then fell back down.

Jack ran after the two Irishmen into the smoke and dust.

He scrambled across the rubble. Bricks still tumbled from the sky, landing in silent puffs of dust. One of the men had fallen into a hole, Jack thought it was someone's cellar. The other man was knocked down by a piece of cartwheel and stayed on his knees, and Jack did not see them any more.

Coughing, he slid down the slope.

Jack found himself standing with ringing ears in an ordinary street. A group of children stared at him in amazement. A dog barked. Every window was broken, and slates slid from the roofs of the tenements, exploding in the road. Several houses had been completely demolished, and he could see through the gap to the row beyond. People began to stir, calling, shouting. Many were injured, surely. Jack heard a scream. Someone's copper bath lay in the road. He stared as two of the children picked it up and ran off with it, carrying it awkwardly between them.

Whistles blew. Jack's thrall broke. He ran through the gap, tripping over broken pots and pans, smoking coals, someone's breakfast loaf with the knife still in it.

Behind him the screams were starting up in

earnest now. They followed him like the calls of wild animals through the rain.

Jack pulled out the knife and hugged the loaf to his armpit.

He crouched, staring back.

Ten soldiers could have marched abreast through the hole in the wall. It had fallen in at the top, broad as a barn. The pile of rubble was fifteen feet high. Huge chunks of masonry had been tossed down. Men wearing brown beaks scrambled hopefully between them, but were easily rounded up by the warders.

Jack watched Detective Inspector Bowler climb onto the rubble.

Bowler put his fists on his hips and looked around him.

One of the plainclothes policemen shouted. He had found the leg of a woman sticking out of the rubble, still with the shoe on.

Bowler glanced across, then began to dig with his hands. He tugged something from the ruins, but it was only a mask. He stood with it dangling from his hand.

Then he must have seen something else, because he took a few paces and dropped to his knees, digging over there.

Mr Bowler will never give up, Jack realised. He'll never give up as long as he lives, because this is what he is. This is what he does. He'll never rest, and he'll never pause, until he's done his job.

Jack wished he had a gun.

Bowler stood and brushed his hands. He looked around him, straight at Jack in the shadows, then his gaze moved. Someone called, 'Ten to one we find the bastard somewhere under the rubble, sir.'

Bowler shook his head, then turned away. The whole lot would have to be dug out to make sure. The body of another woman was found.

They might find children under there, Jack thought.

The rain fell heavily.

Jack ran through the maze of alleys and courts, climbing steps, making his way along the narrow turnings towards Clerkenwell.

But he knew he was not going anywhere.

Running was all he was doing. He did not have a place to go. He knew he was going to get caught.

He ran looking over his shoulder.

No one followed him. No one saw him. He leaned back against a wall struggling for breath, peering through the eye-slits. The rain had shrunk the leather.

He crouched, sawing hungrily at the bread, then stopped.

Someone was watching him.

Jack realised that he was still wearing the mask.

He took it off, laughing at his weakness. The prison mask had become so much a part of him that he had not realised he was still wearing it. He dropped the mask and held out his wrists to be taken.

'Fair cop,' he said.

The thickset, white-haired man watched him for what seemed like a long time. He leant on an ivory stick, well worth stealing. His eyes were featureless, white with cataracts, perfectly blind.

He reached out to Jack and gripped his sleeve, then his hand.

'Will you save yourself?'

V

The day started misty, but at last turned sunny as Mr and Mrs Bowler crossed the Bonner Hall Bridge into Victoria Park. It was Saturday and Bowler observed that the men and women walking arm in arm along the Regent's ride seemed mostly of a reliable class. They wanted a quiet afternoon after a hard week's work. The park was huge, but the Northern Metropolitan tramway across the middle of it disgorged more passengers every minute, and the paths became crowded. Hokey-pokey ice-cream sellers and their dogs were getting into the park somehow, plying their wares without a licence no doubt. 'Careful,' Bowler called to his young daughter, who was fighting her little brother for the bag of duck-bread. The two children leaned over the bridge railing, Megan making a spectacle of the backs of her legs to passers-by. Bowler reddened, but said nothing. Mary was too tolerant at home. At work, people jumped when he gave orders. He said, 'Mary—'

'They just want to feed the ducks, Daddy,' she laughed. Her attitude was frivolous, and he hated being called Daddy by his wife. 'They've been looking forward to this all week.'

She was getting at him about work again. 'Oh, and that's my fault, I suppose?'

The last thing Charlie Bowler would ever do in

the whole world was let his children down. They were everything to him. She didn't understand him.

'Nothing's your fault, Charlie,' she said soothingly. 'You're all ruffled feathers today,'

'Dearest, you always spend my day off attacking me.'

'I do not, dear!' Now Mary would adopt her usual tone of injured innocence, he decided. This conversation, which they had had many times before, was not worth pursuing.

'Megan,' he called, hefting the picnic hamper into his other hand, holding it between them. But Mary came round and slipped her arm through his.

'Megan!' he shouted. 'Timmie!'

'He hates you calling him Timmie,' she whispered. 'He's growing up, haven't you noticed?'

'Don't go on at me all the time,' Charlie Bowler said. 'I just want a quiet break in the park, that's all. Don't spend it nagging me. *I* don't enjoy it, even if *you* do.'

'Autumn's coming,' she said, changing the subject as always. They walked arm in arm along the golden ride by the water, as happily married as everyone else. Bowler sensed secrets all around them. Many of these people were not married of course. Some young hooligans chased rolling hoops close by, dangerously fast, and got a telling off from a park beadle. In the distance a football ground swarmed with figures. Factory lads had formed ranks in the gymnasium areas, an instructor in a top hat coaching them in a brisk no-nonsense voice. Timmie, whom Mary had dressed to go out in his smart new skeleton suit, begged to hire a rowboat on the lake. The fountain had been turned on, sending a plume of spray between the islands. Mary would not like the idea.

'Don't get wet, and you're not to get your sister wet. Is that clear?'

'Oh, Daddy, no,' Mary said, mortified.

'Clear, Father,' Timmie said in a flash.

'Megan?'

'Yes, Father, of course.' She could be dignified when she wanted. 'I'll look after him.'

'Off with you.' He flicked them a couple of pence and the children ran off. 'I'm reduced to buying peace and quiet.'

'In your day children knew their place.'

'Do I sound like that? Well, we did.'

'I love you, Charlie Bowler,' Mary said. She spread the blanket on the grass and they sat. She arranged her dress and put up her parasol, though the trees shaded them from most of the sun. 'I said I still love you, Charlie Bowler.'

'I know,' he said.

'Say it.' She blew in his ear when he did not respond. 'Did you hear me properly, now?'

God, she sounded Irish. He noticed how thick her ankles were, how rounded her face was becoming. 'You know I love you,' he said.

'That's better,' she yawned comfortably. 'What have you got to worry about on such a beautiful day?'

Bowler lay back and closed his eyes. His hands were balled into fists. 'Nothing,' he said.

She watched him, wishing he would worry about the children more. There were hundreds of boats on the lake and she could no longer tell which was their children's. She wished he would talk to her, but Charlie was asleep. The sun moved between the trees, hot now. Mary wore a broad straw hat that he had not noticed, and he had not noticed her new dress either. She held the parasol to shade his face from the sun. She was so unhappy that she did not know what else to do for him.

She might get up, and walk away. But she would not do that because of the children. And her marriage vows were sacred, for ever. And she knew that everything that had gone wrong was her fault. The man she had married was hardly in her life any more, no more than a lodger, a sort of favoured stranger in her home. She and the children saw him but hardly spoke to him, and somehow their words never meant anything new. Charlie worked so hard, and left her feeling guilty for taking up his precious time, and letting the children do so.

Mary didn't know what to do.

Tim and Megan raced back for cheese sandwiches and bullseyes. 'Don't wake your father,' Mary smiled. They ran off to the bandstand. A military band was playing, red and silver.

There was a smell. Mary looked at the river behind her. The foul stagnant water was lined with commercial wharves and factories along the far side, so she supposed it was a canal. The lock gates opened and a plodding nag dragged forward a huge filthy juggernaut, a floating slum strung with dirty washing and equally dirty children. The cargo smelt like rotten eggs. The children jeered at the well-dressed people taking their leisure along the grassy bank, and the woman steering the boat drank from a bottle. Thank goodness canals were not allowed to be built through parks, Mary decided. Everyone knew that they were the open sewers of industry. One hundred thousand people of the lowest sort led an animal existence afloat on the water, swearing and drunkenness their ruling passions. Some scamps dropped stones on the boat as it was dragged from sight below the bridge.

She wished Charlie had chosen somewhere nearer the bandstand. The scarlet uniforms looked very jolly.

Someone called her name. Mary used her hat brim to shield her eyes from the sun. A man crossing the lock-gates waved. He jogged heavily towards them despite the heat.

'Charlie,' she sighed, and woke her husband. 'Work.'

Bowler sat up. 'It's George Steynes,' he said, awake as quickly and completely as a cat. 'I told him we'd be somewhere between Bishop Bonner's bridge and Longford lock.'

'Charlie,' she said, 'why did you do that?'

'I'm sorry.'

'You're not sorry,' Mary said.

Steynes came up. He was red-faced and panting. 'Guv, Mrs Bowler,' he apologised, then wiped his brow. 'Sorry, Guv, but I knew you'd want to know right away. Joy Briggs, sir. We've found what happened to her.'

'Well?' Bowler was on his feet.

'I think you'll want to see for yourself, sir. I've got a cab waiting in Old Ford Road, sir. We're just within the four mile cab radius of Charing Cross, thank God—'

'What happened to her?' Mary said.

Steynes glanced at Bowler for permission. 'She's dead, Mrs Bowler.'

Mary covered her mouth. Her children ran up to her from the bandstand, tugged her, then, when she did not respond, set about the sandwiches.

Bowler and Steynes got in the cab. 'Lisson Grove,' Steynes called up. The two men travelled in silence.

Then as they turned into Grove Road, Bowler roused himself from his reverie. 'Still no word of Jack?'

'Disappeared like a puff of smoke, sir. But we'll get him. They can't hide. He's holed up in some little lodging-house somewhere but he'll show his true colours sooner or later. They always do.'

Bowler grunted. Three people had died in the explosion, and three more had died of their injuries shortly afterwards. Forty people had been seriously injured. Queen Victoria had sent grapes to the homeless victims. One street had been demolished, eight others damaged. It had taken the police three days to dig out the rubble and establish that Jack's body was not underneath. Descriptions of him had been telegraphed as far as Manchester and Liverpool, but despite constant false reports no one had seen him, no one heard of him.

'He's got away,' Bowler said.

'We both know his type, sir. He'll be arrested for petty theft or knifed to death in some tap-room brawl before the year's out.'

The cab stopped on what seemed to be a bridge,

but it had only one parapet. Bowler realised they were over a canal tunnel that had been driven into Maida Hill beneath them. Steynes pointed towards a broad brick cylinder poking from the middle of a children's playground. At first Bowler thought it was a chimney, but it was too squat. Nearby boys played on a seesaw made out of an old shop fascia board, squealing with excitement. The girls skipped ropes quietly, or played jacks. A workman saw Bowler's approach and stood.

'It were I,' he said, rubbing his nose across the back of his wrist. 'I found 'em. Reward, is there?' He fetched a ladder and leaned it against the top course of bricks. 'Maintenance. Inside. Got ter watch yerself the little buggers don't shin up 'ere,' he said.

Bowler went up. The top of the cylinder was closed off with heavy iron bars to stop hooligans falling in or throwing things down. A grille had been unlocked and hinged back. Bowler peered down into the dark. 'Well?'

'Forty foot straight down,' the workman called cheerfully. He scrambled up the ladder and sat swinging his legs unconcernedly over the edge. 'It's a ventilation shaft. The Regent Canal's down there, in a tunnel. That's 'ow they put in the tunnel, see. Dig the air wells first, then drive the tunnel out each way from the bottom, 'til all the shafts is joined. Sometimes they miss the line,' he said hopefully, 'an' then it's more work fer everyone.'

'What am I looking for?'

'I'm a good citizen,' the workman said. 'Do anything ter 'elp the police I will, an' get me reward.'

'Sixpence if it's worth it and a black eye if it's not.'

369

'I'll get the lamp,' the man said cheerfully. 'Yer'll see.'

Bowler took off his jacket and swung himself down. Rust showered past him. His feet found iron rungs set in the brickwork. A miner's hat with a candle in its lamp was put on his head, leaving both hands free to climb down.

The air was chill and dank after the heat above. The candle seemed to cast no light on the sooty mortar, his eyes were still used to bright sunlight. Bowler tried to keep his shirt clean. He came to the bottom rung and stepped by touch on to a narrow platform. He felt a boathook propped against the wall.

Slowly his sight cleared. He made out black water glinting about eight feet below him. It rippled as though it was alive. He heard water pouring down from the tunnel roof nearby, the source of the ripples.

Distantly he heard the cries of the children playing far above him.

Bowler knelt.

By the candle's glimmering glow he discerned a niche in the tunnel wall. The niche was arched at the top. It was just large enough to contain someone the size of a little girl, crouching.

At the back of the niche he saw a pair of pink lambswool slippers.

The slippers had been left arranged neatly side by side, left to left and right to right, as though the wearer expected to return any moment.

Bowler listened to the darkness.

He drew a deep breath. He did not bother to probe the canal bed with the boathook. Even her

370

bones would be consumed by now.

At arm's length his boathook snagged the slippers. Bowler drew them in and held them to his chest.

It was a long climb up into the sunlight.

Bowler sent Steynes back to the Yard. He gave the workman sixpence. The man bit it doubtfully.

Bowler glared at him in a rage.

He made his way through the playing children and walked up Grove Road to Abbey Place. At the gate two beadles in wine-red frock coats were now employed to turn back undesirable elements from the neighbourhood. An immaculate appearance was obligatory for a gentleman. They looked doubtfully at him. Bowler went up the drive to the Briggs house. Belatedly he made sure his jacket and necktie were straight, and rang.

A butler he did not recognise opened the door.

'Who are you?' Bowler stared. 'Where's Otto Worth?'

'I'm Prettiman, sir. Mr predecessor has gained other employment.'

'Detective Inspector Bowler.' Bowler went in. 'Is Mr Briggs here?'

'Of course not, sir. It is Saturday afternoon. He is always at the office at this hour.'

'My compliments to Mrs Briggs and I'll speak with her, if I may.'

Prettiman bowed. 'I'll enquire if my mistress can see you, sir.'

'Then you clear off,' Bowler said.

Prettiman surprised him. 'You can rely on my discretion, sir.' He closed the door, bowed again, and went upstairs. The newel post had been perfectly repaired, Bowler observed, and the wallpaper changed from Chinese to an Arabic pattern. The reception room was open and he snooped. She would meet him in here, of course, and he planned how it would go. He was in a formal drawing room, starched, perfect, unrevealing. The chairs looked hard. Lydia – he still could not think of her by the name he must address her by, Mrs Darby Briggs – Lydia must receive her Morning Calls in here. He imagined her as formal and rigorous as the room, wearing indoor clothes while her Society callers sat uncomfortably in outdoor hats and coats with their calling cards, making the fifteen minutes of polite conversation that good manners required.

How I despise these people, Bowler realised. Everything flows from them, the rest of us could not exist if they did not, they are the glue of our country. But I do despise them, these people I work for.

Bowler stood by the fireplace. Mrs Darby Briggs would sit on a chair. There was a routine form of words, stiffly delivered so that she would not break down or faint. Mrs Briggs, pray sit, I have some very bad news for you.

She would know what it was. They always did.

He looked around the room, admiring its cold perfection.

He heard a footstep and turned. Lydia came through the doorway towards him. She stared at his expression. 'Mr Bowler, how envious you look!'

'Lydia,' Bowler said. He gripped her elbows then pushed her away and stepped back.

Lydia rubbed her elbows. Her eyes did not move from his.

'She's dead, isn't she, Mr Bowler?'

'Yes, Mrs Briggs.'

'I knew it from the very first.' She would not sit. 'A mother does know, it is an instinct with us.' She shrugged emptily. 'You would not understand.'

'I do understand, Mrs Briggs,' Bowler said.

'You need not call me by that name. It is my husband's, not my own.'

Now that he had permission to use her Christian name he could not say it. 'I will,' he said.

She looked around the room with an expression of hatred, then turned on her heel without a word. He watched her walk upstairs and remembered the layout of the house. The family rooms were on the first floor. She did not say goodbye.

Bowler followed her up.

He found Lydia in the parlour. This room was cluttered and homely, with soft furnishings and gilt pictures clustered everywhere on the walls. Photographs were set in heavy silver mounts. She picked up one of a baby sleeping in her arms. Babies all looked the same to Bowler. Presumably it was the dead girl.

'Now she can be buried at last,' Lydia said, and turned it to the wall.

'She can be legally declared dead without a body,' Bowler said. He held out the slippers. 'They were found in the Maida Hill tunnel. The fiend must have taken her in there and left her to—' He could not say that word either.

'Die,' Lydia said. Bowler caught a glimpse of himself in the mirror, and realised the figure he cut. No wonder she treated him with such contempt.

373

There was a smudge of soot on his cheek, another on his collar. He coloured, embarrassed in front of her.

'I would not have visited you alone, ma'am, brought you this terrible news alone. I thought your husband was here—'

'Liar,' she said. He reminded himself that she knew her effect on men, and enjoyed it.

'I wanted to see you,' he said.

She shook her head. 'No, Mr Bowler. You wanted to see my reaction.'

'Perhaps I did.'

'You watched me in the same way the first time we met. Are you suspicious of everyone? Always looking. Examining. Searching. Don't you ever take anything for granted, Mr Policeman? Don't you ever stop working?'

'I am my work, Mrs – Lydia.'

'My husband is like that too. What name does your wife call you?'

The last person Bowler wanted to think of at the moment was Mary. 'Let's not talk any more of husbands and wives,' he said. Lydia waited, and he lied again. 'She calls me Charles.'

'Charles. And you love her.'

'Yes.'

'Are you faithful, Charles?'

'Always.'

'Always is not the same as yes,' she said.

'When I was called to this case, my first thought was that it was your husband who killed Joy,' Bowler said. 'Paid to have the problem go away, perhaps.'

'Darby! My God. He'd never have the nerve.'

'When children are hurt it is usually by someone they know.'

'How appalling, if that's true.'

'Yes.'

'But of course Darby is innocent.'

'None of us is innocent, Lydia. I believe he thought of it. I don't think he did it.' He looked at her steadily.

'At least now we know what really happened.' Lydia took the slippers calmly, then held them to her. Tears squeezed from her eyes. 'I'm sorry. Stupid. Emotions sneak up on you. One doesn't know what one felt until—' She sat. 'Until it is too late.'

'I don't think she suffered,' Bowler said. 'The water would have been hardly above freezing. She would have felt nothing.'

'There's nothing more one can say,' Lydia said.

'Shall I find Mr Briggs at his office?'

'The bank? Yes, he almost lives there.'

Bowler was acutely conscious of the soot on his collar. 'I trust the business goes well.'

She sighed. 'The economy has been booming for three years. In such circumstances it would be difficult for a banker to put a foot wrong, wouldn't you suppose?'

He leaned towards her, but she looked away.

'I am what is known as a City widow,' Lydia said. 'I am married to a man who is married to the City as much as to me.'

'If that's enough.'

'Of course,' she said, with a gesture for her house.

What a deep lady she was, hard as boiler-plate, invulnerable. Bowler knew Lydia was as high above

375

him as the moon above the earth. She regretted nothing she had ever done to get where she was, he was sure. His sort would never have her. That she was unattainable made him want her more.

He took his leave of her and went to the door, then turned.

'In answer to your question, Mrs Briggs,' he said, 'yes, I have always been faithful to my wife.'

Lydia smiled. Bowler closed the door behind him and left.

Chapter Fourteen

I

'You know that running is all you are doing, Jack,' old Samuel called up the stairs. Then he simply called, 'Stay.'

By the light of the candle, Jack got ready to leave the little cottage in Clerkenwell Green. This was the first bedroom he had ever called his home for more than a month of two. It was warm and dry, and safe, and he was welcome. He had no reason to go and every reason to stay. He had been here a year and a month, but he could not stay for ever.

Every day he remained put Samuel in danger. Jack had learned to think of someone other than himself. It had taken Samuel, who could not see him, who was not afraid of him, to teach Jack hope, to show him himself. Samuel had not known he had brought a criminal into his house, and had not cared. 'Eyes don't know a man, Jack,' he'd said. 'You know what you are.'

'What am I?' Jack growled.

'A pot waiting to be filled,' Samuel said.

It would have taken a moment to cut off Samuel's white head with the breadknife, bury his body and white staring eyes beneath the floorboards. Then Jack would have hidden up in the cottage for two or three days, until the smell got bad, and gone on the run again.

He would have been caught and hanged long ago.

For the first week he had jumped at every knock on the door. For a fortnight his balls ached for Maggy, in fact for any woman at all. For a month the blind man fed him, trusted him, asked him no questions, and waited.

'I can't pay yer no rent,' Jack said gruffly.

'Then give me this.' Samuel reached over without moving his eyes and put a book on the table in front of Jack.

'Don't read much!' Jack said.

'I don't read at all,' said the blind man.

Jack had been embarrassed to read to him aloud. But the stories were simple at first, with pictures of men with the sun around their heads. Later they were more difficult, by Bunyan, Blake and Dante.

Until the cataracts blinded him Samuel had been one of the four hundred or so missionaries of the London City Mission. He was no fool and Jack could not fool him. Samuel had worked in the worst places in London, among the most vicious and debased classes of the people where a frocked priest would not dare show his face. As a missionary Samuel still visited some of the several thousand men, women and children who would die in London that year with no other succour but his hope. Once or twice Jack accompanied him, his face well wrapped in a muffler, but going out was fearfully dangerous for him, and always would be.

378

And if he was caught, Samuel would be sent down too, as his accomplice, for hiding him.

This fate, not his own but Samuel's, had weighed increasingly heavily on Jack's mind.

'Can you save yourself?' Samuel had asked long ago. Jack knew the answer was no. In England he would always be a criminal. Here his past would always hang over him, he would never be free.

'I have spoken with my friend Captain Bill Cozens of the *Hougoumont*,' Samuel said. 'I could not afford to pay a passage to Australia, you understand, even steerage, but he has space for a working man. Ninety days to Freemantle. If you must go.' He had shaken his head pleadingly. 'But—'

'You know I must go,' Jack said.

Dawn was still hours away. The cottage stairs were dark. Samuel ate in the dark, bathed in the dark, shaved in the dark. Jack's candle was the only light, and as he packed the solitary flame illuminated the walls. They were a mass of ornamental tracts and religious samplers embroidered by Samuel's daughter, long dead. When he first arrived, Jack had drawn curly French moustaches on the faces of the saints, and he could not now erase them. The old man had never seen them and would never know.

Jack folded his blankets neatly on the bed and slipped his few possessions into the kitbag, razor, brush, spare striped shirt. Then there were the books, and tracts to be handed among the passengers.

'Stay,' Samuel called to him again. 'You're leaving me alone.'

Jack swung the kitbag over his shoulder and went downstairs. He hugged the old man, then went to the door. He put the candle on the table and took a breath to blow it out.

'Jack,' Samuel said, resigned. He held out a sturdy cloth-bound volume with both hands. As soon as he touched it Jack knew this was something real, he'd finished with ideas. He flicked through the pages with growing excitement. This was a practical work about real, honest things that he would need to know. 'Husbandry, farming practices,' Samuel said. 'It will save your life, if you work hard. Man does not live by bread alone, but bread is necessary first, where you are going.'

Jack hugged him again. 'I'll always remember you, Samuel,' he promised. He blew out the candle and left.

Jack walked down through Clerkenwell with the long, open stride of a man with nothing to fear. But his footsteps made no noise. He had learned much, but forgotten nothing. He found his way easily in the dark, crossing lighted streets quickly but without haste, following the gleam of the Thames. Wapping High Street, overhung with ship's chandlers and victuallers, was so narrow that two carts could not pass. The huge warehouses towering ahead of him fell back to reveal the open water of the Gun Dock, and the masts of the *Hougoumont* which would carry him to a new life.

He passed a baker's window, brightly lit even this early by the flames of the oven. A woman's voice said, 'It's you!'

Jack stopped.

'It *is* you, isn't it, Jack?' the woman said uncertainly, coming out of the alleyway.

Jack turned. Maggy wore a brilliant purple dress. She had painted rouge on her lips and cheeks, and her eyes were blackened with kohl. She carried a tassled purse. He could see it was heavy.

'I looked for you everywhere,' Maggy said.

II

Joy slept. She flew. The brilliant blue of the navigation and the *Poca* with its tiny waving figures fell far away below her.

She saw herself standing on a bridge on a hill. The sun had gone in but moonlight glowed around her everywhere. The canal pointed towards a faraway building, ice-white in the moonlight, topped with towers and spikes. *Ice-cream*, she remembered, but the thought flew away from her before it could be captured.

She held out her arms and rose into the air. The streets twisting and turning beneath her were lined with trees and big houses. She fell towards them, gliding towards a single attic window.

She found herself kneeling in there, looking out through the glass.

She wore her dressing-gown and pink lambswool slippers. The windowsill was cold and hard beneath her knees and her hands. The room was familiar and true, every detail perfectly remembered, real. Her favourite toy lay on her pillow.

'Tom,' she called. Everything, everyone was still here, still living inside her exactly as she had seen them and felt about them, and they always would be as long as she lived.

Nothing would ever change here. It was the place called childhood.

In her sleep Joy said aloud, 'T-T-Tuh—'

Then she cried out, *'Tom!'*

Far below, a man arrived next door at number thirteen. The light showed his face as he went inside.

Joy woke with a scream.

Part Three

The Heiress

Chapter Fifteen

I

'Moira!' Joy shouted gleefully. She swung up the ladder from the *Poca* onto the wharf and ran after the others. She wore her hair in a fiery ponytail, a knotted yellow kerchief at her neck, a white blouse, and a black skirt to her ankles. Damian scrambled after her as fast as he could. 'Wait for me!' he yelled. His cottony curly hair flew behind him as he ran across the wharf on twinkling legs, his face scarlet with the effort of catching her. Eleanor, plodding back to the Furnace wharf behind the cheesemaker's dog-cart, watched them with her heart in her mouth. Damian was just six years old and not the superman he thought he was. Joy ran backwards in front of him, dancing beyond his reach but obviously ready to catch him if he fell. The wharfside was treacherous with scattered coals and cinders, wheelbarrows and workmen everywhere. Teams of pit ponies snorted steam from their nostrils, dragging huge coal-wagons along the shiny steel rails of the gangway, but Joy weaved between them expertly, leading him on, keeping him away from danger.

He trusts her – and so do I, Eleanor realised, staring longingly through the rusty railings. I love her the same as my own flesh and blood. But terrible accidents happened to children in dockyards. Eleanor's own little brother, hardly older than Damian, had been killed under a load of hundred-weight sacks tumbling from a broken gantry. She could still remember how slowly they seemed to fall, and then the terrific dust billowing up, and then the noise.

But nothing will happen, Eleanor thought, watching Joy's dress swirl. She's too alive. She won't let Damian get so much as a scratched knee. 'Oh, to be young again!' Eleanor said aloud.

Damian ran out of puff. Joy let him catch her and swung him up.

'Moira?' he said hopefully.

'You're too young,' Joy told him, rubbing noses, then slipped her handkerchief from her sleeve. 'Blow!' Damian had learned to blow into the handkerchief and fart at the same time, which amused him endlessly, for as long as he could keep it up. 'Dirty little bugger,' grunted one of the coal-heavers on piecework, pushing past with no time to spare.

But she's right, Eleanor thought. This is important. This is what being alive is about. These tiny moments that make a life worth living.

Joy put Damian down. He gave her his hand without thinking or looking, and she took it in the same way. Eleanor watched her walk Damian to his brothers, who waited by the building with no windows at the dock gates.

'Moira,' Ham said, so glumly that Joy laughed at him. For once Ham was not referring to a girl. The Moira pits were everywhere beneath their feet and under the canal. Shafts and tunnels reached out below the village and peaceful cow-speckled fields as far as the eye could see. From these mines came the finest glossy handpicked house-coal in England. The Midland Railway had bought the Moira nearly thirty years ago to run the canal down and steal its trade. Steam boats were banned, bridges and tunnels neglected. But still the Moira quietly sent coal all over the kingdom through hundreds of Number Ones, their families and butty-boats. Hidden in the railways' glamorous shadow, the canal network sprawled for thousands of miles, from the English Channel to the Bristol Channel to Liverpool, intricately inter-connected, a secret world, another country.

The cart-dog stopped to sniff a lamp-post. It growled when Eleanor prodded it with the stick. "Ere, this dog don't like me,' she called.

'I don't like Moira,' Ham said. He gave the dog a kick to help his mother and it bit his boot.

'Yer don't like learning,' Shane said. He carried his own slate for rubbing-out work and his own exercise book for neat.

'I don't need ter, brown-nose,' Ham said, bunching his fists.

'He likes girls,' Jaffrey said. Over his shoulder he carried the big bag with the towels in.

'I'm not frightened of yer, Ham,' Shane said, but he was. Ham shaved. While Shane saved pennies for his exercise book and dip-and-scratch, Ham bought his own razor. He kept the blade free of rust with grease from his nose. He shaved for hours, and carried the razor in his inside pocket all day – whether from pride, or to stop Shane or Jaffrey stealing it for their own hopeful use, or as a weapon, Shane was not sure. Ham was much more belligerent with his brothers lately. Shane looked at Joy.

Joy said to Ham, 'Did you need to call him that?'

'Ay, but I wasn't thinking,' Ham said, instantly contrite with her. 'Sorry, Joy. Sorry, Shane.'

'I'm no brown-nose,' Shane said.

'Shut it, Shane!' Joy said.

'Brown-nose,' Damian trilled.

'You shut it too,' she said, then turned on the others. 'Now look what you've started, you two, teaching him.'

'If only I was young again!' Eleanor said. 'Yer as much a mother ter 'em as I am.'

Joy saw the roundels piled on the dog-cart. Her eyes lit up hungrily. 'Cheeses,' she said.

'Business,' Eleanor said, putting the tarpaulin over them protectively. Just as there was a market for Moira coal at many of the villages they would pass through, Eleanor had discovered that she could bolster her housekeeping by selling Moira cheese on the side. Long famous locally, the cheese went down equally well at village stores along the Oxford canal, in Banbury, at Louse Lock for Oxford – two roundels there last time – the little shop by the bridge at Abingdon on the Thames always took some, then any of a hundred family businesses along the Wilts & Berks navigation. Last trip Eleanor had sold out at Swindon, long before reaching the Kennet & Avon Canal. When Shane totted the shillings and pence up Eleanor was amazed. She had doubled her money.

She felt rather bad about it. 'I didn't mean ter overcharge them,' she'd said. This time, meeting around the lantern in the increasingly cramped cabin of the *Poca*, she and Kes and the children had talked long and hard about what she should do. Ham wanted to forget cheese and spend the money, Kes wanted to buy a new mule and put poor old Ramses, who Shane reckoned had walked eighty thousand miles, out to grass. Joy wanted to put all the money into buying twice as much cheese. 'Then you'll have four times the money to play with afterwards.' But the others thought waiting that long was too hard. 'An' suppose the bloomin' cheese don't sell in the end?' Kes said.

'It sold last time.'

'One swallow don't make a summer,' Kes said.

She'd looked at him with her deep brown eyes. 'One load of coal doesn't make a winter,' she said. Kes scratched his head. He never could answer Joy back.

'She's saying everything's risky on the canals,' Jaffrey explained.

Eleanor knew better. 'She's growing up,' she said.

They had decided Eleanor should buy as much Moira cheese as before, then invest in buying half as much again. Of the money left over, half would be spent on themselves, and half would go into the family's Boat Fund.

Ham put down his slate by the dock gates. 'I'll 'elp yer wheel the cheese in, Ma.'

'No yer won't!' Eleanor said quickly. 'I wasn't borned yesterday. Off ter school with yer.' Joy lifted

Damian on top of the cheeses and left Eleanor looking nervously at the dog, then ran after the others under the railway bridge to the Slackey Lane school.

In class Miss Cardew consulted her ledger. 'The elder master Wampsett?'

Ham put up his hand. 'Ay, miss.'

'In this part of the world we say, yes miss.'

'Ay – yes miss.' Boat children were never popular, always coming and going, a morning here or an afternoon there while the boat was loaded or emptied. Someone had splashed Ham with ink. The hooligan who had done it sat at the back of the class with watering eyes, holding a handkerchief to his bloodied nose.

'Ham, we do not yet carry proper records on people like you,' Miss Cardew said. 'However it is certain from even the most casual examination that you are no longer thirteen.' She raised her eyebrows. 'You are no longer a child, Ham. You cannot stay at school.'

'I'm sad,' Ham said sadly. He ran out into the playground and they heard him shout, 'Whoopee!'

Miss Cardew tapped the lectern with her rod. The rows of children parroted, 'Good morning, Miss Cardew.'

'Good morning, children.'

There would be no afternoon school for the boat children. The *Poca* was loaded and Kes trimmed her cargo with the shovel, getting ready to go. Instead of lunch Joy, Shane and Jaffrey, each with a tick for a morning's work entered in their attendance books, ran to the Moira Baths. Invalids came from all over the country for a cure at the salt spring, but the

390

children were segregated and issued with special soap and pumice stone. Joy was the only one to use hers. She emerged scraped, scrubbed and beaming. She wore her long red hair loose, to dry, going back to the boat. The gleaming fan rippled almost to her waist, swinging around her hips as she walked.

'Unnatural,' Jaffrey said with boyish horror. But Ham helped her down into the boat though she didn't need it. Eleanor watched them thoughtfully. 'I carried them cheeses into the fo'c'sle meself, two at a time,' she overhead Ham brag to Joy.

'You should've carried another two on your head, it's so big,' the girl shot back. Eleanor chuckled, relieved. Joy wouldn't let anything stupid happen. But boys would be boys, and Eleanor's expression turned serious again. She set her lads to work with the fine rakes called kebs, dredging the navigation for dropped coals that would suit the stove just dandy. When Kes finished mopping coal-dust from the boat and cast off she went below.

Grandma Pebble sat in the bedhole exactly as she'd been left, in Kes's rocking chair he'd picked up a couple of years ago, when he hurt his back winding a bridge on the Llangollen navigation. When Kes and Eleanor's bed was put down during the night the rocking chair was tied to the cabin roof. "Allo, Gran,' Eleanor put on cheerfulness. 'All right, are we?' She pushed the kettle on the stove and got tea on the go.

Grandma Pebble smiled. It was not her usual smile. It was a lopsided grin. She'd dropped down on the cabin sole this morning and not moved. Eleanor had been afraid it was a fit, but when hauled up the old lady seemed to recover. She just wanted to sit quietly, and she had done so all day, with her hands folded in her lap.

'I remember when all the Number Ones wore tarred 'ats,' Grandma said. 'Shone in the sun. Lovely, they are.'

'Still wear 'em when it rains,' Eleanor grunted.

'Oh, is it raining?'

Eleanor glanced at the bright autumn sun slanting through the slide. 'Gran, yer sure yer all right?'

'Fine as a firkin, Leonora,' the old lady said vacantly. She thought she was talking to her sister. It wasn't the first time this had happened.

Eleanor put in one for the pot and stirred the tea. 'Gran, yer remember Joy arrivin'?' she asked gruffly. 'D'yer remember that day?'

'No,' Grandma Pebble said brightly. 'Was she borned?'

'No, she's not mine, though God knows wot she feels like she is.'

'None of 'em are Kes's,' Grandma Pebble said.

A dreadful cold feeling stole over Eleanor. Perhaps it was the same deathly cold Grandma Pebble felt. 'Wot's that?'

'Castles in the air,' the old lady said. She was looking at her paintings adorning the bulkheads, the Red Indian girl on the water can, the coal-box. 'I'm building castles in the air. It's what we all spend our lives doing. All fer nothing.'

'Yer shouldn't talk like this,' Eleanor said. She put the mug of tea in the old lady's hand, which held it as though it were not hot. Eleanor took the tray and went up out, then turned back so that her shoulders blocked the doorway. 'Don't say anything stupid ter Kes.'

'I'm not stupid,' Grandma Pebble said. She sat without moving, clinging to her tea.

Eleanor placed the tray with mugs and sugar on the cabin top. 'Tea's up!' The boys swarmed round. Joy was walking beside the mule. Eleanor stepped ashore where the *Poca* came close to the towpath under a bridge, and caught her up. It had been a dry month and the trees that fringed the banks were red, brilliant purple, gold. They painted the navigation with the same colours. The mule clopped peacefully.

"Ow the Canal Company 'ates them trees,' Eleanor remarked. 'It's their leaves falling wot's doing fer the Moira. Dropping in the navigation, silting up the banks, see.' Behind them the heavily laden *Poca* kept to the centre of the channel.

Joy sipped her tea. 'What's on your mind, Mum?'

'Nothing,' Eleanor said.

Joy swept her mug around the horizon. 'It's a strange place, this. It looks flat but it isn't. It slopes.'

'That's the mines. The ground's falling down 'em, they say. The bridges are sinking, won't get under 'em one day. There's not a lock on the Moira till Marston stop lock, thirty mile, and yer only need that on windy days. The wind pushes the water ter make a slope, see.'

'I see,' Joy said. By God, Eleanor thought. I think she really *does* understand what I'm prattling on about.

'I'm not really yer Mum,' Eleanor said.

'I know. I wasn't a baby.' Joy hugged her.

'Now yer spilt yer tea.' They ran to catch the mule up. There was no better backerer than Ramses. In its old age the mule would plod by itself for hours if necessary, stopping for bridges, pausing when a boat came the other way to let it slide over the towstrap left slack on the canal bed, and then the animal would pick up its stride again, all without being told.

Eleanor said, 'D'yer remember?'

'I don't want to remember,' Joy said. Eleanor stared. Children were so ruthless – not only ruthless with other children, like Ham was, but so ruthless with themselves. Little savages, they were. It always caught Eleanor out how little could be hidden from the young and the old. It was her age in the middle, the busy grown-ups, who saw least.

'I've always felt guilty about wot I did,' Eleanor said, hugging her shawl around her shoulders. The sky was ablaze with sunset and the air was going cool. 'Takin' yer in.'

'Sometimes I have dreams,' Joy said. 'I'm happy here, Mum. If I had another life it was just a dream.'

'I love yer,' Eleanor said fiercely. 'Yer more my own daughter than if yer really was my daughter. I chose yer.'

Past the Gilwiskaw aqueduct the navigation turned mossy and stagnant, blocked by a green hill with a village on top. The tunnel into the hillside was a black hole in the failing light. 'It's the Snarestone,' Kes called. 'We might as well get on through. It'll be no darker inside than out any minute, an' we'll save ourselves a job in the morning.'

Eleanor returned aboard. She found Grandma

Pebble sitting exactly as she had left her, the full mug of tea in her hand now cold. 'Getting out the quant?' the old lady muttered. She clutched the mug with all her strength when Eleanor tried to take it. 'I'm not finished yet!'

The tunnel roof was too low for Kes to lie on the top planks and walk the boat through with his feet. He got out the pole to push her. Shane and Jaffrey helped him and Joy unhitched the mule's gear, then walked Ramses up the path over the tunnel mouth. There was a track across the fields and she would be waiting for the boat at the far end. At the last moment, as the *Poca*'s square counter slid out of sight into the tunnel, Ham jumped ashore.

'I'll give yer the benefit of me comp'ny,' he said brashly. She knew he would be quite different alone with her.

'All right,' she shrugged.

At first he tried to keep up the cockiness with her that he showed with his brothers, but alone he sounded tentative, almost shy. She took the change as a compliment.

'I s'pose yer'll want ter pick flowers,' he said, and took the reins so that she could.

She laughed. 'In the dark? In October?'

'I thought – girls. You know.' Ham sounded crushed. In silence they followed the track, a lighter stain looping between dark hedgerows. 'Yer leading me on like I'm leading this mule,' Ham said miserably. I'm making him feel like this, Joy thought with amazement.

'No I'm not,' she said modestly, excited by her power.

'Yes yer are. Yer are.'

They turned downhill. 'It's not me leading you on,' she said. 'It's you. You're doing it to yourself. Don't blame me.'

'I'm not blaming yer. I can't 'elp wot I feel.'

'What do you feel?'

'I love yer, 'course.'

'I'm the only girl you know,' she pointed out sensibly, then bit her lip for telling the truth. Ham's pride was wounded.

'No yer aren't! I know lots!'

He made a show of leading Ramses down the steep slope to the towpath. She sighed and made herself look impressed. But it was almost dark here at the far end of the tunnel. There was a pub with a thatched roof and a lantern that cast a glow. She sat on the landing stage while Ham hobbled the mule on the grass. He sat beside her. 'Do yer like me a bit?'

'Yes,' she said honestly.

He put his arm round her. 'Yer getting them,' he said. 'Bubs.'

'What?'

'Yer know. Tits. Soon, anyway.'

Joy was acutely embarrassed, but Ham looked pleased. 'All girls do. An' legs,' he added. 'I've seen yer undress.'

It had never occurred to her until now that Ham could possibly be interested in the sight of her, any more than she was interested in the sight of him. 'You've watched me undress?'

'Why not? I'm a boy, aren't I?'

'I know that,' she said.

'Ma says it's the most powerful force in the world.

More powerful than a railway engine. More powerful'n 'Er Majesty.'

'What is?'

Ham kissed her.

'I don't like it,' she said. 'That's not love.'

'Yes it is.' He fumbled at her blouse.

She said, 'What are you doing?'

Ham kissed her again, fumbling. Then his fingers stopped their frantic pecking. His eyes opened. 'I can't do it wiv yer,' he said. 'It's not the same.'

'I should think not.'

'The trouble is, I like yer,' he said. 'But I can't kiss a girl I owe me life ter.' Ham had never talked of the day he had almost drowned, holding his shame inside himself, and she had almost forgotten what had happened. 'When I kissed yer I saw meself in the deep water an' I was drowning,' Ham said. He groaned. 'Saved by a girl!'

'What's wrong with that?'

'There's something about yer, Joy. I respect yer.' He looked at her earnestly.

She wiped her lips.

'There yer go again!' he exploded.

They heard voices. Ham moved two feet away from her and the *Poca* slid out of the tunnel. The family moored up for the night and went into the pub. The Navigator was someone's front room with a big barrel of mild beer raised on chocks in one corner. Straw covered the bare boards and a couple of dogs snored by the fire. The publican's wife fried up some battered fish and pushed it between slabs of buttered bread. They sat along the settle in the corner and wolfed down the fried fish butties with glasses of black beer, Kes drinking a quart from his own pewter tankard. Jaffrey took out a stump of pencil and sketched the scene on old scraps of newspaper. The room grew hot and fuggy as it filled up during the evening, other canal folk mostly. One of the dogs yelped, trodden on, and the publican cursed it. Joy recognised most of the people. Henrietta Feeney and her little husband had their boat pulled by her two grey donkeys Mick and Mack, who worked as a pair with the tow-line forked, one tail to each swingletree. She saw swarthy Josh McStivens with his muscles bulging in his red shirt, and the Gallup boys came in scratching their beards. They stood together and swore about this and that. The women talked among themselves, and mostly kept the same glasses. But tonight Eleanor stuck with Kes, Damian asleep in the crook of her arm. 'I'll 'ave another,' Kes said, getting up.

"Oo's carrying yer back ter the boat?' she said.

He sighed when he came back. 'All right, wot's up?'

'It's time we 'ad a talk,' she said. He belched. 'Christopher,' she said.

'I'm listening, aren't I?'

'It's time we 'ad the children out of the same bed,' Eleanor said. 'I've decided. It's wrong fer Joy ter sleep wiv the boys any more.'

'She sleeps round the other way,' Jaffrey said.

'Three pairs o' boy's smelly feet, I dunno 'ow she stands it,' Eleanor said. 'Four pairs, when Damian's in there not wiv us.'

'I'm used to it,' Joy said. 'Cheese in the fo'c'sle, cheese in the cabin.'

'That's another thing I wanted ter talk about,' Eleanor said. 'We could convert the fo'c'sle into a forecabin, Kes. We can afford it.'

'*Her* cheese, so it's *her* money, so *she* can get wot she wants,' Kes said. He brushed the foam off his beer and took a gulp. 'I knew it'd come sooner or later.'

'A forecabin of our very own?' Ham said. 'Private, like?'

'A boys' castle,' Joy said. 'A bo'c'sle.'

Jaffrey giggled unstoppably.

'Where would we put the cheeses?' Shane asked.

Ham glanced at his father. 'Where'd we put the ton of cargo we'd lose?' He wanted to sound responsible in front of Kes. But Joy could see he wanted this idea to go forward very badly. A place of his own, even if he had to share it with his brothers. 'All the profit's in the last ton, isn't it, Dad?' Ham said, repeating the old saying. Kes stared at his beer. Still he hadn't said no. 'Dad's got a plan,' Ham beamed.

'Well, I've been thinking fer some time,' Kes said. 'I know wot Ma's thinking of. She's frightened of all this talk about law an' order. A Member of Parliament's been out spyin' on the canals. Mr George Smith. 'E's bringing in an official Act 'gainst us folk.'

'But that's only 'gainst dirty people and drunkenness,' Eleanor said. 'An' a good thing too,' she added.

'That's wot they want yer ter believe,' Kes said patiently, 'but laws don't work like that. Laws is politics, my dears. When they talk about dirty drunken people they mean us. We are, ter them.

Members of Parliament aren't people like us, see. They say they're fer us, but they're against *us*, 'cos they just want ter tell us wot ter do ter make 'emselves big over us. They're fer *themselves*. Lots of 'em is railway directors, or put forward by railway interests, or wined an' dined by 'em. An' then there's the lords and earls. They all got their fingers in the pie an' they want to boss yer an' me about so it stays that way. An' they'll do it, too. The Boat Inspectors won't just go ter dirty drunken folk, they'll inspect all of us, yer'll see, an' we'll 'ave ter do wot they say.'

"E's a blooming Chartist!' Eleanor said. 'Votes for all men, landowners an' directors paid no more'n the rest of us, I don't know wot next.'

'What choice 'ave I got?' Kes said. He sighed. 'The Boat Inspector'll make us put in a forecabin, 'cos we got a girl. That'll cost us the best ton of cargo like Ham says.'

'An' the mule's flaked out,' Shane said. 'If yer bought a good strong Shire 'orse, we could tow a butty boat behind the *Poca*.'

'Money,' Kes grunted. 'New boat, new 'orse, lots o' new gear. The mule's gear won't fit a Shire.'

'A Shire's legs are too long,' Jaffrey said. He turned over the paper and scribbled a Shire horse with feathered hooves and lots of harness. 'Can't get beneath the bridges, often as not. Need a Welsh cob.'

'Need short legs,' Ham agreed.

'Need steam,' Kes said.

That made them sit up and look. Kes shrugged.

'But steam's not allowed on the Moira,' Joy said.

'I told yer it was politics,' Kes said carefully. 'See, there's a pipe factory been built at the clay quarry beyond Moira Furnace, at the dead end by Overseal. Miles o'pipe got ter be got out, very delicate, packed in straw, can't be rattled about in railway wagons. Perfect fer boats though. It can come down the Moira into the Oxford Canal or the Coventry Canal, from there be shipped anywhere in the country. The Oxford and the Coventry companies want the business, sure enough. If yer want my opinion, I think they'll itch fer the ban on steam ter be taken off the Moira.'

'Steam!' Ham said. Joy eyed him. He was almost a man, but all men were little boys where steam-driven machinery was concerned.

'We could convert the *Poca*,' Jaffrey said. He rubbed out the horse towing the boat and added a funnel to the cabin roof. But all the children knew that Mum would never allow it.

'The engine's big,' Kes agreed, forestalling her. But he seemed to have got it all worked out. 'We'd lose 'alf the cabin an' about five ton of cargo, I reckon. Then there's 'alf a ton at least of coal ter be carried. We'd 'ave ter carpenter a round counter on 'er, ter take the propeller beneath. But we'd get six miles an hour instead of three.'

'Like Ezra Jones an' the *Lurcher*,' Eleanor said.

'That's the way it's going,' Kes said. 'Plenty of 'ot water from the steamer fer washing,' he added, with a cunning wink at Joy.

'I'm not giving up 'alf my cabin fer 'ot water, an' that's that!' Eleanor added accusingly. "Ow long yer 'ad this on the boil, Kes?'

'I'm still thinking about it,' Kes reassured her. 'I 'aven't decided. We'll decide as a family. I wouldn't

401

necessarily ask yer ter give up 'alf yer cabin, Eleanor. There might be other ways. I mean . . . we might build an entire new boat.'

Eleanor thought at once of Cody's Bend, and everyone helping.

'Hayes & Co on the Grand Junction could do it,' Kes said.

'Yer could do it yerself,' Eleanor said tersely. 'Peter Pebble knows boats an' 'e's good with a saw. There's Clem, an' Nat's no fool. An' the boys'll 'elp yer.' Then her face fell. 'Nah, I couldn't give up the old *Poca*. All me boys was borned at 'ome in 'er cabin.'

'We'd butty the *Poca* behind the new boat,' Kes said. He looked around their faces. 'If we decide ter go ahead wiv it, that is.'

Ham said, 'Where would we get the money fer the engine?'

'From a bank,' Joy said.

'And me Moira cheese,' Eleanor said. 'We could scrimp—'

'An' there's the Boat Fund.' Kes finished his beer and stood. 'Let's sleep on it.'

Ham whispered excitedly to Joy as they went back to the boat, 'I think 'e's decided on it!'

But the subject was not referred to the next morning. It was as if last night's plans made in the pub were just the booze speaking, and Kes's mood was sour all the long morning's pound to Marston Junction. 'It's only 'is 'angover,' Ham told Joy at the stop lock. But Kes turned the *Poca* south along the Oxford cut and stayed on the hellum all afternoon, staring ahead without a word. Eleanor sold ten pounds of Moira cheese at Hawkesbury. 'Towards the new boat!' she winked, rattling the coins before hiding them in the bottom of the Measham teapot. Her imagination had been caught.

'Sheep-shanks an' clove-'itches yer know.' Kes was showing Joy the more complicated knots that were so much a part of boating life. 'Double Blackwall 'itch, use it fer 'ooking tackle ter rope. 'Ere's a Turk's 'Ead Running, an' now a Turk's Head Standing. Gordian knots I don't do, 'cept fer fending-off. Now yer turn. Take the end o' that strap an' make me a chain splice.' As she rove the strands, her fingers so much slimmer and nimbler than his own, Kes pointed out the other boats. He knew them all. 'Salt from Droitwich, that one, an' there's the *Cyclops* wiv gas-tar from Birmingham.' He held up the splice. 'Not too dusty, girl,' he admitted.

Near Brinklow the *Lurcher* overtook them, Ezra Jones grinning through his gappy teeth and his two po-faced daughters doing all the work as always. The *Poca* tied up behind them at the Stretton Stop toll-office. Kes gave a polite wave to old Ezra then had a quiet word in Ham's ear. 'Why don't yer stroll over ter the *Lurcher* casual-like an' find out wot's ter be found about steam, eh, sprog?'

'Ay, Cap'n,' Ham said, and went more than willingly.

Eleanor put her arm through Kes's. 'Yer serious, aren't yer.'

'Got ter be,' Kes said, then shouted to Jaffrey to give the old mule a smack, and the *Poca* was tugged slowly towards the next lock. 'But it's a risk.'

Ham must have made a good impression, because

403

when the *Lurcher* put up black smoke and pulled ahead across the twelve arches of the Smite Brook aqueduct, Ham was aboard her. There was no sign of him at the Newbold tunnel, getting dark. This was the busiest part of the cut and a new tunnel had been built with two towpaths. No sign of the *Lurcher* or Ham at the far end, either. 'That Jones is showin' off 'er rate of knots,' Kes said.

'Poor Ham, stuck with that horrible old man and those smelly girls,' Eleanor said.

The next day was the Sabbath and work was out of the question. They lay up with Newbold parish church tolling close by, the bells of Rugby chiming and pealing through the distance. Joy strolled alone along the towpath, enjoying the low sun breaking through the mist that wreathed the navigation. She passed the *Lurcher* moored on the far bank, silent and insubstantial in the fog. One of the Jones girls, Blodwen the younger daughter, sat on the counter dangling her feet almost in the water. She looked glum. Joy waved and got a glum wave in return. She walked on and heard voices giggling through the fog. A girl's head bobbed up in the middle of the navigation, all black hair as she swam to the other side. Ham swam after her – or perhaps he had his feet on the canal bed – towing a vee of ripples. The girl's back came sliding out of the water, then her long white legs splashed as she pulled herself onto the bank. It was Blodwen's elder sister, Morwenna.

Joy thought Morwenna, clean, looked quite pretty. She was fat but Ham seemed to like that, because as he scampered up the bank after the girl Joy saw that he, too, was as naked as the day he was born. His skinny figure caught Morwenna eagerly and she turned with her pink nipples bobbing, then danced back, giggling. Ham wrapped his arms around her broad waist and sank his head between her breasts. She lay back between the tussocks of tall grass and put one knee on each side of him. Joy stared amazed.

She walked on with her gaze fixed to the towpath. Ham looked over his shoulder, then covered his backside with his coat and smiled. He surrendered himself to Morwenna's passionate kisses.

Ham came back to the *Poca* that evening. 'Even with a forecabin there's no room at all on the *Lurcher*,' he reported, 'the machinery takes up all the space.'

'I'm surprised you had time to look at the boat's machinery too,' Joy said. Shane and Jaffrey stifled sniggers.

'Wot's got into yer lot?' Kes said.

Ham kept a straight face. 'Dad, the *Lurcher*'s engine an' boiler weighs ten tons, an' takes up ten foot of carrying space, so she's only good fer fourteen tons of cargo. Morwenna told me it's an inverted tandem-compound wiv surface condensers. She knows all about engines.'

'Yer done well,' Kes said.

'Amazed you didn't burst your boiler,' Joy said. Ham blushed.

'I did,' he whispered later. 'Ma's right. It's the most powerful, beautiful thing.'

'What, steam?'

'Love,' Ham said. 'Morwenna's off down the Warwick & Napton tomorrow. It feels like I'll never see her again.' He looked so pathetic that Joy pulled his hair to make him smile. 'It's yer I love really,' he said, 'but I love yer wivout the dirty bits. Yer know wot I mean?' He added, 'Steam's not bad, neither.'

She gave his hair a really sharp tug to make his eyes water.

'But by next week Morwenna an' the *Lurcher*'ll be on the Wilts & Berks,' he said, and rubbed his head with a broad smile, 'just like us.'

Eleanor and Joy sold more than double the last trip's quantity of Moira cheese at Banbury market. They caught up with the *Poca*'s slow progress in the evening – a dozen lift bridges within a few miles of the town made for slow progress on the water. Kes hardly greeted them, chewed his tobacco lost in thought. No one dared interrupt him.

Eleanor sold more cheese at Louse Lock, close under the spires of Oxford, then they came into the broad Thames looping between fields and forests. The cheese shop by Abingdon Bridge took a whole roundel this time, and Joy and Eleanor ran to catch up the *Poca* at Tythe Barn Lock. Next morning, up before dawn, they carried their full cheese-baskets across the common fields to Drayton, then waited with empty baskets for the *Poca* to arrive at Drayton Lock.

'If we sold our coal at Swindon,' Kes told Joy later that morning, 'wot wiv the competition from the Great Western Railway I doubt we'd get a pound sterling fer each ton. So we'll sell at little canalside villages, Uffington, Wootton Bassett, Dauntsey Park—'

'And cheese,' Joy said.

'At Dauntsey yer'll 'ave ter cart it two mile uphill through the park ter the village proper. Earl

Spencer's village took ten ton last winter, so did the Earl of Radnor's—'

'Don't worry,' she said gently. It was obvious Kes couldn't make up his mind whether to go ahead with the new boat. 'Eleanor and I will run the *Poca*,' she said, 'we'll keep the money coming in. We'll pick up Wiltshire or Gloucester coal at Semington—'

Kes chuckled. 'Yer keep yer eyes open and yer wits about yer, don't yer.'

'You've got to go ahead with the new boat,' Joy said.

'Why?'

'Because if you don't, Kes, you'll always wish you had.'

That evening the *Poca* tied up to dog-leg anchors on the Summit pound among the chalk hills of Wiltshire, more than a hundred and sixty feet above the Abingdon level.

'I've been thinking,' Kes said, as soon as they settled in the pub and he got his tankard out.

'Yer mean yer decided fer us,' Eleanor said.

'We're going ter build us a steamer,' Kes said. 'I got it all planned. I reckon it'll take us two months. That'll keep us busy through the coldest part of the winter, when the navigation'll be froze like as not anyway. Ham, Shane, Jaffrey, yer'll come wiv me on the third-class ter Cody's Bend. Eleanor, Joy, yer'll run the *Poca*. Yer got Gran ter 'elp out wiv chores.'

On boat matters Eleanor deferred instantly. 'We'll do it all right somehow, Dad, don't yer worry.'

'I got enough else ter worry about now,' Kes said wryly. 'But yer know, if I didn't go ahead an' do it, I'd always wish I 'ad.'

II

Tom Briggs had Duty.

He knelt on the windowsill. He was six feet tall but painfully thin, and the wood hurt his knees. The establishment contained no clocks, only Dr Gregory's silver watch, which the headmaster kept like a talisman in his fob-pocket. From his perch Tom could see the church beyond the canal and the fields. The church clock was visible over the vicarage roof, and by narrowing his eyes he could just make out the time through first light. It was ten to seven.

Tom jumped down, jammed his top hat on his head, and ran on cracking knees to the bell that hung in the stone hall. He rang it and counted out thirty seconds. First Bell.

'First Bell!' he shouted. Groans came from the dormitories upstairs, the slap of bare feet on boards.

Tom went back to the window, took off his hat and knelt against the glass. On foggy days, or the darkest days of winter, the Duty boy must rely on the tolling of the church bell.

Tom's neck was rubbed into angry boils by his Eton collar. The celluloid collars irritated the necks of all the boys, and they were called the Ring of Fire. In addition Tom wore a short black broadcloth jacket, pointed at the back like tails, brushed but very shabby.

One of the elder boys, a Monitor, came downstairs. His name was Slattery, and he had been smartly dressed by his Fag. 'It's not your duty, Briggs,' he sneered. 'Who is it this time?'

'I'm looking in for Tosser, sir.'

'Your friend Tosser's malingering again, is he?'

'He's sick, Mr Slattery.'

'You bloody Proles,' Slattery said with genuine loathing. Once he had been a Prole himself. It was only human nature that the wrongs done to him he now believed to have a purpose, and inflicted them on others in the name of discipline. No one was more cruel than a child who had been treated cruelly, and Slattery had been treated with great cruelty and indifference by his very rich parents. 'You won't get a second chance at Prefect if you won't learn discipline, Briggs. You could save yourself all this, you know.'

'Yes, sir,' Tom said. 'I know.'

They were almost the same age, and Slattery dropped his voice. 'Why won't you make it easy on yourself, Tom? You let all of us down, don't you understand?'

'Yes, sir,' Tom said.

'You hate me, don't you,' Slattery grinned. 'You hate everything I stand for.'

'I wouldn't put it as high as that,' Tom said. The church clock pointed to seven. He ran and rang the bell.

Slattery found a spot of egg on his necktie that boded ill for his Fag. 'I think you're a rebel, Tom,' he said. 'I think your sort make the most dangerous rebels, because you play the game. And no one realises you're on the other side until it's too late.'

Tom stared after him. Soon it was time for Third Bell, and Baths.

Dr Thaddeus Gregory's private boarding academy at Green Hill Hall, Wootton Bassett, Wiltshire, was a large redbrick private house set in overgrown grounds. As though the property contained dangerous animals, it was enclosed by a redbrick wall and tall wrought-iron gates. Difficult or unwanted children were placed in the establishment by busy parents, not always wealthy. Sixty-six boys lived here for as long as their fees were paid. When the money stopped, or at the age of nineteen, they were let go. These young men could not always find their way back home. Their fathers had often moved away to another job, or perhaps to a posting somewhere in the far abroad of the Empire. In effect the Hall was a fee-paying Barnardo's Home for children who had known their parents. It was one of many.

Dr Gregory's boarding school operated the usual system of Latin and trigonometry, cold baths and the birch. The birch cane was split into seven cuts at the business end, and was called the Cutter. Since the establishment had no teachers or ushers, only the overworked and long-suffering Dr Gregory and his missionary wife, discipline came from the oldest and most privileged boys, the Monitors. A Monitorial was when a boy was given six strokes by each of the Monitors in turn. Below the Monitors were the Prefects, Proles and Fags, everyone in their place. It was every boy's ambition to be a Monitor.

Except Tom.

Tom just wanted to escape.

He wanted to get back home. Tom remembered *home* with almost mythic intensity, better and warmer than it had ever been. He needed to be forgiven by his mother, and by his father, and to have everything in the past forgotten. He knew it would never happen.

The boys streamed out of the gates. They filed across the fields to the river, counted by a Prefect at each hedgerow – boys were incredibly devious and would sneak off for a smoke or an eye at the local girls given the least opportunity. Tom came last, bringing up the rear with Freddie Tosser. The ulcer on Freddie's thigh, caused by a pencil lead, was as large as a cup. It had suppurated in the night and smelt. Freddie seemed fascinated by it but Tom could hardly bear to look. Several boys had gone blind in the school, or died of infection, and he knew of healthy boys who had hanged themselves or run away. Such incidents were inevitable in any school, but he could not come to terms with it happening to Freddie. 'Come on, you women!' Slattery yelled contemptuously. 'Baths!'

They came to the water. Between the wreaths of mist the slate-grey water was crowded with boys' bobbing heads, low cries and chattering teeth. Most boys thought this channel was the Thames, but Tom was sure it was a canal. The water was only four feet deep, and when sent to collect meat from a butcher in the village Tom had seen a headline in the *Wilts and Gloucester Standard.* 'WILTS & BERKS TO BE CLOSED?' This required the permission of Parliament, which for legal reasons would take fourteen years from the date tolls ceased to be charged. He had noticed the bridge was in poor repair, and few boats used the Twine & Co wharf, only private operators. The Great Western Railway

411

claimed it would take over the carrying trade with a station at every wharf, and had already extended its branch lines to Abingdon, Wantage and Calne.

Tom had never heard of these places, neither had the other boys.

Freddie gave a grunt of agony at the cold water. Tom plunged in after him. Most of the boys were getting out by now, drying themselves on their britches. Those who could were smoking or drinking. 'Everyone out!' Slattery yelled. A boat pulled away from Twine's wharf and Tom swam after Freddie, who had not seen its approach. The bow slid by them, the tow-rope passed above Tom's head, dripping through the mist. Then the stern went past them, steam swirling around the counter, mash being boiled up to feed the mule led by the older woman.

Water flowing in behind the boat turned both boys round and round. Tom glimpsed the girl at the tiller.

She was tall, something silver flashed at her neck, her red hair lay in curls across her shoulders.

He stared even after the boat was gone, Slattery shaking him and shouting in his ear. Freddie Tosser was frightened. Tom's face was white as wax. 'Tom,' he said, 'Tom . . .'

Tom looked like a boy who has seen a ghost.

Later that day, Tom began to write a letter. The nib on his pen had splayed, and after each word he had to dip it again into the inkwell.

Dearest Papa and Mama, I hope you are well. I am well . . .

* * *

III

Lydia put pen to paper.

15, Abbey Place
St John's Wood
London, NW

1 November 1876

My dear Bowler,

Kindly come to my house at your convenience, today, on an urgent matter of concern to us both.

Yours, etc
D. Briggs (Mrs)

Still no sign of Mr Bowler.

Afternoon had come, and Lydia sat in the window. Her dress was made of challis, silk and wool woven crossways, warm but light, and around her neck she wore a filmy silk fichu of a paler yellow than the dress. Her hair was tightly bound but her fingers twined and clasped each other and she could not force them to be still. She despised herself for revealing what she felt. Bowler would see into her at once, she knew, however deeply she tried to hide herself. She imagined the policeman's pale blue eyes examining her, merciless, professional. He would make her feel guilty – she, the victim! She should not have summoned him.

Again Lydia unfolded the letter from her son.

She hated getting letters from Tom. They made her very angry.

She re-read it for the hundredth time. It was written on terrible paper that creased easily, betraying her interest.

Yesterday morning Tom's letter had arrived like a bolt from the blue. For several years he had shown better sense than to write, since she always enclosed his letters back to him having cast her eye over them. They were always on that feint paper, the envelope made from another sheet of paper, folded as though smuggled out. His efforts to be neat were pathetic, the words scratched with some awful dip-pen.

Lydia had not slept a wink last night.

Suppose it were true?

Suppose Joy were still alive?

She stiffened as a hansom cab drew up in the road. Charles Bowler got out. He swept his hands down his plaid overcoat to smooth it. A gentleman would have worn wool or vicuna, grey perhaps, with a fur collar. He straightened his necktie. His shoes were perfectly polished, though not by a servant's hand, she was sure. Nevertheless, the tips sparkled as he walked along the drive. He passed out of sight below her.

Bowler had glanced up, and she knew he was well aware she was watching him, but he gave no sign. The arrogance of the man.

Lydia forced herself to wait. The front-door bell. Prettiman's footsteps along the hallway. The heavy brass latch opening, the creak of the hinge. The murmur of voices. Lydia could bear it no longer. She jumped to her feet, went from the parlour onto the landing, and called down.

'It's quite all right, Prettiman.'

'Indeed, ma'am.'

Prettiman bowed, closed the front door, and returned to the servants' quarters. Bowler came upstairs. Lydia went back into the parlour so that he must follow her. As he came into the room she sat.

He closed the door firmly. 'Lydia,' he said.

She held out the letter between her fingers. 'How do you explain this, Mr Bowler?'

Bowler took the letter. He examined it.

'It's from my son Tom!' Lydia burst out.

'So I see, Lydia.'

'He's seen Joy. He says so there.'

Bowler read the letter. She watched his face. Bowler scratched his nose. He went back to the start of the letter and read it again. He finished. Lydia sat up hopefully.

'Do you know how many hoaxes are perpetrated upon the police each year, Lydia?' Bowler said.

'No,' she said. 'Of course not.'

He folded the creased paper and handed it back to her. 'The public is malicious. Each tragic case – every missing child, every murder, every fire – brings another crop of hoaxes to waste police time. If only you knew. It is impossible not to be disillusioned.'

'But Tom saw her.'

'Naturally Tom believed what he thought he saw. Tom has blamed himself every day since her murder, I am sure.'

'I did not find it convenient to inform him of the discovery of her slippers,' Lydia admitted. 'He has had no reason to suppose her not alive.'

'You were letting him live in hope,' Bowler said.

He seemed not to think less of her for it.

'One might draw that conclusion.'

'But look rationally at what Tom says. He says he saw a tall red-haired girl in Wootton Bassett. If I'm not mistaken, Lydia, he doesn't want to stay at that school.' Bowler looked her in the eye. 'Am I right?'

'I'm sure that you are the sort of man who is always right, Mr Bowler,' Lydia said angrily. She stood for him to go. 'Tom is no hoaxer.'

'I did not say so. He wants your attention. Perhaps he even thinks he is telling the truth.'

Lydia trembled. A lump rose in her throat. 'I would appreciate it if you would leave me alone.'

'Do *you* really want to believe she is alive after all this time?' Bowler said gently. 'You must do. You wanted to believe Tom's letter.'

Lydia examined her feelings. 'Would it be too awful?' She was afraid she would cry. 'I think I do, Charles.'

'Even changed as she would be?'

'She is my daughter.'

'You mean *was*, Lydia.'

Lydia went to the mirror above the fireplace. Bowler had that terrifying knack of making her want to tell him the truth. She might blurt out her heart and soul to him. 'One . . . one grows no younger, Charles,' she conceded. 'I'll never have another child. I have only me.' She touched her face. 'When one is young forgetting is easy. Now I admit I cannot forget her. She haunts me. Sometimes she would stand in the doorway watching me eat my breakfast, and sometimes I still think—'

Bowler's reflection studied her. Lydia knew he

416

was wondering if she had told Darby what she felt. She hadn't, and Bowler knew it.

'Damn you,' she said. 'We don't have anything hidden from you. Stop it.'

Bowler turned her round. Lydia's fichu slipped from her left shoulder, exposing her powdered flesh.

'Darby is weak, contemptible,' she blurted. 'The father of his son.'

'You have been married to him for many years.'

'Stop,' she said. 'You intrude. It is a private matter.' But she wanted to tell him everything.

'You have carried his two children,' Bowler said.

Lydia confessed. 'Two indiscretions between husband and wife do not make a marriage, Charles.' She turned her head away.

Bowler kissed her exposed shoulder. She gave a gasp of relief, then shivered.

He took her face in his hands and kissed her mouth. Lydia felt her breasts fill with hot blood. She raised herself on tiptoe. 'No!' she said. 'No. Not here.'

'No,' Bowler said.

'Upstairs. Quickly—'

Bowler knew the way as well as she. He turned left on the landing, crossed the carpet with big dark patterns, pulled Lydia inside her bedroom. She closed the door and caught her breath. 'It's my time for a nap. We won't be dis—'

He pushed her back against the door. Lydia imagined Detective Inspector Bowler lifting her petticoats in handfuls, she imagined taking him here, like this, backed against the door.

'Tell me what to do!' she said.

Bowler lifted her dress and everything else. 'You're

beautiful, you're beautiful, you're perfect.' He pushed himself between the white fork of her legs. 'Perfect woman. Bitch. Adulterer. I've got you.' Their bodies climaxed at almost the same moment, they shuddered and cried out almost together.

He had thought Lydia Briggs was different.

They lay naked on her bed, without sheets. A fire roared in the grate where the loofer boy had come down all those years ago. A couple of dolls with woollen hair sat in the chair as though they were alive, heads lolling, stuffed limbs floppy, passive, endearing. Lydia grunted in her sleep. Her mouth hung slightly open.

'I'm not the second man you've had,' Bowler said.

Her eyelids flickered. She woke and closed her mouth, then cuddled against him, slid her knee sleepily over his. She grinned and sighed. She'd been here before, Bowler knew, sliding her flesh over other men's flesh.

'Did you say something?' she murmured.

'No.'

Bowler knew the way it went. Lydia herself had once admitted to him she was a City widow. Her husband was acquainted with the highest circles of Society, seen at Ascot, Henley, the opera. One day Darby's daughter should have had the honour of Coming Out before the Queen as a debutante. But Lydia was supposed to be content with dresses, jewellery, and the titbits of rumour and scandal from the rich, powerful, handsome men gathered at her husband's table. It was not a woman's nature forever to play second string to her husband's success.

Lydia was beautiful, strikingly beautiful. Such women developed their Bohemian style of living not for money but from boredom. Where Bowler came from they were known as Westminster Wives. In the evenings they met male company through their husbands' business circle. By day the broughams and barouches arrived with champagne, flowers, admiration for the neglected wife while the lord and master was busy in the City. All she needed was a butler whose discretion could be relied upon.

These West End women were whores in the truest sense, Bowler knew. They did it not because they had to but because they liked to. They had no morality.

But he had hoped Lydia was different.

She circled her fingertip on his chest. 'You're hairy, Charlie.'

'Don't call me Charlie.'

'Because she does,' Lydia said wisely. 'Your little woman.' She slid her fingertip down his belly. 'I've made you all floppy for her now.' She fondled him, lifting and caressing. 'I used to do this to Tom.'

'Your son? Good God.'

'When he was a baby.' She laughed at his face. 'Women always have. It's called wrapping the child in the tail of his mother's smock. Fondling makes them more . . . more. You know.' She squeezed him beguilingly. 'For when the little girls grow up.'

'You think you can do anything with me now,' he said.

'Men don't make fools of men. Women do.' She kissed his chin. 'I like you, Charlie. You're strong. Ordered. Successful at what you do. My very own Scotland Yard detective.'

'I wanted you the moment I saw you,' he said.

'I know.'

'The very first moment the very first time I saw you, Lydia.'

'I know,' she said seriously.

'You could have killed your daughter, don't you realise? I mean it, Lydia. The way you treated her. Gaby Daniells had seen the marks, hadn't she?'

'Nonsense. You're stiff again.'

'Gaby suspected.'

'My girl got the best of everything.'

'Yes, I know all that. Otto Worth kept Gaby quiet, didn't he. She was frightened of him.'

'Now you have *two* girls being beaten in the same rather nice house in a leafy suburb of St John's Wood.' Lydia chuckled. 'Really, Charles, do you think so? Do you suspect everybody? Are you *always* a policeman? Anyway, both of them are long gone.' She rubbed him, grinning. 'Do you like me doing this?'

'Yes.'

'I expect your mother did it.'

Bowler groaned. 'I was born in St Luke's. My father died when I was very young and my mother married a man in the next parish.'

Lydia straddled him and took him.

She sat looking down at him afterwards, enjoying her feeling of power as he slipped out of her. 'Why did you call me those things?'

He yawned. 'What things?'

'You know. B—ch. Adulterer. Did it excite you? It did, didn't it.'

'Lydia, may I ask you a question?'

'Go on.'

'Why is a woman like you in bed with a mere policeman?'

She leaned down. 'What made you become a policeman, Charlie?'

'I wanted to catch guilty people,' he said simply.

'An idealist. How banal.'

'I'd seen enough crime where I'd been brought up. In those days I thought there were victims and criminals, guilty and innocent. It never occurred to me that I was no better than the people I caught. I was the policeman and they were the criminals. But the more I put away, the more there were to catch. Crime is everywhere, Lydia. The more we squash it down the stronger it bubbles up. It's inside us all. We're all guilty. All men and all women are capable of murder. Just along the road here a woman was garrotted the other day – a wire slipped round her neck from behind and dragged tight – murdered for the shilling in her purse. Fact.'

'How terrible!'

'The awful Limehouse murders. Fact.' His voice rose. 'When a wife is killed, arrest the husband. Rule of thumb. Fact. When a husband is killed, arrest the wife—'

She sat beside him. 'Ssh, Charlie, someone will hear you.'

'There's a system called Bertillonage, measurements of the head. We may be able to predict crime. Another system called Herschel prints, the detection of tiny unique patterns on the fingers. Criminals will be born and registered and traced all their lives, they'll never escape.'

'Everyone?'

'Yes.'

'Not people like us, surely?'

'Every year is worse,' Bowler said. 'Not just crime. I mean the police strike. One hundred and nineteen ringleaders dismissed from the Force, the others with their careers stalled. I'm ashamed. What are we coming to? The crime rate should have gone through the roof, Lydia. But it didn't. It didn't.'

She put on her dressing-gown and stroked his hair, looking nervously at the door.

'I wanted to serve the good,' Bowler said, going quiet. 'The Queen. The public. Truth. But there isn't any good. The whole system is corrupt because it makes criminals of us all. Who knows the law? None of us is perfect. Not even you.'

'You aren't a criminal.'

'Only because I haven't been arrested.'

'Well I'm certainly not a criminal,' Lydia said. He said something and she covered his mouth with his hand. 'Do you suspect everybody, all the time?'

She released him.

'It's my job, Lydia,' he said. 'Nobody is innocent.'

'Do you suspect your own wife, Charlie?' That jolted him. His eyes widened. 'I thought not,' she murmured. 'What do you think she's doing now, Charlie? Making the supper? Do you suspect your children too? Or have you brought the little angels up so strictly that they know right from wrong and never do wrong?'

She watched him think about his children.

'All children are difficult,' he said.

'I was wrong about you,' Lydia whispered. 'You aren't envious. You're *angry*.'

422

Bowler stood. She watched him uncertainly. He took his clothes and hung them over the chair by the fire, dressed himself matter-of-factly. 'Come on, get your clothes on,' he said, 'I've got something to show you.'

She said coquettishly, 'Even more than you already have?'

'Can't you upper-class women dress without help?' he said. He knotted his chocolate-brown tie and reached for his brown jacket. Bowler was not the sort of man to tolerate delay.

Lydia was embarrassed to dress in front of him. She went into her dressing-room to perform her toilette. Instead of the tea-gown, which would have been her usual choice for this time of day, she slipped an afternoon dress over her head. Her hair snagged the material – she wasn't used to dressing herself, he was right. Rather than bother with her hair she pinned it and returned to her bedroom. 'We're going out,' he said. 'You'll need a coat.'

Lydia's nerve failed her. 'What about my husband?'

'What time does he get home?'

'Ages, usually.'

'Need his permission to go out, do you?'

Lydia tightened her lips. She went back and put on a thick woollen dolman with loose sleeves, half-cape, half-coat. A fur hat and fur muff completed her ensemble. She presented herself in the doorway.

'Darby still loves you, you know,' he said.

'Why do you always try to make me feel guilty?' Lydia said in a breaking voice. 'I won't let you.'

He looked at her in that steady, penetrating way. She brushed past him. 'He loves his work,' she said.

'I only wanted to be loved. I see you are no more capable of showing that than he.' She went downstairs in front of him and waited in the hall.

Outside, Bowler whistled for a cab. Prettiman came up and Lydia told him that she was going out for a short while. A hansom cab pulled over in the road and Bowler directed it to the house. Lydia came down the steps and he helped her into the seat. 'St Luke's,' he called through the hatch.

They rode in silence for a while.

'You mean St Luke's church?' she said.

'You'll see what I mean.'

She glanced from her window, watching the passing streets without noticing them. As always Bowler's silences drove her to talk.

'Obviously you know by now that Darby won't win the game.'

Bowler shrugged. Lydia would not have slept with him if all was going well. He let her talk.

'He . . . he boomed in the boom years,' Lydia said with difficulty. 'The first three years were very profitable. But now times are . . . a little harder. A minor adjustment.'

'I know one or two banks are in trouble.'

'A matter of acceptances – guarantees of payment. Loans to the Eupion Gas Company, for example. Railways in out-of-the-way places that never get built. Honduras. The Argentine. I don't pretend to understand it, of course. I hate talking about business,' she said anxiously.

Bowler said, 'Doubtless people like him make enough in the good times to see them through bad.'

'Doubtless.' She turned from her window and

spoke directly. 'But you did know, didn't you, Charles.' When he didn't answer she turned away from him. 'Did I disappoint you very much this afternoon?'

The horse clip-clopped steadily. A bell rang and a tram overtook them with a metallic squeal. Having overtaken, it stopped in front of them to take on passengers. They waited.

Bowler said gently, 'Don't cry.'

The tram moved on. The hansom jogged forward. After a couple of turns Bowler knocked on the roof and opened the door before the horse had stopped. He got out and Lydia hung on to his elbow. She looked around her in confusion, then recognised the rooftops of the City stretching to the river. The church spires stuck up into the evening light like gleaming nails. It must have been raining while we made love, she thought.

'Welcome to St Luke's,' Bowler said.

Lydia heard rough laughter. A gang of Irish navvies shoved past them and strode down the narrow roadway. Their muscled bodies, hair and tattered smocks were white with plaster. They carried sledgehammers over their shoulders. One man hefted a cannon ball on a length of heavy chain. Lydia squeezed Bowler's arm tight as he followed them. She had never seen houses so horrid and decayed, and she wondered what sort of people had once inhabited them. The doors had been pulled from the doorways, the frames were gone from the windows, bare brick and mouldy plaster gaped. Pale shapes moved in one gutted room. She saw children like ghosts, a woman standing protectively over them.

'Did you see them?' she whispered.

'They'll find somewhere else,' Bowler said.

People were coming against them in a constant flow now, some of them with their goods piled high in wheelbarrows, like refugees. An old man pushed his chair a step at a time. Two men carried a mildewed sideboard very briskly, almost at the run. A small boy dodged past carrying a squealing pig. Dogs yapped and babies cried. Women wailed.

'That's the sound of it,' Bowler said.

Ahead of them police constables were keeping order, going from house to house to make sure the premises were empty. Demolition orders had been tacked to the walls. A crowd gathered to watch the procedure, then a cheer went up as the steam crane whistled. A huge stone block dropped from the gantry, plunged through a rooftop. Dust flew into the air, the walls trembled and sagged inwards. The block was winched up and the process repeated.

'Coming through,' Bowler said. He led Lydia onto a low hill covered with stones. Gradually she realised it was a graveyard. The stones were headstones. Some people came and stood with them, watching. City gents walking home joined them, pickpockets, workmen, traders. An enterprising hot-spud man set up his stall by the well, calling, 'Fluffy, fluffy spuds, nice'n fluffy 'ot spuds.' Sledgehammers clinked against the walls around them, rotten wood was thrown on the bonfire. There came a dull roar of rubble.

Lydia studied Bowler's face. The flames gleamed on his cheeks. He was smiling.

'You're frightening me,' she said.

He put his hands over her ears as an explosion banged. Cellars collapsed. Part of the street dropped down, outlining the warren of stash-cellars and oubliettes that had been burrowed below it.

'Everything's going,' Bowler said. 'I got demolition orders all the way from Bunhill Row to Golden Lane and White Cross Street. The Artisans and Labourers Dwelling Act. They're out. The whole lot.'

There was a warning shout and the bang of a second explosion.

'It's for their own good,' Bowler said.

Lydia said helplessly, 'Where will they go?'

'Not here,' Bowler said. 'That's all that counts. I've broken 'em. The biggest criminal ring in London.'

The fires grew brighter.

Lydia murmured, 'Who were they?'

'What does it matter?' Bowler said. He stared into the crowd. 'Ordinary people.' He laughed, then put his hand in the nape of Lydia's neck and pressed her lips against his own. She could not help responding to his strength, lifting herself against him in the firelight like a shameless hussy.

She opened her eyes. Bowler was not looking at her.

A gentleman carrying a silver-topped cane stood in the crowd on the other side of the fire. He gave no sign that he had seen the people beside him. He wore his Chesterfield coat. He had taken off his hat because of the heat of the fire, showing his thinning grey hair. He ignored the destruction of the houses around them, the crash of the stone block from the steam crane.

Darby Briggs looked at Lydia, straight at her

through the shimmering heat, then turned and walked away.

'Oh my God,' Lydia said. 'Take me home. Take me home.'

Chapter Sixteen

I

It was the bitterest of winter evenings. Everything was grey, grey snowy hills, grey sky, grey rotten ice gap-toothed along the banks of the cut. Only the waves blown down the navigation kept the channel from freezing over. The mule plodded forward against the headwind, mane blowing, ears flat. Joy walked alongside hanging onto the bridle, eyes and nose running with the cold. Her black skirt flapped, her black coat was tightly buttoned against the wind's icy fingers. She had tied her hat on with a scarf, keeping her ears warm. Another scarf encircled her neck twice. The ends whipped.

The wind whined, and poor Ramses dug in his hooves as the empty *Poca*'s windage dragged him back. High in the water, the wind caught the boat sideways, driving it into the bank. Joy heaved on the rope with all her strength, and Eleanor pushed at the reeds with the long pole that Grandma Pebble called a quant.

The old lady sat vacantly in the cabin, close enough to the stove to burn on one side while her other side froze. She wore the same lopsided grin. Her eyes did not move. Sometimes her eyelids closed slowly, right eyelid first, then opened again in the same order.

'She's dyin'.' Eleanor had faced it reluctantly that morning. 'She'd want ter keep going. She'll 'old off till we get ter Cody's Bend, I reckon. Tough old bird.'

'Better turn her.'

'Better get on in an 'urry, more ter the point,' Eleanor said.

'I ain't deaded yet, young Eleanor,' the old lady said. But she had not moved from the rocking chair for days. 'That Eleanor of mine, always was in an 'urry. Can't wait ter see that Kes of 'ers, I bet.'

'And see the new boat,' Joy said.

'Wot new boat?'

Eleanor explained it again. 'Oh yes,' Grandma Pebble said. 'Tough old bird, am I? Looks like wind today.'

She was right, and the *Poca* was difficult to handle empty. All day the two women had struggled. The reeds thrashed and creaked along the *Poca*'s sides as she gathered sternway. Now the wind blew Eleanor's bonnet off. She would have lost it to the navigation but for the drawstring. The pole bent as she pushed into the reeds, finding bottom. The mule dug in. Joy heaved with all her strength. Slowly the *Poca* inched forward, then swung clear, gathering headway. The waves slapped loudly under the front end.

Eleanor pointed. 'There's the blooming viaduct! Nearly there!'

The wind eased as the *Poca* came around the bend. The row of cottages showed their thatched roofs above the canal bank, the bare trees waved their branches around the church tower beyond the water-meadow. A long skeleton of yellow wood, wedged clear of the ground on bostocks, lay along the top of the embankment. It looked like one of Jaffrey's sketches for a boat, bare bones seventy feet long and seven feet wide. Ham, Shane and Jaffrey threw down their tools and ran towards the *Poca* hallooing excitedly. The others grabbed the ropes and pulled with a will, but Ham grabbed Joy, swung her off her feet and kissed her cheek. He winked. 'Morwenna an' the *Lurcher* went by 'ere last week, stayed a night. I do, I really do. I do, Joy!'

'Besotted,' Shane called.

'Can't work! Can't sleep!' Jaffrey said.

'It's sweet, he's writing poems,' Shane said.

'If 'e could write, that is,' said Jaffrey. 'An' wot rhymes wiv Morwenna?' Ham beat him with his hat, then turned back to Joy. His expression was serious.

'Wot d'yer think she thinks of me? Yer an expert.'

'On Morwenna? Am I?'

'Yer a girl, aren't yer?' he pointed out.

'She probably thinks what you think about her,' Joy said sensibly. She looped the *Poca*'s front strap over the mooring post and released the mule.

'I think I'm the luckiest bloke in the world,' Ham said earnestly.

'Then she's the luckiest girl.'

'I wish I knew exactly what yer thinking, some-times,' Ham said. He followed her to the stable and watched her fill the mule's nose-tin. 'I never do know, Joy Wot's-yer-name. Yer got a streak of iron in yer, I know that.' He slopped water in the bucket, watching her. 'Sometimes I'm afraid yer aren't going ter stay wiv us. We're gonna wake up one morning an' yer'll be gone. Empty bed.'

'You're funny in love,' she said.

'Yer've changed,' Ham said. 'A year ago yer would've stuck yer tongue out.' He laughed at her then hugged her tight. 'Don't leave us. Not wivout telling us first. Promise. An' then I won't let yer go.'

'I don't make promises.'

He sucked air through his teeth, startled. 'There yer are. Yer streak of iron.'

She laughed. 'Better watch your p's and q's then.'

He shook his head glumly. 'Yer girls is all the same, if yer ask my wot-say,' he said. 'Morwenna wants 'er own way too. Own boat. Place ashore. An' me.' He sighed. 'Why do they always want as much as yer can possibly give, an' then more?'

'You'll think of a way,' Joy said.

The wind dropped as the light faded. Grandma Pebble was carried ashore in her rocking chair, a rug over her knees, and settled by the fire in Peter Pebble's warm cottage. Joy went with her but the old lady shook her head. 'Let me rest a while.'

Ham pressed an enormous mug of hot, sweet tea into Joy's hand. 'Come see the work us lads been at while yer ladies were swanning about on the Wilts & Berks.'

The men had set up a tarpaulin to work under. An acetylene lamp hissed, casting a white glare full of black shadows. 'The keel's two thirty-five foot pieces of oak scarphed together, the spine of the boat.' Ham pointed through the timbers piled everywhere.

'What a mess,' Joy said.

'Organised chaos,' Ham said, 'that's our name fer it.'

Shane came up behind them and said, 'With the emphasis on chaos.'

Joy waved to Peter Pebble, who toiled with a box saw at the front and back posts. Ham went and helped him. He straddled the stempost and swung the adze with steady sweeps between his legs, forming the curve. Clem and Nat, thinner than ever, were working on the planks. 'Elm,' Shane said, walking after Joy. 'Never rots, long as you keep it wet.'

'How are you, Nat?' Joy called.

'Warm enough, fer once,' Nat said, banging a square spike into a round hole with a heavy long-handled mall. He cursed as he missed, knocking the wood. 'I'm a machinery man, meself, not a blooming carpenter.'

'We can see that,' Peter Pebble said, argumentative as always. He mopped his bald head and threw Joy a grin. 'I 'ope Jaffrey's got 'is angles right, that's all.'

Joy turned to Jaffrey and raised her eyebrows. Jaffrey looked modest. 'I drew the plans.'

'An' I'm building 'em,' Ham said.

'And I . . .' said Shane seriously, 'I shall . . .'

'Don't let 'im touch nothing what can break!' Ham said.

'Shane's not practical wiv 'is 'ands,' Jaffrey said, 'only 'is 'ead.'

'I shall think of something . . .' Shane raised the palm of his hand. 'I shall bless this boat . . .'

'And all who sail in her?' Joy said.

'Especially all who sail in her,' Shane said. He followed her as she walked on along the half-finished hull. 'I've been going to the church school in the village. Old Soames thinks he can send me to college.'

'Can he?'

'I do very much want to go, Joy.'

'The way you're talking you sound like you ought to.'

'Can't hide anything from you.' He looked sheepish. 'Don't let on to my brothers.'

'They'd think you've gone soft.'

'For taking matters of the mind seriously. Yes.'

She sounded sad, as though something had been lost. 'You aren't the little boys I knew.'

'You aren't the little girl either,' Shane said, glancing at her outline against the lamp.

Joy pointed at a long box lying along the ground, a fire and bubbling water at one end, steam blowing past the sacks stuffed in the far end. 'They trust me in charge of that,' Shane said. 'I put the planks inside to steam, makes them soft, then Nat and Clem cripple them round the curves and coachbolt them.'

'Cripple,' Joy said, learning the words. 'Coachbolt.'

Kes came back from the village carrying a bag of clenched and squared bolts from the blacksmith. He hugged Joy then waved a telegram in the air. 'It's official, lads. The Midland Railway's backed down! There's steam on the Moira.'

'Better get down ter some work then,' Ham said, tossing a hammer.

Kes winked at Joy. 'This is how they treat their poor old Cap'n in 'is old age.'

Each day, Joy watched the boat grow as the work moved forward.

The women, of course, were not expected to help. Morning and afternoon Joy brought out a huge pot of boiling tea. Damian helped her by carrying milk or sugar. For lunch she took them a steaming platter of the workmen's pasties Eleanor had taught her to bake, the golden pastry stuffed with meat and potato at one end, marmalade or jam at the other. Damian struggled beside her with the pitcher of ginger beer. Now that Joy understood what she was looking at, the boat changed each time she ducked under the tarpaulin, the planks – 'Strakes!' Ham said – growing a little higher up the hull, the outline becoming heavier and more solid as the sides were filled in. Soon she learned to chuck their talk of strakes and bevels back at them and talk knowledgably of spiles.

'If yer know so much,' Kes said, throwing her a piece of old rope, 'yer can pick oakum.' It was the worst job. Patiently she teased the strands apart, sitting there for hours in company with them, always ready to help any task with a third hand.

Around Christmas it rained torrentially, and Kes looked up through the raindrops speckling his greasy face. 'See?' he said. 'Even got the right weather fer building an Ark.'

Joy learned to use a caulking iron, rubbing linseed oil into the oakum, feeding the threads between the strakes, ramming them tight with the knocking-in iron. 'That'll make 'em watertight,' Kes said approvingly, 'that's good.' She treated each seam three times and finished up with quick, accurate blows from the hardening iron, walking backwards as she went. The boys watched her with admiration, shaking their heads. 'She oughter be the one wearin' trousers, not us,' Ham said. He hugged her.

'You're slowing my work,' Joy said. She boiled a cauldron on the fire to 'pay up' the pitch, then treated the caulked seams. The boys disappeared for an hour. When they got back they lined up with broad grins. Together the three of them handed her a brown paper parcel. 'Proper 'uns,' Ham said.

'We went into the village,' Shane said.

'Ter the tailor,' Jaffrey said. 'Special.'

'I wanted ter go too,' Damian piped up, 'but they said I was too young.'

'Oh . . .' Joy said, remonstrating with the others on Damian's behalf.

'They're a present from yer, too, sprogett,' Ham said, tousling the youngster's curly blond hair.

Joy opened the parcel. They were proper tailor's trousers, the first ones she'd ever had. She held them against her, almost as broad as skirts at the ankle. 'Honor'ry workman,' Ham said. 'Now yer'll 'ave ter work 'arder'n the rest of us, just to show us up.'

'I do already,' she said.

'Whooo-hooo!' the boys said, and Damian joined in. Joy nipped into the stores shed to change, and soon everyone was busy again.

The inside of the boat's hull was smeared with chalico, a time-honoured recipe of gas-tar, pitch, tallow and mule dung, applied steaming and covered with felt. They finished up quite light-headed from the fumes. 'I'll get the tea,' Ham said.

'Don't forget to bring the pasties,' Joy called after him. They set to work hammering on the shearing, oak boards made pliable over the fire, to seal in the chalico and make the boat completely waterproof.

436

Ham reached up and banged the hull with the flat of his hand. 'Last for ever,' he said.

Kes arrived with the mule pulling a cart. He looked at Joy, surprised, never having seen a woman in trousers. 'Looks like the blooming wild west in 'ere,' he said. He'd been to the railway station and taken delivery of the propeller, fabricated in Derby. Kes called it the blades. The propeller was huge, nearly three feet across, and it took the six of them to lift it off the cart. 'Phosphor-bronze,' Kes grunted, 'twice as good as steel.'

'This is where I get busy,' Nat said, taking the propeller shaft and flourishing his engineers' calipers.

The engine was delivered by boat, on a blustery afternoon in February. 'It's the *Lurcher*!' Ham cried, and went running along the towpath to meet it. Blodwen was at the hellum, her expression unreadable as ever. Morwenna stood on the front end with the breeze flapping her skirt and lifting her long black hair. Her expression was serious. She jumped ashore with the rope and Ham took her in his arms.

'Our dad's passed on,' she said tearfully.

'Good,' Ham said. 'Now he can't say no.'

'Yer don't understand,' Morwenna said. 'We'll 'ave ter give up the boat.'

'Give us a kiss,' Ham said.

'Don't yer just 'ate some people,' Blodwen said glumly.

The boys swarmed over the *Lurcher*'s sidecloths, lifting them off to expose the cargo, and gave a gasp of awe. 'It's even bigger'n I thought, sprogs,' Kes

437

said, running his hands over the cold iron. 'Look at the size o' that boiler.'

''Orizontal return tube,' Jaffrey said. ''Undred an' thirty pounds per square inch steam pressure.'

'My God,' Kes said, 'wot 'ave I done?'

Joy read the brass plaque. 'Built under licence by Fellows, Clayton and Moore.'

'How will we lift something that gosh-heavy from one boat to the other?' Shane said.

'I got an idea.' Jaffrey scribbled a sketch and showed it to Kes.

'It might work,' Kes said dubiously.

'Easy peasy,' Jaffrey said. He could visualise stresses and strains in his head, and seemed to know instinctively what structure was required. 'Believe me. The shaft and propeller are already on the new boat, she's ready for wet. We'll do it tomorrow.'

Kes watched them. ''Ow lucky I am,' he said, putting his hands on his hips, 'ter 'ave such sons.'

Next morning they gathered under the tarpaulin at the front of the new boat, Grandma Pebble like a waxen doll in her chair, Constance standing beside her, Aunt Aggie holding their hands. Ham wanted to hold Morwenna's hot hand but he had been given the sledgehammer, and had to be content with making sheep's eyes at her. She giggled. The women smiled at them both and at each other. Nat and Peter Pebble took tallow and greased the two steep ramps that led from the new boat to the water. Now the hull was held back by a single stout oak post, and would be launched sideways. The ramps ended five feet above the water. It looked dangerous. 'She'll overturn when she hits the wet,' Clem said.

'Vera?' Eleanor said. She always turned to Vera.

'If she overturns,' Vera pointed out, 'she was no good anyway.'

Ham spat on his hands and swung the sledgehammer. 'Wait!' Shane said.

"E's right,' Kes said. 'No name.'

'Boats is always girls,' Eleanor said.

'What do I name her?' Shane said.

'It's time I did my bit, or Kes'll shilly-shally all day.' Eleanor pulled Joy forward. 'Get back, yer blokes. Ham, give 'er the sledgehammer. Joy, 'it that bit o' wood. It'll knock out the post an' in she'll go. Big swing, now.'

'Spit on yer 'ands,' Ham called.

Eleanor whispered in Shane's ear. He nodded.

Joy swung the sledgehammer with all her strength.

'I name this boat *Joy*,' Shane said. 'God bless her and all who sail in her.'

Ham smashed a stone bottle of ginger beer on the front end. White foam splashed them all.

The *Joy* slid down with increasing speed. The hull dropped from the ramps well heeled over. There was a surge of dirty waves across the navigation, then the empty boat bobbed quietly, afloat.

'By God, we done it. We all done it!' Kes cheered. 'Rope 'er in, lads. Everyone ter Eth and Eli's fer ginger beer an' rabbit pie, an' the last one's cissy!'

'Look at 'em youngsters,' Grandma Pebble murmured. 'Never thought I'd see this day. It's an 'ole way of life coming to an end. An' I'm still 'ere to see it.'

The towpath was smooth, and Joy pushed the old

lady in the wheeled wicker chair that the lads had knocked together. It was strong but creaked alarmingly.

'Mind yer don't push me in the water by mistook,' Grandma Pebble said, then pointed with her stick. 'Wot are they up to *now*? Birthed yesterday, they was. Why d'they always 'ave ter be *doing*?'

The two boats were moored abreast, the *Lurcher* outside. A mast had been stepped at the water's edge. A jib almost as tall as the mast angled from the collar around the base.

'Gonna sail the canal bank away, are they?'

'They've lowered the end of the jib over the *Lurcher*'s hold.' Joy explained what the boys were doing. 'They've attached a rope. They're swaying up the new engine clear of the hull. Now they're hauling on the jib.' Shane's feet skidded in the towpath ash and he sat down with a bump. He jumped back to his place on the line and hauled. 'As the jib comes upright it's swinging the engine over the new boat—'

'Yer boat.'

'Our boat. All of ours.'

'She ain't a proper boat till she's painted, girl. No personality. No guts. No luck.'

'Now they're lowering the engine onto the oak bearers. Uncle Nat can move ten tons with his little finger while it's in the air. He's lining up the bolts with the propeller shaft. He's done it.' Joy sighed. 'Easy peasy.'

The old lady twisted round. There was life in her eyes.

'The real work's yet ter come.'

Joy found Eleanor in the cottage. 'I think Gran's getting better.'

'Yer don't know nothing,' Eleanor said.

Next morning Joy took the teapot outside. 'Look!' Damian said. Peter Pebble and Jaffrey had taken advantage of the sunny day to fit the cabin top. They were trying to fit out the sliding side doors to the engine compartment and all the other paraphernalia of slides, pigeon boxes, cabin shafts, the funnel, but a scrawny figure dressed in black, nose almost touching the paintwork of the new boat, a fine brush in her hand, seemed to be in their way whatever job they tried.

'It's Gran.' Damian gripped Joy's hand hard. 'She's started painting.'

II

Tom looked behind him. The black wrought-iron gates clanged shut for the last time. He was determined that he would never again see Dr Thaddeus Gregory's No Vacations Academy for the Sons of Gentlefolk. Last night he had been summoned to the Head's Study for the Valedictory. The Headmaster's genial wife, known to the boys as Wampum, sewed by the fire. She looked up and smiled from time to time. Tom had eyed the Cutter in its rack, and the rail over which he had been doubled so many times to receive his punishment. 'A thrashing never failed to improve a bad boy, nor harmed a good one,' Gregory reminded him smoothly. 'I trust, young Briggs, that in the fullness of time you may consider sending your own sons to my establishment?'

To Tom the most incredible thing about Dr Gregory's boarding school was not the stupidity and savagery of the place, but that the Headmaster was right. Most of the boys, having suffered its brutality, would indeed – if they could afford the fees – send their sons here to suffer the same treatment. Tom was expected to say something along the lines of *I hope so, sir. Thank you, sir.*

'You're a vicious thug,' Tom said levelly. 'You're a monster and a hypocrite and you know it.'

Gregory was amused. 'That's the way the world turns, isn't it? That's why I'm sitting here warm and comfortable, and you're standing there. First train tomorrow,' he added carelessly. As Tom closed the door the Headmaster called, 'I'll look forward to hearing from you, Briggs. In about ten years' time.'

The gates clanged, and Tom shivered. He held his lapels to his neck, hefted his scuffed leather suitcase. He had arrived here a child, and now he was leaving as neither a child nor a man. He knew that without this place there would be a hole in his life. Part of him would always want to come back here, subscribe to the School Mag, return grey-haired on School Day to a rosy nostalgic past that had never happened.

'You must be joking,' Tom said to himself.

He set off down the track through the cold dawn light. In the village the church bell tolled as he passed, and on impulse he went into the graveyard. He took off his hat in front of Freddie Tosser's headstone. The stone already looked old. A local councillor had recently died and Tom carried the flowers over, adorned Freddie's cross with them.

The smooth, broad-gauge Great Western Railway

swept him to Paddington. No one was at the station to meet him, not even the butler, Worth, or Dottie and a boy with the dog-cart to carry his case.

Tom walked up Watling Street alone. Abbey Place had changed, of course, the number of gaslights doubled, and the gate was manned by beadles who admitted him only when he gave his name.

He came to his parents' house. The windows had been repainted in cream rather than white. The shrubs had grown tall. When he knocked on the door it was answered by a man he did not recognise.

'Mr Worth left here many years ago, sir. My name is Prettiman.'

It was all horribly strange to Tom. The house looked so much smaller than he remembered, and everything had been redecorated and moved around. He waited in the hall like a stranger.

His mother came down the stairs.

She looked so much older that he gasped.

'Tom?' she said.

He put down his suitcase and reached out. She frowned, and Tom realised his cuffs were threadbare. He stared at himself in a mirror. A wild, stalky figure gazed back at him. His hair stood up as though cut by shears. His shoes were scuffed, his trousers two inches too short, revealing white ankles.

Tom said, 'I'm sorry, Mama.'

Lydia's eyes softened momentarily, but she did not seem to know how to be kind. 'No socks. I'll try – I'll see – you cannot go to your Papa like this.'

She looked vaguely at Prettiman. The butler hastened away and returned with a pair of socks and a brush. Tom sat on the stairs, pulled on the socks, brushed his hair. 'Excuse me, sir,' Prettiman said, handing him a comb, and brushed his clothes.

Tom followed his mother to his father's study. He felt awful about carrying his suitcase but did not know where he should put it down. Lydia knocked and went in. The desk had been put round a different way.

Darby Briggs had white hair.

'What are you staring at?' he said. He looked as old as Grandfather. He was dressed in a frock coat, considered formal and old fashioned now. He put his knuckles on the desk and stood, making himself the same height as Tom. Tom said something and Darby interrupted him.

'You're eighteen years old. That's old enough to work. You'll drag no more on your mother and me. You'll start in the bank tomorrow. You'll learn the value of money. Go out and buy yourself a proper suit. The money will be taken out of your screw, which will be paid quarterly, in arrears.'

So he was to work at the bank. He was not disowned. Tom said, 'Thank you, sir.'

'Don't thank me, thank your mother,' Darby said without looking at her. 'You're my son and heir, Tom, whether I like it or not. That means you're going to behave like it. You're going to be better than everyone else.'

'Yes, sir.' Tom swallowed. 'Sir, that letter I wrote to you.'

'Letter?'

'I did see her, sir. I wasn't just saying it.'

'Nine o'clock sharp,' Darby said. He sat and looked at the papers in front of him. It was a dismissal.

444

Tom carried his suitcase upstairs. Once the house had seemed as tall as a castle to him, but now he took the stairs to the attic two at a time. He went along the narrow corridor and stopped.

The children's door had an elephant and a mouse drawn on it.

Tom opened the door.

Nothing had changed.

Joy's playthings had been left just as they had been that terrible night long ago, as though no time had passed. Her bed was still made up, her teddy bear on the pillow, waiting for her.

But the room smelt musty. Tom opened the window.

He looked down on number thirteen next door, where Mr Goldblum had been eviscerated for the key in his belly, long ago. Now three children played on the grass. The boys wore tweeds and fought each other. A girl in a white dress, red ribbons on her white hat, played with their wooden train.

There was a knock on the door.

'Come in.'

It was Dottie, plumper than he remembered, with her hair grown long. She put the tray on the table. 'I brought yer 'addick an' chips, Mister Tom. Just the way yer always used ter like it. It's good ter 'ave yer back.'

The City of London, Tom realised, was a city of clerks. No clerk could afford a carriage, and the police had banned three-horse omnibuses in Threadneedle Street. In the morning a quarter of a million clerks in black coats, white collars and black

445

shoes hurried on foot up the broad boulevards of London Bridge, King William Street and Cornhill into the Square Mile. They scurried like ants to the City's great institutions of banking and insurance. In the evening they hurried home again. Tom was surprised to see so many old men among them. Few banks paid pensions, and most clerks could not afford to retire. For all the thousands of pounds that passed through their hands each day, the great mass of them were poor men, and burdened with the expense of appearing to be middle-class.

Tom hurried with them. He too wore a black coat, white collar, black shoes, and his hair was neatly trimmed. He would be the perfect clerk, and work his way forward by his own efforts.

A joint-stock bank was expected to be large and ornamental, he realised. The Briggs Bank was built in the Italian style. Tom went up the steps on the busy corner of Cornhill, but female staff hurried past him to a different entrance, in Finch Lane. The ground-floor banking hall where customers queued was called the shop, as in all banks. It was grandiose with marble columns, dark panelled walls and counters, behind which clerks conducted business without raising their heads. Over them hung a large clock. Out of sight upstairs and to the back, behind the Directors' Room to take advantage of the cheaper Finch Lane rents, lay the warren of tiny offices where the work was done, the endless filing out of Bills of Lading, Bills of Exchange, allotments and acceptances. These magical words had been the stuff of Tom's early childhood, conversation casually thrown about at Papa's parties, and now would be made real.

A portly walker, resplendent in a damson-coloured suit with gilt buttons, crossed the Banking Hall and fetched Tom to Mr Mostlock's desk. The Principal Clerk's right ear stuck out due to the pen behind it, Tom noticed, as did the ears of all the clerks. They all had inkstains on their right thumb and forefinger, except those who were left-handed.

'Your father has made it clear that you are to begin at the lowest step,' Mostlock said quietly. He was British but there was a faint bloom of olive in his complexion, something Spanish somewhere. There was a banking notice on the mantelshelf behind him. *Call on a business man in business hours only on business. Transact your business and go about your business, in order to give him time to finish his business.* 'Here, Mr Tom, you will meet with no respect to your person but what is due to any merit you may have, and to faithful service.'

'I understand, Mr Mostlock.'

'Ledgers are to be balanced at the end of each day, no staff allowed home until the reconciliation is complete, any shortfalls to be made up by you. You will copy letters, go out with messages, run to the Post Office and fulfil every duty required of other junior clerks. Sign the book at the start of the day and again at the end. One hour is allowed for lunch. On Packet Days and Post Days you will stay until dismissed. There will be no unnecessary conversation. Begin over there.'

In short, Tom thought, I must learn the business for myself.

'Yes, Mr Mostlock,' he said, and took off his hat.

'It is one of our traditions,' Mostlock said, 'that the hat is taken off with both hands, and replaced with both hands.' No bank acquired tradition more earnestly than a new bank.

Tom went to the counter pointed out to him.

A ledger was put in front of him. He must fill in the names from the papers in front of him, add up the sub-totals, and subtract them down to nought again. Commission was calculated in eighths of percentage points. After trigonometry, it was easy.

The young man in the next chair watched Tom working rapidly, then reached across and shook hands below the level of the desk. 'I'm Widgeon.' He spoke without moving his lips, in the way Tom was soon to learn. 'Don't worry, there's only one tradition that really matters here. "Nine till five, nine till five, brush your hat and get out alive!"'

Tom laughed, and everyone looked round. Widgeon scribbled furiously, then looked up when they were no longer the centre of attention. 'You'll meet old Briggs upstairs, I expect, he always likes to inspect the new intake. There's a man who can still think in millions, even if he no longer deals in millions.' Widgeon explained with a knowing wink, 'He spends a good deal even if he does not make a good deal . . .'

Tom must have looked surprised. The Bank seemed very wealthy to him. The marble alone must have cost thousands, and the banking hall radiated solidity and respectability.

'Briggs makes a good show,' Widgeon whispered, 'but in the Clubs people reckon it was a big come-down for him, chucking up his place at Prideau's. Question of loyalty. Dicey judgement. He's never shaken off the name for it. You'd've been better making a career at the City Bank, or Hambros – or Prideau's.'

My God, Tom thought, the City believes my father is failing. The men who matter believe he is a failure – or at least, that he is not the great success he promised them.

He listened to the cheap, desultory chatter of typewriters from upstairs.

'Psst,' Widgeon whispered. 'What's your name?'

'Briggs.'

'Oh!'

Three months later came Tom's first pay day, deducted of the loan for his suit and stout shoes, and the board and lodging for living in his parents' house. At two minutes past five, the day's transactions totalled, completed and approved, he and Widgeon ran down the steps to Threadneedle Street. At Bannister's the butcher they each bought a pound of steak, wrapped in a page of the *Commercial Chronicle*, and took it into the Fleece and Sun next door. They settled themselves in a box by the window and drank ale while the gridiron sizzled, then paid for claret with their meal, and glasses of ruby port after a large sweet pudding. They emerged on to the pavement happy and staggering.

'Come on,' Widgeon said. 'I know the place to go.' He jerked his hand suggestively.

'No,' Tom said.

'Young girls,' Widgeon said. 'Never been touched.'

Tom pulled away. He felt sick.

'Everyone does it,' Widgeon said. 'I say, you aren't strange, are you?'

Tom stared at him.

Widgeon noticed the ink on his fingers and licked them clean, then disappeared into the crowd towards Aldgate.

But in the City, at their desks, they were the best of friends. Their quarterly tightner at the Fleece was soon a tradition that neither man would have missed.

As always, they parted company on the kerb afterwards, Sammy Widgeon setting off hopefully down east, Tom turning his steps towards St John's Wood. This particular day was a summer's evening and birds were singing in the warm afterglow, and well-dressed children and their nannies were returning from the park. As Tom turned the corner into Abbey Place, he knocked into someone wearing a brown plaid overcoat and brown billycock hat.

The other man braced himself solidly and did not apologise.

'Steady on there. Tom, ain't it?'

'Bowler,' Tom said, wondering at Bowler's remarkable memory. A policeman must see thousands of faces in nearly ten years, and Tom had grown up in that time, but Bowler's air of authority made him feel small again. He was sure Bowler knew he had been drinking, had sniffed the port on his breath. 'Well, Detective Inspector,' he said quickly, feeling guilty, 'what brings you here?'

'I don't stop just because it's five o'clock in the City,' Bowler said. So he knew Tom worked at the bank.

But he had not answered Tom's question.

Tom said, 'Have you been to see my parents?'

'Your father was out, in fact.'

'He never comes in until eight on Fridays.'

'So I have discovered,' Bowler said. He pushed past. 'Doubtless I shall see you around, sir.'

Tom called after him, 'So the case is not closed.'

Bowler stopped. He turned back.

'Did you not know? No, it cannot be closed. Lydia – Mrs Briggs has refused to have your sister declared dead.'

'You know that I saw her. I saw Joy, Mr Bowler. I swear to it.'

'I do recall your mother showed me a letter.'

'Did she!' Tom said. He blurted, 'She never wrote back.'

Bowler took Tom's arm, jerked his head towards Abbey Road. There was a public house with a large livery stable. They crossed the strawyard and went inside. Tom felt as if he was being arrested. He could not resist Bowler's will. Bowler pushed through the travellers and sat down. 'Beer for me,' he ordered. 'Another port for the young man.' He glanced at Tom and showed his teeth, slightly ragged with age. He must be about fifty, Tom reckoned. As a child he had felt wholly in Bowler's thrall, and he still felt that he *ought* to feel the same way.

'The case will never be solved,' Bowler said. He drank half his beer and called for another because the counter was busy.

Tom said, 'The Goldblum case was never solved either.'

Bowler shrugged at the implied criticism, drained

his glass. He thought Tom was a pipsqueak. 'You didn't look out of the window, Tom. No one knew anything until Alfie Nutting found the body.'

Tom said honestly, 'I can never think of that night without a feeling of whole, complete horror at what I did. And what I did not do.'

'Don't be soft,' Bowler said. 'I reckon anyone would have done the same as you, if they only had the guts to admit it.' He raised his fresh glass. 'You had the guts to chase the thief down through the house. As for what happened then, what eleven-year-old boy would have done different, with a knife cutting his throat?'

'Goldblum did different,' Tom said. 'He didn't give up.'

Bowler shrugged and drank. 'Goldblum was a fool and died.'

'You've still no idea who did it.'

'I've always said Jack Riddles did him. The same bloke who nearly got you, Tom. You were lucky.'

'But you never found him.'

'Disappeared off the face of the earth.'

Tom called for a pitcher of beer. He put his elbows on the table and refilled Bowler's glass.

'You're drunk,' Bowler said.

'I'm interested,' Tom said persistently. 'You see, I've never really thought about it before. I mean, what actually happened that night. I've been too busy being sorry for myself and not actually *thinking* about it.'

'What's your point?'

'For instance, that fabulous piece of jewellery.'

'The Bethlehem.'

452

'It never turned up either, did it?'

'Neither hide nor hair.'

'That's unusual, isn't it?'

'No,' Bowler said. 'It was probably put in a bank vault until the fuss died down. It's probably there still. He'll get it out to pay for his old age.'

Tom thought about Jack. 'Do you really think so?'

'Yes,' Bowler said.

'So he stole the priceless jewel and then came to turn over our house.' Tom paused. 'Does it sound likely?'

'You know nothing of the criminal mind, Tom. They don't care, you know, they're not like me and you, don't make that mistake. Maybe it was an inside job –'

'My father dismissed Nanny M'Kenzy.'

'Yes, for dereliction of duty.'

'But no suspicion fell on her.'

'No.'

Tom refilled Bowler's glass with the last of the pitcher. 'You won't find out any more by trying to get me drunk,' Bowler said. 'I live over a pub now.'

'I always supposed you were a married man.'

Bowler shrugged. 'I rent a room above the Eyre Arms from Sergeant Steynes. He's busy with the Special Irish Branch of Scotland Yard and works all round the country now, such is the degree of terrorism and unrest. The Fenians. And working-class radicals in the northern towns.'

'I remember him.'

'I'll give you sound advice, Tom. Let sleeping dogs lie. What happened is all in the past. You'll only hurt your parents if you rake over old coals like this, playing detective.'

'Did you never catch that boy, Monkey, either?'

'He died.' Bowler stood. 'Ta for the beer. You'll do well in your father's bank, Tom. Keep your nose clean.' He nodded farewell. The door banged shut behind him.

Tom stood shakily. Bowler's right, he thought. I am drunk.

But he's wrong, too. It isn't all in the past. He's still here, and so am I. The past is still with us. It always is. Each of us carries the past inside us.

He's still looking, and so am I.

A couple of men shoved past him and sat at his table. Tom finished his drink at the bar.

He went home. Going upstairs he stopped thoughtfully. The door to the parlour was open and he saw his mother's head over the back of the sofa.

Lydia half turned, sensing him. 'Come in, Tom.'

His father was not yet home. 'I saw Bowler,' Tom said. He sat in the armchair.

Lydia didn't deny the visit. She patted the sofa for him to sit beside her.

Tom stayed where he was.

'Yes, Tom, Mr Bowler was here, because he has become a friend of the family.'

'I see.'

'Don't rush off to your room, Tom! Stay here and talk with me. I see so few people nowadays. Your father and I so rarely go out.' Lydia's face split into weary lines as she smiled. 'It is so wonderful to be young. Do tell me what you get up to, Tom. You never bring your friends home. I'd love to meet them.' She hesitated, then continued talking because Tom said nothing. 'Yes, Mr Bowler came for tea. He is much misunderstood, but I do understand him. He is very lonely. It helps him to talk. He feels betrayed by his senior officers.'

Tom sat watchfully. 'He talks to you.'

'He feels uncomfortable with everyone except police officers. I'm the exception, the only one he can confess his feelings to. You know his wife left him in the most brutal fashion. He came back to find a note on the kitchen table. She took the children too. He has been unable to find her.'

'I'm sorry for him,' Tom said. He thought his mother's perfume smelt strong and bitter.

'Oh, yes, it must be heartbreaking to be a policeman.'

'Is that what Mr Bowler says?'

'You've not heard of the dreadful scandal? The head of the Detective Force, Superintendent Williamson, Mr Bowler's superior officer – arrested! And any number of senior officers with him, all implicated in turf fraud. They have been charged and may go to jail.'

'Policemen don't go to jail,' Tom said.

'Wouldn't it be awful? They are the men Mr Bowler has worked with, trusted, all his professional life. The Detective Force is disbanded and an amateur placed in charge of the new department, the Criminal Investigations Department. A barrister.' Lydia sounded outraged. 'What does a barrister know of policing?'

'Nothing, I suppose.'

'Yet Mr Bowler continues his work loyally. The

criminal situation is so frightening. One has only to read the newspapers to be terrified. I'm afraid to go out. I don't think you ought to, Tom. I'm frightened for you walking into the City each day.'

'Perhaps I should take a lodging closer in.'

Lydia's smile failed. 'I could not bear it if you left.'

Tom went and sat beside her.

Lydia said, 'You're all I have.'

'You have Father.'

She made no reply.

'Mama,' Tom said, 'you must know that there are serious difficulties at the bank.'

'There always have been! City men are never optimists. Always cautious. Cluck, cluck. They cluck like old hens. Your father knows what he is doing.'

'Willis Percival, one of Lombard Street's oldest institutions, has failed with liabilities of over half a million pounds. The City of Glasgow Bank has crashed for ten or twenty times as much. At Briggs we cannot get any Bills discounted under the Bank of England rate. Soon we will not be able to keep our balance sheets secret. We are spread too thin.'

'Your father has nothing to fear.'

'He has been lending money to stockbrokers. We are in eight hundred thousand pounds to P.W. Thomas & Co. You used to take such an interest, Mama.'

'I'm tired,' Lydia said.

Tom realised she had not been listening. She did not care.

Tom arrived at the bank bright and early the next

morning. Widgeon, as usual, was even earlier. Tom leaned across his desk.

'Pass me the Post Office London Directory, would you?'

'Which one?'

'M to P.'

Sammy Widgeon watched Tom riffle through the pages of the bulky volume. 'What exactly are you looking for?'

'Putting a name to an address,' Tom said.

Chapter Seventeen

I

'Why d'you wear your hair plaited over one shoulder?' Damian asked, running after Joy.

'It's called a Zarnder,' she said.

'May I walk with you?' he said shyly.

'If yer put a shoe in it,' Eleanor called back from the Paddington dock gates. She carried her wicker shopping basket over her arm.

'What, Mum?' Damian always sounded so eager that both girls laughed at him.

'Yer mouth, Damian,' Eleanor said.

Damian slipped his hand into Joy's. 'But why's it called a Zarnder, Joy?' he whispered.

'Because it's a tubbichon.'

'What's that?'

'Wearing my hair plaited over one shoulder,' said Joy.

'Good job we ain't pulled by donkeys, Damian,' Eleanor said.

'Why, Mum?'

'Yer'd 'ave talked their 'ind legs off by now,' said Eleanor. They turned into the street. She gave him an affectionate slap upside the head. 'I wish I 'ad 'is 'air,' she confided. 'All lovely an' curly an' blond like that. D'yer remember what a beautiful babe 'e made? Our Cottontop. Seems like yesterday.'

'It's a lifetime ago,' Joy said.

Eleanor sighed. 'An' now Morwenna's got two littl'uns of 'er own back at Cody's Bend, an' 'er sister Blodwen married the village baker's boy. My little boy Ham's a proper man, 'is own Number One wiv the *Lurcher*. I'm a grandma, Gawd 'elp us.' She stepped around the loan shark with his baggy apron, who lent lunch-money to Lumpers against their day's pay.

But Damian had stopped at the gates. Joy went back to him. He pointed across the busy wharfside to the *Joy* and its towed butty, the *Poca*, tied up behind it on the far side of the Paddington basin. It was a breezy day and a finger of sun rippled across the roofs of the warehouses, made the water bright, picked out the two boats in their brilliant peacock colours.

'They're beautiful, our boats,' Damian murmured, so quiet that she had to lean close. 'Who painted them?'

'An old lady, you wouldn't remember her, Grandma Pebble. She died when she had finished.'

'Of course I remember Gran.'

Joy brushed her finger across his upper lip. 'Who's getting a fuzz?'

Damian touched it anxiously as they walked. 'D'you think I should cut it off or leave it?'

Joy almost laughed, but she remembered Ham at that age. 'A razor is very impressive,' she said seriously.

460

'Perhaps I ought to consider purchasing one,' Damian said. 'I wish I was as tall as you.'

'You will be, one day.'

Eleanor shook her head, overhearing. 'Listen ter 'im, 'e talks just like yer.'

Joy was hurt. 'I'm no different,' she said.

'Yer are!' Eleanor said. Joy looked away with a swirl of her hair, upset.

That girl's as hard as nails in her way, Eleanor thought, and she looks tough because she's pretty, maybe beautiful one day, but it's real sad how an innocent remark cuts her, sometimes. 'I didn't mean ter say nothing 'gainst yer, dear.'

'Castles in the mist, and Birds of Paradise,' Damian murmured, and Joy knew he was still thinking of the boat, even here on dry land. She gripped his hand.

'I know,' she said.

'Yer sound diff'rent, girl, always 'ave, an' that's a fact,' Eleanor said. 'An' then there's everything else about yer.' They came to the market. It was late and past its best. The costers had been up since three in the morning. Many snoozed standing up, leaning their faces against their stall-posts in the afternoon heat. Eleanor sniffed disapprovingly at a half-empty stall of tomatoes. 'Yer made Shane sound like it too. That's 'ow 'e got into college, I swear. When did yer last 'ear a Cockney Church of England vicar? They don't make 'em. 'Ow much fer these toms?' she demanded. "*Ow* much? Bleedin' outrageous!'

'Half to voo,' the coster yawned. 'Buy net pound I'll vrow in owt pound vree.'

'All right, but none of yer rotten ones yer got

461

'idden underneath.' She winked at Joy. 'Give 'em an inch an' they'll take a mile. Damian, yer do the carrying.' They walked on and Eleanor said, 'Yer made Damian diff'rent too. Birds of Paradise indeed. They're sparrows wiv tails on.'

'And she wears trousers,' Damian said.

'I can do anything I like,' Joy said.

If anyone can she can, Eleanor thought. Her hair plaited like that looking hot enough to burn a man's hands, and those deep dark black-brown eyes of hers that you can't see into, but a man would want to, and think he could. 'No yer can't,' Eleanor said definitely. 'Yer a prisoner.'

'She isn't!' Damian said.

'Of the way she looks, I said. I didn't say she could 'elp it. She can't 'elp what she looks like any more'n yer can.' Eleanor sniffed the air. 'Onions. I'll 'ave a sack of onions. Give us yer shoulder, Damian, ups-a-daisy.'

'I wish my brothers were here,' Damian grunted under the weight of tomatoes and onions, following on.

'Me children are growing up,' Eleanor confided sadly. Joy was her closest friend, perhaps her only real friend now, despite Eleanor's vast range of acquaintances. 'Our family's flying apart, isn't it? I wish me babies were still inside me. Everyone wot once needed looking after fer every little thing an' their noses blowin' an' their bum wiped, well, they've growed up and gorned away. Each of 'em 'as their own life now. Separate. Adult.' The market thinned out and they looked in the shop windows. 'Jaffrey at the Mechanical Institute learning 'ow ter do things

462

I'll never even understand. I'll tell yer fer free,' Eleanor said impulsively, 'I do wish Ham would marry Morwenna.'

'You never married Kes. Ham's following your example.'

'Kes would've. I wouldn't let 'im.'

'Why ever not?'

'Oh, this and that.' Eleanor spied a butcher. She examined the meat.

'Anyway, you couldn't have had a better husband.'

'That's right, I don't deserve 'im, an' that's the truth. I've never loved another man.' Eleanor called to the butcher, 'I'll 'ave two stone o' best beef, not the fatty bit, not the gristly bit. *That* one.'

The butcher recognised her and grinned. He came out of his doorway, tipped back his straw boater with his thumb, then wiped his bloody hands on his blue pinstripe apron. 'I'll get the lad ter take it round on the cart fer yer, if yer like.'

'He can make a proper job of it,' Joy said, adding on the onions and tomatoes. Damian gave a sigh of relief, rubbing his shoulders. Eleanor paid with her cheese-money and they walked towards the bridge.

'Did yer see the look in that butcher's eye at me?' Eleanor said, pleased. 'The cheek of 'im,' she preened herself.

'Mum!' Damian said, scandalised.

'At my age, too,' Eleanor said. 'Dirty old man.'

They stopped on the Warwick Road bridge and leaned on the parapet. The sun was very pleasant, throwing their shadows along the Regent's Canal below them. The canal was lined with elegant houses. In the distance rose a hill covered with buildings. A

463

man led a horse up the steep ramp to go through the streets. Below him two men scrambled onto the top planks of the boat going into the tunnel. They lay back and braced their feet on the tunnel roof, walking the boat into the darkness.

'The other end, that's where we found yer,' Eleanor said. 'Don't know where yer got on. Out we came an' there yer were, that's all.'

Damian said to Joy, 'You don't know where you came from?'

She shook her head.

He said, 'Did you never wonder?'

'Nobody knows where they come from, exactly,' Eleanor said. 'Nobody knows everything about themselves, Damian.' The butcher's donkey-cart came toiling over the bridge. Eleanor stopped the boy and got on the back of the cart. She swung her swollen ankles luxuriously. 'Too 'ot ter walk,' she grinned, patting the boards for them to sit beside her.

But Joy turned away. 'I'll meet you at the other end of the tunnel,' she said. 'Damian, you go with her.'

'I'm staying with you,' Damian said.

Eleanor waved as the cart pulled away, and Damian stood waving after her. He had hardly been away from his mother before. He turned to tell Joy.

But Joy was already gone.

Damian saw her down on the towpath along the left bank. She walked with long strides. He ran down the wooden steps after her, calling, but she wouldn't wait. He caught her up but she said nothing.

He cast her adoring glances, glad just to be with

her, to be seen with her. Her face was set, her nose and cheekbones freckled slightly by the sun.

'What are you looking for?' he asked.

She didn't reply. He fell in step behind her. Towpath ash scuffled around the hems of her trousers. A maid glanced over the wall above them, hanging out the washing. She followed them with envious eyes, pegs in her mouth, then looked away when she was called. A gleaming carriage drawn by two gorgeous black horses went tapping smartly along the broad residential road on their left, then turned out of sight.

Damian realised that Joy had got far ahead of him, already striding up the cobbled ramp into the streets over the tunnel. Damian ran after her. The smell of horse dung and humanity was trapped between the tall buildings crowding around him. Sunlight slanted out of the turnings on his right, shops, houses, vehicles rushing forward. Damian hurried through the shadows and sunlight almost too bright to look at, pushing people aside, running.

He found her standing on a corner.

A man was trying to sell Joy matches. As Damian watched them the man kept coming back to her. Traffic whizzed and rumbled past her in every direction. A driver with a whip spat over his iron-rimmed wheel and called out something filthy.

Damian came up to her. 'We'll look together,' he said.

He put his hand on her elbow. Joy turned to him and the blank look left her eyes. She realised who he was.

'Have you ever been here?' Damian asked her.

She shook her head. 'I remember . . . Kes used to lead the mule over here, didn't he?'

Damian took her hand gently. She nodded. 'All right, we'll look together,' she said. She took a step, then glanced at him suspiciously. 'What are you grinning for?'

'Oh, I just like holding your hand.'

He walked beside her patiently. He knew Joy wouldn't find what she was looking for. All the streets of London looked the same to him. Windows glittered over the heads of the mob. She went first this way then that, cutting down turning after turning, sometimes walking fast, then stopping and staring around her helplessly.

'It's like a dream,' she said. 'As soon as I reach out and touch it . . . it's gone.'

They came to a huge building with pillars. Damian stopped to look at the grinning women painted on the posters. They were showing their legs to the frills. 'Cor,' he said. 'They're kicking as high as their heads!' Joy tugged him on impatiently. They crossed a broad thoroughfare and went along the road beyond. They must be almost over the tunnel again. Damian read the name of the road, Aberdeen Place. From somewhere he heard the cries of children playing. They came to another wide road, and Joy stopped.

At first Damian thought they were on a bridge, because the drop beyond the parapet was almost vertical.

'It's the end of the tunnel,' Joy said. She pointed at a massive ornate structure in the distance. 'Is that the Houses of Parliament?'

'It's only St Pancras Station,' Damian said.

They went down the wooden steps to the towpath thirty-five feet below. Damian sat on the long bench where boaties put their horse harness. He watched the men in the Stone Yard shovelling gravel into a waiting boat. The yellow dust rose high into the air. They wore handkerchiefs over their faces.

'It's changed,' Joy whispered. 'It was a steep grass slope. The grass has been concreted over. I threw Jack's knife in the water from there. It's probably still down there somewhere.'

Damian, waking, realised he had dozed.

Joy gripped something to her throat. A flash showed between her fingers. 'I remember . . . it was dark. Jack was running. I remember Tom saying, *Take her, she's yours*. I wanted to go with Jack. I wanted to save Tom.'

'Mum's little brother was called Tom,' Damian said.

'What happened to him?'

'He was killed, I suppose. She doesn't talk about it. Dad told Ham about it one night in the pub. It was long ago.'

'I want to go away from here,' Joy said. She shivered as though cold air blew from the tunnel mouth. She took a few steps into the sunlight along the towpath but Damian stopped in front of her.

'What's that?' He touched her fingers.

She opened her hand, showed the silver coin in her palm. 'It's a child's toy. Play money. I've always had it. I think my father must have given it to me to play with.'

Damian touched it. 'It's not a toy,' he said.

467

'Everyone has one. He called it a Talent. His own father gave it to him.'

'*I* don't have one,' Damian said. He showed his bare neck. There was only the tiny silver cross Shane had given him before going off to college, one to each brother.

'I thought everyone did,' Joy said. 'Or something like it.'

'Well, I don't. You're special.'

She laughed. 'Damian, you *do* have one.' She touched Shane's little gift. 'Of course you're special, you just don't know it. Everyone's special. You are too.'

'If you say so,' Damian said.

'Look, I scratched my name on it with the point of a knife.' She leaned close, showing him the coin, the three ragged letters followed by a full stop, JOY.

'They were much deeper,' she frowned. 'They're faded.'

He leaned close, examining it. Suddenly she realised he was looking down the front at her breasts. She pulled away, buttoning up her blouse. 'What do you think you're doing?'

'Don't you know how beautiful you are?' he said.

'Oh, stop it.'

'I won't stop it.'

'You're just a silly little boy.'

'You're not the same girl who wrote that,' Damian said. 'You're twice as tall for one thing, and you've got boobies.'

They turned as water piled up, swirling from the tunnel entrance. The *Joy* swept into the sun in a brilliant burst of steam and smoke, paint shimmering, buttied by the faithful *Poca* towed behind. Kes waved and pulled in close by the towpath. The steam engine didn't change its breathy, familiar chuffing, foam sloshing under the counter from the blades, travelling at the steady six miles per hour that the boat could keep up all day, and all night if need be. Joy and Damian ran along the bank, keeping up.

But this time it was Damian who jumped first onto the sidecloths, clinging expertly to the ropes, and reached out his hand to Joy.

He pulled her aboard.

That night they slept aboard the two boats, Joy in her cabin kept warm by the slumbering steam engine, Kes and Eleanor aboard the *Poca* with Damian in the forecabin, moored under the elegant arches of the London and Blackwall Railway viaduct. Only one lock separated them from the Regent's Canal dock. They went through at first light, navigation lights burning and anchor strung, crossing the choppy Thames tideway to the Surrey canal. They unloaded their cargo of pipes at Peckham, then sold the packing straw at canalside pubs in Camberwell and were back on the Thames by evening. Sleeping grounded on the mud at the Lion Brewery wharf, they were woken by the chimes of Big Ben. The morning tide swept them upstream to Brentford with a full cargo of beer. Kes dropped off and picked up cargoes where he could as they ascended the locks of the Grand Junction. At Newport Pagnell they moored alongside Ham, who was getting lonely aboard the *Lurcher* without Morwenna. They swapped news and passed the evening in the pub like the good old days, waving goodbye at the first calls of birdsong.

Within the week, after Sunday spent as usual resting at Cody's Bend, the family was back at Moira taking on a full load of pipes for the huge works at Plas Kynaston in Wales.

And so it went, two trips a week, only the Sabbath for rest.

II

Across a landscape so vast and featureless that he and his horse seemed not to be moving, a man rode alone.

Here, in the midst of nowhere, he stopped. The dust behind him drifted away, disappeared. He swung down from the saddle and hitched the reins to the horns of a skull.

His horse grazed the white grass, and Jim Palmer looked around him.

He swept off his broad-brimmed hat and wiped his arm across his forehead. The air was too dry for a man even to sweat. This was the Western Australia cool season, but the heat was pitiless, over a hundred degrees. No wet for months, and maybe not for months more, here inland of the coastal hills. On the coast it could flood a bucket, flush out the soil from the hills in torrents red as blood, and steam dry again in an hour. But out here in the bush he was on the bone-dry limit of his property – not of what he owned, but of what he could use.

His yellow-white pastures simmered under the superheated blue bowl, not one cloud in the sky. The rim was at least fifty miles away, dry as a sunstruck bone, chopping and changing with mirages. He narrowed his eyes. He could count on his fingers the number of trees. Each tree held beneath it a deep black pit of shadow. Each shadow was full of sheep, poor little buggers. Their pale shapes clambered over each other as the sun moved the shadows.

Jim Palmer looked at all he had fought for, and thought of Home.

He had paid cash for this land, but it was a strange, wrong land, not his. He grazed fewer sheep each year. A few steps away one of the dry runs, like a wide shallow ditch, would take the rain when it came, but its whiteness hurt his eyes. The soil was turning to salt, dry salt. He didn't understand why. He owned everything from horizon to horizon, but somehow it wasn't his.

He spied a group of Aboriginals in the distance. They loped indian-file through the white glare, their spears hanging from their hands. Their shadows stretched beneath them in the mirage, as though they were part of the land. He waved, but they did not respond.

This was not his home, and his name was not Jim Palmer.

Home was St Luke's. Home was the spires of the City below, and wet mist drifting in from the Thames. Jack Riddles unhitched the reins and swung into the saddle. He stared down at the sunbleached skull. He had grazed Hereford beef on this land profitably for the first year, broke even the second year, and last year was a dead loss. As soon as it was put to use, the land died.

Cruel, pitiless, heartbreaking land. The cruelty he could understand, but no man could live without pity.

A wallaby hopped by, grazing his sheep's grass. They had little enough, and next year there would be less. Jack levelled his pistol, then uncocked it and slipped it into his belt. He clicked his tongue, pulled lightly on the rein. His horse cantered back to the hills.

The grass was green here. As he topped the rise he came into the cool, steady breeze of the Indian Ocean, intensely blue ahead of him. Below him the Royal Mail coach trailed red bauxite dust between the stands of gums, heading for Margaret River, the mighty karri forests of Pemberton and all points south. In the days of the Prisoners Of Mother England, Australia had been separated from Home by up to nine months under sail. Now, with steam ships and the Suez Canal, England was only a couple of weeks distant. Jack heard the faraway thwack of the Mail's whip, then silence fell again, except for the angry, alien cries of the birds. The sun blazed off the tin roof of his shack.

This was where he'd started. In town he'd heard Aboriginals talk of a place called Nirrup, and round here any Aboriginal word ending -*up* meant there was water somewhere about. He'd got the skinny black binghis drunk on Domain cocktail, his old standby of methylated spirits mixed with bootpolish and bluestone, and saved the last bottle for the guide. Jack had left Maggy blowing the last of their money at the hotel and come out to the valley alone but for his tottering blackfellow guide, and a donkey, and a shovel. Within a foot Jack was digging moist soil. Three feet down he was standing in water to his waist.

He'd built the shack by the first well.

Now Jack crossed between his vineyards, came past the ponds, and rode up to his house. His voluble black servant wordlessly took his horse. 'What's up?' Jack said.

The man flashed a glance at the stable. A scrawny Government roan drank from the trough, Her Majesty's V-R crown stamped ornately on its saddlebags. Jack closed his eyes and groaned.

'Day to you, Mr Palmer!' For a moment Jack went blank on his assumed name – and for a moment he almost did not care.

'What?' He plunged his head in the trough, slapped his hat back on, stuck his thumbs in his belt, and strode up the steps onto the verandah. 'Constable Joller, good, eh?'

The constable from Margaret River touched his cap. 'Sorry, Mr Palmer.' A woman's voice cursed in the shadowed rooms behind him.

'What's she done this time?' Even Jack heard the weariness in his voice.

'Drunk and disorderly covers it, Mr Palmer. The gentleman won't press charges. Might be a broken mirror.'

'Can't thank you enough for your time and trouble, Constable. That's for the mirror.' Jack folded some notes and tapped them into Joller's top pocket.

'Thank you very nicely, Mr Palmer, sir. Don't know how much longer we can keep this quiet, though, do you?'

Jack watched him ride away then went into the house. Maggy sat on the couch. She crossed her arms and legs and sulked at him. There was vomit down the front of her dress but it had dried in the sun. She did not look ashamed of herself.

'Still having fun?' Jack said.

She said what she always said to get round him. 'I love you, Jim.'

'No,' he said. 'You don't.' When she tried to speak he said, 'Maggy, you don't know what love is. You really don't.'

She nodded at the walls. 'You and your bloody books, you effing Christians make me sick. Where's your forgiveness? *You* made me what I am, Jim.'

'I've forgiven you enough,' Jack said.

'Now I'm worse than you, aren't I,' she said gaily. 'Done something better'n you for once. 'Cos you can't love me as much as I love you.' She dragged the front of her dress and showed her tits. 'Here, these are what you want.'

'Maggy,' Jack said so sadly that she thought his heart was broken.

Then her face suffused with rage. 'It isn't me, is it! Who is she?'

'She's no one, Maggy.'

'What sort of a bloke are you? Who is she, damn you?' Maggy struggled to get up. 'Come on, Jim. I know what love is all right.' She grinned, then trotted out her old line. 'I waited for you, didn't I? On the Ratcliff Highway . . .'

Her eyes glazed over. She put out her arms and Jack caught her, as he always did. Maggy had the unpleasant habit, when dead drunk, of passing out with her eyes open as though she really was dead. She was out cold.

What sort of a bloke are you?

'Maggy,' he whispered, 'it would have been different if we'd had children. I promise you.'

He closed Maggy's eyes with the side of his thumb and carried her upstairs to her bed. He worked her limp body out of her clothes, washed her, then sat her up, her arms flopping around his shoulders, and slipped her nightdress over her head. He lay her head on the pillow and pulled the embroidered hem demurely down to her ankles. He covered her with a sheet and a light blanket then pulled the blind, shadowing her room from the harsh afternoon light. He poured a glass of water from the pitcher and left it beside the bed. At about sunset she would wake, groaning, and drain the glass, then she would turn herself over and sleep until dawn. Then, he knew, she would be filled with unhappiness and recrimination until breakfast time, when she took her first drink. After a few, when she was feeling sufficiently bright, she'd make it somehow or other into town. There, he knew, the blokes would get her drunk, give her a good seeing-to, and beat her up. And Jack knew she was right. He had made her what she was.

He bent to kiss her and she exhaled her vomity breath on his lips.

Jack went to his room and put on his warm bluey coat because the night would be cold. He took a thousand pounds from the safe, put half in his pocket, went into her bedroom and put the other half in her shoe. Downstairs he cooked a steak and ate it. By then it was dark.

475

III

Tom crossed London Bridge and walked down into Southwark, navigating by the Phoenix gasometers. This time, having found the place yesterday after work, he went straight to Waterloo Street. Number thirty-two was in the terrace closest to the gasometers, three large ones and nine small rusty ones, and like much of the street the house would probably be shadowed by them for most of the morning.

The lamp was not yet lit upstairs and no smoke came from the chimney. Tom put up his collar and waited.

Women started shuffling from the houses. They gathered round the Southwark Water Company's standpipes and filled their kettles, eyeing him. The water was brown. One of the women called to him to sod off. Tom told them he was waiting.

"Oo fer?"

'Mr Nutting.'

"'E's a bobby,' a woman said.

'Yes, that's why I want to see him.'

'Wot yer done wrong then?' Another of the housewives put her hands on her hips. Her voice rose. "Ere, I'm not 'aving this. Go an' wait on the corner, we don't want people like yer in our street.'

The door behind Tom opened and Abigail Nutting came out, stepping over the step by force of habit so as not to mark it, though she was wearing house-slippers. 'He's all right. This is Mr Briggs. He came here last evening to see Mr Nutting, but my husband had already left to start work.'

'That's all right then,' the fat woman said, taking her hands off her hips. 'Can't be too careful.'

'Indeed not, Mrs Bushell.'

'Working nights all this month, is 'e, Mrs Nutting?'

'My husband never turns his back on his duty, as you well know, Mrs Bushell.'

'By the way, there was a boy wot was rude ter me on the Blackfriars Road yesterday, yer might ask yer 'usband ter look into it—'

Gail tugged Tom into the doorway and shut the door. 'Nosy old biddies,' she said. She went back to the kitchen and fetched the kettle. 'I'll do it,' she said.

'I don't mind running the gauntlet,' Tom said.

'Hold this bit of muslin over the spigot to filter the water,' advised Gail cheerfully, 'else we get rat hairs and you can imagine what else. When Alfie retires in a few months I want to move to Croydon, my cousin's got a farm there, there's clean water and clean air and light work. Our two daughters have fine families of their own now. He deserves a peaceful retirement.'

'I'm sure he does, Mrs Nutting.' Tom glanced anxiously at the parlour clock. It was already half past eight, and he had to be at his desk in half an hour.

'But you know what men are like,' she said. 'His pride won't let him admit he's getting on. He won't even take a desk job.'

'I work at a desk.'

'How nice. I wish he did,' she said.

Tom stepped carefully over the step, went to the standpipe and put the muslin bag over it as instructed. He recognised Alfie Nutting coming round the corner at once, though he had never seen him close. Eyes did not change, and the police constable had kindly eyes in a web of firm lines. Neither had the shape of his long walrus moustache changed, though now it was white. He wore his policeman's cape and helmet too, which made him look very old fashioned. A key concession from the police strike was that officers need not wear uniform off duty, though they were free to if they wished, and nowadays many young coppers were anonymous even in their own street or the pubs where they drank. But Alfie Nutting even walked like an old-fashioned policeman, with a long measured stride, steady, but as though his feet were slightly sore.

Tom called, 'Police Constable Nutting?'

Alfie stopped. He looked from Tom's face to the kettle he was holding, then back again.

'Who wants to know?' he enquired ponderously.

'Tom Briggs, sir. I found you in the Post Office Directory.'

'You can see I'm not wearing my duty band. If you want a policeman—'

'You're the only person who can help me,' Tom said.

'Tom Briggs.' Alfie sighed thoughtfully, then nodded. 'You'd better come in. And bring my kettle with you, or I won't get my morning cup of tea.'

They stepped over the step and went down the hall. Gail put the kettle on the range. Alfie sat on the kitchen chair, put his helmet on the table, yawned, and started unlacing his boots.

'Sir—' Tom began.

478

'Not now,' Alfie said. 'Here. Pull.' He gave Tom his foot, pushed Tom's backside with his other foot, and Tom pulled off the boot. Alfie groaned with relief. He wriggled his toes. They repeated the process with the other boot. The kettle boiled and Gail warmed the pot, then made the tea, bustling about. Alfie put on slippers – 'Couldn't train the puppy to bring them,' he grunted – then took off his jacket and hung it neatly in the hall, where kitchen steam and grease would not mark it. Gail started frying his breakfast. Tom felt as if he was interrupting some hallowed routine.

Alfie lowered himself into his chair. He looked tired. He had been up all night. 'Right, Tom Briggs. What's so important? Why me? Why now?'

'I came here yesterday evening to see you but you had already left to start your night shift,' Tom apologised.

'And here you are again.' Alfie sipped his tea. 'It must be *very* important. Do the boy an egg, Gail.'

'Hard or soft?' she said.

'Soft, Mrs Nutting.' Tom sat.

'Fried bread? Tomato?'

'Thank you.'

'The bacon's for Alfie,' she said. 'I hope you don't mind.'

'I have to be at work at nine anyway,' said Tom.

'You're going to be late,' Alfie said as the parlour clock *tinged* quarter to nine. 'Your father's bank – you are that Tom Briggs, aren't you?'

'Yes, sir. I see you haven't forgotten the case either.'

'Alfie was a detective for a while,' Gail said, holding

479

down the spitting frying bread with a spatula as though it might escape. 'He was involved.'

'Detective Force,' Alfie said, surprising himself that the pain of his unfulfilled ambition had not quite abated. 'I'll be a police constable until I die.'

'You know there was something wrong about the whole case,' Tom said.

'Was there?'

'Alfie always said so, didn't you, dear,' said Gail busily.

Alfie threw her an annoyed look.

'You're the one man I can trust, Police Constable Nutting,' Tom said.

'Am I? I'll ask again, why me?'

'Because you found Goldblum's body,' Tom said. 'He wouldn't have been found for hours otherwise, like as not. You must be innocent.'

Alfie looked down as his breakfast was slid in front of him. He shook salt and pepper over it, then passed the shakers to Tom.

'Innocent of what?'

'Of whatever was really going on.'

Alfie cut his egg, then stopped and held out their mugs for more tea. 'What was really going on?'

'You tell me,' Tom said.

'Have you been to Scotland Yard about this?'

'Scotland Yard is full of detectives.'

'Have you spoken with Detective Inspector Bowler?'

'He said Jack Riddles did it and that's all.'

'Detective Sergeant Steynes?'

'Away in the country somewhere.'

'Steynes was there on the night,' Alfie said. 'He

would know what was going on if anyone did. *He* hasn't said anything.' Alfie picked up his fork to spear his egg.

'You see my difficulty. I've always thought it was odd that Steynes happened by chance to be by the Lodge Road stables.'

'He made a statement that he was walking from the Eyre Arms to catch a bus in the Edgware Road.'

Tom said, 'Why did he make the dogleg detour down Lodge Road, behind the houses, instead of simply walking straight down Abbey Place?'

'Where's the bus stop?'

'Bang at the end of the road.'

Alfie said patiently, 'Why did he?'

'He wasn't walking. He was waiting.'

'You're spoiling my breakfast,' Alfie said.

'Alfie, you know you've thought the same thing for years,' said Gail, and he threw her an angry look. 'And there's all the other things.' She poured herself a mug of tea and drank it defiantly. 'But you said no, shut up, keep your head down, keep your nose clean, be loyal. My superior officers know what they're doing, you said. Well, they haven't been loyal to *you*. They're as criminal as the criminals they were catching, it seems. They were just cleverer about fooling us, that's all. They don't deserve you, Alfie.'

Tom said, 'What other things?'

'Tell him about the nanny,' said Gail.

'I can't. I'd be guilty of slander. I can't prove anything.'

'If you don't tell him, Alfie, I will.'

Alfie sighed. He cut his bacon in half and put it on Tom's plate.

'Nanny M'Kenzy didn't jump off Waterloo Bridge. I think she was thrown.'

'Then it wasn't suicide.'

'It was murder.'

'What did the coroner say?'

'There was no investigation into the two men who were seen near her, so obviously the verdict was suicide.'

'And you've known this for years?'

'What could I do?' Alfie said. 'There was no struggle. She was accompanying them willingly.'

Tom ate. 'But why should Nanny be killed?'

'Perhaps she saw something that night. Perhaps she *could* have seen something. Her window was near yours. She may have seen the killer—'

'Then my life is in danger,' Tom said, then contradicted himself. 'No. I'd sworn I hadn't seen anything from the window.'

'Monkey could have seen from the chimney-tops,' Alfie said. 'He didn't trip under a bus, he was pushed. Arthur Simmonds, the lookout – he was lucky, he jumped the roost before he was pipped, luckily for him. Or I think he'd be dead now, too.'

The clock *tinged* nine times. It was nine o'clock. Tom finished his meal and put his knife and fork together. He wrapped his hands around his mug of tea. Gail put on the kettle to brew another pot.

'Alfie, tell him the rest of it,' she said.

'I spoke to Mr Meulenhoff, Goldblum's diamond-cutter. Mr Goldblum's security was such that he must have invited the thief into his house. He wouldn't have asked Jack Riddles inside in a thousand years, it's a ridiculous idea. No, Goldblum obviously knew and trusted the man who killed him.'

'Gaby Daniells might have seen him, or remembered something later,' Tom said. 'It was her duty to lay the fire in my mother's room, she could have looked out—' He stood. 'She's in danger. Do you know where she lives now?'

Alfie took the kettle off the hob. 'I know where she is,' he said.

'Here,' Alfie said.

The two men stood with their hands in their overcoat pockets, gazing at the mossy headstone in front of them. Dew and spiders' webs made the grass silver in the early sun. Alfie's black labrador puppy, Jet, sat with her pink tongue lolling, then scratched her ear and looked up adoringly at her master.

'Gaby Daniells.' Alfie bent and cleaned the letters with his thumb.

GABRIELLE DANIELLS
1848-1871
All life death does end
And each day dies with sleep

'I found her by chance, one Sunday. My mother, also, is buried here at St George the Martyr's.' Alfie told his dog to sit but she jumped up at his leg. 'I could look up the coroner's report, but I know what the cause of death will be.'

'What?'

'Anything but murder.'

Tom saw a bench and sat on it, careless of the dew.

'You know as well as I do where this leads us, don't you, Alfie.'

Alfie dried the seat with his handkerchief and sat. He cleaned the muddy paw marks from his trousers.

'There's a line in Latin,' he said. 'You're a bright boy, you'd know it. *Quis custodet custodes.*'

'Who protects us from our protectors,' Tom said.

'If I was a clever man,' Alfie said, 'and I believed in the truth, and goodness, and law and order, and in my opinion I saw a little of it die each day, perhaps in the end I would believe everything was a lie. In fact I'd be a fool not to.'

'You're no fool,' Tom said.

Alfie found a stick and threw it. The dog dashed away between the headstones, tail wagging. 'I worked for what I believed in all my life,' he said. 'What if it's just a big lie, Tom?'

Tom murmured, 'If Jack Riddles didn't steal the jewel, who did?'

The dog brought the stick back and Alfie chucked it. 'The Bethlehem wasn't stolen because it was worth a lot of money, it was stolen because it was priceless. Once it was called the Bloodstone. Simple in its perfection, complex in its flaw.'

The dog retrieved the stick and Alfie tossed it.

Tom murmured, 'And Nanny went quietly with her killers.'

'Middle-aged ladies often do go quietly when they've been arrested,' Alfie said.

Tom stared at the police constable.

'The way from Miss M'Kenzy's house to Scotland

Yard goes over Waterloo Bridge,' Alfie said. 'At Scotland Yard half an hour later Detective Inspector Bowler refused to investigate the incident. Listen. Bowler knew Goldblum. When Bowler was a sergeant with G Division – the division that covers Hatton Garden as well as St Luke's – some thugs tried to break into Goldblum's workshop with sledge-hammers. Bowler arrested them, and ever after Goldblum had great faith in the British police.'

'That doesn't mean—'

'The guard on the door recognised Detective Inspector Bowler without being told.'

'Oh my God,' Tom said.

'Bowler has steel-tipped shoes. He uses a clasp knife. He is the same build as Jack Riddles and might be mistaken for him in the dark.'

'You know what you're saying.'

'I do,' Alfie said. 'For me it's treason.'

He sent the stick flying between the headstones. 'We're not going to say a word about this, Tom. It's circumstantial, and think of the damage it would do the Force. This ends here. We can't prove anything, it's air. Everyone's dead or missing.'

The dog brought the stick back, wagging proudly.

Tom said, 'Joy is alive.'

Alfie threw the stick. 'I'm sorry, Tom. I understand.'

A man called out. 'Oi, you can't throw sticks in here, you know!'

'I *saw* her,' Tom said urgently. 'I'm not just saying it, Alfie. The thirtieth of October, 1876. A red-haired girl on a canal boat—'

'What was the name of the boat?'

'I couldn't see, there was a mist on the water,' Tom said wretchedly. 'I know I can't prove it. I'm just asking you to believe me. Just believe me.'

Alfie Nutting tapped his tooth with his fingernail, thinking. Tom Briggs was a liar. He had concocted the story that tried to cover up his cowardice. He had been the nanny's accomplice in hiding the fact that she had been drunk.

St George's bell clanged ten o'clock.

'You're going to be late for work,' Alfie said.

Chapter Eighteen

Detective Sergeant Steynes's bluff, blunt features stared back at him from the window of the Manchester, Sheffield and Lincolnshire Railway Company carriage. He had brown eyes and a steady gaze, and his hair was still black and short though he was in his middle fifties. The hairs jutting from his nostrils and ears were grey.

He sat back and looked at the other passengers riding in the compartment, summing them up one by one. People behaved like a herd, but everyone thought they had something personal to hide. His Guv'nor, Mr Bowler, had taught him that. A sufficiently confident demeanour persuaded even the innocent to fidget and spontaneously, in the course of conversation, often to confess to some small oversight or self-doubt. It was remarkable to see them break down, and the sense of self-esteem it gave Steynes made him feel almost invulnerable. There was a man in wire glasses. Steynes looked at him. Mr Wire Glasses fidgeted then got up and went to the window, pretending to anticipate his station, then got down his case and umbrella, and went into the corridor. But the train did not stop. He must have gone into a different compartment, Steynes surmised. Probably Mr Wire Glasses was cheating on his expenses, or his wife, or was capable of doing so. No doubt he had not possessed a First Class ticket and was finding his conscience easier in Second Class, the milksop.

George Steynes loved travelling First Class. It was unbelievable, the polished wood and deep carpets, white linen tablecloths and roses in the buffet, and a choice of teas. He had acquired a collection of silver MS&L teaspoons since commencing his weekly London to Manchester return. What an amazing life. His mother had never walked further from London than Edgware, and she could never have believed that her plodding, affectionate son, almost female in his conscientious-ness, would travel First Class at sixty miles an hour in all this luxury – and not pay a penny for the privilege.

The Special Irish Branch gave him an allowance for a room at the railway hotel, too, with hundreds of rooms and hundreds of tables in the dining room, and waiters in white jackets just like on the train.

The woman opposite Steynes wore a feathered hat. She did not take her eyes off him. He had enjoyed a good breakfast and began to wonder if he had a spot of egg on his lapel.

Steynes moved across to the vacated seat, away from the annoying flicker of telegraph poles across the window. He turned up the gaslight. While he studied his papers, he brushed his lapel absent-mindedly with the back of his hand.

Until recently there had been talk of renaming the SIB the Special Branch. The English industrial towns were hotbeds of radicalism, with revolutionists intent on unionising the great factories, recruiting men loyal to their class above their country. The Special Branch would keep an eye on these troublemakers. This would require more money and hundreds if not thousands of officers, which meant promotions.

But for now, the Fenians were active again.

During the Lord Mayor's Banquet in the City, a bomb had been placed on a windowsill of the Mansion House. It failed to detonate, but after an enormous police search an Irish Republican arms cache was turned up in a stable by Farringdon Station. Inside the packing cases Special Irish Branch officers found four hundred rifles, pistols, ammunition, explosives. The stable had been rented by an Irishman named Sadgrove and the rent was in arrears. The landlord had a forwarding address for Mr Sadgrove in Manchester.

The rifles were replaced with dummies and the stable placed under observation. 'Sadgrove' was now believed to be a terrorist named Walsh. The interest of the Special Irish Branch had switched to the Manchester address, and their patience paid off. John Walsh had been arrested yesterday.

Detective Sergeant Steynes got off when the train stopped at the Manchester Piccadilly station. He booked in at the Railway Hotel and unpacked his change of clothing in his room, unclipped his braces and relaxed. The hotel's telephone rang and he jumped. He answered it awkwardly. It was a girl. It felt strange to be talked to personally by a girl he did not know. He did up his braces while she talked. Her thin, metallic voice informed him that a man was waiting for him downstairs.

In the foyer Steynes met one of the detectives who had arrested Walsh. 'He'll be arraigned in twenty minutes,' said Detective Constable Ockerslee. His hair was meticulously parted in the middle. 'We can just make it.' They walked along the busy street to the magistrate's court and pushed through the crowd in the vestibule. 'Court number four, here we are. You can have a quiet word with him afterwards if you like.'

'Wouldn't miss it for the world,' Steynes said. 'Two years, we've been snapping at his tail.'

The detective went ahead of him into the full courtroom. Steynes glanced back. He stopped. Someone with a Mancunian accent asked him to kindly get out of the way. Steynes pushed past him back into the vestibule. He raised himself on his toes, peering over the heads of the crowd. He glimpsed that worried face again, from a different angle. There was no mistake.

'Smart Arthur,' Steynes whispered to himself. 'Got you, you bastard.'

The years had not been kind to Smart Arthur. His plum-coloured coat was gone, his hair white and scraggy, lying shoulder-length on his threadbare black jacket. He was scrawny, as though his skin had folded in upon itself, and he walked with a stoop that made him shorter than the woman beside him. She supported his elbow and spoke to him soothingly. Steynes remembered her. Elsie, still a strong-looking,

490

handsome woman. She wore a lilac coat with a fur collar, shiny brown shoes, neatly turned out and authoritative. Arthur gazed around him with quick flinching jerks of his head, seeing enemies everywhere. No policeman had him in custody. Arthur had been nabbed for some minor crime, no doubt.

Steynes moved behind a pillar.

They went into Number Three court.

He followed them and sat at the back.

Arthur Albert Simmonds was up on a charge of shoplifting. The list of goods was pathetic, a bar of soap, one left shoe, a celluloid shirt collar. He seemed to understand little of what was said to him of the seriousness of his offence. Several times Elsie whispered in his ear before he replied to a question from the bench.

The defendant was found guilty and given the choice of five days in prison, or a ten-shilling fine. It was a lenient verdict, too lenient in Steynes's opinion – a man like Smart Arthur would steal until the day he died. But both Arthur and Elsie looked devastated.

Elsie stood. 'My Lord, we don't have ten shillings.'

Steynes beckoned the usher and spoke quietly. He reached into his pocket. The usher went and spoke quietly with the clerk, who nodded. The fine had been paid.

Steynes waited in the vestibule. When Arthur came out he did not seem to understand his good fortune. Elsie explained to him several times that his fine had been settled by an anonymous benefactor and he would not go to prison. Arthur's face lit up, then fell. They came close to the pillar, not realising

491

Steynes was on the other side. He heard their voices become clear as they approached, and he could see their shadows. They stopped.

'But I've already packed me things,' Arthur was saying. 'We told our boy I was going off on 'oliday, didn't we?'

'Bert will be happy to see you home,' Elsie said. Steynes watched her shadow put its arm reassuringly round Arthur's shoulders. 'Now, you won't be silly again, will you?'

'No dear,' Arthur said.

'He's at the cab-rank by the station, I expect,' Elsie said practically. Their son Bert had recently married Gabriel Paz's daughter, a Second Class Buffet waitress at the station, and he was driving a cab. He was ambitious and wanted to buy his own vehicle and a good horse, set up a company based on station trade. 'I'll go and tell him you're feeling better,' Elsie said. 'All right, dear?'

Arthur sounded worried. 'Where yer off ter?'

'Don't worry, I won't be long.'

'Yer taking yer coat an' shoes back to the pawnshop,' Arthur said.

'Don't get into trouble,' Elsie said lightly. Steynes heard her kiss him.

'Yes,' Arthur said. 'I mean—' She left him reluctantly and he took a couple of steps after her, into Steynes's view. Arthur put his fingers to his lips as if remembering her kiss, then wandered with the flow of people towards the doors.

Steynes followed him.

The streets around the railway station, as always in such places, were broad boulevards with fine

492

shops and hotels to attract travellers. There were cab-ranks and carriages everywhere, and good well-fed horses. Arthur slipped between them. No one seemed to notice him, and even Steynes was hard put to keep up.

Arthur turned a corner into a narrower road, and Steynes pushed people aside to catch up. As he came round the corner Arthur looked back, straight at him.

Steynes turned immediately to a newsstand. He bought a paper.

When he glanced up Arthur was crossing the road. Steynes folded the paper under his arm, took off his hat and went after him.

Arthur went into an alleyway. Steynes walked past the entrance, saw nothing. He turned back and ran down with long, heavy steps, coat flapping. A woman carried out her washing and he bulled past her. She dropped the lot and groaned, then shouted after him.

Some young girls were playing jacks in a courtyard. There was no sign of Arthur.

There were half a dozen ways out he could have gone.

Girls in a place like this wouldn't talk. Steynes remembered one of the Guv'nor's tricks. 'That man's dropping his money!' The girls ran squealing towards the way out down the steps. Steynes ran after them, using his size and weight to shove past them in the narrow passageway beyond, ducked under the archway. He got black brickdust on the shoulder of his coat and ran forward cursing. Washing obscured the sky like flags, cutting out the light.

It was bright ahead. The buildings ended. There was a cutting below and a brick bridge with a locomotive chuffing beneath it, maroon livery and white steam, then shabby coal wagons sliding out of sight under the bridge one after the other, clickety click.

Steynes leaned back against the wall. Arthur stood between two empty wagons in a siding. He must have thought he saw someone on the bridge because he scampered across the rails, round the back of the moving wagons, past a miserable straggle of workmen's huts, then paused for breath. He scrambled up the embankment on the far side.

Steynes followed him.

He found himself on a terraced street, black bricks, broken windows.

Steynes grunted, panting through his open mouth. He was sweating and his collar chafed his neck.

Some children were shouting insults at the far end. Steynes ran down. They shouted at him too. He was too puffed to swear back.

The turning at the end was a cul-de-sac lined with shabby dwellings. It finished in a brick wall, the railway beyond. There was no other way out.

A door slammed.

Steynes pulled back before he was observed through a window.

The kids looked up at him with innocent sooty faces.

'That's A'tha,' the eldest said, rubbing one bare foot over the other. 'Mad as May-butter, tha's why we throw t'stones a' tha'.'

Steynes caught his breath. He found his way back

to the hotel. In his room he threw down the newspaper on the bed and loosened his tie. He picked up the telephone.

'Whitehall, one-two, one-two,' he said, rubbing the sweat from his face. After all, he told himself, it was only a telephone, and the girl couldn't see him or tell from his voice what he was doing.

He sat on the bed and pulled off his shoes while he waited.

'Arthur Albert Simmonds,' he said when the telephone was answered. 'Found him.'

'Where is it exactly?' Detective Inspector Bowler said.

'Over there, Guv'nor.' Steynes pointed. Bowler leaned on the parapet of the bridge, surveying the railway below and the houses beyond through the smoky glare. All these northern towns seen from the train this morning had seemed made of smoke. Everything was greasy with soot.

'I kept an eye open all afternoon yesterday,' Steynes said. 'It's a cul-de-sac but there's kids and nosey parkers everywhere.'

'And his woman,' Bowler said.

'His wife. Elsie.'

'I remember her. I won't fool her a second time. They know us.' Bowler looked up at the sky. No gaslights on the bridge. 'What's on the other side of the houses?'

'More bloody railway tracks.'

'So he'll come this way.'

'Unless he wants to get run over by a bloody train.'

Bowler stuck his hands in his pockets. The cinders that covered the bridge crunched beneath his shoes as he turned and looked at the pub behind them. It was not the sort of pub that had a name or a welcoming gas-globe over the door, and curtains were nailed over the windows.

'A man like Arthur works at night,' Bowler said definitely. 'And if he doesn't work at night, he drinks at night. Whichever, he'll come this way.' He looked at the sun. 'Let's find somewhere not too close for a cup of tea.'

The best thing about the north was the sunsets, Bowler decided. It was probably the smoke. He settled himself at the end of the bridge nearer the pub. Steynes was hiding somewhere beyond the other end of the bridge.

Women and children started arriving at the pub carrying empty jugs. After a while they came out carrying full jugs. Bowler knew he was part of the shadows by now. Their footsteps shuffled past him on the cinders. A train rumbled beneath the bridge, then he heard their shuffling again, their low voices.

Factory whistles blew, making an odd piping discord across the gathering darkness. A couple of men went by carrying implements over their shoulders. They shook hands and parted with good wishes for tomorrow. A whole bevy of girls wearing dirty aprons went over the bridge.

Bowler looked up at the sky. It was clear, he was sure, but there were no stars. The lights of wealthy areas reflected from the smoke above, making a glowing haze.

Half a dozen men pushed into the pub and slammed the door. Others arrived. Night sounds began, the same in any city the world over, Bowler supposed. A child crying. A man and a woman shouting. The rumble of a train below him rising to a roar. It was an express. The brilliant acetylene lights illuminated the rails ahead of the locomotive like two silver arrows pointing into the distance. The bridge shook.

Silence again. A girl's scream, then an older woman's voice shouting at her. A dog sniffed Bowler's foot.

A match was lit at the other end of the bridge. It was Steynes's signal.

Bowler rubbed his legs to get the blood flowing.

He walked out onto the bridge. His boots crunched on the cinders and warned the shadow in front of him.

'Someone's following me,' Arthur said in a frightened voice.

'Smart Arthur,' Bowler said.

'Oh, it's yer, Mr Bowler.' Arthur sounded surprised but relieved. 'I'd recognise yer voice anywhere. 'Ow are yer? I s'ppose I've done something wrong again.'

Two faint silver lines appeared below the bridge.

'It's a fair cop,' Arthur said. 'I wish I could've 'ad me drink first.' He held out his hands. 'I'll come quietly.'

Bowler took Arthur's wrist and Steynes took the other side. They lifted Arthur up and hefted him over the parapet. Arthur kicked the bricks, dangling.

'Wait,' Bowler said.

Arthur looked up. He struggled. Air rushed out under the bridge, the rails shone, they heard the steamy roar of the approaching express.

Arthur screamed.

The train's whistle shrieked. Steynes peered at Bowler's face against the light.

Bowler's lips moved.

'Now.'

They let go. It was as easy as that, just letting go.

Arthur dropped down into the light. He shrank. His writhing shadow rushed back along the tracks to meet him. Steam and smoke gushed up.

Bowler and Steynes stepped back. They brushed their coats.

'You'd better stay and finish up the Walsh business,' Bowler said.

'All right, Guv'nor.'

'Strike another match, would you?' Bowler asked. He opened his watch. 'Good, I'm just in time to catch the last train home.'

Chapter Nineteen

I

On Monday morning Mostlock, the Principal Clerk, descended the Carrara marble staircase of Briggs Bank. He crossed between the marble pillars of the banking hall towards Tom's desk, nodding to left and right at favoured accounts, as stately in his approach as a Spanish galleon.

'Psst,' Widgeon hissed. Tom looked up. He memorised his running total, slipped his pen behind his ear and stood attentively.

'May I be of assistance, Mr Mostlock?'

'Your father presents his compliments, Mr Tom, and wishes a word, if you would be so kind.'

Tom was surprised, first that the Principal Clerk had come to him personally rather than send a walker, secondly that it had been phrased as a lengthy request rather than a terse command. Banks prized efficiency above manners. A City man was supposed to sum up a situation, however complex, in three plain sentences and a decision.

'Do you know why, Mr Mostlock?' Tom asked.

'He wishes you to attend him in the Directors' Room, Mr Tom,' Mostlock said cautiously.

This too was unusual. Usually Darby Briggs worked in his office, where he felt most at home — more at home than in Abbey Place, probably. His office was a dull, not very big room dominated by a very large oak desk with a single swivel chair. Clerks taking dictation did so perched on a wooden bench.

'Do you know what it's about?' Tom said.

'That's not my business, sir.' Mostlock resumed his stately progress.

'You won't get the push, Mr Tom,' whispered Sammy Widgeon. 'He's your father. He'd put the rest of us on the street before you.'

'You've got it the wrong way round, Sammy,' Tom said bitterly. 'My father would get rid of me first.'

'Why?'

'I don't know. To demonstrate his fair-mindedness, I suppose.'

'Then he'd be cutting off his nose to spite his face! You're a natural at this business, you are. You were almost born to it, you've always wanted to do it, you grew up with it for the early part of your life. All you need is confidence, Mr Tom.'

'Thanks, Sammy. But somehow,' Tom said ruefully, 'I don't expect I'll get that from my father.'

He went to the stairs, then came back to his desk and stuck his pen properly in its holder, ran his hands over through his hair. 'Inky fingers,' Sammy whispered.

'Do you know what's really odd?' Tom said. 'Old Mostlock called me sir.'

He cleaned his fingers on his handkerchief as he went upstairs. His father's correspondence clerks, well paid and mostly foreign, worked by the

Telegraph Room in all the languages of the world, guaranteeing beef shipments from Buenos Aires, guns to Cape Town, a whole lighthouse shipped out in sections to Australia.

Tom straightened his collar. He knocked on the door of the Directors' Room and went in.

'You asked to see me, Papa?'

Darby sat alone at the head of the long, dark hardwood table, the tall window behind him.

'Come in,' he said.

Tom closed the door behind him. It was a silent room, hushed, almost reverential. A portrait of his father hung on one wall. Opposite it was placed the grouse-moor Landseer painting from his father's study at home. Seeing it gave Tom a sudden shock of familiarity, though he had never been in this room before, and as far as he knew his father had never actually succeeded in hitting a grouse or a monarch of the glen. He stayed where he was, unsure how to behave – as confidant or outsider, as his father's son, or as his employee.

'Come here,' Darby said. Tom walked behind the empty high-backed chairs to the head of the table. It must nearly be lunchtime, for over his father's shoulder he saw the City ant-swarm beginning to converge along Cornhill on the ancient taverns and dining rooms squeezed into every niche, every alleyway, every hole in the wall between the great façades of the banks. Tom knew he should feel hungry.

'Sit down, my boy,' Darby said.

Tom sat, and for the first time noticed the bottle of brandy in front of his father. Darby cupped a snifter in his hands, drank from it, put it back on the table. The glass had left rings on the wood. Darby smeared them with the flat of his hand, knocking over a second glass. He set it upright carefully.

'I'll get a mat,' Tom said, horrified.

'I know what I'm doing.' Darby must have pushed one of the chairlegs with his foot, because the chair closest to him moved out in invitation to Tom.

Tom sat. He was close enough to touch his father. Darby offered him a drink. Tom refused.

Darby put back his head and drew a great breath, then let it out as a sigh. 'The things I have put my faith in have let me down, Tom.'

So Tom was being sacked. 'Father, I am sorry I could not live up to your trust in me.'

'No, no, I'm not firing you. My dear boy, I wouldn't hurt a hair of your head.' Darby refilled his glass. Usually he did not care for brandy very much, preferring whisky. 'You're going to have to learn something, Tom. A hard lesson. Harder than anything you have endured so far.'

'What is that, Father?'

'You're going to have to learn to stop saying sorry, Tom.'

'I'm—' Tom stopped himself. 'I'm not sure that I understand.'

'I'm sorry about everything, Tom, but I can't say so. I'm sorry about the way I treated you, but I can't admit it. I seem to have made rather a mess of my life, but I can't change it. It's lived.' He burped. 'See? No apologies.'

'I'll call a cab to take you home, Papa,' Tom said.

'I'm going to sit here,' Darby said. The most

extraordinary thing happened. He reached out and took Tom's hand in his own.

'For pity's sake have a little drink with me, Tom.'

Tom heard himself say, 'Thank you.'

Darby poured. He filled both glasses to the brim. 'To us, Tom.'

He held up his glass, waiting. Tom held up his own glass. The glasses clinked, spattering drops on the table. 'To us, Father.'

They sipped. Darby sighed. Again he swept the table with the flat of his hand.

'There are certain things that can no longer be hidden, Tom. Forgive me if I speak with total frankness.'

'I presume you mean the bank's loans to P.W. Thomas & Co, the stockbrokers.'

'No. I mean I knew of Lydia's mistreatment of my poor dead daughter—' Darby's face distorted. 'I did nothing. I excused Lydia. I understood her disappointment. I connived. I told myself Lydia was worth it. I would have died for Lydia, held my hand in the candle flame for her, anything you like.'

'Sssh, Papa,' Tom said.

'I loved her. I still love her. When the opportunity came to excuse Lydia and myself too, I grasped it with both hands. I put all the blame, all the guilt I felt on you, our son.'

This was so awful that Tom did not know how to respond. 'How great is the bank's exposure to P.W. Thomas?'

'I shall love your mother to the moment of my death. Even if she is an imperfect woman, I am lost to her.'

'Papa. Father.'

'Remember.' Darby touched his son's face. 'Never say you are sorry.'

'But I am, Father.'

'You're a stronger man than I am, Tom. I'm making the right decision.'

'What decision?'

Darby drank. 'To business. It is an old City saying that to eat well, buy shares. But to sleep well, buy bonds. We have eaten well. We are exposed by nearly a million pounds to P.W. Thomas. We shall be lucky to see two shillings in the pound. I see you need more brandy. I do, anyway.'

Tom said, 'When will the news be known?'

'When P.W. Thomas folds, a run on deposits will begin, and I shall have to close the doors of the bank.'

Tom shook his head. 'If we acted at once, we could reconstitute the bank as one of the new limited liability companies, with a smaller capital base, and make it profitable again.'

'I wish I could live my life again,' Darby Briggs said.

'We may be able to sell the bank. I hear Lloyds of Birmingham are in the market to take over London banking houses.'

'No. This was my great dream. I gave up everything for it. I won't have it taken over.'

'We could move to a smaller premises, in Princes Street perhaps.'

'I won't be a damned Princes Street banker at my age.'

Tom said, 'If you would only let me help you.'

504

'I am certain that young Winston and Ernest Prideau will not place money into any venture of which I was a part.' Darby turned his chair to the window. 'I wanted you to be aware of the situation. There is nothing I can do to prevent it. Take the afternoon off.'

Tom could not credit what he had heard.

'Take the afternoon off,' Darby repeated. 'Consider the position of the bank. Go and throw sticks off London Bridge, or sit in one of the parks. It's a hot day. Have some fun in Cremorne Gardens.'

'Cremorne Gardens has been closed,' Tom said absently.

Darby stood and shook his hand. 'Goodbye, Tom. I'm sorry.'

II

Detective Sergeant Steynes travelled in a black mood. John Walsh, the Irishman, was being transferred to London. He faced questioning by the City of London police as well as Scotland Yard about the Mansion House bomb, but this formidable prospect had daunted Walsh not at all. He had turned out to be a thorough spoiler. It was a fact of life that most criminals knew their place and went quietly once they were caught to rights. But Fenians were different. These scum did not believe they had committed any crime. Walsh had been put aboard the train with uniformed constables in front and behind, and he was handcuffed to Detective Constable Ockerslee. Usually criminals did not like the public to see them handcuffed, and Ockerslee was prepared to be discreet. But Walsh threw up his arm in the busy corridor, revealing the glittering chain to the shocked passengers. 'Political prisoner!' he shouted.

'Shut it, spud,' Steynes said. He pushed Ockerslee and Walsh into their reserved compartment, but to his dismay it was full except for three seats. Everyone looked at them. Walsh grinned, relishing the attention. Steynes called the guard.

The Manchester, Sheffield and Leicestershire Railway guard was an old soldier, and an old private soldier at that. Resplendent in the railway's maroon uniform with gilt buttons, lovingly polished, he wouldn't budge. 'Sorry about't, gent'men, but they's paid them fares and I'll not turf paying passengers out, have 'em standing in't corridor all t'way t'Lunnon.'

Walsh put back his head. He hummed, then broke into a keening song, 'Kathleen Mavourneen'.

'He can't do tha',' the guard warned.

Walsh sang at the top of his voice.

Steynes, Ockerslee and Walsh rode in the guard's van. Walsh's hands were nipped behind him by the handcuffs and he shouted obscenities. 'All the same, these spudeens,' Steynes said. He balled his handkerchief and pushed it in the prisoner's mouth, held it there with string knotted at the back of Walsh's head, gagging him. One of the Guv'nor's old tricks. Walsh breathed through his nose. Steynes grinned at him. The Irishman's eyes rolled, but he was quiet. The guard's van was very noisy anyway.

Steynes perched on a bale of newspapers in the corner and tried to sleep. Ockerslee sat on the mailbags playing solitaire, glancing up occasionally. He was normally a talkative man.

Occasionally the racket died away, on a hill perhaps, or at a water halt. It was hot. Steynes dropped the window and stuck his head out. Country air always smelt of manure.

The train started again. Ockerslee unwrapped a package of greaseproof paper and ate tongue sandwiches. He offered one to Steynes and said something about his wife. Steynes fetched tea from the buffet. From time to time the guard came back, waved Ockerslee off the mailbags, opened the rear door and carried one of the bags onto the platform. It had an ornamental cast-iron railing. After a few seconds a station or country halt would roar by and the mailbag would vanish into the net. The guard looked at Walsh sympathetically.

'You mind your business, I'll mind mine,' Steynes said. He leaned back, at least half-asleep. The silence woke him.

'It's been like this for ten minutes,' Ockerslee said.

They were stopped on a curving viaduct. Steynes saw trees and a church tower below them. In the distance rose the smokestacks of some huge industrial city, Sheffield or Derby maybe, they all looked the same. Steynes dropped the window and stuck his head out. He could hear cows lowing. Because of the curve he could see right to the front of the train, the locomotive puffing quietly. The signal was down, red. The canal beneath the viaduct looked very blue from up here, the water cool and inviting. Steynes watched three boats, two of them brightly painted, the one in front blowing steam from the funnel, moored near some thatched cottages. 'Cody's Bend,' grunted the guard. 'T'valley bends, t'canal bends round't, t'railway bends over't.'

Steynes watched a girl walking on the towpath. The boat's name was painted in three large ornate letters, gold on green, along the side of the cabin. The girl's hair was red. The boat's name was *Joy*.

Steynes pulled his head back into the van. His face looked twisted.

'What's wrong?' Ockerslee was alarmed. 'Guv'nor? All right, are you, Guv'nor?'

'Stay with the train!' Steynes said. He opened the rear door. 'Wait for me at the next station, Detective Constable.'

My God, Steynes realised with a moment of pleasure, I sound like Mr Bowler.

'But—' Ockerslee shut his mouth loyally. 'Anything you say, sir.'

Steynes jumped from the platform onto the track. He crossed the cinders and leaned over the railing. It was much too far to jump. He ran back along the line, stumbling awkwardly on the ash, then ran on the wooden sleepers, which was easier. The railing ended in a wooden fence that stopped cows wandering on the line. Steynes wished he had left his overcoat in the van. He scrambled over the fence and half ran, half skidded down the slope beyond. The cows scattered in front of him towards the towpath. Some farmworkers looked round, baggy trousers, dirty faces. The girl had almost reached the boat. A thin-looking boy was walking with her now. Steynes came up behind them and grabbed her by the arm.

'You're coming with me,' he said.

'That train's been stuck a while,' Ham said. 'They'll be going mad, them townies in top 'ats.' He leant back against the side of the *Lurcher* and chewed a straw. Kes had put his back out lifting a bale this morning – they could feel the rubbery curve of the disc sticking out of his spine – and he was in the cottage trying to find a way of lying that was not wholly agonising after ten minutes.

Ham wore a cap these days, another change Morwenna had made. She was leaving the children with her sister in the village and coming with him on a trip for once. He was looking forward to it. They would make love every night without being interrupted. He'd have her to himself for a few days, but then she always started worrying about the little ones, imagined sniffles and falls, and wanted to rush home. Morwenna had got very settled in her ways since moving ashore. Her life revolved around their children, and she wanted them to stay ashore and go to school, no boating life for them. Ham hoped to shake her out of it. 'She wants to make 'em like yer an' Jaffrey!' he told Shane.

Shane grunted. He hadn't taken his eyes off Joy. He was on holiday from the college, pale with learning. Ham squeezed his arm muscle playfully. 'All that reading's lost yer strength.'

Shane pulled away. 'Leave it alone, Ham, please.'

'I wouldn't rib yer if I didn't like yer,' Ham said. 'Yer know me. Don't yer? I'm yer elder brother an' I got ter look after yer, I'm a nice bloke really.'

Shane ignored him, walked along the towpath to

509

meet Joy. 'Wot did I say wrong?' Ham muttered.

Jaffrey, lying apparently asleep on the top planks, opened one eye and put his finger to his lips. 'Not Shane? Me and me big mouth,' Ham said cheerfully. 'Yer shouldn't lie out in the sun like that, Jaff, it'll curdle yer brains. They won't take yer back at the Mechanical Institute if yer curdled.'

'Me and Shane always have had curdled brains,' Jaffrey murmured. 'Twins, see.'

'Does 'e, yer know, got it fer 'er?'

'Love,' Jaffrey said patiently. 'Yes, Ham, Shane does love her.'

'Does she – d'yer think they'll—'

'Who knows what Joy thinks,' Jaffrey said.

Ham agreed. 'She's a woman.'

'I love her too,' Jaffrey said simply. 'Always have. Always will. And I'll be like Shane. I'll marry some other girl.'

'I—' Ham took the straw from his mouth. 'Lookathat! One of 'em's gone stir crazy!' A man had jumped from the stalled train and was sliding down the grassy bank. ''Oi, Damian, see this.'

Damian came out of the engine room. His pale curly hair was streaked with black grease and he held an oilcan. 'He's frightening the cows,' he commented. The man grabbed Joy's arm.

'Something's about,' Ham said. 'Come on, lads.' The brothers walked towards the fuss.

Joy struggled. Shane remonstrated with the man and got a push that sent him sprawling. Ham stepped over him and squared up his fists to the stranger.

'Get back if you know what's good for you,' the man panted. Joy tugged at him and he slapped her head. She dropped to her knees.

'Let 'er go,' Ham said. He stood on his toes, sighting over his knuckles.

'Police,' the man said.

'My arse,' Ham said. 'Let 'er go!'

Jaffrey stepped forward. 'You heard him.'

Shane scrambled to his feet.

The man stared them down. Damian squirted the oilcan. Black oil splashed, then trickled down the man's overcoat.

Ham jerked his fist. ''Op it,' he said.

The man let go Joy's arm. He backed away from them, then jumped down into the water-meadow. 'You haven't heard the last of this,' he said. The lads jeered at him.

Ham put his arms round Joy. 'All right? Yer shaking.'

'It was awful. I was so surprised.' She shuddered. 'It was like a nightmare. Who was he? Ham, if you hadn't – all of you—'

'It's all right,' Ham grinned, putting a brave face on it, worried about her. 'I owed yer one. Yer never seen 'im afore?'

She shook her head. She was crying.

'Yer never knows 'oo's about nowadays,' Ham said.

Steynes splashed across the water-meadow. He was humiliated, faced down by that young hooligan with white knuckles. Steynes had smeared the oil trying to wipe it off and his overcoat was ruined.

The train had pulled away but he saw a plume of steam rising beyond the trees. The village station

511

must be there. Where there was a station there would be a telegraph.

III

When Tom got home that evening there was no answer to his summons on the door. He was drunk and couldn't find his key. 'Prettiman!' he shouted. He hammered on the door panels. When there was no reply he relieved himself behind the oleander bushes and went through the tradesmen's entrance to the back of the house. He came down the steps and saw the kitchen door was open. The servants were sitting round the table. Cook leant back against the range with her arms crossed. Their mood was anxious but stern.

'What's this about?' Tom demanded. 'Some sort of servants' council? Get to work, all of you.'

Prettiman jumped up. 'I'm terribly sorry, Mr Briggs, sir. I didn't hear—'

'Our condolences, sir,' one of the little maids said, a girl of about thirteen. She handed Tom a flower.

'Are you all mad?' Tom said. A cold feeling stole over him. P.W. Thomas must have folded this afternoon, and the bank had crashed.

Cook called out in a strong voice, 'Will we be let go, sir?'

'You'll have to ask my father that!' Tom said. He crossed the kitchen and went up the steps.

'Mr Briggs, sir,' Prettiman said respectfully. 'Don't you know?' Tom stopped with his hand on the iron railing.

'He's dead, isn't he?' Tom said.

'Your father died this afternoon,' Prettiman said. 'I'm terribly sorry, sir. We all are. He was a real gentleman.' His jaw moved angrily, as though he knew more than he said. 'A *real* gentleman.'

'Thank you,' Tom said. 'Thank you, all of you.'

He closed the door behind him and leaned back against it for a moment.

Then he went along the servants' corridor. He opened the green baize door to the dining room, skirted the long table and chairs, and came out into the hall. His mother was standing at the open front door, wearing what looked like her nightdress. Even against the daylight Tom saw that she held a note crumpled in her hand.

'Mama. I heard.'

Lydia turned. 'I thought you were knocking on the door, Tom!' Her face was puffy and tears trickled down her cheeks, slid quickly into the lines round her mouth. Her rouge had run. She put her fingers to her nose and sniffed, unladylike. She must have lost her kerchief. 'Oh, Tom. My dear son.'

She ran to him. Tom put his arms round her and patted her back.

'Mr Bowler was here earlier,' she sobbed. 'He brought the news. He wouldn't stay, a telegram came and he had to rush off as usual, there is so much work for him to do, so much grief, this is only a small part of it. I understand him. We are not really so very important—'

'Lydia,' Tom said. He shook her gently. She fell silent. Tom said, 'How did it happen?'

'Your father had an accident. He shot himself somehow. He was in the Directors' Room. He hadn't even eaten his lunch.'

Tom closed his eyes. 'My father sent me out, and then he committed suicide.'

'Don't say that, it's a terrible word,' Lydia said. 'This was found under his hand.' She held out the crumpled note.

Tom took it.

To the moment of my death, I love her.

'How will this affect the bank?' Lydia asked anxiously. 'Will we lose our money?'

IV

What sort of a bloke are you?

The tall man walked down the gangway on the dockside. It was Tuesday night. Most of the other passengers had already disembarked from the old *Corona*. He swung his kitbag over his shoulder, pushed through the small circle of remaining porters, and walked into the dark and fog.

London dark, London fog. It settled on his face like sweat.

As soon as he was alone he got down on his knees on the moist cobbles. He clasped his hands in prayer. If anyone could have seen him, he looked like a man in pain.

Home. He had come home.

He might swing for it.

He walked, finding his way by calls, shouts, the

514

squeal of winches around him. At the dock gates lights glowed through the fog, illuminating the kitbag but not his face.

The name stencilled on the side of the kitbag was J. PALMER.

He walked to Sairey's Hotel, but it was gone.

All the lodging-rooms he remembered were blocked up or taken down. He heard only Irish voices. He hardly recognised Wapping High Street, it was so changed.

Jack walked. Three policemen patrolled together, shining their bull's-eye lanterns in shop doorways. He walked past them openly.

The sailors were gone from Ratcliff.

Jack put up his collar and plunged his hands in his pockets. It was a warm night, which was why the fog was coming up off the river, but he was getting cold to his heart. Moisture dripped from his long black hair onto his face.

He came to a decision. He walked to Clerkenwell Green, knocked at Samuel's cottage. He waited and knocked again. Though the house was dark, he told himself Samuel's house was always dark. A blind man had no need of light.

Jack shivered and knocked for the third time.

A lamp was lit at an upstairs window. It opened and a woman looked out. She held up the lamp. 'Who is it?'

'Is Samuel – tell him Jim's here—' Jack changed his mind. 'No, tell him *Jack's* here. Tell him Jack is home.'

'Never heard of no Samuel,' she said, 'never heard of you. Get off afore I call the police.'

Jack walked away. The window slammed.

Within a few moments everything was behind him. He felt like a shadow slipping through the dark, no one could see him. He was back in the old days. The feeling brought back to him everything he had thought was lost.

This is your place, Jack, the feeling said. *You always carry the place you were born inside you.*

Jack came down the steps into St Luke's. Even if Mrs Oilick wasn't there to welcome him, plenty of others would be.

He stopped.

They were gone.

St Luke's was huge blocks of flats surrounded by paving. Even the streets were gone.

He leant back against the church wall. It was the only place he recognised.

You know why you came home, don't you, Jack. What sort of a bloke are you?

It was very late now, and his footsteps tocked noisily as he walked. There was a real danger he would be stopped by the police.

He imagined it happening. Just routine, sir. Where are you coming from, sir? Where are you going?

Jack didn't know how he would reply.

I was coming from there, officer, and I am going to here. I am so weary of running.

He was running now, running along the City Road. He would be stopped if he was seen, and they would hang him for sure. He would be tried and convicted and kept for a week in the Stone Hold of Newgate Prison, and then he would be taken out and hanged in the prison yard for the murder of a little girl twelve years ago, who would have been a woman by now.

But he would always remember her just as she had been on that night, her little face turned fearlessly up to his, she would always be that age to him.

Jack walked up to the parapet. The moon came down through the fog and gleamed on the water going into the tunnel beneath him.

This is all I know. I never was a child.

He heard her little-girl's voice. *'You'll have to take me back home, Jack. You know you will.'*

Jack groaned, remembering his reply.

I'll be back. Promise. Promise.

Jack knew why he had come home.

Chapter Twenty

I

The Croydon Railway ran into London along an artificial valley, the course of the old Croydon Canal. Long ago the Croydon Railway Company had bought the canal, closed it, drained it, laid tracks along the canal bed, and opened one of the earliest railways to the City from south London.

The carriage was antiquated, probably fifty years old, and the slatted wooden seat bumped Alfie Nutting unmercifully. As the train puffed up onto a bridge he gave up trying to read his newspaper and glowered instead at the Grand Surrey Canal passing below. Retirement to rural life at the little thatched cottage in Croydon had not suited him. He'd not been sleeping well, and last night his fidgeting had finally driven Gail crazy. 'What's wrong with you?' she'd demanded, as he tossed and turned. 'You're like a bear with a sore head. Five o'clock on a Wednesday morning and you haven't got anything better to do than—'

'Once a policeman, always a policeman, I suppose,' he muttered.

'You've got your silver watch and that's the end of

it,' she said. 'I've had enough! You aren't a copper now. You've got to get up in an hour to feed the chickens.'

Alfie lay thinking night thoughts.

She sighed, woke properly and sat up. 'What is it, dear?'

'I am not proud of myself,' Alfie said.

She struck a match and lit the lantern.

'You've done nothing to be ashamed of. The Divisional Superintendent himself said your career was exemplary. You're an example to all young police constables entering the Metropolitan Police Force, he said—'

'I know what he said,' Alfie said uncomfortably. 'But I keep thinking, *what if.*'

Gail snorted irritably. 'What if what?'

'What if . . . *what if* Tom Briggs really did see his sister that morning in Wootton Bassett?'

She put up her hand to stop him pulling his moustache. 'We'll never know, will we.'

'It's not that simple,' Alfie admitted. 'Suppose I believed him?'

She stared. 'What if you did?'

'A canal has locks on it, and wharves. The lock-keepers and wharfingers keep records, detailed records. Cargoes, weights. Tolls paid. Names.'

Gail said, 'But you don't know—'

'Seven-thirty a.m., the thirtieth of October 1876, leaving Twine's Wharf. If I really believed his story, I could check it.'

'Detective Inspector Bowler didn't.'

'He didn't believe in Tom. He didn't *want* to. Perhaps he was even afraid to. I would be, in his position.'

'Do you believe what Tom says?'

Alfie had stood and gone to the window. 'Gail, what if I did turn up something? What do I do then? Keep quiet about her, hide it like I hid what I suspected about Bowler? Or be disloyal?'

'You aren't a policeman any more.'

'What does that mean?'

'You're free to do what *you* think is right, Alfie.' Gail swung her legs out of bed. She went to the wardrobe and took out Alfie's best – only – suit hanging ready for church next Sunday. 'There's only one way to find out what you'll do—'

He made an excuse. 'No, I've got to feed the animals.'

'—and that's to just go ahead and do it.' She added, 'I'll feed them for you, this once.'

Alfie grunted.

The Croydon line joined the London and Greenwich Railway at Rotherhithe New Road. At Spa Road he was held up for nearly half an hour on the viaduct by stuck points. The other travellers took the news phlegmatically and flapped open their newspapers at pages they had not yet read. Alfie looked across the rows of smoking, sooty rooftops below him with affection. This view was all part of an ancient borough where he had spent his life, and Waterloo Street was still his home in a way the fields of Croydon would never be.

The train jerked him out of his reverie. A few minutes later it pulled into London Bridge Station. Rather than walk and miss his connection, Alfie endured the choking filth of the Circle Line to Paddington. He settled himself in a comfortable

521

Great Western Second Class carriage just as the guard blew his whistle and waved his green flag. Gail had provided him with a sandwich and an apple which he ate on the journey. As he walked down the dusty lane from the village of Wootton Bassett to the canal, the church clock struck midday.

Alfie swung his stick pleasurably and tipped his hat to a yokel or two. He was having a pleasant day out. At the water's edge he stopped to watch a heron flap away from him to the far bank. On the hill beyond stood a large redbrick building, probably Dr Gregory's school. Nearby a large peeling board announced Twine's Wharf, and Alfie crossed the creaking timbers to the wharf office. No boats lay alongside. 'Shop!' he called. There was no reply.

Inside the office a man in shirtsleeves lay curled asleep on the desk. Alfie knocked his foot.

'Books?' the man said, when he had woken properly. He got down with a display of energy to show that he had not really been asleep. "Course we keep Books! My life is Books! My old man's life was Books. We got Books 'ere going back ter the opening of the canal, eighty years ago. 'Oo d'yer think we are?' He stuck out his lip aggressively. "Oo d'yer think *you* are?'

Alfie was sure that if he admitted honestly, as he had intended to, that it was purely a personal enquiry, he would get nowhere. He was sure that in the way of book-keepers everywhere, this man had plenty to hide.

'Detective Constable Nutting, Scotland Yard,' he lied.

It worked horribly easily. The man stuck out his

hand. 'Gardiner, Company Wharfinger. Police? I never done nothing wrong! We 'aven't 'ad plainclothesmen 'ere afore. I don't suppose we'll take eight hundred pounds in tolls on the canal the whole of this year—'

'I'll see your Book for 'seventy-six,' Alfie said.

Gardener pulled the tome down and with increasing nervousness watched Alfie turn the pages. 'Wot's this ter do wiv the police, then? Everything's accounted fer proper.'

'Keep your nose clean and hope you've got a job tomorrow,' Alfie said.

He ran his finger down the page. The thirtieth of October was empty of entries. 'Here's an irregularity!' he said.

'Irregularity? Can't be.' Gardiner shook. He pulled on a coat for a little extra dignity. Alfie hid his sympathy for the poor scrimper as his detective skills came back to him.

'Mr Gardiner,' he said ominously, 'I have reason to believe that a boat quitted this wharf early that morning. Why is there no record of that event?'

'I'm sure – there must – traffic comes an' goes, we 'as busy days an' slack days.' Gardiner swallowed audibly. 'I know wot it must be, sir. Under the powers vested in me as Company Wharfinger under the Rules, Orders and Byelaws of the sixteenth day of June 1819, on busy days I 'as Discretion.'

'Discretion,' Alfie said coldly.

'Yes, sir, very important.' Gardiner turned anxiously to the previous pages. 'Under Byelaw 27, see, nobody's allowed to sleep aboard a boat tied at the Wharf, an' no fire allowed to be made aboard any boat at the said Wharf. But sometimes, sir, if we're late finishing an' they asks respectful like, I turns a blind eye.' His finger stabbed the full columns with relief. The day before had been busy until well into the evening.

There she was.

29th October 1876. *Pocahontas*. Eleanor and Joy Wampsett, Mrs Pebble. Ten tons Moira coal unloaded to Vincent's the coal-merchant.

'I remember 'em,' Gardiner said nostalgically. 'The old *Poca*. Sold cheese, too. Don't get that nowadays.'

I was wrong about Tom, Alfie thought. Tom was telling the truth.

The consequences of this were so large that he could not think about them yet.

'How would I find out where they are now?'

Gardiner shook his head. 'I ain't seen 'em fer years. Leaky old scow, the *Poca* was. Wot's it about? Broken the law, 'ave they?'

Alfie said carefully, trying to show no trace of his excitement, 'Do you remember the girl called Joy?'

'Got into trouble, 'as she! Always thought she was the type. Looked yer in the eye.' He shook his head righteously.

'*What did she look like?*'

Gardiner thought about it. 'Red 'air,' he said.

II

Tom and his mother rode in the funeral carriage. It pulled out of the driveway. The cortège, all in black, black horses wearing black plumes and black harness, fell in behind the bier along the street. The beadles wore black armbands and held their hats respectfully over their stomachs, and a tall man standing behind them did the same. 'I wish Mr Bowler was here,' Lydia said.

Tom stared at her. 'How can you say that?'

Her face was a pale blur through the black veil. 'He's always in charge and he always knows what to do.'

'Well, you'll find I'm in charge now, Mother,' Tom said, 'and I know what to do.'

She chuckled. 'Dear little Tom, you're still so young. You'll always be my little boy.' She lifted the veil and kissed his cheek.

'I know my own mind now,' Tom said.

She waved her face with a fan, it was so hot. Summer funerals had to be arranged with great speed. The coffin was mahogany and Tom thought it looked strong enough to last until the Day of Judgment. The bier had been draped with black crepe and surrounded by flowers for its short journey to St John's Wood Church. Lydia had received hundreds of cards of condolence, he knew, but not half the people had turned up. Most of the carriages following behind were empty, hired and paid for but having to be used just for show. Mostlock, the Principal Clerk, rode sombrely. He had followed Darby from Prideau's Bank and he, like Darby, could expect little mercy from Winston and Ernest Prideau when the creditors closed in.

But Mostlock had not shot himself.

Lydia still could not comprehend the enormity of what had happened, and Tom despaired of telling her. Darby's suicide was the sin of self-murder, he could not be buried on hallowed ground – it was not so long ago that Morland, the murderer, had been buried here at the crossroads with a stake thrust through his heart – but Tom had prevailed mightily on the doctor to enter his father's cause of death as a shooting accident. Lydia knew nothing of this. She knew nothing of affairs at the bank, or of how their lives were falling apart. She had taken hours dressing up this morning.

The carriage drew up at the church. Lydia looked out eagerly. 'Mr Bowler may—'

'All you can think about is Bowler,' Tom said so scornfully that she recoiled in her seat.

'What's got into you?' She put her hands to her face, then laughed pathetically. 'Don't be so silly. Why shouldn't I? Tom, you're jealous.'

'Mama, you are foolish.'

'If you speak to me like that again I shall slap your face.'

'Like you slapped Joy,' Tom said. The words could not be unsaid.

Lydia burst into tears. She had to be carried into the church by Tom and the pallbearers, and the congregation marvelled at her grief.

As the cortège dwindled from sight, the tall man melted back through the passers-by crowded behind the beadles.

Jack slipped through the gate of number fifteen and ducked under the trees. No one would see him. He yawned, put down his kitbag and sat on it. Faces got fatter or thinner, hard or soft, but did not really change very much. He'd recognised the child hidden inside her brother's adult face at once. The woman must be the dead girl's mother. These were the same people he had hurt so grievously all those years ago, and now it seemed some new harm had befallen them.

Perhaps, he thought, it's even the same old harm working its way forward. He supposed no family ever completely got over the death of a loved daughter. Jack Riddles could no more imagine now than then what love felt like, but he knew he would never forget what he had done that night, or forgive himself.

He could not bring her back but he could give them their revenge.

Jack lay in the shadows of the leaves, waiting, using the kitbag as a pillow.

He had not slept since getting off the boat. He napped like a cat, his eyes open at every new sound. When he did not move birds fluttered round him, going about their business. A dray rumbled past. A couple of maids walked by, giggling. He could have reached out and touched their legs.

The black carriage came between the gates and turned in front of the house. The woman half fell from the carriage. 'Tom!' she screeched. The young man came around the other side of the carriage and walked calmly away up the steps to the front door. The driver and postillion sat impassively as she ranted. 'Don't you dare turn your back on me, Tom!' The woman pulled her dress up to her knees the better to run up the steps after him. She smacked at his shoulders with her open palm.

Jack swung his kitbag from his hand and walked

across the gravel. They saw him as he came by the oleander bushes.

'Oh,' Lydia said. She looked flustered. 'It's that way.' She pointed to the tradesmen's entrance.

Jack stopped at the foot of the steps. 'Hallo, Tom,' he said.

'You,' Tom said.

Lydia's skirt rustled as she dropped the hem. She touched her fingertips to her hair. 'You haven't introduced me, Tom.'

Jack said, 'I've come back to give myself up.'

Tom interrupted him. 'You'd better come into the house, Mr Palmer.' He kept his hand at his side, so that Lydia should not see, beckoning with his fingers.

Jack stared at him. He realised Tom had seen the name on his kitbag. Tom coughed and put his finger over his lips.

'If that's the way you want to play it,' Jack said. He tipped his hat to Lydia. She, of course, being a lady, preceded them into the house. Jack came up the steps.

He stopped two steps below Tom. 'You know who I am all right, chum.'

'You're Jack Riddles,' Tom said evenly.

'That all you got to say?' Jack held out his hands. 'I murdered her.'

Lydia's voice came from inside the house. 'Aren't you two coming?'

'*I murdered her.*' Jack gazed into Tom's dark brown eyes. There was something hard in them. Jack realised what the difference was. Tom had grown up. The young boy Jack remembered was not here.

Tom bent down. 'You frightened me once, Jack,' he murmured. 'I've always remembered it.' He bunched his fist. Jack saw it coming. Tom knocked him down.

Jack rolled. He sat up on the gravel.

Tom came down the steps.

'I won't fight you, chum,' Jack said. He wiped his mouth.

But Tom put out his hand. 'I don't care what else you've done. I need your help too much.' He put his hand under Jack's arm and pulled him up. 'You must be a decent sort at heart, if you mean it about giving yourself up.'

'I mean it.'

'I know you didn't do it,' Tom whispered.

Jack followed him into the house. He felt numb. Lydia returned down the hall and held out her hand to be kissed. Tom murmured over his shoulder, 'Don't say anything to her.' He turned gracefully. 'Mr Palmer, may I introduce my mother, Mrs Briggs.'

'Lydia,' Lydia said.

'Good, I'm sure,' Jack said briskly. He shook her hand.

'I hear from your tone that you are a colonial, Mr Palmer.'

'Mother, you've had a very tiring and distressing day,' Tom said. 'You must go to your room now.' For a moment it seemed Lydia would resist, though she did look tired, then Tom said firmly, 'I'll send Dottie up with some tea.' He took his mother's elbow and guided her upstairs. He pointed Jack towards the parlour.

Jack went through. He looked at the photographs and realised he was thinking – even though he was wealthy and middle-aged – that the frames were worth stealing. Sadness swept over him that he couldn't change who he really was, inside.

Tom came in. He closed the parlour door and leaned back against it.

Jack said, 'All right, split it, chum. What's it about?'

'She doesn't know,' Tom said decisively. He reached into his pocket and pulled out a piece of paper. He held it out to Jack. It was a telegram, only two words, but Jack was still a slow reader. He deciphered their meaning letter by letter.

SHE'S ALIVE

'Stone me,' Jack murmured. 'It isn't true.'

'That's what my mother said six years ago. She wouldn't believe it either. It is true, Jack.' Tom unfolded the telegram so that the top line showed, 'General Post Office, Wootton Bassett, timed at half past two this afternoon. Delivered here just before three, when we were about to depart for my father's funeral.' For a moment Tom looked exhausted, as though he carried an enormous burden on his shoulders. He blinked back tears. 'My father will never know.'

'You can't believe one little note, Tom. It might be a hoax, or a mistake.'

'It was sent by Alfie Nutting. If Alfie says it, it's true.'

'Then I am innocent,' Jack said.

'He might bring her back with him for all I know,' Tom said.

'You didn't tell Lydia.'

'She didn't believe me last time. I won't cry wolf twice.'

The butler knocked and came in. He bowed. A maid with a trolley followed him. Jack watched them nervously as the tea-things were set out. The cakes were arranged on a silver cakestand, the tea in a silver pot on a silver tray, with cups and saucers of bone china so fine they were almost transparent. The mantelshelf clock chimed five o'clock. 'Tea-time,' Tom said. He waved Prettiman and Dottie away. 'I'll do it. Kindly take another pot up to my mother in her room.'

'Please, sir, Mrs Briggs is asleep,' Dottie curtseyed.

'Very well.' They went out and closed the door.

'How can you be so calm, Tom?' Jack said.

'I *always* knew she was alive,' Tom said. 'I felt it.'

Jack watched him pour the tea.

Tom handed him a cup and saucer. Jack poured the tea into the saucer and drank it. 'We have about an hour before Alfie arrives,' Tom said. 'He's an ex-policeman.'

'Christ!'

'Jack, there's something I have to ask you first,' Tom said.

'Fire away.'

Tom said, 'Did you steal the Bloodstone?'

'The bloody what?' Jack laughed. 'Never bloody heard of it.'

Tom breathed a sigh of relief. 'Then there are some things you should know,' he said.

Alfie walked from Paddington Station. It was six o'clock and people were already packing into Turnham's for Gilbert and Sullivan's new opera, *Patience*. Buses and cabs swerved around him and a horse shied. Alfie realised his long day's travel had tired him. His bones weren't as young as they used to be.

He turned down Abbey Place. When he knocked on the door of number fifteen Tom opened it personally. 'Did you see her?' he asked eagerly, staring over Alfie's shoulder. 'Did you bring her?'

'Saw where she'd been,' Alfie said wearily. 'I reckon you'd have a shock if you saw her close, Tom.'

Tom took his coat and led him to the parlour. Jack stood up from the most comfortable chair, thumbs hooked in his belt.

Alfie said dubiously, 'Who's this?'

Tom said, 'May I introduce Mr Palmer, also known as Jack Riddles.'

'Him! Still on the run.' Alfie shook his head. 'This puts me in an awkward position, Tom. I can't turn a blind eye to this.'

'I know,' Tom said.

Jack swept back his hair. He stuck out his jaw. 'Going to take me in?'

'Where have you been hiding, son?'

'Where I've come from I got used to buying coppers,' Jack said pugnaciously, 'not running from 'em. And ex-coppers don't frighten me at all.'

'That's enough,' Tom said. 'You're not a policeman now, Alfie. We need Jack, he understands what it's about. I call this meeting to order.'

'I never did nothing wrong I didn't have to,' Jack said.

Tom poured a glass of whisky and handed it to Alfie. 'What did you find out? Put us out of our misery,' he said.

'I'm not sure if I can do that. Tom, the name of your sister is now Joy Wampsett. She seems to have been taken in by a pack of itinerant canal folk, dirt poor, probably drunk most of the time and out for what they could get. They might have sold her or ditched her, but this lot didn't. All along the Regent's Canal there's trouble with boaties, theft, affray – here today, gone tomorrow, you see. No catching 'em. The worst of it is, they go all over the country . . .'

When he had finished Tom said, 'So we have no idea at all where they are now?'

'That's the size of it.' Alfie put down his whisky half-full. 'I had a stroke of luck. While I was at the wharf Mr Twine came by. He's part-owner of the Wiltshire canal now, but way back his father was lock-keeper at Seven Locks, and he was brought up there. He reckons that family often worked out of Moira.'

'Where's that?' Jack said, helping himself to the whisky bottle.

'Up north. Twine reckoned Scotland Yard would find them in the records of the Ashby de la Zouche Canal Company,' Alfie said.

Tom and Jack looked at him. 'Scotland Yard?' said Tom.

'Yes, we're reporting what we know to Scotland Yard,' Alfie said.

'Not me,' Jack said.

'Then we have to inform Detective Inspector Bowler of our allegations.'

'He's got a pistol,' Jack said.

Tom said, 'I'm worried about Mr Bowler. My mother expected him to be here today. But he was called away on Monday afternoon, the day of my father's death.' He cleared his throat awkwardly. 'Mr Bowler has become something of a friend of the family.' He added, 'Alfie, you once put it that Scotland Yard was full of detectives. I suppose that's like a family too. Families don't like scandal. *Quis custodet custodes*, they keep their own secrets to themselves, so that we have faith in them.'

'But we'd be breaking the law,' Alfie said. 'We know something for certain now. We'd be making ourselves accessories after the fact. Gentlemen, I'm no criminal. I have never broken a law in my life.'

"Course you have,' Jack said. 'Everyone does, all the time, and gets away with it. There's laws as high as the Man in the Moon. That's why you need lawyers when you get caught. I bet you've spat on the pavement or crossed the road without looking, or smacked a cheeky kid too hard—'

'I don't want anything to do with you,' Alfie said.

Jack said seriously, 'Let's be clear about this. When Mr Bowler finds out Joy is alive, he will kill her.' He stared into their soft faces, nodding. 'I would.'

Tom waited for Alfie to speak.

'Smart Arthur Simmonds threw himself in front

of a train in Manchester,' Alfie said. 'He was insane, talked to himself. I read the report just before I left the force.' He felt for his whisky glass and drained it. 'Joy is the last living witness against Mr Bowler.'

'And we don't have the Bloodstone,' Tom said. 'It's been lost since that night, Mr Bowler told me so himself. But Bowler would say that. If we could find it—'

'We don't know where he lives,' Alfie said.

Tom said, 'I know.'

They crossed Abbey Road. The Eyre Arms was a long clapboard building on the corner of Blenheim Place, and it was busy. The branch-coach had arrived from Hitchin, horses milled in the yard. Their hooves struck sparks from the cobbles under the layer of ash. The three men pushed through and came into the bar without wiping their feet. Alfie leaned one elbow on the counter. He crooked his finger and the barman came over, smartly dressed in a blue striped apron and red striped shirt.

'What's your pleasure, gentlemen?'

Alfie looked him in the eye. 'Detective Constable Nutting. I need Mr Bowler's case notes from his room.'

The man slipped the towel off his shoulder and wiped spilt beer from the counter. 'Mr Bowler's h'away,' he said cautiously.

'That's why he sent me chop-chop to get them,' Alfie said impatiently. 'Sergeant Steynes about, is he?'

The man pointed upstairs. 'Try 'is door.' Jack

went up and knocked. He shook his head.

One of the barmaids called, 'Steynes is in Manchester, 'e was due back Monday but 'e 'asn't showed up.' She flicked her eyes prettily. 'It's a martyr's life, being a policeman.'

Alfie clicked his finger. 'Key,' he said.

He opened Bowler's door, left the key in the lock, and went in.

It was a small, strangely proper room. Framed commendations were hung along one wall. The bed was neatly made, a spare blanket folded at its foot. There was a desk. Bowler's bedroom had no more identity than his office. His hairbrushes were arranged tidily on the dresser. There was a bottle of macassar oil.

'His razor's gone, but he sure left in a hurry,' Jack said. He glanced at the photographs on the dresser, one of them a cheap faded daguerreotype of a toddler holding her brother, who was just old enough to sit. The others were better quality, stamped by a photographer in Danbury Street. The same boy almost in his teens, with slicked hair, the girl coming up pretty, with dark eyes and curls.

'Not one of his wife,' Jack said.

A few pictures in wooden frames hung over the bed, cheap prints cut from chocolate-box tops, Swiss mountains, waterfalls, the moon seen through a breaking wave.

Tom went through the drawers. Nothing but clean shirts, clean collars.

'No jewel,' he said. 'If Joy was dead, possession of it would be the only evidence against Mr Bowler.' He went pale, realising what he had said.

'Mr Bowler would never go that far,' Alfie said. 'Not a young girl who's been through all she has. You forget, Tom, I know Mr Bowler pretty well. There are plenty of men like him on the force, but he's one of the best. You can't tell me he's bad all through.'

'He will kill her.' Jack was angry. 'He'd be stupid not to, he's got no choice. It's common sense. But you still don't really believe your precious Detective Inspector Bowler is a guilty man,' he said. 'You can't really believe he's betrayed you all these years. He's made everything you've done rotten, Alfie. He really has. You're saying to yourself there must be an excuse, some explanation you haven't thought of that makes him not guilty. And you're still trying to cover up for him. But there's nothing.'

Alfie said, 'I say we put this in the hands of the proper authorities.'

'He *is* the proper authorities.' Jack shouldered past him, heaved out the drawers on the floor, scattered their contents. 'Let's do this properly.' He kicked aside the mess and got down on his knees, feeling inside and out round what was left of the chest.

Tom said, 'What—'

'Looking for secret compartments,' Jack grunted. 'Don't they teach you anything in banks?'

'We should get a search warrant,' Alfie said.

Jack upended the bed, split the mattress. He tore open the pillows and they coughed as goose feathers fluffed up. 'You're the banker, you're clever with papers, you do the desk,' he told Tom. Alfie stood with his arms folded.

Tom licked his finger and pulled out sheafs of bills, receipts.

'Bowler pays every bill by return of post,' he said. 'There's nothing wrong here. His bank account is always in credit. He's perfect.'

'Personal letters?' Jack grunted. He broke open the back of the clock then threw it down, rolled back the rug to expose the floorboards. He pulled one and it came up with a loud bang.

'Nothing personal at all,' Tom said. 'I mean it.'

Jack dragged up the boards, peered between the beams. 'He isn't here. Nothing of him is here.'

The door opened and the barman looked in. 'Police business!' Jack snarled. The door was closed as quickly as it had opened.

Jack tore the backs off the photographs, scattered them. 'Nothing.' He jerked the pictures off the walls, opened the backs, threw everything down. 'Nothing.'

'You're a hooligan,' Alfie said.

Jack's eye lit on the armchair. He overturned it, gutted it of its horsehair stuffing, checked the frame. There was nothing.

At last Jack slumped back on his haunches. 'You're right, Tom. He's perfect.'

'Gentlemen, I have to confess I'm relieved,' Alfie said. 'I'll go up to Ashby de la Zouche tomorrow and ascertain from the canal company offices where Joy is now.'

'It's where Mr Bowler and Mr Steynes are that bothers me,' Tom said.

'Go to Ashby tomorrow? You don't understand what I was looking for.' Jack shook his head. 'I didn't find the pistol.'

'Oh my God,' Tom said. 'Bowler's got it with him.' He glanced at the broken clock. 'We can still get to St Pancras in time. We'll be there tonight.'

Chapter Twenty-one

I

'I feel bad about leaving Kes at the Bend,' Eleanor admitted. 'That back of 'is was real bad, an' it's not the first time 'e's put it out.'

'Vera knows how to heal that sort of thing,' Joy said. She stood in the hatches with the iron swan's-neck hellum, painted white with a scarlet spiral along it like a barber's pole, nestled comfortably in her armpit. That paint had been Grandma Pebble's last bit of work, faded now but no one would ever replace it. Around the scarlet line wound the body of a serpent, round and round to the rope roving where Joy's hand gripped. Whoever the helmsman was, the snake's head almost touched his or her wrist, its forked tongue reached towards the palm of her hand.

'Good old VerVera,' Eleanor agreed. 'I'm wrong ter worry. Strong as an ox, our Kes.'

Joy wore a cheap black blouse. Her long leather skirt, tucked tight at the waist, almost brushed the deck. Her black, broad-brimmed felt hat could be punched into almost any shape. She squinted at the setting sun ahead of the steamer. Its light gleamed off the cabin top, making the paint like the sky, and the cut stretched ahead of them as bright as the sky too. The engine chuffed, steady as a heartbeat, the canal banks golden with flowering yellow balsam slid by at their same remorseless rate. Smoke and steam drifted from the enamelled funnel with its polished brass rings and chains. 'Damian!' she called.

Dabchicks scattered ahead of the bow, a moorhen ran across the water, leaving coloured rings. Damian pulled himself out of the engine room side-hatch. He sat on the cabin top, his hair a glowing nimbus, the rest of him in shadow. He yawned, and seemed to hold the sun in his mouth.

He wiped his hands on an oily rag, then looked back at her and waved. Joy pointed. There were hills and lakes ahead, the canal winding back and forth around them to keep on the level. The *Poca* was buttied astern on the long manila snubber, keeping her clear of the *Joy*'s wash and turbulence. On the straights Damian could strap her hellum, jump ashore and run forward to the *Joy* to perform the tasks he enjoyed for some strange male reason, stoking the boiler, greasing the bearings, putting half a turn on the stuffing gland if it was dripping. He seemed to enjoy the dirt, it didn't seem dirty to him. He always had grease in his hair, and it showed, which it never did in Ham's black hair. And Ham and the *Lurcher* were always dirty, too. But the *Joy* was a woman's boat. Eleanor and Joy kept the outside as immaculate as the inside. The outside brightwork shone as brightly as the plates and ornaments that decorated the bulkheads below.

'Bends,' Joy called. The *Poca* would need steering now to keep her in line. Damian jumped onto the towpath. 'I'm letting the steam pressure run down,' he called as the boats swept past him. 'It'll be dark in half an hour.' He jogged alongside to free his long legs. Damian would be much taller than the other boys. Joy saw Eleanor looking at him and knew she was thinking the same thing.

'It's all the cheese you used to feed him, it's built him up,' Joy said.

'I don't know about that,' Eleanor said. Travelling without Kes made her a different person from when he was aboard. 'Much as I love 'im—' Eleanor would always say, and she did love Kes, but the truth was that she and Joy were much closer without a grown man about, and they had much more fun. Damian still slept in the steamer's fo'c'sle, still called the boy's castle, which he had outfitted as his own place and preferred to the cabin. When it came down to it men and boys didn't really feel happiest with plates on the walls and everything sparkling and in its place. Joy and Eleanor slept aboard the *Poca*, which had no engine but a much larger cabin, and at last they had it exactly as they wanted. 'Eh, Damian,' Eleanor called, 'yer might light the stove.'

Damian leapt across the tussocks of grass lining the towpath. He jumped over the sliding water, skidded on the deck and hung onto Joy's arm.

'Bends, Damian,' she reminded him patiently.

'Aren't we stopping now?'

'There's the Railway Inn at the next lock,' Eleanor said. 'We'll make it afore dark, if yer stop playing about.'

'Got enough pressure for that,' he said. He took off his shoes and before they could stop him stepped

543

over the back of the boat onto the snubber. He gripped the tow-rope with his bare soles. The manila line was three inches thick, hairy and stiff as iron with the drag of the tow. Foam boiled beneath him from the whirling blades. Eleanor saw him and squealed.

'Don't,' Joy murmured, 'you'll spoil his concentration.'

Eleanor was more alarmed than she could say. ''As 'e done this afore?'

'He is a bit of a show-off.'

Damian wobbled, holding out his arms for balance, each hand with a shoe in it.

'If 'e falls the *Poca*'ll run over 'im,' Eleanor whispered. 'There's only six inches 'twixt the bottom of the boat an' the bottom of the canal. Slow down.'

'If I do that the rope will go limp and what you don't want will happen,' Joy said calmly.

'I'm gonna wet meself,' Eleanor said.

From the middle of the rope Damian looked round and grinned. His weight pulled the long length of manila down so that he was standing in the rushing water. Foam brushed his heels, sprayed up to the backs of his knees. Then he walked up to the *Poca*'s front end, the bow wave breaking in front of him, and as the angle of the rope became too steep, he pulled himself over the stem with his hands.

He jumped lightly to his feet, pulled on his shoes, waved and ran back along the top planks to the *Poca*'s hellum.

'Isn't he brave?' Joy said.

'I'm gonna rinse me bloomers,' Eleanor said. 'God, I 'ate it when they're growing up. Yer always tell yerself it'll get easier an' easier, but it always gets 'arder an' 'arder.' She swallowed, and her lower eyelids gleamed. Joy realised Eleanor really had been frightened.

'I'll tell him not to do it again,' she said.

'That's the funny thing,' Eleanor said. "E listens ter yer.'

Joy laughed, then gave her full attention to the bends. The light had lost its colour. The hills rising around them were grey.

She sounded the siren as they passed through a short tunnel. The steady chuffing of the engine died away to a whisper. The *Joy* lost way beneath the railway bridge and entered the lock. They came out on the last few pounds of steam pressure – 'Did I get it right,' Damian said proudly, 'or did I get a bullseye?' They tied up at the Railway Inn mooring. It was fully dark but there was a heavy dew. Lights were strung over the bridge and beneath the station gables, so everything was silvery beneath the stars. Damian bled boiling water from the engine and made a pot of tea. 'I don't know that I can take any more of me own stew,' Eleanor confessed. 'Let's 'ave a night off 'ome cooking.'

A train flew northward over the bridge with a thunderous roar, sending sparks drifting into the canal. The carriage lights raced by, the guard's van disappeared swaying into the dark. 'Birmingham ter Chester,' Eleanor said. She hated the railways with a passion. 'The Ellesmere canal heads west, see, where they can't go. Into the mountains. Mount Ruabon. Mount Llantysilio. Others yer can't pronounce less'n yer Morwenna wot speaks Welsh.

That's 'ow we boaties still got the trade.'

After tea and a wash they went into the cheap'n'cheerful end of the Railway Inn. Without Kes to keep an eye over her Eleanor drank gin. 'Mother's ruin,' she told them seriously, 'but it never ruined my mother, did it?'

'She was a wonderful woman,' Joy said.

'Me Mum's family were thatchers,' Eleanor said. 'Reedham. Norfolk reed, that is. Remember when Peter thatched the cottages?' She swirled her glass cheerfully. 'I say, good stuff, this is.' Her mood turned serious again. 'Oh, yer should've seen them wherries under full sail. 'Ardly see the boats beneath, just them 'uge sails seeming ter sail above the reed-beds. Rust-red sails.'

A man in a long black coat came in carrying a zinc tray. He tipped his cap respectfully to the landlord and went round the drinkers, bowing politely at each table. Eleanor bought three hot potatoes off him. The man split the potatoes and put a big hunk of butter in each one, presenting them with a bow from his dirty hands. They ate the steaming potatoes as the butter melted, blowing on them because they were so hot, juggling them between their fingers. The butter ran down their chins. 'That 'it the spot,' Eleanor said. 'Now I need another gin ter cool me mouth.'

Damian watched her at the counter. 'What's it with Ma?'

'She's worried about Kes,' Joy said.

'We could put her on the train if it's that bad. You and I could handle the boat.'

Joy whispered, 'Can you imagine Eleanor travelling on a train?'

Eleanor tottered genially back to the table. 'Now, where was I in me proud potted 'istory of boatie folk?'

'I see your point,' Damian murmured to Joy.

Eleanor finished her drink. 'I can walk,' she said with dignity. They came out of the pub and crossed by the stables. Eleanor stopped to stroke the muzzle of one of the huge Shire horses. She'd appropriated a Shropshire Union Railway salt cellar from the pub. The horse licked the salt peacefully from her hand. Damian said goodnight and went back to the steamer. They heard the slide to the fo'c'sle bang open, then it slammed closed.

'Peace an' quiet. Just us.' Eleanor took Joy's hand. The two women walked to the wooden landing stage over the shimmering water. 'Me Mum always called a landing stage a staithe, did yer know that?'

'I think I did.'

'Norfolk word. I like talking ter yer, yer always was a good listener.' Above their heads curved a sign mounted on two posts. '"Ruggles's Flying Gigs",' Eleanor murmured. '"Shropshire Union Canal licensed. Fares to all parts." Grandma Pebble could remember when it was busy enough 'ere. Queues o' people, farmer's wives mostly. Farm stuff in baskets, proper Welsh leeks, she'd see a goat on a red leash like a dog, even a calf maybe. All fer Shrewsbury market, or as far as Wolverhampton sometimes, Birmingham even, an' back in a day. Must've seemed like a miracle in them days, afore the railway.'

They returned to the *Poca*. Eleanor pulled down the crossbed. They undressed and Joy swung herself into the sidebed. Eleanor put out the lantern.

After a while her voice came out of the dark. 'Joy?'

'Yes.'

'You awake?'

'No. I'm asleep.'

'I wish Kes was 'ere,' Eleanor said. ''E does keep me feet warm.'

'Send him a telegram if you're worried,' Joy said.

'It's the expense. An' where would 'e send the reply ter? Nah, we'll be back 'ome next week anyway.'

'Might pick up a load of stone at Llangollen,' Joy said sleepily.

Eleanor's voice came again. 'I wish Kes an' I was married proper.' She heaved a sigh. 'It's me guilty conscience won't let me do it.'

Joy rolled over. 'What guilty conscience?'

'Well. I suppose you're old enough ter know about yer-know-what? Yer must've 'eard me an' Kes often enough.'

'I don't listen.'

''E always grunts like that, it's 'is way.'

Joy giggled. 'Perhaps all men do.'

'No,' Eleanor said. 'They don't.'

Joy listened to the older woman sighing.

'Me Mum knew,' Eleanor confessed. 'I keep looking fer meself in 'er paintings. A wicked, evil, witchy woman lurkin' in 'em somewheres. Me. She knew me secret, see.'

Joy slid the sidebed door fully open and peered down into the dark. She could smell Eleanor's feet and hear her breathing but she couldn't see her. 'What secret?'

'Everyone 'as a secret they keep buried inside 'em, Joy. I do. Yer does. Me boys do, or will one day. A

548

secret something. It might not start off as a bad thing, but things grow, don't they. They just keep growing like them Welsh leeks. Finally yer got so much ter lose that yer can't stop 'em. Kes is a wonderful lover. 'E's the best man, I won't 'ear a word 'gainst 'im. But there's something more.'

'I don't want to hear anything bad about Kes,' Joy said.

'It's not bad, it just *is*. See, Kes is all pump an' no squirt.'

Joy sat up.

'Oh, Eleanor.'

'I couldn't 'ave kids by 'im. I don't know 'ow long, fifteen years we was together on the Mon & Breck an' everywhere, an' nothing 'appened. I thought it was God's will. Then one night I 'ad a little bit o' gin, a place just like tonight it was, an' 'orses in the stables, an' Kes'd 'ad too much ter drink an' went ahead ter the boat, an' there was this bloke wot'd been giving me the eye all evening, an' 'e followed me ter the stable. 'E was quite nice as it turned out, lovely an' dark, an' 'ard all over. An' it 'appened in the straw. An' nine months later, Ham 'appened.'

Joy lay back on the pillow.

'I love children,' Eleanor said in a lost voice. 'Shane an' Jaffrey 'ad just the one dad, bein' twins. That was economical.'

Joy said, 'Who is Damian's father?'

'*Was*,' Eleanor said firmly. 'Kes is 'is dad. I never saw 'em twice, see. It was just ter get the kids. An' I was always tipsy, an' it was always dark, I'd prob'ly never recognise them blokes again anyway, or them me. I just used 'em. It wasn't love.'

'But you didn't have a girl.'

Eleanor's hand reached out of the dark, warm. She squeezed Joy's hand tight.

'Yes. There's yer. Me bonus. But yer diff'rent, Joy. I've never understood yer like I've understood me boys. But I'll tell yer wot. Yer as much ours as any of 'em.'

Joy lay with Eleanor's hand holding her own. Gradually she realised that Eleanor was asleep, breathing evenly. But still she hadn't let go.

In the morning they woke and went about their tasks without saying a word. It would be a hot day. Damian swam in the canal, scattering pale drops of water from his blond hair. The funnel spurted a fine haze of smoke, the engine started its steady chuffing. They cast off and at Frankton Junction turned the boats due west, and the sun rose behind them.

Eleanor brought up a mug of tea. She laid it on the cabin top and squeezed Joy's hand. That was all that was said about last night.

II

The MS&L milk train paused only briefly at Cody's Halt, time enough for the milk churns to be swung aboard, the mailbag tossed down in return. There was no platform. Jack jumped from the bottom step onto the planks and looked around him.

The sound of the locomotive faded into the distance, revealing birdsong. He could hear cows lowing contentedly. By God, this land was green. He'd never seen so much green, and clear fresh water burbled in the ditches. And the trees were green, all different sorts of green, and there were many more types of trees than Jack knew the names.

He saw a funny little building like a dwelling made for gnomes, the second floor bigger than the one below. A man backed up the ladder dragging the mail, and it took Jack a moment to realise that here the signalman did both jobs – in fact, all jobs.

'Hey, chum,' Jack called, 'Cody's Bend? The Wampsetts?'

The signalman stopped. 'Boaties, they,' he said. He jerked his thumb downhill. 'Don't get no letters like us ordinary folk.' He sniffed. 'Why's they so popular all of a sudden then?'

Jack said warily, 'Are they?'

'Man all of a state on Monday, then two o' them on Tuesday—'

'Tuesday,' Jack said bleakly. Today was Thursday morning.

'Said they was police,' the man nodded importantly.

So Bowler had already found Cody's Bend.

'Detective Inspector Bowler and Detective Sergeant Steynes, was it?'

The man nodded again. 'Armed police, they was, or leastways one of 'em was, on the lookout for Fenians – I said, I told them, you won't find no bloody terrorists here, we're country folk, as straight and true as English oaks—'

Jack gradually realised the man would talk all day. He waved his thanks and started downhill through the woods. He passed a pretty little church and came out into the water-meadow where the cows were grazing. These were black-and-white Friesians with big soft udders, not the rangy longhorn

Herefords he was used to. They gazed at him curiously as he walked along the gravel track between them and came to the canal bank. The row of thatched cottages must be the place. There was only one boat at the mooring. Its name was the *Lurcher*.

Jack realised he was too late.

That meant she was probably dead by now.

'What have I done?' Jack said aloud.

They should have been quicker. But they'd caught the train from St Pancras with less than a minute to spare, Alfie running along the platform, Tom leaning back from the door to grab his hand.

The canal offices at Ashby de la Zouche had been closed, of course. It was nearly midnight. Jack broke inside soundlessly while Alfie and Tom waited in the street. When Jack returned Alfie said, 'Couldn't you get in?' He'd sounded almost relieved to think that Jack's criminal activity had been unsuccessful.

But Jack had grinned and handed him the ledger. 'Quicker than official channels, mate. I'll put it back before they know it's missing,' he said.

They went into a pub. Tom and Alfie pored over the book while Jack bought beers. There were few other drinkers left and the landlord wanted to shut the place up. He banked the fire and put the dog out.

'Moira Furnace,' Tom said. 'The *Poca*. Coal. Loads of entries.' He turned to more recent pages. 'No *Poca*. Wait. *Joy/Poca*.' He whistled softly. 'That name's a dead giveaway.'

'They must be using the old boat as a dumb barge,' Alfie said.

'They stopped carrying Moira coal,' Tom said.

552

'Look. Place called Overseal. The Overseal Pipe Company. They're carrying pipes now.'

'There it is.' Alfie's blunt finger stabbed the page. 'Mr Christopher Wampsett, Cody's Bend.'

'This is last year's book,' Tom said. 'Well, we know that last year the family was carrying cargoes of pipe from Overseal to Plas Kynaston, wherever that is.'

'Gentlemen,' Alfie said, 'I suggest we find the Overseal Pipe Company manager's house, and spoil his sleep.' He closed the book and handed it to Jack. 'And I don't want to know how you get it back,' he frowned.

Jack just grinned. 'Trick of the trade,' he said.

The manager was Mr Sear, and he did not like his sleep disturbed in the early hours. He sat in his parlour in his dressing-gown, fuming with rage. 'Of course I know them well. Most reliable. Forty tons of pipe, all sizes, from the claypits here to the Plas Kynaston cut for the Welsh collieries around Cefn-mawr, regular as clockwork.'

Tom said, 'When were they last here at Overseal?'

'Saturday afternoon. They usually lie up at Cody's Bend on the Sabbath, Monday mornings sometimes. Mr Wampsett is a Number One, a free man.'

Alfie asked, 'So they wouldn't be at Cody's Bend now?'

'It's unlikely. I would expect them to arrive at Cefn-mawr tomorrow.' Sear looked at the clock. 'I mean today. I shan't get back to sleep now, you know!' he exploded, and slammed his door.

The three men put up their collars and stood beneath a street-lamp, arguing. 'I'll deal with it,

Tom,' Alfie said. 'I know what I'm doing. You'd better get back to the bank.'

Tom said, 'Bugger the bank. I'm coming with you to Cefn-mawr.'

'They may have caught and killed her already,' Jack said. 'I'm sorry, Tom, it's got to be said. If Bowler knew about Cody's Bend, he's ahead of us.'

'We don't know that he did,' Tom said.

'You don't understand the man you're up against,' Jack said. 'I do.'

'Jack had better cover Cody's Bend just in case,' Alfie told Tom.

So Jack was out of it.

Now Jack stuck his hands in his pockets as he walked along the towpath. 'If only I could have been quicker,' he said aloud. He stopped as a couple of young children ran past him, the youngster behind struggling to keep up. A woman appeared from the cabin of the *Lurcher*, her glossy hair flying, her strong bones showing in a face full of life as she jumped ashore. Jack stared as she embraced the children.

For a moment he had really thought that this woman was she.

But the girl's hair was black, and when she called back into the cabin her accent was Welsh. 'Our little ones, it is, Ham! Blodwen must have heard the engine—'

She sensed Jack looking at her and fell quiet. The children looked round at him.

'I'm looking for Joy . . . you know her as Joy Wampsett,' Jack said.

A young man came out of the cabin. He leapt onto

the towpath, bunched his fist, and knocked Jack down.

Jack lay there. 'I'm not getting up. I don't know what's got into people in this country.' He sat cautiously. 'You must be Ham.'

'Yer get up so I can knock yer down again,' Ham said. 'Keep the kids back, Morwenna.'

'Don't you dare hit him in front of them, Ham Wampsett!' she said.

Ham lowered his fists. 'This is the third time,' he muttered. 'That bloke wot tried ter snatch Joy, then the two of 'em wot tried ter frighten the wits out of Vera—'

Jack stood. He picked his hat off the towpath and dusted down his jacket.

'Well I'm going back to the house, Ham,' Morwenna said, shepherding the children away. She looked over her shoulder and smiled at Jack.

'Good kids,' Jack said.

'She thinks no one else can look after 'em,' grumbled Ham. 'Couple of days we been on the cut, an' never a minute when she wasn't thinking of 'em.'

'Those blokes on Tuesday said they were police, did they?'

Ham looked at him suspiciously. 'Wot d'yer know about it?'

Jack told him.

'Yer'd better come an' talk ter Vera,' Ham said.

The woman who opened the door was dressed all in black. Her hair was silver, tied back in a bun by a long black ribbon. She looked Jack straight in the eyes. 'Are you her father?'

'Christ, no!' Jack said.

'I've been expecting him,' Vera said. She stood back so that they could come inside.

'I'm the one who's to blame for this whole bloody mess,' Jack said.

Vera sat. She did not gesture them to sit, and in fact there was nowhere for them to do so. The room was almost bare of furniture.

'I doubt that,' she said.

'Yer listen ter wot Jack's got ter say, Vera,' Ham said.

Jack spoke. Before he had finished Vera stood and went to the window. She stared out sadly.

'And you have told no one else this, ever?' she said.

'Not the complete whole of it, no.'

'And not that you blame yourself?'

'No, Vera.'

Vera said, 'I think Joy knows.'

'I don't reckon I come out of it too well,' Jack said ruefully.

'Don't you indeed!' Vera was fierce. 'You could have slit the child's throat or thrown her straight in the water to drown or freeze. You should have done that, Jack, if you really wanted to be safe. She knew your name. That alone was probably enough to send you to the gallows.'

Jack said, 'I think I fell in love with her.'

'Blimey,' Ham interrupted quickly, 'bit old fer 'er, weren't yer?'

'Sshhh.' Vera went back to her seat. She paused and touched Ham's shoulder. 'It's all right, Ham. I know. I understand. Perhaps you should go and see Morwenna now.'

556

'All she thinks of is the children,' Ham said. He burst out, 'Shane an' Jaffrey's back at college. There's nothing ter keep me 'ere now.'

There was a knock on the door. Everyone stiffened, but it was only Kes. He hobbled in on two sticks. 'I've slept enough,' he said. 'I 'eard yer through the window. Go on.'

Vera sat. 'The men came two days ago. Joy had left the day before – shortly after your argument with that man, Ham. You also had left, with Morwenna. I was here alone when I saw them coming across the field. I didn't like the look of them. They took themselves too seriously, I thought. They said they were police, and they behaved like police, but I didn't trust them. Mr Bowler asked where Joy had gone and I said I didn't know. He walked around my house as though he owned it. I was afraid the noise would wake Kes lying a-bed next door and he'd start groaning, his terrible pain. They could've got the truth out of him, maybe, one way or the other.'

'No kidding,' Kes winced.

'Anyway,' Vera continued, 'Mr Bowler said I would be in serious trouble if I didn't help the police. They tried to make me feel like a criminal. They badgered me until I really did want to tell them what I knew, just to make them stop.'

'But yer didn't,' Ham said proudly.

'I wasn't born yesterday! They talked between themselves on the towpath, then Mr Bowler came back and said he knew Joy lived here, all he had to do was wait. This time I kept my door closed and I said, you can wait out there on the towpath for as long as you like. I knew she wouldn't be back before

557

'Saturday at the earliest, you see.'

'You know she's going to Cefn-mawr?' Jack said.

'Yes, but I didn't tell them that. I was still praying Kes wouldn't wake.'

'I wouldn't have been no use,' Kes admitted. 'Yer don't know wot the pain's like till yer've got it. I would've told 'em anything they wanted to know.'

'You're an honest man, Kes,' Vera said sympathetically. She looked up at Jack. 'Finally Mr Bowler came back and called through the window, all reasonable like, with a cunning glint in his eye, just tell me, mother – he kept calling me mother, cheeky blighter – just tell me which way she went. So I pointed and said, that way. Right, mother, he says, we'll go the other way! Clever, wasn't he.'

'But not clever enough,' Ham bragged. 'She'd told 'im aright!'

Jack said, 'He would have found out at the first lock that the boats hadn't gone through, though.'

'That's not so easy at it sounds,' Ham said. 'Often miles from a road, locks are. An' most of 'em don't 'ave lock-keepers.'

'It was three hours afore they came storming back along the towpath, faces black as thunder,' Vera said. 'Naturally, I'd made myself scarce.'

'But they can take the train miles ahead,' Jack pointed out, 'see if she's reached such and such a lock, and work back to her.'

'Not so simple.' Ham shook his head. 'There's junctions,' he explained. 'That way's Fazeley. She could go straight on up the Coventry canal, or make a port turn down the Birmingham & Fazeley. That's longer, but on the other 'and she'd know there was works at Whittington Brook Junction. Get along the Birmingham and yer got the choice of the Birmingham canal net, 'undreds of 'em. Now *we* know that she'd get through Wolverhampton onto the Birmingham & Liverpool Junction canal, an' from there she'd turn ter port at Hurleston Junction onto the Ellesmere canal. *But*, if yer didn't know that . . . it'd take yer a lot of shoeleather ter find out.'

'You reckon she's on the Ellesmere now?' Jack said.

'I reckon she's passed Frankton Junction,' Ham said thoughtfully. 'She's on the Llangollen cut. She's in the 'ills somewhere, I reckon.'

'Bowler is very close to her,' Vera said.

Ham cast her a respectful glance. He nodded.

'But she'll reach Cefn-mawr soon,' Jack said. 'My friends are there.'

Vera said, 'There are too many people at Cefn-mawr. He won't touch her there. From Frankton Junction onwards he will be certain which way she has gone. It will have been an easy matter to get ahead of her, the canal loops so in the hills—'

'Ambush,' Jack said. He squeezed his fist so hard his knuckles cracked.

Kes said in a hollow voice, 'Eleanor and Damian's on the boat too. Wot about them?'

They all looked at Jack. Jack didn't say anything.

Kes's eyes filled with tears of frustration.

'It's not too late,' Jack said. 'There's the train—'

'That only goes as far as Ellesmere,' Ham said. 'The Shropshire Union Railway owns the canal too, see, so if they built their railway any further, they'd put their own canal out of business.'

'I'm wasting time,' Jack said. He went to the door.

'Me too,' Ham said, opening it for him. 'I'm wiv yer, Jack.'

'Ham, yer'll stay 'ere,' Kes said. 'I won't 'ave yer risk yer life.'

'You've got to let Ham go,' Vera said. 'Kes, let him go.'

'I know the way,' Ham called from the towpath. 'An' there's something I owe 'er, remember?'

Chapter Twenty-two

I

'I'll jump off an' get us a loaf of bread from Usher's Bakery, an' we'll 'ave a late lunch on the 'op,' Eleanor decided. 'Slow down by the bridge, I won't be a minute. Only three miles ter Chirk.' She waved to Damian on the back end of the *Poca* behind them, then pointed at the bakery to show where she was going. Damian gave big nods of approval. Joy used the valve to slow the engine until the boats hardly moved. She looked over the counter at the propeller twisting slowly beneath her in the clear water. She could see each blade glinting in the sunlight. Every day the canal fed six million gallons of fresh Welsh mountain water to the factories of the Black Country.

She yawned, amused to see Damian scrambling up and lying on the *Poca*'s cabin top, sunning himself. It had been a slow day. Earlier there had been a bevy of boats coming down against them, the early boats that had left at daybreak laden deep with Cefn-mawr coal or Llangollen slate, and the toll-keeper at Newmarton Locks held everyone up while he gauged them against slots in the lock sides, working out the weight of cargo from the boats' depth in the water. He was a jobsworth and would not give the proper allowance against the weight of coke fuel in the *Joy*'s bunker. Eleanor had settled the matter with a wink and a couple of pounds of Moira cheese. Later she turned the air over the cut blue swearing about him.

'He was a cheeser,' Joy said. Eleanor gave a bellow of laughter and had decided there and then on fresh bread for lunch.

II

'Yer don't say much,' Ham said.

Jack grunted. 'I'll pay the train driver double if he'll go faster.'

'The express spoiled yer, didn't it. We was doing seventy miles an hour on one straight I reckon.' Ham was so thoroughly enjoying riding the train that Jack couldn't help a smile. 'They call this the Salop Crawler,' Ham said cheerfully. 'It's a local.'

'We should've waited for the express.'

'The express don't stop at Ellesmere.' The locomotive slowed and Ham peered forward. "Ere we are.'

The train rattled over a canal bridge. Ham threw open the door and they jumped down. He led the way past the Railway Inn and stopped at the water's edge. 'Blimey,' he said, 'it's not so posh as I remember it.'

Jack could no longer hide his intense frustration. 'What are we supposed to do, Ham? Row? Run on the water?' Jack stopped, seeing a sign for Ruggles's Flying Gigs. 'We'll hire a gig. With a good horse and a strong vehicle—'

'Yer don't know nothing. On these roads yer'd be all day an' all night.' Ham grinned. 'Trust me. Got plenty of cash, 'ave yer?'

Jack held out a bundle of notes.

Ham knocked on the hut door with the side of his fist until it was opened. 'Mr Ruggles, is it?'

The old man looked at them suspiciously. 'I've paid until next week,' he said, and tried to close the door.

Ham held the bundle of money through the gap. 'Cefn-mawr by three o'clock?'

Ruggles came out. He had forgotten he was wearing nothing on his feet. He flashed them glances and licked his lips. 'Ask that bastard at Newmarton Locks,' he said.

'I'll ask him,' Jack said without smiling.

Old Ruggles became quite garrulous. 'Almost driven me off the cut, he has. 'Course I still gets some work down the Montgomery—' He tucked his shirt cheerfully into his trousers.

'I'll pay a bonus for every minute you cut off the time,' Jack said.

Ruggles pulled on one boot. 'Two-thirty, if you'll help me with the harness—' He hopped across the yard pulling on the other boot, calling for the boy.

Jack and Ham hefted the enormous leather collars that would fit around the horses' shoulders. They followed the old man and his grandson, who came scampering barefoot across the yard, to the stables. Two huge Shire horses, the largest Jack had ever seen not pulling a beer dray or a two-decker omnibus, gazed out at them peacefully.

'Lofty and Silver,' old Ruggles said with pride.

'Not as young as they was, but that's true of us all, isn't it?' He shouted furiously at the boy. 'Get that straw out of your ears, Wag, and get some work going, would you? The *Queen Boadicea* will fly on the water today. Get me my scythe!'

'That rusty old thing,' the boy said.

When the horses were geared up the boy led them out. The old man fetched down two large, strangely shaped felt sacks from the rafters.

'What are those?' said Jack.

'Blindfolds fer the 'orses,' Ham said. 'You'll see.'

The *Queen Boadicea* was a lightly built craft with a cabin for ten or twelve people. The roof was cotton stretched over bamboo, cured for stiffness. Old Ruggles gave the scythe a wipe on his sleeve and tied it to the bow. 'Every boat on the canal gives way to the *Queen*,' he said, 'or their tow-rope gets sliced, right?' He went back to the tiller and waved to the boy, who rode the lead horse. Wag dug in his heels. The boat began to move.

The boat moved faster. A wave piled up at the bow, flooding the towpath, as the horses rose to the trot. 'Seven miles an hour,' Ham said. 'That's why other boats never go much more'n a walking speed. This is different.' The front of the *Queen Boadicea* rose up, then slid forward over the wave. The boy shouted, 'Ya, ya! Ya!' The horses cantered.

'Had her up to fourteen miles an hour, I have,' old Ruggles shouted. 'She slides over the water instead of shoving through it. Even with one horse she'll cruise at ten miles an hour smoother'n the most expensive carriage. Started on the hoolits, I did, the night-boats on the Glasgow & Paisley. Paisley to

564

Glasgow in forty-five minutes. Forty years ago I ran swiftboats 'twixt Birmingham and Wolverhampton. Now I mostly do excursion trips to Llangollen for well-off people,' he touched his forehead respectfully, 'like yourselves . . .'

Jack was amazed. The slipstream made his hatbrim flutter. He stared at the two clear, steady wings of water that fanned into the air from the sides of the boat. It looked as though they really were flying.

III

Detective Inspector Bowler got down from the open phaeton. The springs creaked as the vehicle was relieved of his weight. He wore his plaid overcoat despite the heat of the day, because it had large pockets and he could walk with his hands in them. He felt a packet of Shropshire Union Railway sandwiches in his left-hand pocket, and his pistol in his right-hand pocket. The metal felt hot.

Bowler stretched his legs and called to the driver, 'What's the name of this place?'

'What, here?' The Welsh treated English like a foreign language when they wanted.

'I want to know the name of this village,' Bowler said.

The man sounded surprised that anyone should not be thoroughly familiar with the area. 'Rhoswiel, of course.'

His lilting provincial accent reminded Bowler of Mary, her Irishness that had let him down, and that despite his insistence she had never completely relinquished. Now she thought she was free of him she was probably openly calling herself Màiri again, and she would probably encourage Timmie and Megan to grow up speaking her way too. Timmie would never find a good job in London sounding like that, Bowler knew, or Megan catch a good husband in London Society.

Bowler realised how wrong he had been to marry for love. Love was blind, love was a stupid waste.

He was afraid, desperately afraid, that he would never see his children again.

He'd have to find them somehow.

George Steynes lay asleep in the phaeton, his feet propped on the front seat, his head on the lowered canopy at the back. The hairs twitched in his nostrils as he snored.

Bowler couldn't bear to be near him for another moment. Hands in pockets, he walked to the stone bridge over the canal and leant on the parapet. He was exhausted, he'd not slept properly for two days, and he had been travelling for most of that time. His clothes stuck to him, creased, travel-stained. His shoes were dirty. He felt as though he might never be clean again, and he was sure he had dark circles under his eyes. His skin bristled with two days' growth of stubble.

He took the sandwiches from his pocket and leant forward, nibbling mouthfuls, throwing pieces of bread to the ducks swimming beneath him.

Bowler felt a pain in his chest. For a second, an awful second, he thought it was a heart attack.

He pulled back and opened his coat. The front of

his waistcoat contained two small pockets, one each side of the buttons. One pocket contained his silver hunter watch, and his silver watch chain was clipped across his belly to the other pocket.

Bowler reached two fingers into it and pulled out something which flashed.

He studied the diamond. He had thought once it was the most perfectly beautiful thing he had ever seen, the Bethlehem.

Goldblum's obsession had become his own.

Not until later had Bowler heard its other name, the Bloodstone.

Bowler turned it slightly in the sun, and there it was, the flaw on the other side like a tiny drop of blood. Now that he knew where it was it tainted the whole diamond with pink, made the whole jewel flawed.

Everything he had once thought to be of value, everything he had aspired to be, everything he had dreamed of, everything he had believed in, was worthless.

Bowler let the stone go. Its smooth surface slid on his sweaty palm, then it tumbled through the air, splashed. The ducks quacked eagerly, circling the place, hoping it was bread.

He leant on the parapet, dropping bread to the ducks, helping himself to occasional mouthfuls. The springs of the phaeton creaked as Steynes got out. He yawned and a woman pushing a wicker pram on the towpath looked at him. There were fishermen too, probably miners on night shift. Further along some children were playing with stones.

Steynes pointed. In the distance a plume of smoke

drifted round the hill. A boat appeared among the trees, another boat following it faithfully.

'Here she comes, Guv'nor,' he said.

Bowler went back to the phaeton and studied the map. Half a mile upstream the canal looped almost back on itself along the side of a valley. A river called the Ceiriog ran somewhere below the canal, it was difficult to tell exactly from the chart. But even from where he sat, Bowler could see the open fields giving way to trees. The steep slopes going down would provide plenty of cover.

'Pay off the Jarvis,' he ordered.

'Anything you say, Guv'nor.'

IV

'Why do you keep pulling at your moustache?' Tom demanded.

Alfie gazed at him. 'Just checking it's still there, I suppose, sir.'

'Don't call me sir,' Tom said irritably. 'You aren't on duty now.'

'It feels like I am, sir,' Alfie sighed. 'It feels like I am.' They had stopped in the yard at Plas Kynaston. He didn't bother to get down from the cart. 'They aren't here.'

Half a dozen boats were tied up along the colliery wharf, all of them grimy, most of them unloading heavy machinery for Cefn-mawr or loading coal.

Tom jumped down and spoke to one of the barrow-men. He returned shaking his head. 'Not here yet. Any time after three he reckoned.'

'We'll wait,' Alfie said. 'It's only an hour.'

568

Tom thought about it. 'No, we won't wait,' he said. 'Jack said—'

'I don't want to hear any more about what Jack said. He's got you under his spell, Tom. Always got a bit of glamour about them, that sort. They say the devil always gets the best lines.'

'Jack said we don't really believe Mr Bowler is capable of evil, because he's a policeman.'

'He said *he* was capable of killing her, and I believe that. Jack Riddles is undoubtedly a murderer, Tom. Remember that.'

'You're giving Mr Bowler the benefit of the doubt,' Tom said.

'A man's innocent until proven guilty. Nothing's ever been proved against him.'

'Nothing's ever been proved against Jack,' Tom said. 'But Jack's been guilty all his life, according to you, hasn't he?'

Alfie looked away. 'You're young. You don't know what you're talking about.'

Tom jumped back on the cart's wooden bench seat with a litheness Alfie could only envy.

'Let's look back along the canal,' Tom said decisively. He clicked his tongue and flicked the reins.

The villages were connected by dusty tracks too steep for the cart to use. Tom took the main road towards Chirk. From time to time he glimpsed the cut glinting through the trees on his right, but saw no boats working upstream.

'All these hills,' Alfie said worriedly. 'Suppose the canal goes through tunnels?'

'What about it?'

'If they were in a tunnel we'd never know they were there.'

'You used to be an optimist,' Tom said. On the hilltop opposite them, a castle showed round towers above the trees. An empty phaeton passed them going the other way, the first vehicle they had seen.

'Look,' Tom said.

Chapter Twenty-three

I

'If yer ask me, Mrs Usher's bread is the best on the Llangollen,' Eleanor said, coming up out of the cabin with the breadknife. She helped herself to a scoop of water from the ornamental can on the cabin roof, hooked the scoop back onto the handle, replaced the iron lid. 'I 'ad a bit of a 'eadache earlier, ter be honest.'

'I wonder why,' Joy said.

'I'm better now.' Eleanor buttered a slice of bread liberally, put a spoonful of stew on it, folded it, and chewed contentedly. She turned her face up to the sun. 'This is the life,' she said. 'I only wish the engine wouldn't drop these little bits of soot on me clothes, don't yer? In the old days, remember the mule, wot's 'is name, lives with the cows—'

'Ramses,' Joy said. She ate her fresh bread as it was. The engine puffed steadily, the propeller churned. A shout came from behind them, aboard the *Poca*. Damian ran along the top planks gripping the cloths with his bare feet. He stood on the front end rubbing his stomach, pointing at his mouth. He'd seen them eating. Joy skewered the remainder of the loaf on the boathook and with an expert flick of her wrist released it onto the grassy border of the towpath. Damian used his own boathook to stab the loaf as he passed the place. He ate the bread as he walked on top of the boat, waved to some boys playing with stones, then automatically lay flat as a bridge swept overhead. Probably, Joy thought, he had not even stopped chewing.

'Yer work longer hours wiv an engine, I reckon,' Eleanor said, 'but then it's easier work.'

'It was hard on the mule,' Joy said. She leaned on the hellum, pushing against the force of water. The canal looped along the side of the valley, hills rising around them. 'Sharp corners ahead,' she said. 'We'll have to shorten the tow-rope soon, or it'll cut across them.'

'We'll ease off fer the Chirk aqueduct anyways,' Eleanor said. 'I'm not rushing across that, don't want ter push no water over the edge. I got no 'ead fer 'eights, I 'ate 'em.'

'Look,' Joy said. 'Men running across that field.'

'They're frightening the sheep,' Eleanor said. 'Poor little lambs.' She looked round as something banged on the boat. 'Wot was that?'

'The engine?' Joy climbed on the cabin roof and pushed open the engine-room slide. A gust of heat came up. She listened to the pounding heartbeat, suddenly loud, and stared down at the mass of whirling machinery. 'Seems all right.' If anything went wrong with the engine Damian would have to fix it. She closed the slide and went back.

The sheep were still running. She could hear them now. Two men ran among them waving their arms.

Eleanor waved to them. She popped her last hunk of bread in her mouth, then looked alert. 'Oh bugger it. Me drinking-can's sprung a leak.' She stuck her finger in the hole. 'Look, I'm like the little Dutch girl.'

The boathook cracked in two, skidded across the cabin roof. She tried to catch it but it went in the water. She dropped the drinking-can and it spilt.

'Is someone throwing stones?' Eleanor said. She looked back. Two horses cantered round the bend behind the *Poca*. 'Wot's going on?'

Alfie was closest to Detective Inspector Bowler and saw him first.

Bowler crouched against a tree. He sighted at the boat. He fired again.

Alfie ran. His coat flapped. He saw the boat now. A girl in a leather skirt knelt on the cabin roof, peering down a hatchway. She shrugged, slid the hatch closed, stood up.

Alfie waved both his arms. Sheep milled around him and he was afraid of falling over them. He gestured Tom, who was on his right, to cut towards the boat. In a few moments Tom would for the first time meet his sister as a grown woman.

Where was Steynes? Probably somewhere among the trees on the left, where the boat had appeared. He'd keep his head down to give Mr Bowler a clear field of fire. No accidents, no mistakes.

Bowler fired again.

Alfie shouted, 'Sir!'

Bowler turned towards him. He shot Alfie at point-blank range.

Alfie lay on the ground. He gasped. He could see the trees and the sky. Bowler stepped over him.

'Traitor,' Bowler said.

Bowler walked towards the canal. He had two bullets left in the gun and twelve more in his pocket.

As the *Queen Boadicea* swept around the bend Ham saw at once what was going on. 'It's a fight,' he said, and leapt off the moving boat before Jack could stop him.

Ham rolled on the grass and jumped up. He sprinted. The gig slid almost silently over the water but the horses' hooves made a heavy noise. The boy, Wag, riding bareback and barefooted, looked down at Ham and slowed instinctively. The two men on the boat shouted. Wag kicked on.

Ham saw someone move in the trees. It was the lumbering black-haired man who had claimed to be a policeman. He'd backed away from the threat of Ham's fists a few days ago.

Ham sprinted into the trees. This time the man turned to meet him. The horses went past. Ham put up his fists.

'I've got a bone to pick with you,' Steynes said.

The gig slid by. Ham glimpsed Jack's face. 'I'll 'andle 'im!' Ham shouted. 'Get on!'

Ham swung at Steynes and missed. His arm was grabbed and twisted. It was some sort of police hold. Ham had seen constables use it to restrain drunks. He was humiliated. He was bent double, pushed forward. He felt towpath ash under his face. He sputtered, breathing dust. He felt himself being

574

dragged. His head was pushed underwater.

Ham struggled with all his strength. Water bubbled into his nose. He sneezed. Mud, weed rushed into his mouth, he couldn't close his teeth. He felt drunk, lightheaded. He could feel his hands and feet thrashing but he realised his strength was very small. Slowly his eyes opened wide, bulging. His hands squeezed weakly at the bottom of the canal. He felt himself fading away and he saw his children. Then he saw the sharks.

Joy was afraid Eleanor might jump in the water. She held the older woman in her arms.

'Ham,' Eleanor said. Her voice was broken. 'My son. My son.'

The man with the gun ran along the towpath.

In their grief the two women did not see Bowler.

'My son is dead,' Eleanor whispered.

Bowler was almost level with the *Poca*. Suddenly he dropped to one knee and took aim at Joy, unmistakable with her long red hair over one shoulder. The other woman on the back of the steamer moved, weeping.

Bowler cursed the old biddy.

He sighted carefully. He fired.

Joy looked round as something clanged off the funnel.

She stared straight at Bowler.

'Oh my God,' Joy said.

Eleanor shook her. 'What's wrong?'

Joy looked past Bowler. A young man ran up the field towards them, scattering sheep as he came. The sheep ran away downhill.

'Look out,' Eleanor said. 'We're nearly at the corner – push the hellum over—'

The young man reached the fence and scrambled up the wooden rails, but the boats had already swept past.

'Tom,' breathed Joy.

'Push the bloody hellum or you'll 'ave us over the edge,' shouted Eleanor.

Joy saw that barbed wire had been laid over the top rail. Tom caught his hand, pulled it free. As he jumped down his coat tore, dragging him back. He broke the buttons and ran forward out of it.

Joy made herself look away. She pushed the hellum and the boat made the sharp turn onto the aqueduct. Water piled up in front of the stem, sluicing across the walkway and falling to the river Ceiriog seventy feet below.

Bowler ran on to the aqueduct. The soles of his shoes rang on the golden stone. An old man leant on the railing looking at the view. His black-and-white dog snapped at Bowler's heels. Bowler ran with his revolver inside his coat, clasped against his belly in case it was seen. The leading boat was already off the bridge.

The canal went straight into the hill. The steamer disappeared in the dark, leaving only a few strands of smoke and the tow-rope leading into the shadows showing where it was going.

Bowler sprinted.

He had almost caught the towed boat, the *Poca*, then it too went sliding into the mouth of the tunnel. The boy at the tiller looked at him without comprehension, then abruptly disappeared in the dark.

Bowler didn't stop. He ran in the dark with his hand out, brushing the side of the tunnel, his shoes running silently along the soot and ash of the towpath. He could hear his breathing and the steady beat of the steam engine ahead. A shout came from behind him.

The boy, Tom, was silhouetted in the entrance.

Bowler threw up his arm, aimed and fired. The sound was enormous, booming along the tunnel. Tom dropped, Bowler couldn't tell if the coward was hit or not. He pulled the trigger again but the gun clicked empty. Tom scrambled out of sight.

Bowler squinted against the light. The fly-boat was coming onto the aqueduct without slowing. Steynes had to jump aside or be knocked down by the horses.

Bowler turned and ran into the dark after the *Poca.*

Jack stood in the bow of the *Queen Boadicea.* The smooth water rushed beneath him. The two tow-ropes, stretched taut, led past him to the horses cantering on the path. Wag clung to the back of the leading horse. Its mane flew about his head. Old Ruggles kept shouting from the stern, 'Slow down, slow down.' Wag pulled for all he was worth on the reins.

'We're nearly at the aqueduct,' old Ruggles called from the stern in a panicky voice. 'Can't leave the hellum, I can't. Throw these to the boy—' He chucked the sacks forward. Jack recognised the blindfolds for the horses. There were holes to take the horses' ears.

'Lofty and Silver walk across the aqueduct,' Ruggles called. 'Slow down, boy!'

Wag looked over his shoulder. He held out his arm for the blindfolds.

A gunshot boomed from the tunnel. Pigeons rose from the trees. The horses bolted.

Jack bundled the blindfolds and threw them to the boy.

They splashed in the water.

The boat swerved onto the aqueduct. Water sprayed up on each side. The horses had the bits between their teeth. Lather came from their mouths. Wag could not pull them back. The boy dug his toes under the side-straps and hung onto the mane, terrified. A man jumped aside or he would have been trampled. Jack saw Steynes. A dog barked.

Steynes ran after them, but the *Queen Boadicea* pulled ahead.

Jack saw the tunnel. Tom was cutting across the fields above. He had lost his coat.

The horses bolted into the tunnel. Their hooves drummed, echoing.

More gunshots boomed ahead, deafeningly loud. The speed of the *Queen Boadicea* increased. Jack knew the horses were completely out of control.

He stared into the dark. Flashes illuminated the curved brick roof of the tunnel, sparkled off the water. At first Jack thought they were more gunshots, then realised he was watching sparks fly from the horses' hooves.

* * *

There was a faint glow from a ventilation shaft. Something moved beneath it, the outline of a boat. It faded, passing through, until it was almost gone.

Bowler clicked aside the magazine of the revolver as he ran. There was just enough light to see what he was doing. He pulled the slide and the empty shell casings tinkled on the towpath behind him. There was only time to load one bullet before the light failed completely.

He fired. The flash illuminated the boat almost close enough to touch.

Bowler jumped.

He hung on then pulled himself aboard.

A boy's voice said, 'Who's that?'

Bowler knelt in the dark, clicked open the magazine, loaded five bullets, and clicked it closed.

The boy said, 'What are you doing?'

Bowler aimed at his voice and pulled the trigger. By the gunflashes he saw the boy running forward along the tarpaulins stretched over the cargo.

Bowler rested his elbow on the cabin roof and steadied his aim.

The boy dropped from sight at the front of the boat. He must be lying on the foredeck.

Bowler stuck the pistol through his belt and heaved himself onto the cabin roof, stood cautiously. The tunnel was high and he could almost have walked upright, but the smoke was very thick. He crawled forward beneath it. Through the clouds of smoke he began to glimpse light ahead of him, the silhouette of the *Joy* ahead. The turbulence of its wash gleamed around it. The following waves made silver lines along the walls.

Bowler was almost close enough to see onto the foredeck now. He stopped and reached into his belt.

The boy must have known he was close, because he leapt up. He ran away along the tow-rope, his arms outstretched for balance, a shoe dangling from each hand.

Bowler stared. He had never seen anything like it.

The end of the tunnel opened up around the steamer, blindingly bright. From the arch the figure of a young man without a coat dropped onto the *Joy*.

He stared at the girl with red hair then took her in his arms.

'It's you,' Tom said. 'It's me.'

She hugged him tight. 'I know it's you, Tom.' She brushed his hair out of his eyes. 'Who else would it be?'

'Father said I should never say I'm sorry,' Tom said. 'I am sorry. I'm so sorry.'

'You're crying.'

'Because you are,' he said. 'I wish this moment could last for ever.'

Bowler knelt on the foredeck of the *Poca*.

If they'd had any sense they would have cast off the tow by now.

He levelled the pistol and pulled the trigger again and again, keeping their heads down. They ducked out of sight. The empty drinking-can on the roof flew into the air, fell with a splash. The cabin door banged closed.

The boats passed down a deep cutting. Steynes,

like Tom, had run over the tunnel. Now he ran along the top of the grassy bank. He looked puffed but managed to wave. Bowler pointed. The cutting ended in another tunnel. Grass grew over the top of the entrance arch.

Bowler gestured. Steynes nodded, understanding the order.

The people aboard the steamer must have understood, too, because black smoke and sparks poured from the funnel. Someone had reached the throttle valve. The tow-rope pulled taut and straight like a bar connecting the two boats.

Bowler laid his hand on the rope. The three-inch manila thrummed. It felt as hard as iron.

He looked again at the boat ahead. They wouldn't stay down there for ever.

A head peeped out of the slide.

He fired at it.

One more bullet left.

Tom said, 'Is that full throttle?'

Damian nodded. 'Wide open.'

They crouched on the cabin sole. The only light came through the slide. Joy went to look out again but Tom pulled her back. 'That's what he wants. He's waiting. He'll hit you next time.'

'He's mad!' Eleanor said.

Joy wrapped a handkerchief around Tom's hand where the barbed wire had cut him.

'I think Mr Bowler is absolutely sane,' said Tom. 'Do you recognise him, Joy?'

'Yes. He's the man who came to see Mr Sparkles.'

Tom chuckled, remembering the childish name.

'Mr Goldblum. He killed Mr Goldblum.'

'I never want to go back there!' Joy said.

'You'll have to.'

'I'd rather be dead.'

She got up to look out of the slide again and Tom jerked her back. 'For God's sake!'

'Steynes is running along the top of the cutting,' she told him.

'All right,' Tom said. 'The first thing we've got to do is cast off that tow.'

'There's too much strain on the line,' Damian said instantly. 'The knot's as tight as a fist.'

'Then we'll slow down and take the strain off the line, untie it—'

'If we slow down,' Damian said, 'he'll catch us up.'

'I need a knife,' Tom said.

'Quick!' Joy said. 'Or we'll be in Whitehouses Tunnel—'

Everything went dark. At the same moment there was a thud from forward.

'Someone's on the roof,' Tom said.

Damian said, 'No, that was on the cargo. They're on the top planks.'

'Where's that knife?' Tom said.

Eleanor searched in the drawer, dropping things on the floor. 'My mind's gone blank,' her voice came frantically. They heard her scrabbling at the scattered cutlery.

Tom decided. 'I'm going out,' he said. 'Stay in the cabin and close the door after me.'

The two horses bolted along the cutting, dragging the *Queen Boadicea* behind them. Both horses were white with lather. Jack stood with one foot on the stem, his hand holding onto the scythe. He reckoned their speed at fifteen miles an hour. He had never felt more calm.

Ruggles held onto the tiller with both hands. 'Cut the ropes!' he called.

Jack ignored him. He knew what tired horses looked like.

Their hooves roared as the boat swept into the tunnel.

The *Poca* could not be far ahead now.

Jack stared into the dark.

He could see nothing.

The *Queen Boadicea* bumped on choppy water. Jack braced himself.

In the tunnel the noise of the engine was redoubled. Tom could see nothing of the *Poca* behind. The steamer charged ahead through the dark.

He lifted himself on the cabin roof. The funnel emitted a faint glow, he could sense the solid cloud of smoke pouring back over his head. He crawled forward beneath it. The heat of the funnel was like a warm fire as he passed its side.

He stood up. The roof of the engine room vibrated beneath his feet.

He felt for the tarpaulins stretched over the cargo. Planks had been laid along the top, hardly six inches wide. There was only one way someone could come back – or go forward.

Tom went forward. The cool air of the tunnel blew past him. He could see a tiny white light ahead now, the end of the tunnel.

A shadow moved across the light. Tom could not tell how near or how far away it was.

'Steynes?' he called.

There was no reply.

'Steynes,' Tom called. 'No man could have been more loyal than you.'

He felt Steynes's breath warm on his face.

Tom crouched. Steynes must have swung his fist, but the blow passed over Tom's head.

Steynes staggered. He knocked into Tom, overbalanced. Tom heard the side-cloths tear as Steynes slid down them. There was no other sound.

They came towards the daylight.

The light grew and Tom saw Steynes's white face, white hands. He clung to the side of the boat. Pale foam rose around him. He slipped.

Tom reached out and Steynes let go with one hand to be saved. The bricks caught his shoulder and rolled him back between the tunnel wall and the boat. He shrieked. The propeller sucked him down.

Tom covered his ears. Sparks gushed from the funnel. The engine resumed its steady, pounding beat.

Tom crawled back along the cabin roof.

The boat rushed into brilliant sunshine.

Bowler was standing on the stern.

Bowler raised his pistol. Joy looked past him. The *Poca* slid out of the tunnel. Two horses trotted out of the dark and grazed.

She faced Bowler. Her hair blew in the wind. The hill fell away and there was nothing but treetops around them.

Tom jumped down. 'Don't try me,' Bowler said. 'You haven't got the nerve, remember? Get away from her.'

Tom stood in front of Joy. He was angry with her. 'I told you to stay in the cabin.'

'I'm not that sort,' she said.

The treetops dropped away into the valley of the River Dee far below. Bowler shivered despite the sun. He really could not tell if Joy's deep brown eyes looked at him or through him. Her mother had tried to beat her into submission and not succeeded. Bowler realised Joy was sorry for him, his suit wet and trousers torn, his hands burned from hauling himself along the tow rope. He saw not an ounce of Lydia's jealousy in her, or Lydia's unhappiness. 'Damn you,' he said, 'you were just a child.'

'I still am,' she said.

The wind blew her leather skirt, and he glimpsed her long legs. Her expression didn't change. Still he couldn't tell if she was looking at him. Bowler half turned but Tom took a step. Bowler jerked, tightened his grip on the pistol.

'You know who I am,' Bowler said.

'I don't have the faintest idea,' said Joy.

For a moment Bowler looked appalled. 'You're lying.'

'When are you going to stop?' she said gently. 'Are you going to kill us all?'

'Stop?' Bowler said. He remembered he'd warned Tom about standing in front of her. 'Get out of the way.'

'No,' Tom said.

Bowler shot him in the stomach.

Tom doubled over. He tried to stagger at Bowler, knock him over the side, but Bowler shoved him towards the cabin. Blood poured between Tom's fingers and his body crashed down into the cutlery and crockery on the floor. His feet stuck up the steps. The woman down there lifted her hands to her face and screamed and screamed.

He had a clear shot now. Bowler put the pistol between Joy's breasts and pulled the trigger.

Nothing happened.

She looked calmly over Bowler's shoulder.

Bowler turned, and understood.

A man dragged himself forward along the tow-rope from the *Poca*. His elbows and knees showered spray when they touched the water.

'Jack,' she said. She held Bowler back as hard as she could, but he was much stronger than she.

Bowler jerked away from her and fell on the knot. He pulled at it frantically. He broke his nails.

The knot was stuck, jammed tight by the pressure of the tow.

Bowler flung the pistol at Jack but it missed. Bowler stood and suddenly seemed to realise that here was no canal bank, nothing, no railing to the left of the boat. He stiffened, watching as if mesmerised. The gun fell outward into the empty air, turning over and over, shrinking. It disappeared into the treetops.

The boat charged along an iron trough hardly wider than itself.

'I promised you—' Jack called. 'I promised you I'd come back.'

Bowler grabbed Joy and tried to throw her off the boat.

She hooked her foot under the cabin slide, wrapped her hands around the cleat that held a coil of mooring rope. He couldn't budge her.

'*JACK!*' she shouted.

Jack stood up on the tow-rope, barefoot.

He ran forward along the rope. He teetered.

Bowler jumped onto the counter. Jack threw himself forward and the two men met head on. They grappled, struggling for advantage, evenly matched in height and weight.

Jack's bare feet slipped. He threw Bowler backwards against the tiller arm. The rudder turned, the boat swayed.

'Stay below,' Joy said when Damian tried to come up from the cabin. He gave her a rebellious, determined look, then went back to Tom.

The side of the boat bumped along the iron lip of the trough with loud squealing noises, bumped into the other side, swung back again. Everyone fell down. The iron screeched and water roared over the edge.

Bowler got a loop of mooring rope, twisted it round his hands, dragged it tight on Jack's neck.

Jack kicked. The hellum went over the other way. Both men staggered across the deck and together fell over the side.

There was no splash.

Joy looked over the edge. The rope hung straight down for thirty feet. Bowler stared up at her. Both men clung to the rope, Jack beneath. His bare feet kicked. There was nothing below him but tiny green treetops.

The rope quivered and jerked as the boat dragged

it along the side of the trough. The fibres splayed out, the iron lip cutting them.

Joy pulled. She could not possibly lift the weight of two men.

The rope caught on an angle of stone coping. Bowler and Jack were pulled back up as though on a mechanical lift. Bowler snarled.

The rope twisted free and both men dropped.

The line sprang taut and they span like puppets on a string. A hundred and thirty feet below them the River Dee sprayed slowly down its rocky course, white water, blue pools.

Eleanor looked over the edge of the deck. She screamed.

Bowler had not taken his eyes from Joy's face. He tried to climb up. Jack hung by one hand to the very end of the rope. He reached up and grabbed Bowler's shoe.

Bowler kicked down at Jack's face. The shoe came off. Jack fell. He dropped down through the sunlight, arms outstretched, his coat fluttering, until Joy could hardly see him. She thought she saw a splash.

The boat chugged steadily forward.

Bowler climbed up the rope towards her. His face was bright red with the effort. He looked like a man about to have a heart attack.

They had crossed to the far bank of the Dee. There was nothing but rocks below.

Joy took the breadknife and cut the rope.

II

The steamer lay motionless in its reflection halfway

across the Pontcysyllte aqueduct. The boiler chuffed softly.

'Your brother Tom is alive,' Eleanor told Joy, down in the cabin, 'but my son Ham is dead—' She was going to cry again.

'We don't know that's true for sure,' Joy said. She held Tom's hand. 'You knew he was going to shoot, you idiot.'

'I couldn't let you go a second time,' Tom whispered.

'At least your hand's warm.'

'That's a good sign,' Damian affirmed.

Tom whispered, 'Warm hands, warm heart.'

Damian came on deck with them. 'We'll have to get Tom to a doctor,' he said.

'There's one at Plas Kynaston.' Joy undid the remnant of mooring rope from the cleat and threw it over the edge. 'Wait a minute.' She pointed back along the walkway. 'Is—'

'It's not,' Eleanor said.

Alfie Nutting, distinctive with his long white moustache, was helped along the aqueduct's walkway by a tallish cocky figure. Alfie had his shoulder in a sling made of Ham's red neckerchief. He looked apprehensively over the railing. Ham waved.

'It *is*,' Eleanor said. She forgot her fear of heights, scrambled onto the walkway and ran to them. She lifted Ham off his feet and swung him round.

'Blimey!' Ham said. 'Put me down, yer don't know yer own strength.' He smiled shyly at Joy. 'I saw the sharks,' he said, 'but they weren't fer me. They were fer my children.' He winked. 'Ter keep the little blighters away from the water.'

589

'Morwenna would agree with that,' Damian said.

Joy looked over the railing. She saw nothing moving below.

'By the bye,' Alfie said, 'there's a gentleman called Mr Ruggles waiting with his boat by the last tunnel, asking who's going to pay him the bonus for his day's excursion and demanding to know what's going on.'

Ham went to Joy at the railing. He followed her gaze. 'Jack?' he said quietly. 'I wonder if they'll find his body.'

'No,' Joy said. 'I'm sure they won't.'

Epilogue

It was a bitter winter's morning.

'Do you remember?' Tom said.

Their two figures, thickly muffled, walked slowly along Abbey Place through the snow. The beadles stared at Joy suspiciously, then recognised Tom and let them pass.

She slipped her arm through Tom's. He still walked with a slight stoop, but he swore he had no more pain.

'No, Tom,' she said, 'I don't remember.'

They stopped outside number thirteen.

'Mr Goldblum's house,' Tom said.

There was a Christmas tree in the porch, candles flickering on it in tiny porcelain holders. A nanny opened the front door and children in bulky overcoats ran down the steps. 'Be careful,' she called after them, then rubbed her shoulders and closed the door. She watched them from a window. The children threw snowballs.

'That family moved in years ago,' Tom said.

'Really?'

He looked at her as she walked forward a few

paces. 'You aren't interested, are you, Joy.'

She stopped in a gateway.

'That's our house,' Tom said.

She looked up at the attic windows, the chimneys smoking behind them.

'Mother is inside,' Tom said.

'Is she waiting for me?'

'I didn't tell her you would be here.'

'Does she miss me?'

'She stays in her room all day. She has her dolls. She cuddles them, I suppose. Dolls never fight back, and they never grow up. Won't you go in?'

'I'm not here.' Joy shook her head. 'I knew I could never find my way back.' She touched the gates, looked up at the ornate wrought-iron patterns thickly encrusted with snow, peered through them at the house. The oleander bushes looked like white balls. Beyond them she saw the sign screwed into the redbrick above the side door, TRADESMEN'S ENTRANCE.

She leaned back against the gate, studying Tom.

'How are you, Tom? How are you really?'

'I've been charged with the manslaughter of George Steynes. Getting bail has taken all the money I possess. Fighting the police case will take all the money I can borrow. That's the way the system works, they get you one way or the other.'

Joy nodded.

Tom said, 'You were lucky that you had witnesses to the way your rope came unknotted and dropped the heroic Detective Inspector Bowler to his death whilst he was trying to arrest Jack Riddles – and that the body of neither man was found.'

'Very lucky,' Joy said.

'I can't formally continue at the bank, of course, while this is hanging over me. But when P.W. Thomas went bust I was able to go to the Prideau brothers, cap in hand, which Father could never have done. Ernest Prideau wouldn't give me the time of day, but Winston's got a mind of his own. He saw the sense of guaranteeing the bank's commitments. One bank falls, a dozen follow. A crisis of confidence benefits nobody and harms the reputation of the City.'

'Well done, Tom.'

'Mostlock manages the day to day business. He reports to Lydia as the bank's major shareholder. But she won't leave her bed, and I invariably happen to be in the hallway when Mostlock arrives.'

'I can see you'll be a great success.'

'No, not just me. All this is yours too, Joy.' Tom swept his hand at the house. 'Come back.'

He waited for her reply, but there was none.

'Our father left a will,' Tom said. 'I think part of him didn't want to believe you were dead. Perhaps in the last few moments of his life, as he raised the gun to his head—'

'It's in the past,' Joy said.

'But it isn't, don't you see? Lydia will contest the will's provisions, since I am the main beneficiary, but I will win. *We* shall win. What's mine is yours, Joy. There won't be much, but you'll be an heiress after all. We're still your family too.'

Joy unwrapped her muffler. She undid the top button of her coat and pulled out something that flashed on a silver chain. She let the coin turn in the

593

snowy light, then took off her glove and held it out to him in her palm.

Tom said, 'What's that?'

'Our father called it a Talent. He believed everyone has one, whether they know it or not. I want you to know that you have this one.'

Tom said, 'But what exactly is it?'

'It's my love,' she said, and he took it.

Tom ran after her. He pulled Joy round.

He burst out, 'Shall I see you again?'

Tom walked from Cody's Halt into the trees. Everything was so green here. He inhaled the scent of new-mown hay. He asked the way along the paths winding through the woods several times, then realised all he had to do was follow the people.

The church in the glade was small, its square ancient tower dappled with leaf-shadows.

In Tom's pocket was a card, rather bent from the heat.

Mr Tom Briggs
is most cordially invited
to the Occasion of Two Weddings
at the Church of St Peter's ad Vincula, Cody's
Crossing
20th June, 1884

There was a small oak gate to keep sheep out of the churchyard. Tom saw Alfie and Abigail almost at once. He crossed the grass to them. Alfie looked very at ease in his morning suit. 'Hallo, Alfie. You always did look good in a uniform.' Tom bowed to Gail. 'Mrs

Nutting. Pleasure to see you again.'

'I'm glad to hear I'm not consorting with a jailbird,' Alfie said severely.

'Alfie, really!' said Gail. She patted Tom's hand. 'I can't take him anywhere.'

'I'm glad your shoulder is better, Alfie,' Tom said, 'and I hear you kept your pension after all.'

'You were lucky too, Tom,' Alfie said.

'Fortunately for me, the coroner's jury at the inquest into Steynes's death put the cat among the pigeons,' Tom explained to Gail. 'They returned a verdict of justifiable homicide. The coroner accused them of being against the police, and threatened to dismiss them and appoint a new jury. But the foreman of the jury was a brave man and said they were not against the police, only against the way the police behaved, and he refused to change the verdict.'

'I hope too many people don't get such self-important ideas,' Alfie said.

'Still, all's well that ends well,' said Gail.

Alfie said in a stage whisper, 'Good news, Tom. While I was out of commission Gail decided she doesn't like getting up early to feed animals any more than I do. I think I've persuaded her to move back home to Waterloo Street. Good old Southwark.'

Tom looked over as Joy came out of the church. She looked very tall, confident, grown-up. She wore a lovely long challis dress that flowed with her footsteps, its glossy shades of russet matching her hair. She smiled to see Tom. 'You look so much better! Colour in your cheeks.'

'The doctors admit that I have made a complete recovery.'

Joy took his elbow and they walked towards the church. She looked serious for a moment.

'I heard about her.'

'Our mother died in the new year,' Tom said.

'I hope she has found happiness.'

Tom shrugged. 'It means law and litigation is behind us, Joy. She had more than I thought salted away. You're truly an heiress now.'

'You mean I can afford this dress?'

'You could afford to buy a new boat, anything you want,' he said.

'Money couldn't buy that,' Joy said.

Eleanor welcomed them at the door. 'Isn't it a wonderful day? Shane arranged the weather special. Look at 'im, I'm so proud of 'im I could kiss 'im, cleric's grey an' dog-collar an' all—'

'Yer leave 'im alone, Eleanor.' Kes pumped hands with everyone. 'Let 'im get on wiv 'is officiating. All the aunts an' uncles are 'ere, I've even 'ad ter kiss Vera . . .'

Jaffrey shook hands with Tom. 'I hear they're letting you design a bridge, Jaff,' Joy said.

'It's a railway bridge I'm afraid,' Jaffrey said.

'Who exactly is getting married today?' Tom asked.

'Me an' Kes, of course!' Eleanor laughed. ''Oo better ter marry 'is mum'n'dad than our very own reverend boy? I shouldn't be here yet, I s'pose, but I just 'ad ter admire 'im.' Shane blushed shyly and bowed to Joy.

'I'm more nervous than they are,' he said.

Tom said, 'Whose is the second wedding?'

'That's me!' called Ham. He ran back down the aisle. 'I mean, us. Morwenna an' me. She wants ter

596

make an honest man of me in case I leave 'er an' run off an' marry Joy.'

'Ham!' Eleanor said, scandalised. He winked and went back to his seat.

Joy glanced across as the church door opened again, then held her finger to her lips. 'Oh, and here's someone you don't know,' she told Tom and Alfie as the man came in. He took off his hat.

'Mr Palmer,' Joy called. She took his left hand and brought him forward into the light. 'I'm sure you two gentlemen haven't met Mr Jim Palmer.'

'Pleased to make your acquaintance,' Tom said, then looked startled.

'Good God,' Alfie said. 'It's—'

'Good to meet you,' Jack Riddles said. He shook Alfie's hand, then Tom's. 'Never say die, eh?' He grinned as Eleanor hugged him.

'I've told yer 'bout talking like that,' she ticked him off, mock-severe. 'We don't talk 'bout nasty things in this family.' She turned proudly to the others. ''Ere 'e is, our Jack, the man 'imself.'

Jack explained to Tom. 'For the last couple of years I've had a little smallholding down by the canal, cattle. Herefords.'

'And someone to keep you in order,' Joy said.

'Yes, someone who cares for me a little bit, I guess.'

Tom and Alfie looked at her.

'You see,' Joy said, 'he promised me he'd come back.' She looked up at Jack and squeezed his hand.

'And he did come back,' Tom said, understanding.

'Even when he was sure he'd hang for it,' she said fiercely. 'He kept his promise.'

Jack said simply, 'I was in love with her. I always was, I guess. And she—'

'Don't keep going on about it,' Joy said. She wiped a fleck of shaving soap unsentimentally from his ear.

'She never did like being taken for granted!' Tom laughed.

'Yer'd be good fer 'er, Jack.' Eleanor added slyly, 'We could make it three weddings.'

'But we all love 'er,' Ham called. The others murmured.

They looked so young. Shane fiddled nervously with his order of service. Ham leaned his arm on the back of the pew, watching intently. Jaffrey stared in apparently rapt contemplation at the vaulting. Damian played with the rose in his buttonhole.

'You know I love you all,' Joy said. 'But there's only one man I'll marry.'

More Enchanting Fiction from Headline

GLORIA

THE STORY OF AN UNFORGETTABLE WOMAN — AND THE CITY SHE MADE HER OWN

Philip Boast

"A girl's got to get on in the world,
and Gloria's just the girl to do it!"

Gloria Simmonds is a girl who's going places. At
seventeen, the life and soul of Marylebone's
Wharncliffe Gardens Railway Settlement, up until
now she's been happy to stay there, apparently liked,
certainly loved and, though she doesn't know it,
sheltered from the realities of turn-of-the-century
London. Then, in a matter of hours, her world falls
apart and Gloria senses she will never be able to
piece it together in Wharncliffe Gardens. She must
find another life . . .

That night she fetches up in a part of London she
never knew existed, a warren of Regent Street's
thieves and whores where pimp Willy Glizzard rules
supreme. And for the first time in his loveless life,
Willy Glizzard falls in love, a love that is Gloria
Simmonds' first real taste of the treacherous,
turbulent city she will one day make her own . . .

FICTION / SAGA 0 7472 4555 X

LONDON'S CHILD

THE SAGA OF A TURN-OF-THE-CENTURY FOUNDLING

PHILIP BOAST

London – a man and a city
London – the first child of the new century

January 1st 1900. A Yorkshire servant girl abandons her illegitimate son on the frosty steps of the London Hospital. A lonely nurse takes the infant home and gives him a name – Ben London – never dreaming that the foundling born in a cemetery will rise to make the city his own . . .

First Ben must endure the hardships of the Workhouse and learn to survive by his wits. It is Ria who teaches him to fend for himself – Ria, the tough and fiercely loyal slum girl who will never forget him. And it is her brother, Vic, who challenges him in such a way that Ben vows never to be powerless again . . .

But the Great War brings escape from the sordid East End backstreets and a chance to prove himself as a fighter pilot. Ben's heroism turns the tide of his fortunes and takes him into the highest echelons of European society – the beginning of an extraordinary rise that will make him owner of London's most elegant emporium. His sights set high, Ben struggles for success, fuelled by the memory of his first love – and by a desire for revenge . . .

London – a world of crime and passion where a foundling can win fame and fortune

London – a self-made man who must truly live up to his name

FICTION / SAGA 0 7472 3186 9

A selection of bestsellers from Headline

LAND OF YOUR POSSESSION	Wendy Robertson	£5.99	☐
TRADERS	Andrew MacAllen	£5.99	☐
SEASONS OF HER LIFE	Fern Michaels	£5.99	☐
CHILD OF SHADOWS	Elizabeth Walker	£5.99	☐
A RAGE TO LIVE	Roberta Latow	£5.99	☐
GOING TOO FAR	Catherine Alliott	£5.99	☐
HANNAH OF HOPE STREET	Dee Williams	£4.99	☐
THE WILLOW GIRLS	Pamela Evans	£5.99	☐
MORE THAN RICHES	Josephine Cox	£5.99	☐
FOR MY DAUGHTERS	Barbara Delinsky	£4.99	☐
BLISS	Claudia Crawford	£5.99	☐
PLEASANT VICES	Laura Daniels	£5.99	☐
QUEENIE	Harry Cole	£5.99	☐

All Headline books are available at your local bookshop or newsagent, or can be ordered direct from the publisher. Just tick the titles you want and fill in the form below. Prices and availability subject to change without notice.

Headline Book Publishing, Cash Sales Department, Bookpoint, 39 Milton Park, Abingdon, OXON, OX14 4TD, UK. If you have a credit card you may order by telephone – 01235 400400.

Please enclose a cheque or postal order made payable to Bookpoint Ltd to the value of the cover price and allow the following for postage and packing:

UK & BFPO: £1.00 for the first book, 50p for the second book and 30p for each additional book ordered up to a maximum charge of £3.00.
OVERSEAS & EIRE: £2.00 for the first book, £1.00 for the second book and 50p for each additional book.

Name ....

Address ....

....

....

If you would prefer to pay by credit card, please complete:
Please debit my Visa/Access/Diner's Card/American Express (delete as applicable) card no:

Signature .... Expiry Date ....

CITY

The epic novel of London

Philip Boast

TWO THOUSAND YEARS FROM THE CRUCIFIXION TO THE TWENTIETH CENTURY

Fifteen years after the Crucifixion, John Fox, a man others instinctively fear, a barbarian wearing a prince's cloak, returns from the Holy Land to the city of Luan-dun, bearing thirty pieces of silver . . .

ONE LONDON

The city of Luan-dun is a shell, a Roman encampment from which the occupying army is making Britain its own. But Fox understands the conquerors and, a survivor, is determined to forge a place for himself and the family he almost lost. And to create a dynasty which, bound together by the tragic gift of Judas Iscariot, will flourish over two thousand years, its roots in the great city whose destiny is intertwined with their own . . .

ONE FAMILY

In this novel of epic scope and hugely impressive achievement Philip Boast tells the story of London, the story of one strife-torn but ultimately triumphant family. And, in many ways, he tells the story of us all . . .

ONE CITY

FICTION / SAGA 0 7472 4726 9